Before The End

G J Stevens

Copyright © GJ Stevens 2019

The moral right of GJ Stevens to be identified as the author of this work has been asserted by him in accordance with the Copyright, Designs, and Patents Act 1998.

British Library Cataloguing-in-Publication Data
A catalogue record for this book is available from the British Library

Cover Illustration Copyright © 2019 by James Norbury Cover design by James Norbury
www.JamesNorbury.com

ISBN: 9781718027992

Other Books by GJ Stevens

IN THE END (Nov 2018)

DEDICATION

For Jayne. You make me.

For Sarah. My inspiration.

ACKNOWLEDGMENTS

To my friends who inspire me every day and sometimes let me work on my passion, despite being on holiday!

To Laura Laakso, talented author and hard-nosed beta reader without whom this novel would be terrible!

Thanks to all those who helped me along the way, be it big or small, I am grateful.

1

The first I knew was the phone call from an old friend; my blood pressure calming when I saw it wasn't the newsroom. I'd just arrived at my parent's house mid-morning on Christmas Day and her picture smiling back with full lips and bright white smile felt at first like a season's treat.

I pushed away any hesitation as our only Christmas together flashed into my thoughts, but as she skipped the festive greetings, that perfect day hurried from my mind. With her panting breath my heart rate climbed as she told me a story reminiscent of the TV horror series which had just finished its millionth season. Experiments gone wrong. People rising from the dead.

Invasion of the Bodmin Snatchers.

I could almost read my headline scrolling across the screen.

But it was a well-timed prank, the one day of the year my guard would be at its lowest.

I listened, amused throughout the short call. Her hurried tone told me it wouldn't do to interrupt her tall story. But when I caught Jamie's muffled words egging her on in the background, she'd lost me.

With true dramatic climax, a slap to the mouthpiece and what sounded like an over-dramatised fall to the floor, the line went dead before I could speak.

She was once my best friend and I hurried to collect my thoughts, trying to understand why she would do this on her first call in such a long time.

I turned to my mother who was stirring one of the many steaming pans on the stove.

"You remember Toni, don't you?" I said as I looked back to the small screen, apprehensive for Toni's face to appear again in want of a proper conversation, or at least a reason.

Mum did, of course. We were inseparable at school. Like sisters until we had to grow up. It had been so long since we'd last spoken.

Even when I had been glad to receive the calls, we missed each other so many times; either I was following a scoop around the world, or she was locked in some government lab for months at a time. It had been a year since we'd met in person. We'd grown too close, too young and maybe providence had stepped in to make the decision neither of us could. If they only knew, my parents would have said her absence was God's will.

My head came back to the room to hear mum talking about Terry and Anne.

"Does she ever talk about her parents?" she said, and I could see the sadness creeping on to her face when I didn't speak, when I didn't tell her we weren't that close any more. "Did she ever say why it happened?"

I shook my head as I pulled the open bottle of Prosecco from the fridge and topped up her glass, setting the empty bottle to the side. Our parents had been friends for almost as long as Toni and I, but Toni had never spoken about why her parents split up so suddenly; why they had gone their separate ways after twenty years of marriage, leaving each other and the area with nothing but a short call to my mother to say goodbye.

Toni had long left the family home and although I'd asked so many times, she was always too distracted to want to chat about anything so depressing. I swallowed down my guilt for not trying harder.

Toni's call stuck in my head as I ate through half the late-cooked breakfast Mum insisted on making. When I couldn't finish the pile of food it triggered the same old lecture about my weight.

I wasn't in the mood for the usual debate about how the British public were wrong to want their TV presenters emaciated. Dad reminded me I was an investigative journalist first as he nodded to the row of framed awards he insisted on hanging on the dining room wall.

I didn't have the heart to tell him about the world I lived in. It would break his heart for him to know they wanted me as a presenter because of my looks and not because a few stories had landed in my lap or the years I'd spent at university and on the lowest rungs during my training.

Still I took pride in their beaming smiles, even if my achievements didn't mean the same to everyone.

Out alone in the garden even though I'd given up smoking so long ago, I plucked up the courage to call Toni back, ready to give her a piece of my mind. It wasn't right for her to do this after so much time.

It wasn't fair on either of us. Yes, I'd told her to stay away, but maybe now, after so long, we could be friends again.

I softened with every unanswered ring, with every echo of the chirps down the wire. By the tenth I'd changed my mind. I'd already forgiven her and was ready to say I'd be on the first train. We could spend the next four days together if she could handle it. If I could.

Still part of me was glad she hadn't answered when the call rang out. I knew deep down I should calm my impulse to think everything would be okay between us. I drew a deep breath and tapped my finger on Jamie's image instead.

Nearly dropping the phone as his voice pulled me from where I'd wandered someplace back in time, I glanced at the video call lit up with Jamie's eyes, the bottom half of his face obscured with his index finger as he frowned at the unexpected shout in the background.

They were together and playing games.

My parents came out to the garden, Mum offering me white wine, and I took a beer from Dad's hand before waving them away.

"Not funny," I said, knocking back half the bottle as I strode to the bottom of the garden.

I let Jamie talk, defend himself, dig deeper as he denied all knowledge of the one-sided call with Toni.

3

Jamie, our mutual friend was someone we'd both grown close to as we went through school. The third musketeer in our dysfunctional pack. I thought I'd lost him so many times. First when the world cracked down the middle as Toni and I crossed the line; the second when it ended, the first time at least.

Thumbing to end the call, I couldn't help analyse his tone, using my professional tools to dissect the conversation as I walked back to the kitchen. Jamie was at home only ten minutes away with his husband and their two kids. Of course he was, it was the season for family.

My breathing grew shallow and Mum asked me if I was okay. I nodded, leaning against the counter to keep myself upright whilst realising it could mean only one thing; Toni was playing a game. She was trying to tell me she was here in town. She was just down the road at Jamie's.

Neutral ground.

I looked up to see Dad offering me a beer, the empty gone from my hand already. He could sense my tension. He wanted me to relax.

I took the bottle wet with condensation. I thought of downing it to bolster my courage but instead placed it on the side as I grabbed my car keys and slipped back into my heels, telling my parents I'd be back within the hour.

I drove slowly, wanted to arrive and at the same time not. I had to fight to force my concentration to the road, conscious of the bottle I'd emptied so quickly and the thoughts of seeing her again. The good times had been so good and the bad times were fading into the background.

With my breath pluming white, I knocked using the brass and counted the pounding beats in my chest as I waited.

Before I could run back to the car, the door spread wide to Jamie's face lit with surprise.

"Where is she?" I said, pecking at his cheek, peering over his shoulder and into the kitchen.

"She's not here, darling. I haven't spoken to her in weeks."

"So it wasn't you in the background," I said, the mix of emotions draining as I watched his brow lower and head slowly shake. "Fuck. So she's really in trouble then."

2

Back at the car and despite Jamie's protests for more information, I scrolled through my list of contacts, determined not to chase after her but not able to bring myself to leave her on her own.

Each of the names from the newsroom group scrolled by as I imagined what I'd say, watching their reactions in my head. They didn't know her, they hadn't heard the fear in her voice. In their shoes, would I believe?

No, I wouldn't and what if Toni's call was one of her elaborate tricks to get me to come to her so she could say it was me who made the first move?

I thought of the time she made me cry with joy, surprising me in America whilst I was on assignment, or the time the tears flowed for the other reason.

No. I wouldn't let myself think about that.

If this was all a ruse then one of my over-ambitious colleagues would be embroiled in the soap opera of our relationship and it would be all across the newsroom. I could be the next celebrity gossip in the magazines.

No. I couldn't send someone else. If I was going to help, I would have to do this myself.

We hadn't spoken in so long. I'd made my decision; we needed a long break and she agreed, by her actions at least. She was nothing if not head strong. She would wait for me to call. She would wait for me to come back to her.

It had been so long I thought she and I had come to terms with it being this way forever.

She would never call unless she was in trouble.

The good times had been so amazing.

She'd shown me her weakness. She'd reached out and I couldn't help but go to her rescue. The words she'd used, the fear in her voice. In all our time together she'd never lied. She'd been brutal with her honesty.

I thought of her words again. The headline.

Maybe it was a chance for another certificate on the wall and perhaps it could be enough to be taken seriously again.

I thumbed her number and listened to her generic answer phone message.

Where to start?

I knew people. I knew her boss's boss.

I knew the minister in charge of the department she'd worked for the last ten years. Favours for silence were owed all over the place. Some for second-hand information told in confidence, others of my making. A misplaced hand here, a quiet dinner somewhere special. Right or wrong, married men were so easy to add to the list.

Still, no one answered my calls. No one gave themselves a chance to tell me I was making a fool of myself over some woman playing a cruel joke.

Swerving to avoid an oncoming car, I juggled my ringing iPhone and pulled over to answer the call I wasn't expecting from Stan, my Editor-in-Chief.

He was calling from his house and not best pleased with the interruption to his celebrations. After my series of calls, word got through and this was my warning under the excuse of it being the season to be jolly and that's what everyone was trying to do.

I tried to tell him about her call, about the fear I'd heard in Toni's voice, but he cut me off and wouldn't let me speak.

It was bollocks. These people never switched off; their work was twenty-four-seven. I was being pushed off the path because something serious was going on. I knew it more with every unanswered call.

My mood turned to regret as I tried to erase what I'd called her in my head, tried to remember the joy at seeing her frozen image lighting up my phone barely an hour ago.

I skipped my parents' house, sending a message with fewer characters than I should before heading up the motorway. Stopping for a freshly cooked bribe at the only place guaranteed to be open and parking in the underground car park, I took the only space left in the line of news vans which normally wouldn't move until Boxing Day.

Dan Huntley and Mike Pollage were on the only shift that was always quiet; the shift which pulled in a triple wage, but still no one wanted.

"No," was their immediate response when I asked nicely if we could go for a ride, neither turning their heads from the TV as they each lay back on the mess room sofa.

These guys came as a pair, both old school, or maybe difficult for others to work with as some would describe, but they'd always been fine with me whenever they were my crew despite being more than double my age.

Dan had long, grey eyebrows I couldn't help stare at over his thick glasses and wore a dog-fur-covered fleece no matter the weather. At least Mike wore different clothes every day, even if it was always from his large collection of check shirts, the combination of colours and patterns seeming to run into the thousands.

"No," was their second unified reply when I explained about my friend in trouble. It was just a quick trip down the road, an hour of their time and they probably wouldn't even need to unpack the cameras.

"I just need it to look like you're ready to do a day's work," I said, making my eyes as wide as I could. "All you need to do is sit in the van and look like you're hungry for a story."

"Is there a story?" Mike said, glancing towards me for the first-time.

"Perhaps."

"No," was Dan's response, his face contorting when I took the keys from the hook on the wall.

Mike was coming around to my bargain, despite his head shaking. The silence of his questioning told me he'd already given up fighting.

"Plus I bought pizza."

We were on the road within five minutes, the three of us lined up along the front seats.

Mike drove, which was his only clause in our forced contract, Dan already digging into the pizza still hot enough to steam his glasses.

With no traffic, we parked across a heavy set of black iron gates just off the road ten minutes later.

I was at the video intercom before the pair of square-jawed protection officers in festive jumpers had left their spots by the two colourful trees flanking the front door, the call picked up before they'd reached the other side of the gate.

It was another few minutes before I was in, leaving the windows of the van to steam. With my message relayed as I walked across the wide block-paving forecourt, the Home Secretary was at the door as I arrived, the two officers waved away to separate corners.

"Ms Carmichael," the secretary said in his trademark low voice. He was still wearing a shirt, the loose top button and missing tie his only nod to the season. He stood with the opening spread just wide enough for his thin body, making no motion for me to enter.

"Jessica, please," I replied with my on-camera smile.

"What is it that cannot wait until my office reopens?" he said, the deep lines around his mouth curling to a glimpse of a smile.

"How's Mrs Secretary?" I said, and watched as he tried to pull the door tighter against his body.

"The family is well, thank you," he said. "Is this a social call?" he replied, raising his brow.

"No, sorry. Business." His brow stayed raised. "Invasion of the Bodmin Snatchers?" I added and watched as the smile fell from his face, his gaze shooting behind me.

I turned as I saw one of the protection officers looking my way, turning back to see the secretary shake his head. I glanced back to the van for effect.

"I don't know what you mean."

"Is that your final comment? I have a source," I said, raising my eyebrows.

His face had paled and his hands were shaking. This man had signed off war. He'd signed off benefit cuts to put millions into poverty. He'd taken money for the party that should have gone elsewhere and he'd done it with a smile. Still, the professional liar couldn't keep this down.

"Shit." I let the word slip. "Shit," I said to the percussion of my heartbeat. Fear for Toni ballooned in my chest, excitement bubbling through my brain.

What the hell have I stumbled into?

"Okay," I said. "I'll just have to take the crew and find out for myself."

"Jessica," he said as I turned, but I didn't look back. "Leave this alone."

For a moment I thought I heard a tremble in his voice.

With my heels clicking on the paving, I watched as the two officers headed in my direction, only diverting when at arm's reach. The gates slid open.

The call came through before we'd left the curb. Stan again, this time his temper boiling over.

I held the phone away from my ear, cringing at words shouted down the line. Watching the road as we headed back to the office.

This was big, bigger than I could have known, but it looked like it might cost me my career. I wasn't scared of losing my job. Turning the other cheek was my fear and letting something big out of my grasp. There were other channels. Other stations. If I cracked whatever this was, I'd have my pick.

I wasn't scared of going it alone. It was just a little bigger than I expected.

We sat in silence as the miles rumbled by like a countdown to my fate, not knowing what waited for me as we headed back to the office. Stan with a torn-up contract probably.

I thanked them both, apologising for taking them out of the warmth, but when they both looked back, confused, I told Mike to stop the van.

Dan jumped as his phone rang, handing it over after he answered the call.

"It's for you," he said, his face screwed up. The screen showed a withheld number, but it was Stan's gruff voice on the line.

"Stick with it, but you're on your own kid," he said, before the line went dead.

Handing back the phone, the two conversations tangled in my head and I watched as the tall door mirrors lit up in a sea of flashing blue lights.

3

The strobe of blue light grew as we slowed, the phone's tone ringing in my ear only twice before the flat voice answered.

"How's your Christmas going Mrs Commissioner? Did you get any unexpected presents this year?" I replied.

The call went dead before she spoke and before I had a chance to make myself blush by describing the details of the photos of her locked in a naked embrace with a man who wasn't her husband.

With the empty echo still in my ear, I watched in the tall door mirror, counting in my head the few moments I imagined it took for her hurried call to connect and for despatch to find the right car.

It was a full twenty seconds before the police car behind veered right as it neared, its lights winking as if still not sure if it would cut across at the last minute and bring us to a stop. As it sped into the distance I knew I'd burnt another bridge and it would only be fair to burn the photos hidden in my safe deposit box.

Mike continued to brake.

"What the fuck?" he replied as we slowed to the curb, his voice as always sounding on the edge of a cough. That along with a scar on his throat reminded everyone of his surgery just as I joined the team.

"Let me out," I said, motioning for Dan to shuffle out of the way. He glared back with a furrowed brow, but without moving to let me by.

"What are you on to?" he said, shaking his head with none of the usual cheer in his voice.

I turned to him, his face hanging with the same fixed expression.

"It's big, but I need to do this alone," I replied.

"And your friend?" Mike said. "Is she in danger?"

I nodded. It was all I could manage, knowing the words would force tears I didn't want to show in front of my colleagues.

Mike and Dan swapped looks across me and the van pulled away from the curb.

"Where are we going, boss?" he said with his cheer returning.

"Cornwall," I replied, my head already filling with ideas while Dan recovered from his double take at my words, Mike nearly choking on his breath. "Thank you. Take the back roads. I want to avoid the ANPR cameras as much as we can."

"You owe us more pizza," Mike said, flicking his gaze to the empty box at my feet as he turned us down a side street, leaving behind the only other car on the road.

"You owe us a pizza shop," Dan said with a great smile.

Gratitude welled in my chest, a renewed optimism I was doing the right thing. The feeling subsided as I saw the phone in my hand. I wanted to throw it away.

About to pull the sim card and snap it in two, I paused with Toni's wide smile flashing before my eyes. It was the only way she could get in touch.

Breathing back the welling pressure, I unlocked the screen and slid my finger to turn off data. It would have to do for now.

The journey was slow, the van not meant for a high-speed getaway along the A-Roads, but at least the tarmac was clear in the most part. The drive was pleasant enough, watching families as they travelled, their exhausts white in the cold, Christmas jumpers on show, winding their way between friends and family.

Joining the motorway, Mike asked for directions or a postcode for the Sat Nav, but I had none to give. Bodmin was all I could say, was all I'd got from the one-sided conversation over four hours ago.

I spent the time holding back the worry for what had become of Toni, thinking of how her words couldn't be true.

Experiments, yes. She was a biologist of some sort.

Experiments on the living? It wasn't a big leap to make. But the mention of the dead rising and the fear in her voice chilled me, but at the same time pulled at my need to know more. My need to spread the word. That need had given me the success I'd already achieved. And some might say helped a few people less fortunate along the way.

Turning off the motorway I was already planning what I would say when we met again. I would say hello, exchange small talk perhaps. I'd get the story and make sure she was safe, then I'd be on my way. No complications. No lingering in the past, determined not to jump back in headfirst, remembering why I'd had to pull us apart.

Maybe this was just what I needed to close that chapter of my life and find another to write the rest of my story with.

We stuck to the main road, heading in the general direction of Bodmin, crossing into Cornwall after forty-five minutes. No signs highlighted our approach to the moor, but as the red and white warnings appeared at the roadside, I questioned the words which had started this all off.

Repeating for the hundredth time, I replayed her voice in my head with my stomach sinking further every time I read the evenly-spaced signs declaring the 'Foot and Mouth Infected Area'.

"Slow down," I said, squinting through the cold air.

The van slowed, halving the speed as sign after sign went past the window.

I'd seen this before. I'd reported for Bare Facts as a Student Features Editor in Surrey.

Back in 2007, I'd stood at the roadblocks, cleaning my boots so many times. I'd chatted with the police manning the road closures. I'd watched as trucks brimmed with carcasses, hoofed feet jutting over the top as they moved the culled to their resting place. I'd watched the smoke rise into the sky and seen the fear for their livelihoods in the farmer's weary eyes.

Each side road we passed on the A30 had a sign declaring 'Road Closed', accompanied with a static line of cones. The turn off for Bolventor was the only open junction. We took it, slowing to take in the line of army trucks on the grass verge as we turned the first corner.

Moving closer to the hamlet, we watched the line peppered with police cars. The crests were different to what we'd expected; military, not Devon and Cornwall Constabulary.

Eyes peered back, mouths pulling on cigarettes. We didn't stop, kept up the momentum.

At the centre of the small collection of buildings was a pub, The Jamaica Inn. The car park to its side was full of heavy canvas olive-drab tents. We didn't stop.

Driving back towards the dual carriageway, we saw the same line of trucks repeated as we built up the distance.

Mike was the first to spot our tail, the low sun reflecting from the Range Rover's white, blue and yellow paintwork. Two dark figures stared towards us as they kept two car lengths behind.

Still we drove on, re-joining the slow lane and getting up to speed before we hit our first traffic jam.

Still, it was reminiscent. I remembered the archive footage; Tony Blair with rolled-up shirt sleeves in the command centre, over-viewing the massive operation during an outbreak as the century turned. I remembered the headlines, the cancelled sporting events. The restrictions on country pursuits and mass graves with carcass after carcass dropped from the scoop of a JCB. The government had taken it seriously.

I took a second look at the road ahead and saw the few cars in front, watching as they released each one to crawl around a pair of green trucks parked on the inside lane at obscure angles.

Without a word, Dan jumped in the back, already unpacking the camera to film what looked to be a traffic accident, while a soldier in a yellow hi-vis vest stood by the

Armco central reservation, motioning the cars forward to squeeze past a third truck blocking the second lane.

Soon we were next in line, the hand motioning for us to slow as Mike negotiated the tight turn, micro-correcting the wheel to the soldier's instructions so we could get through the gap.

We were through and he turned hard left to avoid the truck in our way, but slammed on the brakes.

I looked up and saw I'd been right all along. We were in the right place, the three-pointed rifles clearing away my doubt.

4

The doors pulled wide before we could slam the central locking into place. They gave us no chance to come quietly, hands bundling us to the cold tarmac.

I didn't put up a fight and tried to tell Mike to do the same, but I knew the words would be in vain. The compulsory training for all foreign reporters told me to relax, watching as the moments blurred past as I tried to pay attention to the details.

With my wrists held together with zip ties, I could no longer see Mike, but could hear his language explode with emotion as the ex-Royal Marine gave the young soldiers a verbal beating I hoped stung harder than a punch in the face.

I kept quiet. There would be no changing course; instead I watched as the soldiers left the van with just a cursory glance in the back, leaving Dan, who must have hidden in one of the tall cupboards.

Bundled into a waiting Snatch Land Rover, I saw only the inside of a musty canvas hood pulled down over my head. Mike's voice stifled, with what remained evaporating into the distance as the engine note rose.

There was no Foot and Mouth Disease. I knew for certain.

I'd found what I'd been looking for even though I didn't quite know what it was. At least I was closer to Toni. I hoped.

We didn't arrive in the car park of the Jamaica Inn. The road surface was too loose, too uneven. I had no idea where we were when we stopped. I heard the rattle of a chain-link fence, the collective tap of boots marching on the hard ground and the turn of keys, the rumble of engines and a pervasive odour that smelt like the Portaloos needed emptying.

As the engine cut and light invaded from below, hands helped me to stand, guiding my feet down to the solid ground but not before pulling off my heels and letting my tights split, sharp stones jabbing with each step.

With my feet grateful for a smooth new floor, bright, cold air glinted from below, but just for a moment.

The air turned warm and the hum of electricity filled my ears. The whine of a generator perhaps?

Doors opened and closed at our backs as I counted my steps. A confusion of boots against the floor were the only sound until chair legs scraped along the floor, causing me to flinch back. The hands holding tight at my bound wrists wouldn't let me budge, instead forcing me forward, pushing down until all I could do was bend my knees and sit.

With a snap of plastic my hands were free, but not under my control; each wrist dragged forward, held firm and re-tied in place.

Light poured in as the hood pulled away with a sharp tug. I tried moving my hands to waft chaotic hair from my face, but I saw my wrists tied to a metal ring either side of the surface of a stainless-steel desk. The desk held firm as I tested its weight.

Flicking my head back, I still couldn't move the loose strands.

I let the irritation from my hair pass, moving my head slowly so not to aggravate, just as the door clattered closed at my back.

The room was a small box with no windows and just the one door at my back. The walls, painted white, had dulled with time, covered with the sheen of grime.

Along with the table and my chair, another cheap plastic seat with metal legs waited opposite. I forced a deep breath to let my mind settle and tried to form the words I would use in the documentary. Every few moments Toni's face would invade my head, my thoughts turning to what I would say when the moment came.

The words dried up as the minutes went by; the dull ache in my full bladder was enough of a distraction to pull me back into the room.

The door opened. I took a deep breath and dressed my face in a smile, sitting up straight whilst trying not to flinch at the hand which appeared from my side to push the hair away from my face.

Thankful for the gesture, but at the same time taken aback by the invasion of my space, I watched as a woman in a white coat sat, her smile bunching wrinkles in the corner of her eyes.

She had a resemblance I couldn't quite place. Underneath her white coat I saw the stiff fabric of a pressed green shirt, exposing a triangle of sagging wrinkles at her neck. When she talked, the grey hair at her temples moved.

"Sorry?" I said as I missed her first words.

She tilted her head to the side, her smile growing but her eyes didn't mirror the gesture.

"Are you well?" she said.

"No one's above the law. I know what you're doing here. I know all about it," I said, despite questioning how I could back the words up as they came out. "You will go to jail for a long time." But my words didn't cut through her wide smile.

"Are you well, Ms Carmichael?" she said with an insistence in her voice.

I stared at her deep green eyes, not flinching when she said my name and tried to visualise her in the dock, then in the grey prison tracksuit she'd wear for the rest of her life.

"Yes, I'm well," I replied, as her mouth moved to repeat the question.

"Could you be pregnant?" she said.

I couldn't hide my reply, my mouth opening to laugh as I squinted at the question.

"Not a chance."

Her smile dropped and she nodded at someone beyond my back.

Before I could turn to see who stood there, arms appeared from behind. Their great thickness wrapped around my throat, a solid weight hugged tight against my head before dragging me back in the chair to pull my arms against my wrists still bound to the table.

Straining to see what the hands were doing at my side, I couldn't catch the detail but I could feel my clothes being cut. Panic flooded through my body with the cold of the scissors, the warm air like a blanket as my skin exposed, the breath forced from my lungs as I realised my earlier confidence had been misplaced.

With the flash of a syringe across my view, I tried to move. I tried to thrash out of their grip, but the hands only tugged harder, the plastic digging into my wrists.

I locked eyes with the woman opposite as the needle pricked, watching as the corner of her mouth rose.

Warmth soon raced up from my stomach and to my chest, blanketing me from the inside as the lights faded to an image of Dan and Mike and the realisation of what I'd led them into.

5

A light touch pressed against my cheek as if a fingertip ran down my face.

Cold air chilled my skin. I couldn't move, except the involuntary shiver. I couldn't react to swat whatever hand touched at my skin. All I could do was listen to the rise of my pulse.

The memory of the small room flashed across my view, the image dissolving when I realised I lay with my head to the side, resting on a soft pillow sleeved in plastic. Breath panted, my lungs not listening as I tried to calm, as I tried to take in the air I needed to blow away the cotton wool in my brain.

I wanted so much to move, but my body felt as if encased in lead. The touch came again; this time my eyelids opened, electrified to search into the darkness.

What had she given me in that injection?

Another stroke ran down my face.

I managed to turn, the muscles aching in my neck as I peered up to nothing while willing my hand to rise from my side. The length of my arm felt as if I'd been in a fight as it slowly rose, convulsing left and right with the shakes despite my efforts.

After missing with the first attempt, my hand reached my cold, pallid cheek and my finger came back wet.

Knowing it was water and not another's touch brought me little relief. What had she given me to cause my body to feel like I'd been in such a battle?

Moving to dodge the drops, sensation rose from my limbs as I swayed to sit, my feet edging down to the cold tiles. Had I been left in a fridge to freeze to death?

Head throbbing, I tried to twist in the darkness to see where I'd lain, but the tension fixed me forward to stare into the unknown.

My neck ached and felt on the edge of cramping as I tried to move my head. My arms were heavy and my stomach churned like I'd eaten a bad meal. I sat numb, unable to do anything but try to slow the shivers and concentrate on keeping the rising panic at bay.

Toni's call came into my head, the words 'human testing' ringing in my ears as my stomach clenched.

An echo in the distance almost made me lose control over my breath and, without warning, light came through a square glass panel in the wall.

Pain screamed up my arms as they rose to shield my eyes from the brightness. Lifting my hands slowly after a moment, I realised the glass sat in a door when I saw a line of bright, artificial light piercing low to the ground. Through the glass and my clouds of breath, I saw the white tiled wall and heard the pounding of steps growing closer.

Taking a moment, I told myself my worst fears hadn't been realised and somehow I gained control of my breath. My attention fell to my hands and the wrinkled, swollen fingertips, like I'd spent far too long in a hot bath, not in a freezing damp room. I couldn't help but wonder how long it had been since I first arrived.

Turning around, I caught the detail of the white tiled walls forming the small rectangular room, the plastic mattress on the stainless-steel shelf where I'd lain, but not much more. The room reminded me so much of a police cell, minus the leaking roof.

The light disappeared and my breath sped again. The light came back, bright this time and focused, shining in my face. I flinched away, turning to the side to see the torch beam run down my body and down the hospital gown covering my torso before it flickered out.

The realisation came that I was naked apart from the thin gown. I bit back the panic and the questions about where the hell my clothes were and who had undressed me; it wasn't the time to let my mind wonder what had happened while I'd been unconscious.

At the window, a pair of eyes squinting through the visor of a gas mask sent the questions away. For a moment at least.

Tears flowed, a reaction normally so foreign, a grief pressing down on my shoulders when the corridor light cut off. I cried for Dan and Mike. For myself and my stupidity. I cried for Toni and what should have been.

Curling into a ball, my spine aching as I closed myself in.

A mechanical crack sounded from somewhere deep within the wall and I got to my feet as the door slowly opened.

Dan, I thought, as relief took over my face, both hands wiping tears to the side.

I stood, unsteady at first and moved to the door, guided by a new dim light the other side. The door felt heavy but opened out as I heaved it further open.

Warm air spilled in from the corridor as my breath sucked in, my toe smacking hard against the raised step.

Taking deep breaths through the pain, I pushed harder, peering around to the left and the small bulkhead light over a door at the far end of the white-walled corridor. The door below the light gave me hope. The line of darkness to its side gave me even more.

Warm air wrapped around me, speeding me on towards the door until I forced myself to concentrate on my steps. Twitching my head side to side, I walked along the corridor and saw more metal doors, each ajar, the metal bulk open inwards.

A thought rushed into my mind and I turned around too quickly, my brain moving slower than my skull, my hands pushing out to the walls for support.

Behind me were more doors either side of the corridor, all open, but no one came out. I was alone.

Creeping forward, afraid of my shadow, I looked to the corner, pleased I could see no camera.

Arriving at the next cell, my thoughts turned to Dan and Mike, a sudden realisation that I could be leaving them behind.

I pushed at the cold steel, quickly glancing away from the motionless body lain on the bed, its arm hanging down to the floor and the stench of decay greeting me.

With a churn of my stomach I turned and continued my walk, each step bringing bile up my throat and a metallic sting, growing a fear I was bleeding from the inside.

Step after step I somehow kept it together, focusing on a mental picture of that woman in her grey prison tracksuit.

My hands soon touched at the far wall where I waited a moment to let the cooling breeze from the cracked open door wash over me. The bile subsided and I pushed my palms to the door's surface, pushing it wide until greeted by a bright light which forced my hand to shield my eyes. A gust of wind rattled though my robe.

Wrapping my arms around my chest, I took a first step out into the open and let the harsh lights bear down on my skin. Blinking away the pain searing through my eyes, I pushed my hand to my brow.

I squinted into the dark shadows of the night. I was outside in a square of concrete bordered by a chain-link fence. Beyond the first I saw another, then only darkness. A single gate waited in the far corner. It was open.

I couldn't wait, pushed through the pain in my leg muscles, hurrying towards my escape.

I stopped only when it slid shut, slamming hard, echoing against the steel post buried in the concrete.

Gasping, I turned and watched the door at my back seal tight against the wall.

Trapped outside, the wind felt as if it blew through me, but my thoughts soon turned elsewhere as I saw a figure, a woman dressed much like I was, in the furthest corner. Hunched over on her feet, her knees tucked up to her chest, long dark hair flowing toward the cold concrete as her body rocked.

"Hello," I said, my voice quiet and dry as I took slow steps towards her whilst trying to keep my heart rate slow and ignore her resemblance to who I was looking for.

Her movement was too quick for me, too quick even if I'd had full control. She rose, her eyes glazed white. Dark, dried blood ran down the front of her gown, her face lined with open wounds as she leapt.

I tripped, falling back, my head cracking against the ground. Her teeth were deep in my arm before the spinning calmed.

She convulsed, shaking as static coursed across her body and I turned, following thin wires trailing from the side of her head to the yellow gun poking through the fence. I saw the short barrel and heard the dull thump of air, felt a sharp sting to my thigh before losing control, my world fading to black for the second time.

6

A light touch pressed against my cheek as if a fingertip electrified my skin on its journey down my face.

I lay with my head to the side, resting on a soft pillow of plastic. Breath slow. Senses sharp. Mind clear despite remembering what had happened when last awake.

I sat bolt upright, listening to the slow tap of water as it fell to the metal below me. A sheen of perspiration covered my brow.

Although still dark, I could see across the room. I watched my breath billow out in front of me, despite having no sensation of the cold and looked down with surprise to see I still wore just the gown.

I peered around the room and saw the featureless walls and the handle-less, reinforced door. There were no windows, other than in the door, and no lights, no openings to the sky but still I could make out my hands in front of my face and the wound on my arm which issued no pain.

I gave thanks, realising my stomach had settled, but the gratitude disappeared as the griping was replaced with an emptiness so deep I felt I hadn't eaten since birth.

I caught a faint nectar in the air, smelt a sweet flavour titillating my nose. I turned, somehow knowing the light beyond the door window would go on and its bright burn would not force me to turn away.

The golden smell grew with each new footstep and I stood without thought, pushed my face to the glass at the door, waiting for the veritable banquet of food I expected on trays across arms of the people I knew would be walking the corridor.

No suckling pig came with an apple in its mouth. No bowls of sweet gravy to accompany it. Just three figures, men by their gait, marched into view, bodies bound by thick armour and gas masks covering their faces.

The masks couldn't hide their surprise, couldn't prevent me from seeing their eyes going wide, watching them stop in their tracks as they reared back when they saw me peering through the window.

My mouth fixed in a wide oh as I tried to keep my breath steady, tried not to claw at the door to get to whatever feast they'd hidden on the other side.

They exchanged nods and turned, giving up their disciplined march to hurry away and scurry back out of sight with a mixture of fear and excitement, only leaving me somehow to just about see in the dark and the glimmer of sweet meats in their wake.

Disappointment grew, my stomach pulsing as the anticipation retreated. I stepped back away from the door as it snapped ajar with a noise sharper than before.

I gave a high laugh to myself; sat back on the bed. Did these people think I was stupid?

With the door remaining slightly open when I didn't move, I listened to the silence whilst trying not to linger on the questions flying around in my brain. Try as I might, I kept coming back to the question of what these people were trying to achieve.

I'd been drugged and it had sent me to sleep, but it wasn't just a straight tranquiliser, something to keep me quiet. I'd interviewed many victims of rape, women whose drinks had been spiked. None had reported symptoms like mine. Confusion and nausea yes, but the pains, the aches, the hunger; none of those were the same.

When I'd awoken, they'd engineered for me to be bitten. I looked to my arm; should I be concerned that it didn't hurt, despite the great teeth marks exposing the flesh underneath, thin scabs already forming?

I'd heard what Toni had said on the call. The tests on humans. Those rising from the dead.

Despite the deep cavern in my stomach trying to take my attention elsewhere, in that moment of clarity I realised that instead of turning me away or arresting me and the crew,

I'd become part of their test, but what the hell could they be testing?

A second thought soon broke through the struggle between my head and more base thoughts.

They knew who I was. The woman had used my name. They knew I was a prize-winning journalist and in that moment I realised they couldn't let me see the light of day again.

The void in my stomach wouldn't let me linger on the thoughts and what seemed like the very next moment, the lights were back on full.

Before I could taste them heading back my way, I could tell their number and bounty was so much greater than before.

Riot shields came into view first, POLICE in bold black letters across the top as they pushed between the gap in the door.

I didn't move, didn't leap to take what food they'd hidden, despite the desperate instructions from my belly and the demands for satisfaction pushing saliva to fill my mouth, forcing me to swallow it down.

When I spoke, the soldiers reacted as they had before, their shields twitching as they jumped back like they'd never seen a woman talk.

"I need food," I said, my voice clear, but desperately dry.

The pack backed off, stepping aside as a man was pushed into view. He was not a soldier and wore a dog-haired fleece and unmistakable eyebrows.

Dan, unsteady on his feet, squinted in my direction.

I stood, the soldiers leaping back, the door slamming as I caught him in my arms. Hugging tight with my nose against his neck, I drew in his fabulous scent.

I could so easily pull my lips back, sink my teeth into his flesh. The instinct overwhelming, so near to being sexual, I could feel myself losing control for the first time over a man.

His deep voice murmured something I couldn't quite tell as the lights in the corridor went out.

All I knew was my colleague and friend wished me well.

My head snapped back and I threw myself to the bench. Eyes wide, I watched him hold his hands out, feeling for the walls, the room pitch black for him.

Pains cramped tight in my belly. My mouth kept drawing wide. Each time I had to force back the feeling.

With the smell in the room so overwhelming, I curled in a ball until I felt him stumble at my feet.

I lunged forward, unable to stop my teeth from bearing.

7

His arm pulled back as my teeth touched light to his flesh. The salty, sweet taste of his sweat exciting my tongue as I inhaled.

About to lunge forward again, about to wrap my arms around him and drag him back, a high animalistic scream sent a painful fissure deep through my brain, forcing my hands to my ears.

With the demonic, pained cry growing higher, it was like a deformed child screaming for its mother. The scream flattened with a great thump to its cell door, the piercing feral noise rising high in between the smashing of its flesh against the metal.

I couldn't make out Dan's words but could feel the shake of his body, the sting of his hot flesh radiating against mine. His hands were over his ears as he cried, collapsing to the floor, our bodies rearing each time the possessed creature filled the air with its terror.

The lights came on in the corridor, with boots barely heard over the animal call, their rainbow scent back despite the air already thick with Dan's powerful pull.

I leapt up, standing to shake out my tense muscles and to ward off the desire to fill my belly. Leaning hard against the door with my hands still at my ears, I fought to get my shoulder tight so I could see around the angle.

The black-armoured back of a man came into view, his shoulders tense as he stood ready, but I couldn't tell what he held. Others unseen shouted and screamed, barking instructions near impossible to hear over the deafening din.

The door mechanism cracked and by instinct I pushed, but it was only an echo through the metal, not my door opening.

A slap of metal reverberated in the corridor, sending a shock wave through the wall, the man spilling backward, his feet tripping as the armoured figure stumbled to the ground.

The scream relented, replaced with a barrage of gunfire; round after round from automatic rifles.

My ears felt stripped back. The drums exposed. The bullets blasting off every surface, men screaming and the high-pitched zing of metal against metal.

Soon the chaos receded and I saw no movement in my narrow angle, just the light haze of smoke and the spray of blood up the walls. Whatever had issued the screams, however many there were, they'd won the battle and from the light pad of feet, the victors did not wear heavy boots.

Still, I peered out as my ears relaxed and took in the view as wide-eyed as I could, whilst trying not to remember the hunger in my belly which had hidden by the terror of the wail.

Peering out, a face shot up at the window, blocking most of the light and sending me backwards as I struggled to keep my balance.

Dan screamed and the face at the window erupted with a noise so high I thought the reinforced glass would cave and pelt us with clear shrapnel. The whites of his eyes were deep red and sunken and locked on to Dan at my side, the skin on his forehead missing. Beside dark patches of blood, I saw the white of his skull.

He reared forward, but the glass stayed intact to leave only a dark, sticky film on the window each time he pulled away, only to smash his head again.

The air pressure changed; distant boots ran on the tiled floor. Shots leapt out and I stumbled further until my back was against the wall.

The face had gone and the cell lit again, but between the scrape of lead running down the walls and the bang of each gunshot, I could hear the wail losing volume.

I looked to Dan curled in a ball on the bed, but I couldn't comfort him; the temptation brought tears as I fought the urge and the question burning my senses.

What had they done to me?

All was soon quiet again, the cell bright from the lights in the corridor. I closed my eyes, pushed my hand on my mouth, but still the scent licked at my nose, the sweet taste dancing on my tongue.

I took a step forward, a step closer to the bed. Perhaps it was for the best.

Dan lay ruined, gently sobbing in the foetal position.

Perhaps it was the right thing to do to put him out of his misery and do the deed I knew would fill the aching cavern inside me.

But what was the noise I could hear from the corridor?

It was a sound I'd heard before. The slight cry of a child, but it wasn't from a kid.

The rupture of terror filled the air with a feral scream as my hands pushed again to my ears.

I barely noticed the second call soon adding to the chorus; barely noticed the third and the fourth.

My ears could take no more pain. One thought remained.

There was only one way this could get worse.

As if by command, the lights in the corridor went dark and with a snap, the locks released their heavy steel doors.

Our door relaxed open and the din magnified, searing through my brain.

8

With a collective breath, the pained echoes died away. My hands held out to the wall, hoping to keep upright. As my head rolled from side-to-side, movement in the corridor shifted.

I heard the change in mood as clear as if I'd watched from above.

Footsteps. Bare feet padding, stalking with a single aim; slow and cautious in the dark.

I turned to Dan, still on the bed. Listened to his desperate low whimper. Listened to the thoughtless steps outside, each in time with his low, self-destructive cry.

I moved, keeping my feet slow. Outside theirs were quickening and I pulled Dan reluctantly to his feet. His eyes were so wide, his weight nearly empty as I pushed him against the wall.

I could almost see the shadows in the gap as I leant against him with my back, a foreign instinct holding my arms out wide to shield him from their arrival.

But they didn't come. All I saw was a shadow pass the door. A figure bent low. There and gone in a flash, right before a confusion of scents caught me from the corridor.

Gunfire burst out, tiny flashes lighting the corridor for an instant. Each peppered with a riot of movement.

Screams ripped again through the loud bangs. Dan grabbed around my waist, holding me tight as he sobbed.

The chaos was soon out of the corridor. Soon beyond the far door, echoing further away, leaving just the two of us behind.

I hoped.

The lights in the corridor flickered on and I jumped out of Dan's grasp. A breath unbidden pulled into my lungs. Dan's smell wafted all around and I turned, wide-eyed, a painful emptiness raking at my insides.

Dan looked up and I closed my mouth. He stood watching my silhouette as I backed up to the doorway. I wondered if he could tell I was weighing up if I should take this last chance to kill the pain. To take his life. To fight against these new feelings and not take the step I knew I could never come back from.

I welcomed the scream echoing in the distance, forcing my attention to the call rushing down through the corridor. I turned, placing my hand on the cold of the metal door and peered through the gap.

I stared at the floor strewn with bodies, my gaze roving the blood soaking into almost every space; the white of the floor only visible through the smeared foot marks. The rush of boot prints scattering shattered tile with plaster from the walls, lead and flesh crowding its surface.

I counted seven bodies, four of them soldiers, but could only tell by their thick body armour, doubting their mothers could recognise what remained of their faces. The other three I didn't have enough words to describe, but knew they were like the man, the Bodmin Body-snatcher, who'd smashed his head against my door. Now he lay at my feet, a dark ooze of clots filling where his eyes had been.

Stepping out, blood sucked around the sole of my foot. Warm to touch, it felt like stepping into a lukewarm bath, sending tingles of pleasure along the inside of my thighs.

I peered along the corridor and saw the door at the end ajar. Light burned bright the other side and I pulled my foot from the cell, breathing slow and considered as the blood wrapped around my heel.

A gentle waft of air passed my nose and I turned, following the scent and beckoned for Dan to follow. I didn't wait for him to move.

As I passed each door, I peered in to find every cell empty, the former inmate either dead or a player in the melee echoing in the distance.

The lights outside were brighter this time, the place lit up like a football pitch with no corners in shadow. The gate in the fence hung to the side and I ran before someone could play their awful trick again.

I knew Dan followed, even though I didn't turn to look. Beyond the gate was another doorway, lit from behind. The body of a soldier lay across the threshold, his gun still cradled in his arm, both limb and weapon out of his reach.

The next corridor was much the same, but with the bodies of two of the former inmates mown down, side-by-side halfway along, each riddled with wide gaping holes strafing their bodies. At least half of their heads were missing.

The doors in this corridor were glass, had been at least, but none remained; each shattered into cubes blown across the floor of the examination rooms, laboratories and store cupboards.

I continued to add my red footsteps to the jumble of prints whilst gasps from Dan confirmed he was close. By now the screams had lessened, the gunfire more sporadic and way off into the distance. Cold chilled my bones and I knew this chance would end soon, my time to form a plan shortening with every moment.

I ran.

Precious seconds had passed since the last gunshot, since the echo of the demonic scream, since any sound could have hidden the loud crack as I kicked the locker room door, sending a throb of pain up through my toes.

To my surprise, the metal caved in, but stole my breath as I marvelled at the inhuman feat.

Beckoning Dan into the room, I pushed the door closed. Paying him no further attention as I busied myself, barehanded, I pulled open each of the small metal doors, the locks snapping with my effort.

Glancing at Dan, I wasn't sure if he was gawking at my feat of strength or my naked curves as I dressed in someone else's clothes. I soon lost the thread of thought, caught between adding to the list of questions, asking myself what this could all mean whilst trying to stop myself freaking out when I couldn't stop fantasising about how his flesh would taste.

I'd heard the steps long before the door swung wide, but still we cowered in each corner at the sight.

The burst of flavour almost leapt me to my feet, despite the red dot on Dan's forehead and the scream of the voice to get face down on the ground.

9

I expected a bullet as he barked orders for us to get to our feet. I knew he would shoot as his gaze locked with what I feared would be my new mutated features.

I expected a bullet, but he gave himself no chance to recognise someone else's ill-fitting clothes underneath the lab coat.

I expected a bullet as footsteps built to a roar in the corridor, heavy boots sending cubes of glass scattering in all directions.

I expected a bullet as he herded us through the doorway, turning right as he led the way.

I expected to be shot, falling to the ground as I forced my hand across my mouth, trying to lock out the dreamy wake of flesh left by those who had once raced in our direction.

I expected a bullet after each instruction, each left turn, each wait.

I expected a bullet as he spoke to someone else, a voice on the radio as we arrived at a braced metal door twice as wide and half as tall as those barring the cells.

I expected gunfire from within as the door slid.

I expected the beast of a black soldier on the other side to swing his gun down from his shoulder, to smash the butt across my face and send me spiralling to the ground.

I hadn't expected him to look surprised, his eyebrows twitching and mouth curling to a smile. I hadn't expected that recognition I'd grown so used to; those words no one could hold back.

"Are you...?" he said, stepping aside to let us in the room.

I walked past, not able to talk, fearing the deep breath I couldn't hold. It came with a surprise; a lungful of smoke, a great blanket blocking out everything else.

My nostrils filled, the buds on my tongue clogged. I took in more of the thick air, twisting to see all around.

My vision no longer blurred with the need to fill my urge.

I saw people. I saw the small, under-lit room, an old incandescent lamp hanging bare from the ceiling.

We were in a kind of strong room, dining chairs set around the edge, each alternating its space with white plastic crates stacked to the low ceiling.

I saw pairs of eyes on me. A small collection. Four young women huddled in lab coats in the dark room and a man sat on the floor in the corner, a laptop on his lap and a cigarette dangling from his lip.

Surprised, I felt no desire to tear their flesh. I wanted to know who they were. I wanted to get their story. I was me again.

A rush of hope warmed my insides as the soldier ushered us to seats in the corner. Dan joined me to sit meek at my side, with his head in his hands as I watched the soldier who'd found us walk away with his huge colleague pushing the door closed at his back.

Guilt pushed the hope away as I searched the room again in case I'd somehow missed Mike sat in the corner.

The soldier came over and I smiled, forcing my public face to the surface whilst trying to hide my surprise that I could hear his words.

"Are you the woman off the tele?" he said, his accent thick with West Midlands rhythm.

I shook my head whilst hiding my pleasure that my face had not turned hideous.

"I've just started," I replied. "A week ago. Graduate programme."

He smiled, showing teeth as white as snow. I didn't think he believed me, but I lived a few moments more to tell the tale.

"What's going on?"

I couldn't help saying the words and watched as, despite my low voice, two pairs of eyes glanced in my direction.

He shook his head, turning to the rest of the group as if for show, shrugging his shoulders in an overactive move to add to his point. The cigarette smoke thinned and I watched the wisps of blue air glide up into the ceiling vents.

Dan's smell came first as he leant over, still with his head in his hands. Panic rose as new tastes soon followed. The hope had vanished as I sampled the air, thick and meaty. The soldier's scent, I guessed.

The group of women were delicate and perfumed. I hadn't quite got the older man's scent until I stood next to him. Pale and gamey, like mutton.

"Have you got another?" I said, nodding towards the rectangular package on the floor. He smiled up, showing yellow teeth, his flesh strong as he breathed in my direction. I'm sure I would have found out his taste if he hadn't flipped up the lid of the box next to him to reveal long cartons of white-boxed cigarettes.

The first draw was bliss, the taste empty, saliva retreating down my throat as my vision cleared.

The women in the huddle coughed as I passed. If they'd kept that up, I might have shown the alternative.

A cold wave of fear rushed across my face and it felt as if the blood had drained to my feet when I realised what I had just thought.

I took a long draw of the cigarette, holding my breath to make sure it filled every part of my lungs. Letting the smoke slowly escape, I pushed on a smile to the women, thankful the need to tear their eyes out had passed.

Dan had grown quiet, but flinched up, his red-ringed eyes wide with the dull knock rattling the heavy door.

Words boomed from someone new after our guard pulled up the bolt and swung open the metal with his pull.

"Five unaccounted for."

It wasn't the soldier who had escorted us but another. I wanted to say rescued us, but that wasn't right. A Scouse accent hung heavy in his voice.

The right words tried to form in my head as I savoured my blank taste buds and listened to the drivel. "I had to bring her here. Watch her. She's trouble, the brig's overrun."

I looked up hearing those words and knew before I saw her face in the orange light. I knew it would be her stepping through the gap.

I hadn't guessed about the hands cuffed at her front. Hadn't guessed at the side of her face black and blue. I hadn't thought I'd see her swearing under her breath, the muscles in her neck tense and face fixed with anger as she kept her head low.

I stubbed the unfinished cigarette under my foot and flushed with panic as my smile dropped.

10

She wore a bright orange jump-suit, three or more sizes too large, the kind lifers wore in American jails. Her feet shuffled across the floor, restricted by manacles clipped at her ankles. What could she have done to prompt such fear of escape?

A great black hand reached my way as I stepped forward, but with all eyes on me I let myself cower back, watching her downward face as her escort led her to the opposite side of the room.

Thankful the huddled women gave her their attention, fixing their sneers in her direction, I turned my back to the four women to make sure our eyes didn't meet as I half listened to the soldier's chat, catching only some of their words as a bunch of keys changed hands.

Soon the new soldier left our guard to his task of pushing the metal bundle into a pouch on his utility belt.

Still, she hadn't looked up. I wasn't ready for her to see me.

Lighting another cigarette, I pushed away my returning senses, smothering the sweet honeyed scent I could almost see drawing out from her like an aura. Remembering my determination as we'd driven here, reminding myself I needed to do this on my terms.

Staring at the top of her bowed head and as the door sealed closed, I spoke loud enough for everyone to hear.

"What's going on?"

Toni looked up, my plan a success. The anger fell from her features, her eyes fixing wide in my direction but her left not as much as her right. Her chest heaved as she struggled with pain from the sharp intake of breath.

She couldn't have looked more surprised to see me if I'd been dead for ten years. I could feel my determination crumble.

I turned away after lingering just enough. The soldier stood at the door with a wide smile shining back, his voice booming when he spoke.

"It's under control, but we'll be moving as soon as they clear the compound."

"Moving where?" said one of the women who'd broken from the pack, a chorus of repeats at her shoulders, but I didn't dare move to look.

"I don't know. All they've said is we're going mobile. You have work to do," he said, and letting his rifle relax on the straps, he held his hands in the air. "That's all I know." He turned toward me, raising his brow to test my satisfaction.

I gave a shallow nod and waited until he turned away before I let my view radiate in Toni's direction.

Staring right at me, I saw the pain clear in her hanging features as her view moved from the stick between my fingers with tears rolling down her cheeks. But they were tears of joy. Tears of elation, plain to see from her wide grin and the affection pouring my way.

I'd already done all I needed to do. I knew my only choice. Sit and wait this out. I had to keep smoking to stop myself from going crazy.

Pushing away the air thick with mouth-watering smells, I stared at Toni while fighting my growing anger at the damage to her face, whilst trying not to imagine what they'd put her through.

Her phone call made more sense now, although the words were fading. She must have found out the terrible truth. She must have discovered they were testing on humans; were testing medicine for a new disease I hadn't even heard of.

They'd silenced her. Shackled and chained. But why hadn't they killed her? A shudder ran down my spine at the thought.

Shaking off the growing tension, I let myself fantasise as another option came to mind. Stub out the cigarette and burn no other. Let the smorgasbord of flavour engulf me.

I didn't kid myself about what would happen next.

Despite the abhorrence of the thoughts, I knew I would rend flesh, would pull heads to the side and bite my teeth deep into their necks. I knew I wouldn't stop, couldn't hold back once I'd tasted the sweet warm meat straight from the bone.

These thoughts didn't scare me one bit and I felt my heart beating and my vision haze. I barely heard a cackle of coughs from the side of the room, the sound more like braying lambs in a field. I thought of the blood spurting from their veins, heat raining down my face to cover my naked body.

"Are you okay lady?" the soldier's voice boomed somewhere near, but I saw him only as a shadow.

Breath pulled fast as I snapped forward, sinking my teeth, but only in my head. Sweet, tangy scent filtered down my nostrils while electricity coursed along my veins and blood pumped to my extremities.

Fingers, toes, head, breasts and everywhere else felt engorged, bulging heavy. More words came at me as my head lolled back and forward. I fought the feeling as it took control, knowing if I leapt forward and sunk my teeth, the race of oxytocin would be better than the greatest climax I'd ever felt.

A sting of pain cut through the mist and I looked to my fingers to see the orange ember kissing my skin. Through the fog I pulled it to my lips and sucked the deepest breath I'd ever taken, blowing out with as much control as I could manage.

My heart slowed and the moment passed with the disappointment we all knew when we'd pulled back from the cliff edge, our partner out of energy, or the batteries dead. Hand too weary.

A fear rose to take place of the energy, but I wasn't afraid of the moment; instead afraid of why I thought all of this was okay. Why didn't I feel utter revulsion at the need I'd only just held back from?

My gaze fell past the soldier who'd stood back as I took the drag. I looked past his bulk to Toni.

Plan A was my only option. I couldn't trust myself to be in control, knowing I wouldn't be able to stop. Her flesh would taste the sweetest and would be the most familiar.

The soldier spoke and I looked up, taking another drag. In his hands were the carton of cigarettes he'd taken from my side as the women coughed a chorus.

"We'll just hold off with the smoking until we get outside," he said, his mouth and cheeks bunched in a smile.

11

They made the choice. Not my decision.

What could I do?

At a guess I had a full five minutes before I couldn't hold back, maybe ten if I distracted myself. Then again, what did I know?

Perhaps I could sleep and think happy thoughts, but not those already crowding my head.

I glanced at Dan, his head still bowed with his arm clutched around his stomach. As each of his tears dripped to the floor he looked less and less like the man who'd shown his usual initiative as he tried to hide in the back of the van.

I looked back at Toni, her eyebrows raised in a solemn communication.

Sorry, but thanks for answering my call, I guessed, turning away.

Yes, I'd come to her rescue on the flimsiest of information, but what good had I done?

My situation was so much worse. Pumped full of drugs, or whatever was in that syringe, I'd lain unconscious for who knows how long and had to swallow hard as I tried not to think of what they had done while I'd been out cold. It was bad enough to know I'd been bitten and one way or another I was changing, the first symptoms of which were eroding my humanity.

At least Toni still had her life. Battered and bruised, broken maybe, but she would recover. The future was less certain for me, I knew that much; put down like a rabid dog, or locked in a cage for however long I had left.

And Dan. Poor broken Dan. I watched as he rocked back and forth on the plastic seat. What had they put him through before they'd forced him into the room with me? What had broken him so completely?

I daren't move closer to comfort him and stood, breathing through my mouth and took small steps across the room, ignoring the soldier's words.

"Miss, please stay away from the prisoner," he said, turning my way.

I carried forward my advance, standing my ground as his wide-spread hand blocked my path and he stepped in to follow. Looking him up and down I tried not to linger on his pistol. A Glock 17. A weapon I'd learnt to handle; trained by my Israeli bodyguard on a six-month stint covering the peace process in Jerusalem.

I saw his pouches packed full, guessed which one should hold the ammunition. I could smell a packet of chocolate on the other side that would melt in the building heat of the room. Only as he copied my look did I sit back down.

He'd got the wrong idea, but I'd found a way out.

Closing my eyes, I let my mind drift, turning away from the thought of food and of urges I needed to satisfy.

I thought of my parents sat in front of their TV, each with a glass of sherry and a box of chocolates spread across their laps. Still, the scents rolled in and I knew the four women would be standing in front of me as I opened my eyes, their perfumed notes exciting the thin hairs along the inside of my nostrils. I could almost see the cocktail of scents in the air, their flavours becoming distinct with my attention caught by one in particular. An undertone of burnt caramel.

There they were, silhouetted against the lamp and after shooting a look to Toni to find her watching on, I closed my eyes, but couldn't help opening them again, their words already losing definition as I looked at each of them with a growing desperation to know which one would make a great dessert.

I glanced again to Toni to see her shallow nod and I stood, feeling saliva pour from my glands, the liquid hot in my mouth as I tried to concentrate on their words, but at the same time kicking myself for checking with her.

She was no longer my keeper. She never should have been.

"Karen," the tallest of the four said, with a high-pitched voice she tried to keep quiet.

Blonde hair flowed down each side of her red, perfect cheeks, her curves hidden by the white coat which hung high off her chest. I only noticed her hand held out as the other three gazed down.

I held mine out too, hers so warm. My breath rose and the knots in my shoulders I hadn't noticed relaxed as if she had a healing touch.

"Where do you work? I've not seen you around," she said, her face alarming as she yanked back her hand. "You're freezing."

In unison each of their eyes went wide, fixed on my hand and then my face.

"Do we…" the tall one said, but stopped herself as she stared down at my bare feet. Before I could find my sweet treat, she'd pushed up my left sleeve and then my right, rearing back at the already healing bite wound.

"She's infected," she screamed, almost tripping over her feet as she hurried backwards.

The world slipped down a gear, their shouts slowing as if their batteries had drained. They moved back with a speed like they were stuck in treacle, the screams building as my arm fell to my side. The game was up; their widening faces told me all.

I had just enough of a chance to catch a glimpse of Toni's face as it fell, before I spotted the soldier's moving gaze.

He showed his skill and had his rifle up. With his head turning side to side, the fat in his cheeks carried its momentum as he checked twice either way that his decision would be right.

The first bullet was easy to dodge, the round fired in a panic and like a fly, my body and brain were on overdrive whilst time had sped for those around.

The second bullet grazed my arm, sending pain along its short course before twanging off the wall. A third ricocheted twice before one of the women fell to the floor in the corner of my vision.

I hoped it wasn't in the sweet taste of pudding.

He had the Glock out as I closed the distance. I saw it too late and heard the trigger operate the first internal safety pin, felt the second vibrate through my temple, knowing the third noise would be the sound of my brain exploding.

12

I expected the end. Perhaps it would be a good way to go.

A clean kill. Over and done with before I could commentate.

Instead, his hand went down, the gun slipping from my temple and I snatched it away, grabbing the top of his head and pushing him face down on the floor before any more thoughts could slip in.

Looking up from my foot between his shoulder blades, I saw Toni stood with what remained of the plastic box in her manacled hands, the box she'd used to hammer into the soldier's head with the paper contents still settling on the floor amongst the jagged white splinters.

On her lips she held a wide, lopsided smile, beaming in my direction as the world settled to the speed I was more accustomed to.

No one moved. I'd told them not to. Toni watched as I snatched a cigarette from the carton, only just able to get it lit as my hands shook. She read my distress as I regretted shoeing her away with the smouldering stick between my lips.

I took a moment. I took my time to collect my thoughts whilst drawing in the thick air with the scents evaporating.

The three remaining women huddled over the fallen where I'd been sat. The tallest had taken the hot lead, the price of her height. Each dropped to the floor in shock as her obvious state became undeniable.

The man who'd sat at his laptop continued to type as he looked up with his mouth hanging wide, his fingers speeding as if curating his own narrative.

The soldier shook under my foot, but obeyed the only command I'd given as Toni bent at his side, pulling off the helmet, yanking the radio cables from their sockets and digging out the keys from his pouch.

For the first time in an age I took a moment to think and the first question spilled when I realised I might be able to get out of this alive.

Can I be fixed?

Before I let the torrent of doubt I knew waited just around the corner to crush me, I couldn't help but think how the hell was I going to get this story out.

With the manacles freed from Toni's wrists, she pulled up each leg of the orange overalls and I winced back at the sight of her black and blue ankles, my foot between the soldier's shoulder blades getting heavier with every second.

She looked up and saw my pain, pulled the trouser legs down once the leg manacles were loose and launched herself at me.

She grabbed tight around my upper body, her head buried deep into the crook of my neck as I fought the urge to draw my arms around her. Instead, I took a long drag to push away the growing distraction and fixed my gaze to the three, although they were looking anywhere but in my direction.

Dan stared my way but he wasn't focused on me, perhaps on nothing. He just shook his head from side to side as he rocked on the seat, wringing his hands.

A double clang of metal reverberated out from the heavy door.

Toni pulled away, her gaze catching on the cigarette in my mouth to return a look, a scowl I knew well; the same set of her features I told myself I should no longer care about.

Just as I began to breathe away the thoughts and remind myself of the resolve I'd agreed on the journey, I watched with intrigue as her face snapped to the door, reaching for the rifle and sliding back its mechanism in what appeared to be a well-practiced flow of movement.

"Radio check, dumbass," were the cotton wool words just about making it through the steel. "Open the fucking door. I've got two more for…"

We glanced together as the words cut off and I leant forward, keeping my pressure on the soldier's back as I tried to make out why the voice had stopped so suddenly. I'd heard other sounds, but I couldn't describe anything but movement; heavy footsteps perhaps with the steel of the door blocking out all definition.

A voice? No, a shriek? I shook away the confused pictures forming in my mind.

I looked back to Toni and her nod gave me the will, taking my foot from the soldier's back whilst making sure he was aware two guns pointed at him should he wish to be a hero.

Without words, I motioned for all to move behind the door. The man at the laptop took the longest to comply, almost upset to close the screen and let his fingers leave the keyboard.

Left with silence coming from the other side of the door, our hostages were in the crook and Toni and I were standing at the centre. Whoever was on the other side would see us only when the door pushed fully open. Then we'd have them.

I padded forward, pushing the gun into my white coat pocket whilst gripping around the handle and forcing the bolt across. Pulling the heavy door by the handle, I let it fall open to a crack before I jumped back to my position with our aim centred on the gap.

The door didn't move and no words came. It hadn't crossed my mind that a plan might have been in place for this situation; a procedure ready should they get no answer.

We should have opened the door straight away with our guns blazing. Now, on the other side, backup would be on its way or already there, waiting in the silence. Gun barrels would point our way, doing to us what we'd planned for them.

They were professionals and it made sense when no sound came. No boots ran down the corridor, but they made no final calls just to make sure.

I'd covered enough sieges in my time. Terrorists, bank robbers and plain old stupidity. A canister would soon roll with a casual pace through the gap. A bang and a flash would overwhelm our senses and in those moments they would have control.

We'd be dead or in chains soon after. Or maybe they'd just run and no one was waiting the other side in the silence.

I chanced a look at Toni and with surprise I saw her gaze already on me as if I was the one taking the lead.

Buoyed by taking control, I drew a drag of foul smoke, letting the rest drop to the ground, knowing the only sure way out of this situation would be to lose control and let myself go where my body ached to be. I'd just have to hope I could reign it in when the job was done and not destroy my reason for being here.

By not holding back, I could already taste the change in the air. I could feel blood swelling, muscles tensing and coiling, ready to spring.

Toni's words halted the march, made me pause enough to follow her outstretched finger down to the growing line at the door's gap. I watched the dark fissure of a viscous liquid glinting in the light.

As my gaze locked to the view, I could taste it on my tongue. I could smell the thick iron-rich tang heavy down my throat, all before I heard the structure of her question.

"Is that blood?"

13

Gulping down the heavy air and with the Glock planted back in my grip, I pushed my hand out to my side and forced myself to continue the step. The room stayed quiet, silent if not for the low whimpers. The loudest sound came from my pounding blood.

My gaze fixed on the gap, the smell of its liquor spiralling up my nose. My forward leap only held back by curiosity of who the owner could be.

Stepping around the door, I still couldn't see the start of the trail of scarlet glinting in the bright corridor lights as it disappeared out of the view provided by the gap.

Warm hands burnt at my shoulder and I saw the fear in Toni's eyes as she pulled back. I knew we couldn't wait here for the same fate and I pulled the cold metal wide like it had no weight.

Out into the corridor, I leapt forward to gasps from the room. My head twisted left, my aim following, not lingering on the pair of bodies, a soldier and a bald man in a once-white lab coat as the muffled sounds I'd heard now made sense.

I scanned along to the door in the distance before turning the other way as a piercing scream echoed down the passage.

I took a moment, the shriek sending my body into itself, but I was soon back and turned to see a figure with his head stooped low, glaring in my direction from the other end of the corridor.

Despite his features long gone, the muscle and skull not recognisable without his skin stretched over, I picked out the scar just below his Adam's apple and the checked shirt he'd worn as we drove to this place.

I pulled the trigger all the way back, sending his torso stuttering as the bullet slammed through his bones.

Without my finger on the trigger, a second bullet shattered the centre of his skull. Turning, I watched Toni lower the rifle from her shoulder. When did she learn to shoot so well?

He dropped like a rag doll as I twisted back, his body collapsing to the floor.

We'd done him a service, I knew, and my focus went to searching beyond the body to the corridor and the bloody footsteps disappearing into the light.

Forging forward, I stepped around the body, not glancing back despite Toni's aroma calling me to turn.

It wasn't until another shot came that I twisted around with the gun pushed up, lowering only when I saw her lifting the rifle from the point-blank aim after shattering the bald man's head.

A name called from a great distance and repeated, Toni's sharp tone reminding me why I'd been so reluctant to come to her rescue; her voice like that of a parent disciplining a child.

The name was mine and as I twisted back, I watched her step over the blood and disappear back through to the room we'd just left.

There was enough of me left to stop and accept the order to wait. I stood and stayed the breath I hadn't realised had been racing. I held back muscles itching for the hunt as my stomach groaned, with my gaze fixed to the soldier's body with less of his head left from when I'd stepped around him.

I heard the click of a lighter striking as Toni came through the door. I tried to peer around but her body blocked the view. When she wouldn't relent to my frustration, I looked up to see the carton of cigarettes in one hand and the soldier's Glock in the other, which I hadn't noticed her take from me, the rifle nowhere to be seen.

A wisp of smoke trailed from the cigarette in her mouth.

My God. She understood.

I almost broke down, something heavy draining from inside me at the memory of the connection we'd had not so long ago.

Still, I pounced towards her, like a dog jumping to her side, into her cloud to find her taste potted with a blank space. With the cigarette soon in my mouth, the blood in my veins already calming, replaced with warmth and gratitude after understanding my plight.

I heard her calm, sweet words crystal clear as she grabbed my hand and led me down the corridor to the sound of the heavy door slamming closed.

"I know somewhere," she said as questions formed, but was forced to wait until I could remember how to get my mouth to work.

"Dan?" I managed to whisper, but she shook her head.

"They're better off staying where they are," she said, holding the door at the end of the corridor open and leading me to step over more bodies. Soldiers and civilians, but only one wore a gown, killed by a gunshot shattering his head open.

I didn't care that not once did she check for life before she pushed the gun to each head, setting the air alight with each explosion.

My only concern was the pointless waste of bullets, or did she know something I didn't?

14

Toni drove me through the corridors at a good pace, with my head twitching to noises which could have just been in my head. With each few steps I peered through open doors, out through windows and into the darkness, but never with enough time to fill the picture as Toni pushed on.

We climbed three storeys with my hand in hers. It felt wrong, but right at the same time. There was way too much going on in my head to even think of pulling away.

As we wound our way higher, I wanted to ask why we weren't just heading outside, but I couldn't find those simple words.

We came to a great sliding door which should have barred our way, but instead lay strewn to the side.

Blood streaked across its front, and at its foot lay a guard. Not a solider, but a man in a blue shirt, a great bunch of keys hanging by his side. Only as we approached did she let go of my hand to unclip the ring from his belt.

She didn't administer the gun to his head. Someone had already done the job, the pool of blood slowing its escape.

The carpet felt soft and let my bare feet bounced; the sensation so alien.

Toni lit another cigarette, handing it over before we reached a door with metal letters across its front, forming words I only recognised as her name when they passed out of sight.

She let go a second time and using the great bunch to unlock the door, she led me in, turning the thumbwheel at her back and slapping at the light switch.

I took in the spacious office with a great oak desk taking over half the space in the centre. Everything ordered. Neat and clean. Just as I would have expected.

She didn't stop for breath as we entered, instead ushering me to the long sofa filling the right-hand wall.

Sitting, I pulled on the glorious cigarette whilst watching as she raced around the room, pulling open the drawers of her desk, rifling through cupboards lining the floor and the wall.

On top of the floor-standing cupboards, a sink sunk into a countertop and tall laboratory instruments lined the surfaces, all clustered around a tall microscope. Beneath the counter sat what looked like the front of a white fridge that would seem at home in any kitchen.

I watched as she seemed to slow before glancing in my direction, glaring as if inspecting what she saw.

"You look like a granny," she said at last with a smile.

I glanced down. With the white coat spread wide, the tweed skirt and frilled blouse caught my attention as if for the first time.

"She'll be pissed if she sees you in her clothes," Toni said, then burst out laughing. "If she sees you at all."

"Who?" I said, but the ridiculousness of my reply made me speak again before she could. "Toni, what's happening to me?"

Her laughter cut short with my question and the lights in the room went dark.

I turned to Toni wide-eyed, watching as she held her palm in my direction, only lowering when the dim glow from the emergency light blinked to life above the door.

I turned to the great window, stood and walked around the desk, my gaze fixing on the yellow line appearing on the horizon. I had so many questions, but I struggled to fix on one. Thoughts raced around my head, each battling to fight against the growing fear of the hunger rising again.

"How long's it been?" I said, the question blurted out, dry and hoarse. I turned to the window to hide my face as I winced at my choice of question. I drew a deep breath, trying to force myself to focus on the important questions.

Glad when she didn't reply straight away, I was about to speak again when my gaze fixed on to the light on the horizon before turning down to the rest of the buildings bathed in darkness. Hadn't I been able to see in the darkness when I was in the cell?

"Too long," she said, her words turning muffled as she looked away, draining to silence. "I thought…" she started to say, but stopped herself as if she would choke on the words.

I winced again, this time with her reply, regretting leading her down this line.

"Toni, what's going on?"

"A year, give or take," Toni said, her voice flat.

"What's…" was all I could get out until the words dried.

"I thought we'd never be together again," she said, her words tailing off before her voice came back.

I was about to tell her that's not why I was here, that nothing had changed between us when she spoke again.

"But I see you every week," she said in a playful voice, as if changing her mood with a flick of a switch. I could tell from the muffle she looked away, still searching, but for what I didn't know.

With each moment the sun seemed to rise more, highlighting the roofs of the shorter buildings below.

"I don't get it," I said, remembering her words as I turned back to the darkness. It took a moment for my vision to catch her shape moving in the corner.

"The little flared red dress you wore in Istanbul last week. That did it for me."

"When I interviewed the president?" I replied, stepping away from the window and toward her shape.

The orange jumpsuit lay crumpled at her feet. With her hand at her back she unclipped her bra strap whilst stepping from a lace pair of knickers.

Blood raced around my body, filling me up, urging me on. I took a long drag of the cigarette and turned back to the window, but my thoughts fixed on her curves, the image of her slender body in the dim light stuck in my head.

Was I seriously letting her distract me from the shit going down all around? I took a deep pull on the cigarette, but still I couldn't shake the image.

"It's been too long. There's no escaping from our reality. I know that, but..." Toni said, again cutting herself off.

She was talking like we hadn't seen each other because there was too much going on in our lives.

Yes, when we were together the weeks would pass by like hours. The rest of life set aside, blurring past the window unnoticed, but all it took was for one of us to remember we had other lives, or she'd see me glance at someone else or a call would come from an editor or her boss, and our time would be over.

At first, I thought neither of us could ask the other to make the sacrifice it would take so we could be together forever.

"Too many distractions," she added.

Determined not to be drawn away, I spoke again.

"Why haven't you answered my questions?" I said, turning back, but the rest of the words held stiff in my throat as with the clink of coat-hangers on the rail I marvelled at the jeans hugging her form. The dark marks across her face as she pulled down the tight jumper made me regret my tone.

I turned back through the window and caught movement below, people moving between the buildings. Soldiers. A rescue party perhaps.

Shoulders hunching tight, I realised they weren't here to rescue me. They were here to rescue survivors. They were here to recapture Toni, my fate separate.

"The rescue party's here to save the day," I said.

"Look again," she replied, but I was still watching.

My gaze lingered and I held back from taking another drag. After a moment the pain in my stomach gripped tighter, the light seeming to grow and with it my vision sharpened.

Dull forms took shape. I watched as civilians and lab coats came into focus. I watched their slow movement, their direction without aim. The mass of people seemed to grow in number with the light. I watched their stilted movement, turning only as they bumped into each other, changing direction only as they reached the walls. Like maggots writhing in a bowl.

As the light grew, I saw the mass swelling in and out against a chain-link fence, ebbing and flowing like the tide. I saw another fence beyond and rubbed the bite on my arm. A long drag helped the growing pressure slow and took away the detail.

"What is this place?"

"A research facility," she replied, her voice getting near.

I recalled our conversation as the figure's injuries took shape and dark marked clothes grew clear, each face radiating a blank expression.

Now I knew what I was looking at. I knew what they were trying to do. I knew what I'd been infected with.

"What is it you do here exactly?" I said. With surprise my breath remained even.

"Head of infection control," she replied, her words louder than I expected.

I turned, my gaze catching at first on her bruised face so close. The cigarette dropped as my mouth shot open and my hands pushed to the syringe lunging for my thigh.

15

I lay on my back in the darkness, warm for the first time in what seemed like an age. The left side of my body felt heavy, paralysed under my weight; a soft cushion nestled beneath my head and I waited for the drip to fall to my face.

I couldn't move my left arm, my body unresponsive despite the rising panic. Just as it seemed like all was lost, I opened my eyes to the dim light and glared down at the dark head of hair resting on my chest.

A memory flooded back. My last. The needle stinging at the top of my leg before collapsing as she pulled back.

"What the fuck?" I screamed, my voice building with every syllable as my right side reared up.

The head stirred, soon tilting around. Toni's bleary eyes looked back as I scrabbled to the floor.

"What the fuck?" I repeated, pulling down my trousers and seeing the small circular plaster just below my hip.

"What the fuck?" I repeated, pulling them up, my anger towards her so familiar as she dropped back to the sofa, fists rubbing at her eyes as a deep yawn spread her mouth wide.

"What have you done this time?" I said in a desperate voice. "You'd better answer, or I'll…" I said, cutting myself off, fascinated with the washed-out colours as if I wore sunglasses to smooth the edges of my vision and take the vibrancy from my senses.

Turning back, I glared with my impatience rising.

"Wait," Toni said, getting to her feet.

I backed off, turning to look for any signs of what had happened whilst I'd been out cold. My gaze passed over the pistol on top of the desk, then stopped on a red jacket and skirt hanging on the back of the door. I lingered on the scarlet which seemed the only real colour in the room as our conversation from earlier pulled at my thoughts.

"Before I answer," she said, holding her palms out as I turned back, "tell me how you feel."

"Feel?" I said, snapping forward. "I'm fucking livid," I said, my volume building.

She pushed her hands out, her mouth twisting in laughter as she fought for control.

"Take a moment, let yourself wake. Calm down and tell me how you feel." She sat back, keeping her attention my way, her eyes doughy as she tilted her head to the side with her lips in a petite smile.

I turned away, knowing I had to fight that look. Taking a step to the window I tried to figure out what she meant. I looked out to the horizon and the perfect blue sky. My gaze caught on the carton of cigarettes and panic pushed into my chest.

Snapping back to Toni, I expected to see her leap in my direction, but instead her eyes were wide and hopeful as she perched on the edge of the couch.

I let my breath catch and sampled my feelings, tentative at first, noting all that came. As hard as I searched, the smell in the air stayed benign. Blank. Empty, with no earthy taste drawing my attention. My body gave no reaction, blood didn't course like a tsunami and my heart didn't pound out of my chest.

"I feel great," I said, the words quiet, unsure. "What have you done? I feel like…" I said, struggling for the words. "Like…" I said again, not knowing how to get it out.

"Human again?" Toni said, standing, her eyes widening as I gave a slow nod.

"You've cured me?" I said with tears welling in my eyes, but she stepped towards me, shaking her head, her hands opening to pull me close. "I don't understand."

I had her in my arms, the rage from before replaced with a compassion, a gratitude that I didn't feel the need to pull away her flesh from bone. I didn't feel the overwhelming need to lap at her open veins.

Her arms tightened around me, pulling closer as she spoke.

"It's not a cure," she said, her voice soft. "But it will suppress the symptoms for a while and with enough doses it might work."

I tried to pull away, but her arms held me in place.

"How do you know? How can you be sure?" I searched, frantic for her answer when no reply came. "Please, tell me or my brain will explode."

Her arms tightened further, clamping on for dear life. Her lunge flashed in my mind as the sound of distant gunshots rang in my ears and an explosion shocked the fabric of the building.

"They're coming," Toni said.

"I don't care who's coming. Just tell me please. How do you know?"

After a pause, she spoke with a soft voice.

"It's my formula."

My knees gave way and I staggered back.

16

"You did this?" I shouted, struggling to stay upright, my legs like jelly.

"No," Toni shouted back as she stepped forward, trying to gather me up.

"But you made the drug," I said, slapping away her outstretched arms.

"It's the same thing you were given when you arrived. It was developed as a vaccine," she said as I scrabbled back, bumping against her desk. "But it wasn't ready. Wasn't for human testing. They didn't give me enough time. I told them it wasn't for use on humans yet."

I stopped, confused thoughts racing around my brain and I listened to my panting breath as she continued to hurry out the words before I could process.

"I need more doses?"

"Yes," she said. "But I don't know how many."

"Why didn't you just tell me when we got here? Why attack me?" I said, but already my mind raced onto the next question.

"We didn't have time. I could see it in your eyes. I'm sorry, okay. I should have spoken to you first," she said holding her hands out into the gap between us.

"Wait. How do you know what they've done to me?" I said, a sudden rush of cold air blanketing my shoulders.

"There were more tests to do, more protocols to follow. They refused to let me finish the work and when they told me to jump straight to the trials, I threatened to go to the media."

"Why such a rush?" I said with the shake of my head as I wiped away the last of my tears across the back of my hand.

Toni paused, swallowing down as she took a moment before her words came slow and quiet.

"There's been an outbreak. A small village south east of here." She paused again, her eyes widening as she watched the alarm on my face. "One of our team took himself off sick."

I reared back, already seeing where this was going. Already seeing the shame in her face as I opened my mouth.

"Bitten?"

She nodded. "But, of course, we didn't know at the time. He shouldn't have had any contact with the subjects so he wasn't followed up or put in one of the quarantine quarters downstairs."

"Bitten by what? You said you weren't testing on humans yet."

"You can't call them human. Not at that stage." Toni watched intensely as a scowl set on my face. "I promise," she said, moving forward. "We didn't infect him."

I pushed the weight of the new questions to the side and wound back to one I needed the answer to.

"The outbreak," I said, urging her to finish the story.

She took another deep breath and turned away to the window before speaking. "The village is sealed up. Nothing's going in or out. The problem will be resolved soon."

"But?" I said when she stopped talking. All our years of being so close told me she was holding back.

"There's a small window where anything could have happened."

"You mean someone could have been bitten and hasn't been contained," I said.

Toni nodded.

"How likely is it?"

She paused again as if weighing up her words. "There were calls to the police. A fight."

I could feel my brow rising as she spoke.

"We haven't traced all those who were involved in the incident."

I waited for a long while before I could bring myself to speak. When she edged closer, I backed off, my shoulders tensing.

"I still don't get it. One outbreak and it's like we're in Nazi Germany," I said, watching her purpling cheeks twitch at my words.

Toni leant forward. "It's like nothing we've ever seen. Forget Spanish Flu, Pneumonic plague, Ebola. Those are like the common cold compared to this. Our predictions show a mortality rate of one hundred percent. We're talking global killer. Full stop. The decision came from very high up."

"So why not go to the media? Tell the people something so they would cooperate?"

"Not my decision," she replied in a sharp tone, as if she was losing patience with the questions. "I called you."

I raised a brow. "Yes, you did," I said. "And they singled me out to become the first human test subject."

Toni looked away, but her reaction was so different to what I was expecting. Her arms had fallen to her side, but lifted to wrap around her stomach as she turned back.

"I thought I'd..." she started to say, but again changed her mind, taking a great breath before she spoke. "They knew about you. I had to tell someone. I couldn't sit back. I had to call. They found me on the phone, beat me until I told them what I'd said. If you hadn't come here, they were coming to get you anyway. Some sick revenge for my betrayal. I'm so sorry. I knew what they were going to do but I was powerless to stop it."

A single tear ran down the purpling skin on her face as she barely reacted to the growing echoes of gunshots filling the background.

We stood, neither of us able to talk, neither of us listening to the litter of explosions and the chatter of the gunfire until, finally, Toni pulled in a great breath and let her arms fall as she straightened up.

"We have to go, or we'll never leave this place alive," she said, her gaze near, but she wasn't able to look me square in the eye.

"I know why they'll kill me, but you? You're part of the solution."

"I won't let them do anything to you. I saved your life and I'll do it again. I'll do it every minute of the day if you need me to. I've lost their trust. I'm a security breach and I have to be silenced for the greater good of the project."

I turned away, ignoring her words, then felt her grip around my upper arm. She tugged, pulling me to the window.

"Look," she said, and I turned to face the glass. The swarm was still there, but now lines of camouflaged soldiers streamed from trucks out in the yard, each looking left and right, their rifles levelled as they piled into every building.

A door burst open in the courtyard below, a creature leapt out, its hunched-over form the only sign of its humanity. The arc of its jump was a feat greater than an Olympian in his peak. Only tattered rags remained of its blue gown circling around its neck as dark veins spidered out across its skin.

Heads turned its way, followed by rifles. Soldiers dropped to their knees, their eyes peering through the scopes, but each gave an inexplicable pause. None pulled the trigger and I asked myself what they'd been told to expect as I watched on, rearing back as the creature tangled to one of their colleagues whose flesh flew from his face, ripped and discarded into the air.

My head shook as I took in the melee. I'd seen this before and worse already, but those images felt like I'd seen them through someone else's point of view. Like on TV; my consciousness removed.

Taking this in for the first time, my body shook, panic radiating in waves. Only Toni's hand held tight in mine stopped me from curling into a ball and giving up.

Machine-gun fire burst out from the side-lines, a frantic chatter of bullets exploding into the crowd. I counted three soldiers down before the creature and its victim took the brunt of the barrage. A hundred other rounds swiftly joined the onslaught, every soldier cutting them down.

I felt my breath heavy as I watched, Toni's warm hand clutching at mine, but I couldn't press back; my body so numb I thought I might collapse.

"You'd be dead if I hadn't helped. You'll be dead when they see you. We have to go. They can't let you get out. You're already their best chance. They'll want to pull you apart and see why it worked when so many before you hadn't."

"But," I said, turning away from the reforming line, soldier's rushing in to check for survivors, "I'm not immune. It didn't work," I said in a low voice. "Before. Before," I repeated, "I was like them. I wanted to do so much. The hunger felt so overwhelming."

Her hand clamped tighter and she turned me around by the shoulder, peering into my eyes.

"No, you're not like them. Won't be. You're alive. They're dead. You're human and I've given your body a chance to fight back. We've got to go. They're in the building already."

I stayed where I stood, unable to move as I watched her rush to the wardrobe, pulling out a rucksack while shouldering a rifle.

Beckoning me forward with the pistol in her hand, I paused while I asked myself why the hell she had a rifle in her wardrobe. I started towards the door as she pulled down the red outfit and stuffed it into the bag before opening the fridge, but with her back to me I couldn't see what she'd pushed away.

As she took hold of the handle I stopped, hearing a noise the other side.

Toni heard it, too, and threw herself to the floor just in time for an explosion to destroy the lock and fling the door wide.

17

The metal handle stopped spinning as it reached my feet. With the noxious smoke dispersing, a stocky figure appeared at the door which was somehow still on its hinges. A gas mask wrapped around the figure's face and a short rifle tracked up in our direction.

Toni leant back on her elbows where she'd fallen, her brow lowering as she stared at the figure taking tentative steps across the threshold.

His look shifted to meet mine. A deep but muffled sound came from behind his mask. The words seemed as if not meant for us.

He took a step forward, shifting the weight of the backpack on his back with his gun still on Toni.

Another figure arrived from behind. At first look they were identical.

A burst of gunfire lit up the corridor. Muffled shouts followed as if from all around.

Anger rose in my chest. These were the people who had done this. These were the people who had beaten Toni.

An urge to let my guard down built. I wanted the rage back, wanted the animal hunger to return so I could defend myself, defend Toni, despite the consequences. But I couldn't feel it build.

The second man stood with his shoulder at the doorframe, peering around a shallow angle out into the corridor. The soldier in the room shouted something whilst shaking his head, but I couldn't catch the meaning through the mask as his chest heaved with the effort.

Behind him followed a heavy chemical odour, the burn of plastic thickening the air. A great line of splattered blood criss-crossed his dark, earthy uniform as if an artist had flicked a brush.

The inside of his mask misted, the words muffled with the race of breath through the protruding filter.

Gunfire in the corridor wouldn't let me concentrate. All I could do was stare back wide-eyed at his noise, shaking my head, the point of the muzzle snapping between us.

His hand stopped steadying the machine gun. Instead, he hurried to unclip his helmet, dropping it to the desk as he flicked his view between the two of us. His aim soon settled on me.

Holding the rifle in one hand, he pulled off the mask and dragged in air. His short dark fringe ran with sweat rolling down his red face and his bloodshot eyes flicked open and closed, frantic to rid the sting of salt.

Gunfire burst down the corridor.

The rifle's report at the door surged through me and I flinched in its direction, not sure where I would see the gun pointed. The lack of pain could have been a delayed reaction, but no, the aim peered down the corridor and another volley rattled off as I stared, my feet fixed to the floor by indecision as to which threat they considered the worst.

I looked to Toni out of the corner of my eye. She seemed calm, locking eyes with the soldier as he shook his head, muttering under his breath.

"Stand up," he'd been saying all along. "You're coming with us," he said, his words robotic, rehearsed, but with no conviction.

The unmasked soldier drew my attention back as he spoke whilst moving deeper into the room. With a high voice and pink features, he looked so young; so much younger than me. The shake in his voice betrayed his recent loss of innocence.

"Stoppage," came the muffled shout from behind the other's mask.

Our guy's eyes lit up, face alarming and his head rearing back as he heard the click echo from the rifle.

I glanced to see the solider at the door raking the slide at the side of the weapon, pushing forward and pulling back. Each of us watched as his motion grew more frantic, staring as he disappeared in a blur of movement, his scream quickly muffled to leave only the echo of the rifle hitting the floor.

I looked to the boy soldier to make sure he'd seen it too.

He stared back, reflecting my disbelief. I couldn't tell if sweat or tears ran from his eyes.

Toni didn't pause. Her hand pushed the pistol in a slide across the floor before grabbing at her rifle.

Our eyes locked. I knew she'd seen it. Seen it there, a shadow darting past the doorway, grabbing the masked soldier and he'd gone.

"Aim that weapon somewhere else," Toni's sharp voice boomed.

I turned towards her to see her standing at my side and I followed the aim of her rifle to the young soldier's dripping face, his mouth hung wide, his face turned from the corridor. The gun dropping in slow motion.

Sound came from the corridor. A noise I couldn't at first describe, but soon I recognised something heavy being dragged across the carpet.

The young man and I froze, the shake of his head his only movement, his eyes pleading in her direction.

Toni continued to point the rifle at him, motioning with her head towards the doorway.

"Do your job, soldier," her voice bellowed like a drill sergeant.

His eyes unblinking, I could see his indecision. He gave no reaction to the dark mark appearing at his crotch as he snatched a look between the gun in her hand and the corridor, then to the window at his shoulder.

"Soldier," Toni screamed, but he stepped to the glass and peered down, all with the noise in the corridor multiplying.

I watched his eyes go wide as he peered lower, watched as he let the short machine gun down on its straps.

Toni turned her gun to the rising activity beyond the door, but I couldn't keep my stare from him as with the pant of his breath growing ever faster, he unclipped the top of his holster and drew his pistol whilst shaking his head.

"No," I said, slowly standing with my hands reaching towards him. "What's your name?" I whispered, keeping my voice as calm as I could, but he couldn't take his gaze from below.

He shook his head and I glanced to Toni to see her stepping to the door with the rifle at her hip.

His gun was already under his chin as I turned back and I screamed for him to stop.

My breath caught, head numb as I dropped to my knees. Pressing my hands to my cheeks, the spent cartridge rang like a tiny bell as it glanced off the desk.

I heard his breath push out as he slumped to the floor.

In the corridor, the scrape on the carpet had stopped, replaced with an orchestra of drumming feet.

18

Without thought I rose. Toni was already at the door, slamming it closed before running to the other side of the ornate desk and hopping over where the soldier had fallen.

She pushed.

The heavy wood didn't move until I came around the other side and leant down, heaving with all I could whilst trying not to look at the soldier's legs. It was too late to unsee the spray of red across the ceiling.

I looked away as I pushed with everything I had. The desk built its pace towards the door, slamming hard to the wall. Both of us stared at the gap between the desk and the door, its feet protruding out further than its surface, giving a big enough gap for a hand to fit through sideways.

Silently we agreed nothing could be done and adding our weight to the wood, stared back to the window.

"Sealed shut?" I said, jumping as I finished my words, the door slapping hard against the wood and sending a wave of vibration through our bodies.

We turned around and pushed back, twisting again as the door held firm. My gaze fell to the floor and the sprawled body despite my command, fixing on the slow darkening of the carpet.

"And bulletproof," she said, as I raised the pistol towards the glass, dropping my hand as I scoured the room for inspiration.

"Why the hell did you bring us up here?" I said as the realisation came that we were trapped.

"I need the vaccine," she said. "You were in no fit state to move once I'd administered."

I glared at her then surveyed the room again.

"I'll check his bag," I said, feeling the desk move with me as I leapt away, snapping back around to the door to make sure Toni had kept her hold.

I lunged back as another great smack of flesh thudded against the entrance.

The scream came next, but the effect was different this time. I felt numb to the emotion of the call, but couldn't help stare past Toni with her fingers in her ears.

A pale, white arm came snapping through the gap, the skin along its length scraping against the door, bunching black veins under the surface as it drew back only to return and claw at the air.

Kneeling to the carpet, I held my breath as I crouched over the dead soldier. I tried to keep my survey from his head, huffing breath with the effort of turning him over.

Pinching the top of his small pack open, my fingers slid on the sticky blood. I was in, but found the pack empty of anything we could use.

Letting the body settle on its front, I jumped to my feet at the sound of Toni's effort and ran to the edge of the desk, hunching my shoulders, slapping the wood hard and reclaiming what she couldn't help give up.

Shaking my head, our eyes met, separating to take in the rest of the room.

"Come on," I said in a hurry. "You're the clever one. How do we get out of this?"

She laughed and I reared back.

"I'm serious."

"You ain't too stupid yourself," she replied putting on a thick West Country accent.

I squinted back. "There's no time," I said, scanning the empty surfaces of the room whilst pushing hard against the desk. A realisation came as the door smacked against the wood. Bursts of gunfire no longer peppered the air.

"Sorry," she said with a laugh. I could only reply with a shake of my head. "Bullet proof glass stops bullets, right?"

"What else?" I said to the odd question.

"The glass works because the lead in a bullet is actually pretty soft and spreads when they hit something that's harder. A lot of the damage is done because they're hot, often melting through their target."

I nodded with excitement, but my energy drained as I spoke. "So we need something small, cold and hard?"

I could see the thoughts forming as she squinted around the room, her face straining in time with mine as we pushed against the desk to fight a renewed surge.

As the pressure released, the desk moved again and I pushed back as she leapt away whilst ushering me to shuffle along where she'd been. As I moved, I watched her open the right-hand drawer, sliding it out as far as it would go, the stop slapping hard as it reached its limit.

Her hand grabbed for a small pink fabric-covered box. I knew its contents before she jumped away.

Our eyes locked in the shared moment. She wore a small smile, her head tilted and brows ever so slightly raised. The battering at the door behind me couldn't dismiss the memory.

The ring was my first ever gift for anyone outside my family. My one and only gift for her. I'd used all my money, my head in the clouds after I came to terms with being different to everyone else, different to everyone apart from Toni.

I was in love.

I'd fallen for her so deeply I couldn't imagine it wouldn't work.

When we realised it wasn't meant to be, I told her to get rid of it. I didn't want it back. She gave it to charity, so she'd said, telling me it meant nothing the first time we split. The only time we'd split. The only time we thought we knew what we were doing, a time when we thought we could see into the future.

But she'd kept it. She had it near.

As the confusion welled up in my chest, warmth radiating from my heart, I watched as if viewing CCTV images.

She went straight to a floor cupboard, pulling a heavy weight from the bottom shelf and then a roll of surgical tape from another. Placing the ring on the worktop she let the weight drop from her hands before I could squeal in disbelief. I turned back from a renewed shove at the desk and saw Toni at the window, pulling the diamond from the mangled golden setting, glancing back, sorrow in her eyes, before taping the stone.

Yes, it was real.

I didn't see the glass crack as she raised the weight and hit it over and again. I didn't see it splinter before I had to turn, putting my hands at the edge of the desk to renew my effort.

Shrill screams radiated from the corridor, the wood moving towards me despite my weight's insistence. I turned to see her bending down and saw a great slice along the fabric of her jeans, felt the rush of the breeze in the room, the floor littered with finger-thick clumps of glass.

I turned back despite her urges, saw three black vein-ridden arms at the door. I saw the door bending at the top. Saw what I thought was the wall swaying inward.

"Come on," she said, but I couldn't move knowing the desk would give. They'd overrun us in seconds.

With Toni back at my side, I gave all my effort to push against the pressure. She shrugged the rifle off her shoulder and pushed the muzzle through the gap, unleashing fury with a sharp pull of the trigger.

The first explosion numbed my ears. The second and the third left them ringing, but the tide relented and I could release.

A great breath pulled into my lungs; for the first time I smelt the stench, the soiled soup of sewerage from the corridor.

Toni dragged me away, pushing me towards the window. I had to skip over the body, had to steady myself as I landed on the glass, hoping to stop my bare feet from cutting to ribbons.

With her hands at my back, Toni helped me climb. The door creaked against the wood, but I couldn't look; I couldn't do anything but keep my eyes set on the horizon.

I was soon up and on the ledge, looking along the side of the building at the decorative bricks protruding just enough to give texture at a glance, but were surely not enough for me to balance my weight. Not enough to get me to the metal drainpipe and relative safety just out of arms reach.

"Go," she said, her voice frantic.

I had no choice, the door opening wide, pushing the desk to the side.

"Go," she said, and I saw her rucksack being pushed along the floor with the desk.

"Go," she shouted. As she ran behind me, the first of the creatures came through on the top of the desk, limbs at its back already following.

"Go," she screamed and I took the step, my weight holding as I gripped the thin of the brick below. With my arms almost at their full extent to reach, my fingers scraped for a grip at the edge of the flat roof.

With her following at my side, my foot slipped, scraping toes, but my grip felt strong, fingernails digging into the soft bitumen skin of the roof. I held on, waiting for my breath to recover.

"Shit. The bag," I heard her say.

"Leave it," I shouted, but as I turned I saw her disappear back through the window, a deafening scream howling from inside.

19

With my concentration on where she'd stood, I felt my feet slipping. My fingers ached as they pinched into the roof, my once-long nails already sheared flat. I turned, lunging for the drainpipe, giving my trust it wouldn't fall away; hoping it wouldn't release from the wall as I gripped around its surface and dug my toes hard as they came to rest on each side of the metal bracket.

The round metal pipe moved, but didn't give out all the way. At least not by the time my weight settled. The wind had picked up and with every movement as I clung on, the metal rubbed against itself. Creaking, Shifting. Complaining as if it could go at any moment.

My hands numb with effort, I knew I couldn't last long like this, but I wouldn't look down; couldn't let myself head that way.

I refused to acknowledge what had made the soldier give up and take the easy way out, despite the constant pull of my thoughts in that direction.

I turned back to the space where Toni had been not so long before, but she hadn't returned. I had to help, but I knew I couldn't cling on for much longer to the metal rattling with the slightest of movements. I'd be no help if I fell to the ground.

Somehow I climbed, letting the stack take my weight as I gripped around its girth with each hand, pushing my feet flat against the brick. I could see no other way and somehow I rose, at least at first, getting three paces up the wall before I was high enough for my hands to scrabble at the roof and find the ledge on the other side, just as the stack collapsed. My feet fell from under me as they fought for traction in the air and my grip tested to the limit on the coarse brick roofline.

It held. I heaved myself up by my arms, scraping my front over the edge before I finally had my feet on the solid ground.

My last effort sent the downpipe ringing as it released the last of its grip, clattering against the brickwork as it fell to the ground.

I lay face down against the rough surface, drained, empty and savouring the solid roof beneath me.

My breath calmed with each intake until I thought of Toni left behind, guilt pounding in my chest that I didn't go back for her.

Scrabbling to the edge, not taking in my surroundings, I stayed low. Leaning over, my breath caught as I reared back at the distance to the ground below. It was only three storeys, but enough to send my head into a spin even before I'd processed the movement between the buildings.

Soon the bodies gained definition and I realised it wasn't the ground in motion. Still wandering aimless as before, they'd grown in number with a low hum radiating with the same stench we'd left behind in the corridor.

I pulled my head up, my vision extending across the distance, past the trucks and the Land Rovers and the scattered weapons. Nausea rose up through my body with a great sense of dread when all I could see were the infected. What hope could there be if the lorry loads of soldiers had been overcome so easily?

The horizon ran out before I could see what I wanted, but relief came in the form of gunfire, distant at first; the best sign there was still resistance out there.

Close gunfire replied. So close. I shook with its force, until hope rose again in my chest as I realised it came from below, the sound bursting from the window.

Then came Toni, her body rearing back as she fired again from the pistol in her hand. With her precious pack slung on one shoulder, she swung it under her arm as she climbed out of the window backwards into the nothingness.

I pushed myself out into the air as far as I dared, just below my ribs and reached down, letting my arms drop.

"Grab on," I said and she gave a start, sending her balance off, but I took her hand as it flailed, the other pushing the gun into her waistband before reaching up to take my other hand. A great smile sparkled on my face as we touched, my grip encircling her wrist. Together we scraped and shuffled sideways.

Clear of the window, I felt strong again. I felt ready to help drag her up, confident as she gripped me tight, shuffling her feet along the wall as I scooted back, anchoring my torso to grip the shallow ledge. With her feet flat as mine had been, she climbed higher and I knew soon we would be safe and together. I could hold her in my arms and we could take our time to think. We would have all the time in the world to wait and contemplate the right moment to make the next move to escape the chaos.

Toni climbed higher, my gaze locked to hers, her speed increasing as a scream seared through the air from below.

I peered down as a dark flash burst from the window.

I expected to see the shape fall to the ground. I didn't expect Toni's body to go tight, to pull against me so hard as I took her full weight, dragging me down.

It all made sense when my gaze fell on the snarling beast lined with dark veins, its claw-like grip around Toni's ankle as it swayed, its mouth snapping wide and its other hand clawing at the air.

20

With no time to think, no energy left to slow their weight from dragging me from the roof, I felt no movie-like surge of inhuman strength rising within me to pull them both up.

My options were clear. Save myself, sending Toni to her death, or be dragged down so all three of us could be dead together.

"Let the bag go," I shouted, as it swung at her shoulder. It would make no difference, neither did reaching for the gun. She'd have to let go of one of my hands to do so.

Her eyes just stared deep into mine in reply.

I lingered longer than I should.

I knew there would be no miracle.

I knew the creature's grip would hold longer than I could keep mine whilst staying anchored to the roof. Only as a shot rang out somewhere in the far distance, did I snap out of my hopeless stare.

My joy seemed greater than it should; the creature's weight felt no more. I looked down, watching as it fell, my stare catching on a cloud of blood drifting in the air.

Toni scrabbled over the edge of the roof before the slap of the creature's body hit against the concrete.

Dragging her the last few paces from the edge, I gripped her tight around the waist as I collapsed, exhausted, to the flat of my back.

Our breath heaved as she buried her head in the crook of my neck with her body coming to rest on my side, much like she had as I'd woken on the couch beneath us.

With breath slowing, a low background hum took over and it felt as if the building beneath us shook. When I couldn't stand the noise anymore, I spoke, my words sharper than I'd intended.

"Tell me everything," I said. "Full disclosure." My hands dropped from around her back and I tried to sit, but she gripped around my shoulder, holding me tight.

"Stay down. That sniper might change his mind. If he figures out who we are, we might be his next target."

I hadn't connected the distant shot and the puff of blood which saved us, not having considered the cause before now. Another shot echoed through the air.

"He saved us," I replied, pausing when I didn't hear the shot land close by.

"He might have missed," Toni said with a voice devoid of emotion.

I let the words sink in and repeated my question.

"What the hell is going on? I need details."

She didn't reply straight away and my hearing settled back to the hundreds of low calls writhing below us.

"It's bad," she said, looking up.

"No shit," I said, shaking my head. "Tell me everything, unless you have other things to attend to?" I added, raising my brow.

Toni moved her head to the side and spoke.

"Twelve months ago, a group of American researchers found a new fungus in the Amazon. A member of the Ophiocordyceps family," she said, before pausing for a breath. "When initial research hailed it as a possible cure for influenza, a universal vaccine, work began across the world, fast tracking the R&D to confirm the breakthrough. Within two months, our government received reports that independent labs in the global research network were being taken over by their country's governments.

"They switched to sharing findings only on official channels. There was a big delay before the news broke. A H1N1 influenza strain infected the fungus in the American lab where the initial analysis took place. After some poor containment practices, the first known case of human infection was a research fellow who died of a heart attack. Natural causes as far as we can tell. He died at his desk while carrying out tests. The fungus must have fruited whilst being worked on, transmitting the mutated virus."

82

She paused, tilted her head up, locking eyes with mine.

"He rose from the dead and attacked his colleagues."

Realising my body shook, her grip tightened around me.

"But," I said, my throat drying as I tried to get my head around it, "how does it bring someone back from the dead? How could that be possible?"

"We still don't know. No one does. There's still so much work to do."

I paused, swallowing back the questions piling up in my head, but when a gust of air brought the stench from below, I spoke again.

"When was the first death?"

"Six months ago."

"Six months?" I replied, raising my voice.

Toni nodded. "Since then we've been racing to find a cure. The virus is such an effective delivery system."

"Six months?" I repeated.

"Aside from a few outbreaks which were all controlled, in the UK anyway, there's been very few problems."

"Problems?" I said, and she buried her head back in the crook of my neck. She nodded, keeping quiet before I spoke again. "So this fungus…"

"Virus," she interrupted, pushing herself closer.

"This virus," I said. "It turns people into zombies with inhuman strength, giving the ability to leap into the air and chase down an Olympic sprinter?"

She didn't reply.

"What aren't you telling me?"

"Those abilities are not from the mutated virus," Toni replied, and I tried to pull away, but she wouldn't let go. "They're a side effect."

"A side effect?"

"Of the work we've been doing." She looked up. "The work I refused to administer to human test subjects."

83

It was my turn to hold back my reply, but I couldn't for long.

"But someone did. So they're different?"

"These creatures you see down there, well most, they're infected with the virus. It doesn't kill unless you're infirm or otherwise compromised through a large wound. After death the virus takes over and drives the host to kill. They need the flesh, the protein, to sustain the raging virus."

"So they're just out to feed?"

"Yes. For some reason they're not concerned with spreading the infection as such, although it's a by-product if the newly infected survives the initial bite. The creatures go into a frenzy, biting anything, even if it's too much to eat. They'll do nothing else if faced with a source of protein and if they can't find it, they'll search it out. We've never seen a subject where this is not the case. The original virus doesn't affect the living," Toni said, then added, "in its unadulterated form. It only takes over when the host dies. It takes control. We don't know how, but it does. You have to admire the mechanism though."

"And the other…" I paused as I took in her final words. "Things?"

I shuffled out from under her when she didn't reply.

"They're still alive."

I could feel my heart beating hard. "But you said…" I blurted out as I raised myself to my feet. "I've seen them with terrible wounds no one could survive?"

"Get down," she whispered, her hands reaching up.

When I backed away, she sat up and let her arms drop.

"Unless the central nervous system is damaged, they can't be stopped.

"The people with you down there each had different versions of the trial vaccination. It had different effects, some of which you mentioned. The result is an amalgam of the original mutation and human physiology. Each a different engineered strain."

"But they're super humans with an insatiable thirst for death," I said, staring at her stony-faced.

"If you will." She fixed her view to the roof.

"And you made them," I said. "Like me."

Toni shook her head. "That wasn't our intention," she replied, not looking up.

"But it was the doctor I met that used your drugs on living people and caused all of this?" I said and could feel my eyes squinting more with each word.

Turning away, she nodded and I spoke again.

"I'll say it again. Have I woken up in Nazi Germany?"

She didn't reply. Instead I thought of Iraq and Syria, Darfur and the Congo, and those were just in recent history. But this was Britain. Had we lost our principles so easily?

"And what do you mean about admiring the virus?" I said, her words coming back to jar my mind for a second time. There was no pause before her reply.

"From a biological perspective, our virus is awesome. The way it infects whilst keeping the host alive and in the process imparting so much, like the strength and enhanced senses. All we have to do..." she stopped speaking as my interruption burst out.

"I'm not a fucking host," I said, pulling back.

"I'm sorry. It's just the way I talk. The people. They're people. I know."

"And they're all gone now?" I said when she didn't reply.

Toni turned back, biting her bottom lip as she shook her head and stared down to the bitumen pitch of the roof.

"But everyone I've seen had their brains blown out or smashed against the concrete."

"You saw one corridor," she said, standing, pointing to the long, low building which housed my cell. Still holding her finger out, she turned me around and I took in the building shaped like a child would draw the sun.

Where we stood side by side was the ball in the middle; the cell blocks were the lines out from the central circle.

With the ground writhing between the buildings, I stopped turning as I completed the circle and finished counting the twelve cell blocks.

21

"Each one?" I said, pulling my mouth closed.

Toni nodded with her eyes almost shut.

"Full?" I added, and she continued the nod. "And human testing started when? Where did all these people come from? It's been two days since you called me."

Toni snapped her head to the side at the echo of a distant shot.

"Not here, not now. Please."

I barely noticed the call of the weapon; it was the sight of the birds startled into flight which caught my eye.

"All in the last forty-eight hours?" I said, my voice lowering as I fought to hold back a volley of questions.

"Not here. Please," she insisted again, grabbing my arm.

I let her draw me to a crouch.

"You said you wouldn't let them do it," I said in a soft, almost childlike voice.

Toni slowly shook her head as she scoured the skyline. Another shot rang off as a blast of wind rattled through my clothes, sending a chill through my body. A memory of hunger pulled my lips tight.

She was right; there had to be better places to have this conversation. I did my best to push the thought away, joining in the search across the roof.

After twisting around, still bent at my knees, I wasn't sure what we were looking for, but I was certain we hadn't found it. There was no shelter on top of the roof. No stairwell rising out with a door we could open or break through.

The tallest feature was a metal tower twice higher than the building. On the top sat satellite dishes and mobile phone masts. Halfway up were thick cables running tight to a smaller version of the mast on each of the twelve outer buildings.

Across the roof were small upturned plastic boxes no larger than my head, each face slatted with a ventilation grill. None of these were our way back into the building and, anyway, the infested corridors were not where we should return to.

Toni seemed to agree, ignoring the square hatch we found at the edge of the building. Instead, I followed her on hands and knees as she crawled the perimeter.

Copying her motion as she peered over the edge, I watched as Toni flicked her head away every few moments to take a deep breath and clear away the foul sewerage stench I could taste on my tongue after only a moment staring at the writhing mass of bodies over the side.

Every area of ground swam with creatures squirming against one another. I stared at their unrelenting hunt for human protein. I watched as they walked into walls, turning without stumbling, heading in a new direction before hitting the next object in their way.

In amongst the slow tide it was easy to see those who were different, those I'd shared a cell block with such a short time ago. Their hands swung out, clearing a path wherever they headed. I could see the hunger in their eyes, the hunger I wanted only to be a memory.

If this was what it was like after forty-eight hours then what would it be like after a week?

"What?" Toni said, turning at my side.

My look must have said so much.

"This after such a short time?" I could feel hope draining as I stared on. "If it was just the original mutation," I said, pushing down the lump in my throat, "if it was just those you didn't create, then I guess we would have a chance. But when these creatures…" I paused, searching for the words. "Your amalgam, the ones who are still alive, when they spread their version of the virus we won't have a chance."

Toni shook her head.

"No," she said, reaching her warm hand on top of mine at the edge of the roof. "Those things, the mistakes, they're not the same. When they bite, only the original virus passes on. So it will only bring back someone once they're dead. It's just these we have to deal with. No more."

Questions rose as I processed her words, but as a pair of eyes from below snapped up in my direction, the thoughts dissipated in the shared look.

Their pause was less than mine. His black-lined faced stayed fixed as he forced his way to the edge of the building, smacking aside the dead creatures in his way.

My heart raced as he pounced into the air, his feet landing to the window ledge on the first floor.

"Toni," I squealed as it took another leap, not looking where it would land; the window above.

Leaning forward, she followed my view of the creature slapping against the second-floor pane of glass to fall backward, its landing cushioned by bodies who took no notice, only squirming while he rose to his feet to try again.

I couldn't crawl. I had to stand, frustrated at the pace, but dropped back to my knees as we completed the wide circular perimeter. My heart pounded in my chest with a great sense of dread when our miracle escape didn't materialise whilst knowing it would only be a matter of time before the creatures would get a footing and make the next leap to the roof.

"Get up," Toni said, and I twitched my head to look at her stern face, her hands out for mine. "Get up. We need to get there," she said, pointing to one of the twelve outer buildings.

Standing with my mouth agape, I felt like laughing as I saw the cell blocks were only one storey high, but as I lingered I could see the double perimeter fence intact with none of the dead filling the space. On the far side stood the wide space of a car park full of vehicles we could use to the get the hell out of here.

But to get there we would have to bound across a gap of over three car lengths wide. Unless we'd sprouted wings or gained inhuman strength. I felt like asking if she had a potion for that; instead, I pulled back the barbs.

"Have you gone mad?"

My words fell away, a scream piercing through my head giving no chance to hear if she'd mouthed a reply.

I watched as Toni pulled out the pistol with her left hand, pushing me toward the base of the tower with her right.

With my head rolling to the side, I caught a blur of motion, my body shaking with every shot launching from the barrel which did nothing to slow the creature's race towards us.

22

Puffs of blood, skin and bone burst out from every angle as Toni continued to hit the target. This was it. This was the end of the line and all before we'd got started. Before I could set this outrage straight; before I could tell the world Toni's story. My story now.

No. It couldn't be.

I hadn't got this far in my life to go down as a footnote in a history never told.

I sat up straight, landing on my knees and lunged forward just as the creature blurred across my view. I caught its sodden flesh; tacky thick blood sticking to my fingers as I pushed, only stopping just beyond the edge of the roof with Toni grabbing my ankles.

The creature stared, snarling back as it fell, its jaw snapping at the air before its head smashed against a short wall and its neck set forever at a right angle.

I watched as it rose, my breath getting out of control, but coming back as I saw its slow movement, its eyes already whitening over.

Toni pulled me back and into her arms, squeezing tight until our gaze followed to the cable from the high mast above running down to the centre of the shorter building we hoped to be a haven.

"You first," she said, pointing halfway up the tower. She'd had the same idea. Her other hand pulled a tissue from her pocket, its white ruined by the dark blood coming back as she dabbed at my face.

A shot rang off in the distance and we fell to a crouch.

"Take off the lab coat," she said and I did, the cold air biting through the blouse. She pulled a penknife from her pack, slashed at the material halfway down and tore it in two before rolling one half in on itself.

Holding each end of the improvised rope, she wrapped as much as she could around each fist as she held on tight.

I understood, I said, but only with a nod.

"*You* first," I said, my hands shaking as I tried to wrap my half of the lab coat into a rope. Toni handed hers over, trying not to let it unravel as she took my half and repeated the twist.

"You," she replied with force in her voice, taking me by the arm and guiding me towards the tower.

Movement caught in my peripheral vision and I turned to see a hand on the edge of the roof. We were too far away to see the detail, but I knew it would run with dark veins. The scream confirmed it, stopping only as it thudded to the ground.

I stood and a second scream lit the air; a third call joined it and I didn't need to be asked again. I ran, the thin metal of the mast cutting into my feet as I climbed with Toni close behind on the opposite side. The mast creaked, swayed and moved, tightening the cables as we rose.

The calls grew so loud I wanted to push my fingers deep into my ears. The shout of the distant gunfire grew more frequent, but still we didn't know who the target could be.

We climbed, stopping only when I could reach out to the thick cable.

Breath pulled in fast and I wrapped the rope as tight as I could, loosening back a turn as I felt my fingers numb. I held the rolled-up coat over the cable; it was much harder to wrap the left side without letting go of the right. I would just have to hold on for my life.

And there it was, right on cue, another creature had made it up to the roof, its back arching, already in a full sprint toward us as a second summited.

"Go," Toni shouted over the ear-piercing din.

I took a deep breath, leant forward and let myself down onto the cable with a leap, trying to ignore the creatures I could see altering their path to intercept me.

As I dropped to the cable I saw my news van on the horizon. The folded satellite dish forced a smile, but my lips tensed as I pushed all my energy to my grip. The smile fell as the tower bent with my journey less than half complete.

The cable sagged as if another weight had added, the movement so great I had to tuck my legs under to stop my feet hitting the roof as I went over the edge. At least I'd picked up speed and the creatures wouldn't get close.

Only just over the side of the building, there was nothing I could do as the cable gave out, snapping with a pop greater than the distant shots.

With its length retreating through my arms, I plummeted through the air, my view filling with the building coming toward me faster than I knew my bones could take.

23

My vision filled with clay bricks, concentration fixing on their symmetry as I raced toward them. Without thought I traced the neat white lines between each course, but the view changed, the world spinning as the top of the chain-link caught at my feet.

I heard the rattle of the thin metal links, feeling weightless for a breath until pressure slammed at my side and I paused, hanging upside down.

With what seemed like just enough energy left inside me, I curled into a ball, rolling as the air pushed out when I hit the concrete. The smash of the chain-link came again, and I looked through blurring vision to see Toni at the foot of the other fence, still swaying, sprawled on the floor, motionless with a hundred eyes on her as she lay between the two rows.

I ignored the aches, the pain shooting up my legs as I climbed to my feet, gaze tracking the thick cable slapping to rest on the hard floor, its weight bearing down on top of each fence.

She'd jumped on the cable as I descended.

She'd had no choice with those creatures so close. The inner chain-link fence had caught my feet, slowed me down. Turned me over and I survived the fall.

She'd fallen much further, hit the other side of the fence and bounced into the perimeter.

We'd succeeded in getting down from the rooftop, but were being followed. The air filled with the piercing calls as the creatures jumped from the tall roof, pulling through the sea of stench and would be on us again any minute. We had to go, but first I had to get to her.

Hooking my fingers between the links, jabbing my toes into the space between the thin metal, the fence swaying forward and back as I climbed. Pain shot up my spine as I lurched in my attempt to keep steady.

Toni still hadn't moved. I pulled myself away from the sight, turning to the sea of bruised faces staring with white eyes.

The dead were cast to the side, thrown out of the way by the creature I knew I would see; a version of what could so easily have been me.

Turning away, I was over the top and with one last grip to slow my fall, I landed. Pain electrified the sole of my foot, stealing my breath as I reached for my pocket.

With the burning sensation subsiding, I remembered the lab coat in tatters, my gun lost as I climbed the side of the building. No sign of Toni's pistol or the rifle too, cast aside in the panic.

Around me were hundreds of guns. A pistol at each soldier's side. A rifle slung over every other's shoulder, as they scraped and clawed, rattling, chattering on the other side of the thin linked metal.

The only weapons I had were my hands. I had to think quick. The creature hung prone and slow as it climbed the fence, but it would be here, the first of many, any moment.

I ripped open the rucksack, ignoring Toni's lack of movement, ignoring the thin red liquid swimming inside the bag. I felt no gun, only thin broken glass and I pulled my hand back, a river of panic washing over me as I launched my rage towards the creature gaining height on the fence.

Pushing hard, I screamed my own terrifying call as I raced toward it. Making contact in a blur, I sent it sprawling and slapping to the ground somewhere in the sea of death. Choking back the surprise at what I'd achieved, I ran with the realisation I'd bought myself no time at all.

I scooped Toni's light body up in my arms. She'd always been so dainty, but I had to push away the building thoughts.

I ran as fast as I could around the perimeter between the two fences, ignoring the snarls of the dead and didn't look back.

Toni's tiny movements urged me on. She wasn't dead, despite the new bruise spreading out across her head.

The relief fell when I realised movement was no longer a good sign. A heavy weight closed around me like thick curtains. Lost in her pain as she moaned in my arms, the pad of feet slapping to the concrete wouldn't give me time to check if she was still alive.

The race was on, but I knew I would lose. There was no way I could outrun what was chasing us down. No way I could climb quick enough. No way I would leave Toni behind.

I felt what I thought was its breath on my neck and stopped, laid Toni at my feet and turned, letting out a deep breath, locking with its eyes, its clawed fingers swiping at my face as its teeth bared down.

24

Stunned by the sharp explosions of a gun at my side, I watched like a passenger in my body with the creature lurching forward, its black-veined face smashing against my chest and sending me tumbling backward. Despite using all of my reserves fighting to stay upright, its weight overcame me, pushing me to the ground.

My punches curled to its face, but it gave no reaction as my knuckles dug into its loose skin. The volley forced on, weakening as my resolve ebbed, until a warm hand encircled one fist and then the other to hold them back.

The creature slumped to the side, its hideous, bent features replaced by Toni's pained face peering upside down over the top of my head. She leant down, her lips landing soft on my cheek, but I couldn't calm, twitching around to check the coast was clear and the other creatures hadn't made it into our haven.

There we stayed, held tight as our breathing slowed, until a shot echoed in the distance.

The wake-up call lifted us to our feet, taking in our surroundings as if for the first time, the moans, the soft snarl of the dead ever in the background.

As I stood, the creature's thick blood slipped down my front on a slow treacle-like journey, dripping to my feet. As my arm encircled Toni, she handed over the gun pulled from her waistband, its weight too much as she limped at my side.

Somehow we climbed the fence, with Toni being the first to the top, wincing as she fell, not able to make the last few links. She was on her feet by the time I finished leaving a bloody trail over the metal.

We padded into the car park, my gaze turning this way and that, searching for the next battle as we headed toward the news van.

The few creatures who'd made it this far ignored our slow walk as we kept low, using the cars, trucks and SUVs for cover.

With surprise, I found the van unlocked and I helped Toni up the tall step and into the rear, half expecting Dan still to be hidden, hoping his appearance would push this reality back into a dream.

I let my gaze drop and I gave a shallow sigh as I helped Toni settle to the director's seat fixed to the carpeted floor and took her hands in mine as I stood in her warmth. With her breath settling, I pulled the back door closed, wincing with the click of the lock engaging.

Toni pulled the rucksack from her back in slow motion as I watched the drip of liquid trailing from the canvas.

After searching by fingertip, she drew out two unbroken vials of the red liquid.

"The cigarettes?" I blurted out when I didn't see her pull them from the bag.

She shook her head with a solemn look to the floor of the van.

"You won't need them now," she said, swallowing hard as she clutched the vials tight in her fist.

We didn't speak for what seemed like an age, neither of us able to put words to what we'd just gone through.

The first to move, I pulled away, opening the long cupboard to find it empty. Time flashed back to Christmas Day when, unsure how long had passed and for the cost of pizza, I'd convinced Dan and Mike to come here to die.

Holding back the pain in my chest, the physical form of my guilt, I stared into the empty wardrobe which, had this been an assignment, would have been full of my outfits. I would have to remain blanketed in the creature's drying blood for the duration.

"What next?" I said, turning to Toni.

She stared at the doors as if they had windows in the centre. When she didn't reply, I moved over towards her, but held myself out of her reach.

"If we leave here, we'll get picked up when we hit the perimeter. They'll have people covering the perimeter, won't they?" I said, looking to her for answers. "Unless they're still in shock, overwhelmed, waiting for reinforcements. What do you think?"

Still, she gave no movement, no hint of a reply, just continued to stare through the non-existent window.

"If we stay, eventually they'll round me up. You, too, and do whatever they were going to do anyway. Right? Do you think?" I let the words hang in the air, trying not to raise my voice as I spoke again. "You know these people better than me."

She gave no reply.

"Toni?" I snapped and watched as her head turned away.

Taking a step, I knelt to force myself back into her view. "What next?" I said again, raising my hands to cup her chin as I stared into her vacant eyes.

"We have to find her," she said, her words low.

"Who?" I said, letting my hands down from her face.

"The woman who did this," she replied. "The woman who did this to you."

"Why?" I said, brushing the front of my hand against her undamaged cheek, drawing back with a sudden discomfort at the intimacy as I remembered the promises I'd made to myself.

"There's not enough…" she said, but stuttered to silence. "There's not enough…" she said again, this time taking care of the words. "There's not enough to give us time."

"Time for what?"

"For your immune system to have its best shot."

"Of beating this thing?" I said.

Toni nodded.

"I feel fine," I said, doing my best to raise a smile and it wasn't a lie; apart from the aches and pains from our escape and a hunger which felt like I hadn't eaten for days.

"For now," she replied.

"What can this woman do?" I said, standing, my gaze fixed on her face. I wanted to rest her head against my stomach. I wanted to comfort her, but it would be no great comfort to rest against the blood flaking to the floor as it dried and I didn't want to give her the wrong impression.

For a second time I looked around the contents of the van, trying to find something I could change in to.

"Everything," she said, and turned back away from my searching look. "She can do whatever she wants. She's the head of the whole program and holds the key to getting more of this," Toni said, opening her palms and showing me the vials resting in the centre.

"Who is she?" I said, remembering a cupboard above the camera boxes.

"You've met," she replied, as I pulled out the hi-vis jacket with PRESS written along the back in black letters.

Trying to keep my fingertips from the blood as much as I could, I picked open the blouse buttons and slung the shirt to the corner. Looking down my chest, bare apart from the streaks of dried blood, I stared at the remains of a red river running between my breasts.

"You met her when you first arrived. She would have wanted to look you in the eye."

I pulled on the warmth of the jacket. Feeling the hug of the material against my skin, I turned back to Toni staring back through the imagined windows.

The conversation caught up in my head, my fingers stopping the zip halfway up as I remembered the older woman with grey hair as she sat across the table with those deep green eyes.

"Who is she?" I said, my eyes narrowing. I watched as Toni took a deep swallow.

"My mother," she replied, and her head fell into her hands.

25

"Your mother?" I said, lurching forward as I pulled the zip to just below my neck. If I'd blinked, I'd have missed her nod. "She's not your mother," I said, not able to hold back the laughter as I shook my head. "I knew your mum almost as well as I know mine. Why would you say that?" I stepped back, my surprise turning to anger at her obvious lie.

"I'm adopted," she said through her hands, her shoulders stooped as she stared at the floor of the van. The words sparked through me like a shock wave.

I should have paused and taken the time to think this through, but instead the words just came along with the anger of only just finding this out now.

"How long have you known?"

"Just over a year."

The frustration turned to guilt as I saw the conflict on her features. The last time we'd seen each other, the last time we'd spoken would have been about that time. It had been almost a year since I'd told her we needed to keep away from each other.

"Did you know when…" I said, not able to finish the sentence as I questioned if maybe it was the stress of the news that made her so much worse than she'd ever been. "You never mentioned her," I said, trying to hold back a torrent of emotion whilst unpicking how I felt.

The pain she'd gone through was so clear on her downcast features and the way she slumped in her seat. Still, there was no excuse for taking it out on me at the time. When I made my decision, the arguments had grown so frequent I no longer wanted to be near her for fear of the anger spilling over and one of us doing something we would regret forever.

Toni looked up with her eyelids low and her battered face so full of sorrow.

"There was a lot going on at the time," she said.

She snorted a laugh, but her lips fell flat before they could form a smile.

Maybe if she'd talked about it, maybe if I had helped her open up rather than just walking away, things might have been different. Guilt weighed heavy and I stepped forward, kneeling back beside her and pulling her undamaged cheek to mine.

I didn't know how to reply. I wanted to know so much. I wanted to know if I'd made the whole situation worse.

"What about Terry and Anne?" I said without thought as a vision of their faces sparked into my head. Their names sounded weird in my voice.

When she pulled away, pushing her head into her hands, I kicked myself as I drew a deep breath and rubbed the back of her head.

Toni tried to stand but fell back to the chair before trying a second time. Breath sucked through her teeth as she put weight on her feet.

I stood, taking a step back and watched a brightness appear on her face as she looked around the van, eyeing the boxes of cameras and equipment secured by cargo straps to the shelves.

"Does this stuff work?" she said, her features pointed to a frown.

"Of course it does," I said, scowling at the question, but my annoyance disappeared as I watched the smile rise on her lips.

"Do you know what we should do?" she said, but spoke again before I could answer. "We should get this story out there. Break this wide open."

"You think?" I said, a wide smile hanging from my lips.

"Our bargain. Fill the tapes with what they want no one to see," Toni said, her tone rising. "Then she'd have to give us what we need. Come on, let's get moving. I know just the shot we need."

My head filled with excitement at her words. She was saying what I wanted to hear and my mind raced through the possibilities. Then I realised the obvious flaw.

"One problem," I said, and she turned back, raising her eyebrows. "Who's going to film it?" I replied, my brow matching hers.

She stopped before she spoke with her mouth hanging wide. Her lips then pursed as if the words would come out, but didn't.

"I'm in front of the camera," I said, trying to flatten out my scowl.

"You don't..." she said, stopping herself, then laughing before her brow furrowed again to ease the pain. "You don't know how to use the equipment."

"Stop staring at me like I'm an uneducated ape. I'm a journalist. A professional. I have qualifications, experience. This equipment," I said, looking around and repeating her waving hand gestures, "is state-of-the-art."

I paused as my crew's names stuck in my throat. "The crew who use it train for years. They have special places they go to learn this stuff. It's not like a compact camera where you just point and shoot."

A lopsided smile appeared on her face despite her best efforts; the Toni of old, the Toni who thought I was playing a joke.

"That's what they told you, right?" she said, undoing the straps of a rugged plastic case at waist height. She was only just able to take its weight as it left the shelf. I watched with interest as she laid the case down, grunting with relief as it landed to the floor.

With the clips either side undone, she hovered over, peering in as the lid fell back. She surveyed the large hulk of black plastic and metal sat on the dimpled foam, its surface covered in tiny buttons, each with a foreign symbol or minuscule white writing beside.

I looked back, my cheeks bunching with a closed-lip smile. My brow raised as I waited.

"Go on then," I said when she didn't move.

"There must be a smaller one, right?" she said, turning but looking away as she saw my expression.

I shook my head, watching as she closed up the case and helped lift its bulk back to the shelf.

We barely had the strap across its front before a metallic thud came from the back doors, the echo repeating somewhere inside.

Our eyes locked, peeling away before turning to the back doors. Our collective breath drew in as we saw the small hole in the door, its jagged metal pushed out towards us.

I followed Toni's look as she turned, stopping when we saw a matching hole by the director's chair where Toni had been sitting only moments before.

26

"Stray shot. Right?" I said before Toni had the chance to speak.

Wide eyes were her only reply.

"It's not safe here," I said, turning towards the cab.

"You can drive?" Toni said, her voice slow.

I half expected a smile, but as I turned I saw a cold, blank expression.

She knew I could drive. I'd driven to meet her so many times. I'd driven halfway across the country full of anticipation, my head bursting with excitement at what lay ahead. Days later I'd driven home. Deflated. Tears spent.

After a week of heaven, the bubble would always burst and I'd promise myself never to open up again, never to think we could be any other way. Never to daydream we could be together. Could never build on the good times, ditch all the pain.

"You know I can drive," I said, turning away, climbing between the front seats as I peered through the windscreen. My gaze caught on the sea of movement, the car park dotted with people walking.

But they weren't people anymore. Their slow walk told me they weren't making their own decisions, told me their desire to fill the burning hunger drove them.

I found the keys still in the ignition. I was so overjoyed to see them dangling my mind didn't consider there could be a good reason.

Looking through the right-wing mirror, my survey caught the white side panel and the flared hole in the centre before falling to the mess of flesh slumped to the tarmac.

"Stray shot," I said under my breath.

Toni caught my eye as she settled into the passenger seat, pulling her belt across with the engine roaring to life.

"Where now?" I said, as I pulled the van from its space, scouring the surroundings for the exit.

I flashed a look in her direction when she didn't reply; the raise of her hand told me she didn't want her thoughts disturbed.

Still, I saw no life as I slowly drove through the narrow lanes, the dead following between the cars to cut across our path.

A soldier appeared from around a drab olive truck. I slammed on the brakes, the belt pulling tight against my chest.

My first thoughts were for the sniper who'd saved our lives. The second for those who'd come to take us.

I stepped on the accelerator before the third thought came to mind, steering the wheel into the figure as I saw the huge welt down the side of its face and the milky white eyes fixed in a stare as its mouth snapped open and closed.

Bile rose from my empty stomach as the crunch of bone carried up through the suspension.

I turned to Toni to see her eyes closed and head shaking as if trying her best not to spoil her concentration.

I couldn't avoid the next few; took them out one after the other. Each time my reaction lessened, my pause grew shorter and my gaze scarcely stopped on their shape as I scoured the horizon for a break in the fence.

I found it moments later; not a break, but the way out. A thick sliding gate of green steel barring our exit. On both sides a white and red barrier stretched across the deserted road.

I headed towards it without waiting, steering to take down anything that stood in our way whilst ignoring their gawking faces, knowing they fixed any thoughts on how they could get to our taste.

I sped to the gate but without surprise it stayed fixed in place. There was no way we were getting through without a tank and I hadn't seen one of those yet.

"Toni," I snapped in her direction and she opened her eyes, fumbling in her pockets.

I turned around to the side of the gate and noticed for the first time a panel with a green LED blinking at its top.

"It's on," I replied and I turned to Toni, still searching. My gaze passed her by, instead landing on the small crowd of the dead I saw through the window heading in our direction.

A soldier headed the shambling group of five. Behind him, other soldiers followed, as did an Asian man in a white coat, shuffling forward with a pronounced limp. Around his neck hung a white card on a lanyard, swinging from side to side.

"No," Toni snapped, and I caught her turning back from the same direction. "I'll go."

I couldn't let her do that. Only moments earlier she'd been out cold.

"Give me the gun," I said, but she shook her head, unable to stop her gaze darting back toward the rear compartment.

"No," she replied, her voice sharp as she gave her command. With her tone, the guilt I'd felt only moments earlier fell from around me and I stood before she could rise and reached between the seats.

Toni didn't try and follow.

She stayed watching from her seat as I took the gun from the side where she'd placed it to pull the vials from the bag.

With one in the chamber and five bullets in the magazine, I would have a spare.

Cold air bit between the gap as the door opened wide and, regretting leaving the warmth of the van, I pushed it shut at my back.

Turning as I felt the sticky handle, I saw the ink blot of dark blood splattered above the jagged hole in the metal. I shuddered as I caught the air, the chill of the icy wind carrying the foul stench of sewerage, but my gaze turned to find the source of the moaning voice.

I had no time. The group were only a few paces away.

Pulling the gun up, I took aim, choosing the soldier at the front. Closing my left eye, I centred on his forehead.

The shot missed, but I'd got their attention. In one fluid motion, each of the creatures turned, faces electrifying with energy, mouths slapping shut and eyes gaping to show their full whites.

I took a step closer. I couldn't miss at this distance, with barely the length of the van between us. I centred my aim again whilst trying not to let the incessant groan distract me.

I fired. The shot might as well have missed as it pushed through the soldier's neck, thick blood hardly filling the space left before I fired three times more to put him to the floor.

With a single shot left, I looked to the van, turning just in time to catch a clawed hand as it swiped for my back.

The final bullet ripped through a scientist's head, sending my eyes wide as I stared at the white plastic pass hanging from its neck.

I twisted back around, breath panting as I aimed, the click of the empty chamber echoing in the cold wind.

With the group's slow procession nearly at its destination, I turned with one last dash, bending over and snatching the lanyard from the fallen scientist's neck.

About to stand, I felt fingers claw down my back and I swung my fist in an upper cut with all my strength, hoping it was enough to send the creature's jawbone into its head.

27

There was little time to pull the punch before Toni's head deflected left, my knuckles glancing along the side of her face. Her teeth clamped together as she grabbed me up with her face in a scowl, sending me surging into the open back of the van.

Her hand slammed the door against limbs reaching through to the sound of distant gunfire. Blood sprayed between the gap; metal crushed soft tissue until the fingers fell loose to the van floor and let the lock catch.

Scrabbling back along the floor of the van, I pushed my arms out in front with my palms out as I tried to put as much distance between us as I could, waiting for Toni's voice to boom.

When the tirade hadn't come, I looked between my hands to see Toni curled up on the floor with her hands covering her face as she sucked through her teeth.

Jumping up, I leapt to her side at the sight.

"I'm sorry. So sorry. I didn't know it was you," I said, the words alien to my lips as I couldn't help smear blood from my hands on her t-shirt.

Breath panting, I turned away as she stayed curled up with her hands to her face.

Pulling my skirt down over my cold legs she eventually lifted herself upright, her face tensed with pain and she pulled away her hands.

"Sorry," I said as she raised her eyebrows in my direction.

"It was a good shot." She continued to rub her cheek.

"No, the opposite. I didn't mean... I thought..." I said, but she cut me off and stood.

"I know," she replied, stepping past me as I stayed sat, doing my best to keep my breath running out of control.

"They split because of me," Toni said, and it took me a moment to realise she was answering the question I'd regretted earlier. I paused but when she didn't speak I spoke softly.

"It can't be your fault," I said. She looked up, her face sharp and features pointed with anger.

"They lied to me for years. I didn't know it at the time, but the pressure of keeping up appearances for so long, working out answers to the questions I had growing up. Why was I the only one with dark hair? Why was I taller than everyone else in the family? Why didn't I have my dad's nose?"

"I'm sure it wasn't…" I said but she wouldn't let me finish.

"I left home and they realised the lie was all they had. They had nothing to be together for and boom, their marriage just collapsed. Dad had an affair and Mum, the one who brought me up…" She paused as the emotion caught in her throat. "Mum just vanished. Just over a year ago she came back and told me the woman I'd been working for all this time was my birth mother. She'd got me here. She engineered for me to join the team. Looking back, I can see it now. Looking back, I can see how she manipulated all my choices from behind the scenes. And now here we are."

I didn't know what to say. I edged forward and pushed my arms around her, but she stood with her hands out just enough to push me away.

"Not here," she said and moved past me, slumping to the passenger seat and stared off into the distance as I sat in the driver's seat, checking in the mirror as I wound the window down.

"I guess we have a friend out there," I said, almost in a whisper whilst letting my breath run out.

"You shouldn't have gone out," she said, ignoring my words. "It was a stupid thing to do. A risk we didn't need to take."

"I got the pass," I replied, dangling the bloody lanyard at the reader.

She didn't turn. I knew this Toni, too; it was the Toni that came out each time we got to the end of our bliss, each time we figured out the fun and the long carefree days had to end. We would be back to our lives, each time realising it should be the last. Time to move on.

It was the Toni that came before the arguments. Before the real pain. It was the Toni I knew I had to get away from before one of us flipped up the cover and pressed the self-destruct button, jabbing it over and again.

This time I couldn't leave; we couldn't separate. Our lives depended on being together, helping each other.

The gate slid without a noise, a beacon flashing either side. The barrier lifted as we passed through, closing at our backs with gunfire clearing the air.

The strays fell as they tried to follow in our wake. We were free. Out. We'd saved ourselves.

The realisation came again. Only Toni was safe and I knew she wouldn't be for long if I couldn't get more of those vials which kept me feeling human.

"Where do we go?" I said, letting the van coast around the winding road, cutting through the shallow hills either side. "Where did your mother go?" I added when she didn't reply.

"Don't call her that," she snapped back and I felt an all too familiar emotion circling my head.

I waited for her to offer out her name, despite not being able to bring myself to ask.

"Where do we go then?" I repeated, raising the volume, my head not turning away from the road.

She didn't reply until I slammed on the brakes, rounding a corner to find the road blocked with sandbags and at least five rifles aimed in our direction.

"I don't know, but I think they might," she replied, her hands raising at her sides.

28

I killed the engine, raising my hands to match Toni's stance and setting my mouth in a grateful smile while bunching my cheeks. I thought of Dan and Mike and the first tears began to drip down my face.

The soldiers didn't move and the rifles stayed steady as I paid attention to each of their faces, looking for signs they weren't the real enemy.

Each stared back, no doubt doing the same as I was, their weapons making them no less anxious. I saw enough pigment surrounding their pupils to slow the beat in my chest in time for the call from somewhere in their line.

A soldier in the centre turned at the command. I could see his reluctance as he looked back towards us.

Keeping his rifle high, a pasty white man side-stepped the sandbags and started the journey in our direction. He didn't call out, didn't shout commands, but as the young soldier walked, the aim of the other rifles drifted either side.

"Open the door," were his first words as he came around in a wide arc to the driver's side. I knew his eyes should have remained fixed on mine, but he couldn't keep from looking down to the front of the van. His eyes twitched, travelling along the side. After longer than he should, his gaze snatched back and his aim snapped up from its fall.

"Do what he says, Jess," Toni said.

I hated the way she could make me feel with just her tone.

I pulled the handle and let the cold air in.

"How d'you get out?" the young man's voice called as I placed my bare feet to the cold tarmac.

"It was awful. Help us, please. We have to get away from here, where they can't get us," I said, pushing the emotion to catch in my voice.

He didn't reply; instead, looked back, his eyebrows raising as he surveyed me, tilting his head up and down. I saw the same look I always saw in a young man's eyes, in a man of any age's eyes, as they caught my sight, but this time his mouth hung wide for other reasons.

I looked down my fluorescent yellow front, following the black lines running down the jacket and I turned as the white of the van caught my eye. It wasn't white anymore. Most of the surface was flecked red, clots streaking down the dented, once pristine paintwork. Tattered remains of cloth and flesh hung where they'd caught between the bumper and the metal.

"We hid. Waited for it to all die down, then ran. Found this thing unlocked, the keys in the ignition," I said, pointing over my shoulder. "It saved our lives. God only knows what would have happened if we'd not found it."

"Ask her," came the call from another voice. The young soldier's gaze shot back to my face, running up and down the jacket before falling to the scratches on my legs.

"Were you bitten?" he said, his voice quivering as he spoke with his gaze locked to mine.

I forced myself not to flinch to my arm underneath the sleeve of the jacket and shook my head before shooting a glance back to Toni as he spoke again.

"Her?"

"No."

"Take off the jacket. We've got to see," he said, motioning with the rifle.

I paused before I replied. "I'm not wearing anything underneath."

His gaze came up from my torso and he latched back onto my face, his head turning in Toni's direction, glancing back quickly when I spoke.

"I got covered in blood when we were trying to escape. You've got to help us, please?" I said, biting down my annoyance at myself as I let the tears flow.

He paused, moving to look off into the distance as if leaving the conversation for a moment, then he turned back to the line before returning to stare wide-eyed in my direction.

"What is it?" I said, leaning towards him.

"They're coming," he replied, before the call from the group could shut him down.

"Private, stow that," came the booming voice.

I turned back to him, almost putting a hand out in comfort as I realised he was yet to face the horror in person. His gaze was no longer on me, was no longer on the van, instead fixed across the horizon as he stepped backward to the roadblock.

"Get back in the van, Miss," he said, as the distance between us grew.

I followed his gaze out to the horizon, but couldn't see anything new. I turned back to the roadblock and saw the soldiers leaving their defences to fan out so they could see past the van.

"Miss, get back inside," he said, but his eyes had never left the horizon.

"Get back in, Jess," I heard Toni say. "Get in the van," she said again, the words loud and controlled.

I turned and I felt the wind change. The foul stench of sewerage filled my nostrils.

I knew what it meant before I saw the two figures running down from the high ground; before I had a chance to tell if their stance was controlled enough. Not too animalistic. Too fast or too slow to confirm my fears.

They were still human and I knew what they were running from.

29

I watched in the wing mirror as the pair of soldiers ran with their wide expressions fixed forward, neither looking back as they hurried to cover the ground. Their hardened faces and the disbelieving look in their eyes told me they'd seen at least as much as we had. A breath pulled unbidden as I spotted the barrel of a long sniper rifle rising from behind one of their backs.

"It's him," I said, not turning to Toni.

She made no reply and I lost the train of thought as I turned to see a soldier shouting through my window.

"Move it," the tall man called, his top lip consumed with a bushy moustache. His confidence, more than the stripes on his chest, told me he was in charge. With breath misting against the window, he pointed to the left side of the roadblock where two soldiers were pulling down the sandbags while another revved the engine to move one of the two Land Rovers.

By the time I'd turned my back he raced up the side of the hill to meet the pair. He turned only when they didn't wait, running at their side as they shouted their report.

I turned the ignition, wheeling the van up the first of the incline, the tilt unsettling as I leant in the opposite direction with my hands correcting the steering left and right to miss the remaining sandbags. As the wheels settled back to the tarmac, I pulled open the door and jumped out onto the road while not listening to Toni's calls for me to get back in. To stop being so stupid. To get us away from the danger.

The words disappeared as my door slammed shut.

"Give me a pistol," I shouted to the three soldiers settling back behind the roadblock. None looked up from their rifle sights as they knelt against the sandbags. "Give me a gun," I said, nudging the closest at his shoulder.

He looked up and shouted across to the three returning.

"Sarge," he said, flicking up a look in my direction.

"Hundreds," said the sniper, as he swung the long rifle from his shoulder, the deep blue of his eyes lingering on mine for more than a moment.

Jumping over the roadblock as he broke the connection, he gave me the slightest of nods before running to the back of the closest of the Land Rovers without chance for me to reply.

The stench caught in my nostrils and I looked down the road, watching the valley cut between the hills as it wound out of view. The sergeant stood at my side as he looked, stone-faced, in the same direction.

"Give me a pistol," I said. "I trained in Israel. I may not be able to hit a bull's eye on a target, but I can bring the odds a little more in our favour."

The sergeant double took, looking down across my spoilt front and turned to the van before snapping back in my direction.

"Get in your vehicle, Ma'am. Get in the vehicle and get the fuck out of here," he said.

I turned to the van, saw Toni's stern wide-eyed command repeat his words, her head leaning out of the open driver's window.

I bit my lip, her scolding look only deepening my resolve as I told myself she had no control over me.

"Where do we go?" I replied, folding my arms in the cold.

He double took again. "You know what's coming?" he said, looking down the blood stains across my front again.

I nodded.

"Then get anywhere. Get as far away as you can. What you see..." he said, looking back to his men. "What you see is everything, you understand? There's a hundred or more of those. I don't know what they are, but they were my regiment and they're coming here with one thing on whatever remains of their minds. I don't have to tell you what will happen. Now go," he said, his voice raising. "Or do I have to waste one of my men forcing you back inside?"

They had no chance. Their colleagues had been overrun with such ease. One minute they were jumping from their trucks, the next they'd joined the ranks of the dead risen up.

I could use a gun. I wasn't the best shot, but maybe one more bullet could be the tipping point.

"Toni," I shouted, remembering how she handled the rifle.

Despite knowing I should run, knowing my job was to get the story out, still I stood my ground as he turned away and watched him raise his rifle and peer through the sight.

I flashed a look down the road to see the tarmac clear until I blinked. The moment my eyes opened I saw the first movement, saw the camouflaged legs, looked up the body and half an arm hanging loose at his side, swinging in time with its slow, casual stroll.

I jumped as a bullet leapt from the long rifle, snatching a look to the sniper crouching to my right, the double legs of the long gun leaning on a sandbag.

I turned back to the road and watched the sea of legs trampling over the fallen figure. With the awful creatures in view, the stench felt like it poured from the sky. My heart raced, but I couldn't just walk away. Toni needed to know where her mother was if there was any chance she could stop me being consumed by what had taken over those creatures. I wanted her for another reason altogether and I couldn't let this pass by.

The rifle snapped over and again, my body's reaction lessening each time. Each time a hit. Each time a kill, despite my mind's trouble with those words. Ten, maybe more, fell down, but still they continued on, stumbling over their fallen.

Some veered up the hill, nudged by the piling bodies before falling back, drawn down by the incline, funnelled by the valley back to the road.

This was a stand. This was where history could be made. If they broke through here where would the next be? From here they could move out into the open and I'd seen too many movies to know how this would end.

I thought of my parents and my friends. I thought of Jamie and his kids. I thought of the villages, the towns, the cities. The people. The children. The lives to be lost. The lives that would live again and add to the battle that would have to be fought.

I couldn't run. I walked to the back of the van, avoiding Toni's eyes and the scorn I knew would be pouring out of her. I pulled the rear doors open to the sound of the dried blood cracking and took the empty gun from the floor. I shouted just as the door slammed.

"You go. The keys are in the ignition."

Moving to the rear of the Land Rover, I took a magazine from an open crate, pushing it into the base of the pistol and re-joined the line as the sergeant gave the order to open fire.

30

The machine gun jumped to life, hot lead spraying in a furious chatter, consuming the belt of finger-length bullets as the soldier swept it across its wide arc. The first shots were too low, the bodies rattling with each impact, but as the spray moved across the line, skull and brain erupted under its power.

The first in line were down, with rifles picking off those missed in the rain of metal. The soldier's pause caught us all by surprise, their gazes catching on the next targets stumbling through the red mist as the wind added a thick metallic hint to the acrid swirl around us.

"Fire," the sergeant screamed and all rifles joined the chugging rhythm of the machine gun. Shot after shot, round after round exploding flesh as they hit their targets.

Dead flesh sprayed to the ground. Blood and guts showered the air with gore. Slowing their advance, they stumbled, moving to their hands and knees, if they still had them, to cross the carpet of bodies, only to be cut down.

Shouts went through our line, an excited rumble of voices as the bodies piled ever higher. The gunfire fell quiet when all movement stopped, the masses unable to cross the hill of camouflaged bodies.

Weapons reloaded as the rifles went quiet. Voices died to nothing with the slap of metal against metal.

The sergeant called the line to order and silence surrounded to let us hear the low rumbling chorus of moans in the background.

A chill ran down my spine and I let my gun drop without a round being fired. I knew my limitations and was pleased enough the advance had halted beyond my useful range.

I turned as the van's engine sprang to life at my back, smiled to Toni in the driver's seat as she peered out, beckoning me toward her with her head shaking.

I pushed my hand to the air, gesturing for just a few minutes more.

The soldiers were talking amongst themselves, their voices high, excited at their easy victory. Not even the sergeant held the rise of his bushy moustache as his mouth parted in joy.

Until the first screams brought back their silence.

Only two remained calm, their heads not snapping sideways; their mouths not hanging down, eyes not wide with questions.

The sniper and his companion had seen it before. They'd taken them down and had saved our lives.

The wretched calls were more distant than we'd heard before, but were no less terrifying, forcing the cold into my bones.

"Get ready," came the sniper's voice, not turning to the faces who didn't know what would happen next.

I levelled the gun, trying to ignore as my arms refused to steady, the shake of my hands only pronounced by the cold. I knew before the first of the dark shapes sprung high from behind the line my gaze would catch on a second as the first landed.

In a tattered orange jumpsuit, the colour only showing between the dark patches, his legs bent like a gymnast dismounting from a pommel horse. His face as dark as oiled hardwood, thick black lines spidering across. A beard of dried blood matted the skin around his jaw. His left ear was missing; so, too, was the skin on the top of his head. With it went the long hair covering the other side, brown locks matted and clumped like dreadlocks.

For a moment I wondered if it was how I would end up.

A single shot pierced the air, the sniper the only one not paralysed with fear, but his bullet went wide, thudding a red spray out from the pile of bodies at their backs. The leap of the second, his pasty naked form riddled with the dark lines like roots through snow, took his attention.

Silence returned as the shot's echo fell. Even the moans in the background seemed to pay their respect and quiet. The pause felt as if it lasted for an age. The only movement came from their jaws, slow and considered as they opened and closed in time with each other to the metallic click of the new round worked by the rifle's mechanism. With the orange jumpsuit's single step, the pause ended, its companion back in the air and surging forward.

The line of fire lit the space between us. Hurried shots flashed against the barricade of bodies, ripping flesh from bone and shattering each form, but not those racing towards us. The sergeant screamed for focus between each of his shots as he stood, calling for concentration of fire, splitting the squad.

The first three pumped their shots to the crazed creature on the ground, whose distance had just shortened enough for me to open fire. The second group, of which the sniper joined with his sidearm, aimed to the target high in the air, his form only just falling back to the ground in front of his companion.

Fire continued until the explosions were replaced with well-drilled shouts at each position as they hurried to reload and retake up the battle.

"Bayonets," came the next call, his voice breaking, but there was no time. Despite the near continuous fire, the expert shots falling to their targets, the rest of the pack were on us, the numbers just too great and were just the other side of the short defences.

The knives were taken in hand, the sergeant jumping the barricade, the blade held in his fist with a great warrior call as he ran forward. Leaping across the sandbags, he led with the sharpened metal.

I stayed my shots, forgetting how many I'd taken as his knife hit high, the creature only catching the advance when it was too late; the blade already through its temple. A panic descended across our group, heads twitching as we searched for the second enemy.

We didn't find it. It found us. It found the last on the line; the young soldier who met us as we arrived. His screams turned our heads, the blood pumping from his neck turned me away, but not his friends, not his colleagues. They stayed true to their calling, pouncing on the attacker. Climbing up with pistols, blades slipping in and out of the monster's skull as the soldier's heart pumped a fountain of blood over each of them.

The creature slumped down within a moment, but with the damage done, the warrior's frenzy replaced with a furious activity of hands on the wound. Red palms fell to his neck, until after not too long it was obvious there was no hope.

I turned away with my eyes closed, the sound of the horn bellowing at my back spinning me around.

Toni's outstretched arm pointing out turned me back to the battle and I watched as the dam of bodies collapsed either side. The walking corpses streamed around the edges, massing in the centre.

Having covered half the distance to us, they were a stone's throw away without our notice.

31

"Fire," was all I could think to say, my voice hardly registering against the bass drone of the crowd. "Fire," I repeated, shouting out across the line.

Faces turned forward and rifles lifted, sending the air thick with hot lead once again. Calls for reloads came too soon, silencing the advantage before we'd regained. My pistol clicked empty with two shots missed and I spun around, fist balled towards what had grabbed me, pulling me by the shoulder.

I let myself fall into Toni's arms as she cupped my fist in her hand and pulled me away from the roadblock. Taking my weight back, she hurried to the van with the rifles and pistols lighting up again.

The shouted commands blurred into one long call and Toni dragged me by the hand, pulling hard as we passed the back of the Land Rover. She wouldn't let me reach out, turning only as she pushed me through the driver's door of the van so she could run around the bonnet.

In the driver's seat I closed my eyes, not wanting to see the chaos at the line.

I couldn't help look.

The guns fell silent, knives swung out and the soldiers stepped away, leaving the line. Ghouls were falling, but not fast enough. As one fell to the floor another would be at its back.

Three of the soldiers were down by the time Toni's calls went out.

"Go," she pleaded. "Drive."

My gaze fixed on the only two remaining by the time her words faded to nothing. The sergeant and the sniper.

I slammed my hand to the horn and faces looked up, dead white eyes set in our direction.

The sergeant turned, soon consumed by the pack, his struggle obscured by those once under his command.

The sniper didn't turn but edged away with three or more of the creatures snapping on his heels, using the one advantage we still had. He ran, moving out of my view.

Only when I heard the doors at the rear opening and weight in the back shifting did I push the accelerator to the floor, whilst doing my best to ignore the bloodied hands at my window.

I didn't pause for the turn. I didn't wait; instead, I let the tyres spin in the mud as they caught the incline of the hill, pushing my foot harder even though I knew there was nowhere further for it to go, my wide-eyed gaze on the expanding line of the undead shrinking in the wing mirror.

Toni slowed me after a moment, her hand on my shoulder when the van almost tipped on its side rounding the corner.

I watched the surrounding land flatten. All I could think of was the village I'd passed on the way in, the motorway near; an artery for the infection to spread.

I slowed at Toni's command, lifted my foot from the accelerator and watched as two police cars came into view. I watched the pair of officers gawking in our direction in fluorescent jackets as they took in what must have been a terrifying view.

I let my breath calm, even though I hadn't realised it had been racing, in a hope my heart would slow. Turning to Toni, I watched as she mirrored my expression and slowed the van as the police cars separated. Neither got out of their cars as we rolled by, but just as our metal passed theirs, I slammed on the brakes and let the window drop.

"You need to call someone."

The police officer paused, his head turning sideways.

"You need to call someone," I repeated. "Then get the hell away from here." I pushed the accelerator, taking the road which led under the motorway. "Where now?" I said, my words without emotion.

"My place," she replied, her face fixed forward. "Next junction, by the Holiday Inn. Can't miss it."

I drove, the motorway deserted, but I wouldn't have noticed any cars if it had been gridlocked, my thoughts so distracted by the growing pain in my stomach. I'd felt it earlier, but with everything else it was the least of my concerns. Now the action had died down, fear and something else grew to take the place of the adrenalin. I could feel it already growing inside; the hunger, the thirst.

I didn't want to return to what I'd been before, what she'd made me into.

"This one," she said, and the road snapped back into my vision.

I pushed the indicator left and slowed, looking up at the ten-storey hotel as it loomed out in front.

Her words sounded muffled, cotton wool in my ears as she gave directions, passing by the hotel, the empty car park. I stopped at a pair of low holiday chalets. The ache in my stomach cranked up as we rocked on the brakes.

"What's wrong?" Toni said and I turned to look, feeling as if the blood had run from my face.

"What's wrong?" I said, and she smiled in a reply which melted my heart.

"Apart from the obvious," she said, holding out her hand.

A wave of pain rushed over my stomach as our hands touched, her skin so warm, so inviting. I craved to be close, to hold her in my arms, to take in her scent. I craved to run my tongue over her neck, to bite, gently at first.

As the air came alive with smells I didn't want, my smile fell and she repeated the question with the raise of her eyebrows. I took a deep breath through my mouth, holding back the ache of my empty stomach.

"It's happening again," I said, and her face dropped.

"What's happening again?" came an unfamiliar male voice from behind us.

32

I jumped, turning through the pain to see the shadow of the solider in the back of the van.

"What's happening again?" he said, his voice again urgent as he drew forward, his gaze falling to my hand resting at my stomach.

"Shit," Toni said, her reaction sharper than mine. She closed her eyes and drew a deep breath. "She's hungry, that's all. I need to get her something to eat," she replied, pulling open her door, turning back as she left. "It's not time yet."

I smiled back in her direction, wincing as I turned away with my stomach aching with emptiness.

"Thank you," I said, my eyes closing.

"For what?" he said. "Are sure you're all right?"

I nodded, unable to do anything else as Toni took me from the seat and helped my feet to the floor.

"What is this place?" I heard his voice join at our backs to the sound of Toni pushing keys into a lock.

She stopped, I felt her turn towards the soldier.

"What are you doing?" Toni said, holding her free hand at the door.

"I need to use your phone," he said. "I need to call this in. Make sure they're sending everyone this way."

Toni paused on his face, then turned, her eyes narrowing.

"You think they don't know?" she replied, and just as she did, I heard the beat of helicopter rotors in the air.

Pain ripped across my stomach, a feeling like something was about to burst. I bent, letting out a stream of air.

His strong hands gripped around my waist, catching me before I could fall.

"Get off her," Toni snapped, and despite my eyes being closed I knew the glaring expression she would fix as she took over, peeling his hands from my body.

She led me through the door, my gaze on the wooden floor as I fell down to a soft sofa and heard her harsh words exchanged through the pain, the detail muffled through the throbbing beat in my ears.

"Jess." It was Toni's voice, near. "I'll get you something to eat, just hold on a minute."

I kept my eyes sealed tight, squirming on the sofa while I listened to the sounds of a kitchen close by, my mind wandering over what she could have to satisfy the ache. A slaughtered lamb? A side of uncooked steak? I felt bile rise in my stomach as it contracted.

"Jess." The words came again and I forced my eyes open and saw the cheese sandwich on the plate offered out in Toni's hands.

I pulled my hanging jaw closed and focused on her smile.

"What were you expecting?" she said.

I shook my head and pulled the bread from the plate, stuffing the food in my mouth like it was the first thing I'd eaten in days. The flavours were out of this world, the taste of the cheese so intoxicating.

"Slowly," I heard her say, as the pound in my ears lessened. My fear subsided, the pain easing with every swallow.

"All because I was hungry?" I said with the last mouthful pushed down.

"Better now?" she said, a soft smile on her lips as she handed over a tall glass of water. I nodded with enthusiasm and took my first look around the room as I drank.

Faded sunflower relief hung on the walls of the open-plan space, with a small kitchen to the right and along the wall exposed steps rose to the next floor. I sat on a three-seat sofa facing an imposing wall-hanging TV, but my attention drew to the blinking light on the black stand where a cordless phone rested under the large screen.

"Where'd he go?" I replied, remembering the soldier's words, but couldn't see him anywhere in the room.

Toni turned her gaze away from the TV.

"To do his job, I hope," she said, dismissing my enquiry to the growing sound of helicopter rotor blades passing over our heads. "We need to get out of here."

"You think he'll tell them where we are?" I said, stretching my back to work out the last of the pain.

"They won't care for now. Too much going on, I hope. It's us that need them." Her eyes drifted to the red vials laid out on a kitchen cloth on a table at the far wall. "I'm astounded by the results so far, but you'll need another dose tonight or tomorrow morning, then more. And we need a few other supplies before then," she said, turning away.

"How many doses do you think it will take?" I replied, looking back to the table.

She didn't reply straight away, her head not turning my way.

"Honestly?" she said, finally meeting my gaze.

I gave a slow nod.

"I don't know," she said, her words quiet. Her hands rested on top of mine clasped at my lap. Her brow lowered as she squeezed my hands. "I don't even know if it will work long term."

This wasn't news.

I gave a nod as I drew a deep breath. It had been the only thought going through my head since the first dose.

"But we've got to try, right?" she said, pulling her hands away to grip me under the shoulders and help me to my feet. "Shower first," she said with a sharp blow of breath.

I stopped and looked down, raised an eyebrow and nodded back. I watched as she stood, then following with my hands out to steady myself on the arm of the chair.

Together we froze as a shadow moved across the window by the door, both of us drawing back in a start as a heavy fist knocked hard against the wood.

33

We stared at each other, breathless for a long moment Toni's eyes matching the stark wideness of mine as I tried to rationalise the panic at the knock. The infected wouldn't be tapping on the door so politely, but perhaps the authorities had come to take us back and continue where they'd left off.

Snapping away from the moment, she shook her head in reply to my screwed-up brow. As she turned, her gaze caught on the flaking stains across my front and followed the scattered dark dried blood trailing in my wake.

I crept to the side and out of view of the door as she stepped toward it. Moving to the foot of the stairs, my view snapped to the news van parked outside and the dark ink blots across its front.

A policeman circled its perimeter, his head turning at an angle as I remembered the blood smeared across the white of the back doors and the jagged bullet holes marking their journey.

Twisting with my mouth agape to Toni, her long hair thick with knots and thin splashes of blood up her arms and across her t-shirt, I wanted to scream for her to stop, but no sound came from my mouth hanging wide as she pulled the door open.

I listened with intent to the depth of the new voice, watching the yellow of his jacket reflecting into the room, my breath halting with the pause in his flow.

"There's been an accident at the chemical plant near…" he said, his voice already hesitant.

I watched as Toni's face turned with what looked like the proper level of concern, her soft features staying high with surprise despite the officer not completing his words. I envisaged the change in his expression as he deserted his practiced script.

"Are you okay, miss?"

Toni raised her eyebrows further, setting her mouth in a toothy smile. With a high voice, she explained about the strawberry jam she was making. The officer gave no response as she swept her hand towards the side of the room you could call the kitchen.

I imagined his raised expression, waiting for the questions to flow when he saw no pots and pans, no ingredients spread across the kitchen work surface. Instead, a question came from further away, the officer who'd been circling the van appearing from behind as my look shot back in his direction.

"Is this your van?" he said, dropping his radio from his mouth.

Toni shook her head.

"Do I look like I work for the BBC?" she said. There was a second pause. "The guy next door," she said, gesturing to her right, "works in film. He's always bringing home the props," she said with laughter in her voice, running her fingers through her hair and pushing out her chest. The moment hung silent in the air.

It all came down to whether he had time for a wild goose chase when there was real chaos unfolding up the road. My breath came back the moment he spoke, the intake of air so loud I could hardly hear his words.

"Okay, Miss. The advice is to stay indoors. Keep your windows closed and stay off the roads. There's a lot of military coming in to help with the clean-up. It's nothing too bad, but best to keep to what I say. Do you understand?"

I watched as she took a moment to think and then let out a nod before closing the door.

"A chemical spill?" I said as she stepped away.

"They had to say something," she said, then pulled her mouth wide, flashing her teeth as she spoke. "Sorry, a group of government scientists just up the road are bringing people back from the dead, only to let them escape. They're coming your way, so stay inside. If you don't, you'll get bitten and you'll join the massing undead army."

I stood still, waiting to see if she would burst into laughter. Waiting for a sign this wasn't real.

"People need the truth," I replied when her face remained flat as stone before I hurried up the stairs.

***

The cascade of water felt as if it cleansed through my entire body. The act of lathering up, washing myself down, watching the water turn from red to clear again. Untangling my hair as I ran my fingers through felt like I cleaned away all that had gone by.

As I dried, I felt shrouded in optimism, the bite wound now barely a scar. I felt an uplifting sense it was all going to be okay.

My thoughts turned to who I'd call first. I had to tell my parents I was okay, even though it was a lie. Then Stan. I'd have to tell him about Mike and Dan. I could feel my head getting heavy as I thought about their families.

I had to remain calm. I couldn't lose it. I was already going to sound like I'd lost my mind when I tried to explain what was going on. Perhaps I should just say I needed picking up. I could set up in the regional offices in Exeter and Stan could come to me. I could tell him in person and make a plan from there.

I stepped from the bathroom full of resolve and retraced my steps to find Toni's wide-open smile greeting me as she stood pulling off her white lace bra which matched the knickers already laying to the floor. I drew a slow, deep breath, determined not to dissuade me from my course.

My gaze fell to the clothes she'd laid at the bed. My clothes, I thought as my heart fluttered. The red jacket and skirt she'd grabbed from her office. An outfit I'd left behind in my rush to get away two years ago now, and for the first time I wondered why she had kept it at her office?

I stared, letting the thought drop as memories of pleasure flooded back and I turned to see her standing beside me, her warmth radiating through my towel.

"What you smiling at?" she said.

"You're smiling too," I replied, glancing down to see her protruding nipples. I thought about letting the towel drop and watching as her grin raised higher.

By the sight of her biting her bottom lip, I could see she was thinking the same.

"No time for that," she said, her mouth bunching in a pout.

I didn't say a word, but my eyebrows lowering did all the talking as I ran my hand between her shoulder blades.

"No," she said stepping away.

"You're right," I said, the disappointment clear in my voice as I kicked myself for the control she had.

Toni disappeared through the door towards the shower, her words echoing before it closed at her back.

"I've found her."

34

The white vest top from Toni's drawer fit as if it were my own, the bra a size too large but would have to do and the jacket, which *was* mine, hung loose and gaped wide.

I heard the two opposing voices in my head. The first, my mother reaching for the cupboard to find me food as she chastised me for not eating properly. The second, Toni's single remark as we ate takeaway at her dining room table to make me push away the plate.

I stood at the mirror, running my hand down my stomach, not knowing whether to curse the inward flow of my touch as I stared at the way the material hung loose, or to celebrate the loss of weight. Either way I had to be ready to meet the world again. I had to be ready to share my story.

I heard the rush of water stop and I stared out of the window, my gaze following the tops of the olive drab trucks rolling along the motorway in the distance.

At the sound of the bathroom door opening wide, I busied myself with a brush through my hair, despite having already smoothed it to perfection.

Turning when she hadn't arrived in the room, I found her leaning on the door frame, a white towel hanging from her armpits to halfway down her thighs. Hair wrapped in another towel, her eyes narrowed as she stared back with a sweet smile, teeth digging into her bottom lip. The smile rose as I took a step. Toni pulled in a breath and walked past me, only turning as she arrived beside the bed.

"You should get something else to eat," she said, shaking the towel loose from her head and rubbing it against her hair with her hand. "You're losing weight."

I tried to push away the comment. I tried not to analyse her intent. Had she changed her mind? Was I imperfect for her in another way?

No. I told myself those days were gone, reminding myself she had no control over me as I watched whilst she continued to dry her hair with her gaze on me, but only for a moment. She turned away, pulling the larger towel tight around her upper body.

Lingering again, I shook away my thoughts and meandered down the stairs, staring out of the window as I arrived at the ground floor. It wasn't until I noticed the bucket and sponge by the front door I turned back through the window and saw the van white again. By the bucket stood a pair of red heels, my size. I could tell without having to look inside.

She was a four, I was a five. I was bigger in all but one way. They must have been mine. I was sure until a thought crept in; they could have belonged to someone else.

Without time for my mind to ask questions I didn't want to answer, my stomach urged me back to the fridge and, flicking on the TV as I passed, I made another two sandwiches, setting one aside.

There was no rolling news, no stories breaking through the seasonal films. The scoop was still mine to break. For now.

Just in that moment I remembered the phone, cursing that she'd managed to distract me.

I looked below the TV to the empty cradle, its light no longer blinking. Before I could survey the room for the handset, I heard her feet on the stairs.

"What day is it?" I said.

"New Year's Eve," she replied, with no smile in her voice and none on her face as she landed at the bottom in jeans and a t-shirt. "You found the shoes."

I turned to see her looking down to my feet, shaking her head as I offered out the sandwich on a plate.

"Mine?" I said without thought, my heart pounding in my ears as the words slipped out.

Her smile went wide, her teeth glistening as they bared, her face alight with joy at my question. She nodded, turning away, only coming back as the smile faded to a shadow in the corners of her lips.

I had to wait, not wanting the relief to show in my voice and ate the other sandwich, controlling my movements with each bite.

"I'm a little over dressed," I said with a smile, hoping and not she'd tell me to take the clothes off.

"You want to film this, right?" she snapped.

I nodded, turning back towards the kitchen. The remains of her smile flattened.

"What now?" I said, looking away, my mind drifting back through the months. We could never bear to be apart for so long, couldn't have been naked so close without having to spend the next hour scratching each other's itch.

Warmth filled my cheeks as I tried to push away the thoughts, but her cold, strict tone did the job for me.

"There's another facility on the edge of Dartmoor. A place called Willsworthy. You know it?"

I shook my head, remembering how it always changed.

"I'll need some trainers as well," I said, my voice flattening out.

A phone call, either mine or hers, and it was like something snapped. A fight would start. I'd take the blame, but they were mostly her fault. Maybe she would say the same, but she'd be wrong. I could feel the warmth inside me turning cold, my stare following as she went around the tiny room squaring the place up. We had to get out of here before the inevitable.

"Are we going or what?" I said, heading to the front door.

"You're ready now, right?" she replied, and I pulled it open, letting the cold breeze wash away the building anger as the door slammed at my back to leave her searching a cupboard.

***

I drove the empty side road in the trainers Toni had found. We'd agreed in a few short words we'd avoid the motorway like the plague, both of us regretting the phrase if the silence was anything to go by.

Passing each closed up shopfront, Toni's frustration grew, claiming she couldn't get the supplies she wouldn't disclose and for which I wouldn't indulge her by probing further.

Only a handful of the shops bothered with a sign telling people who'd dared to brave the chemical leak it was the reason for closure. After travelling half the distance we'd covered escaping on the motorway, Toni's sharp phrase called for me to stop at a petrol station on our left.

With pumps which hadn't seen a new coat of paint since the seventies, to the side of the forecourt stood a building you could barely call a shed.

For a fleeting moment I ignored her call; it was time for her attitude to stop, but my will relented as her head turned my way with a scowl and I pulled the van under the shallow canopy.

"Wait here," she said, already slamming the van door against my protests and heading towards the thick padlock hanging just below the petrol station's iron door handle.

My heart raced as I watched out of the passenger window, gaze fixed on the screwdriver she'd drawn from her pocket. The door soon levered open as the padlock clattered to the floor and I fought the compulsion to pull out the camera and attempt to film the robbery in progress.

As I sat, simmering, glancing around and about, checking the glove box for my mobile phone, my attention snapped to a tap at my window, jumping in my seat at the sight of a policeman in a fluorescent yellow jacket.

His hand slapped at the glass. Fingers stripped of flesh left a trail of thick blood as it returned to take a second hit.

With my lungs failing to muster air for the scream, I stared, fixed on his vacant white eyes as his low growl vibrated through the glass.

35

I recognised his face from before. It was once the policeman who'd moved his car first as we'd raced away from the soldiers' last stand.

How long had that been? An hour, if that.

Missing from his great bald head, half his scalp hung down the side of his face and slapped his cheek each time he moved. A flaking scarlet crust blanketed the left side of his yellow jacket.

I jumped again as his teeth bared, the whites of his snarl smacking into the window. A tooth fell to the ground and a dark gap stared back as he glared with his mouth wide.

I stared on, transfixed, wishing I had a gun filled with rounds to make the problem go away. I felt around the cab, searching for something sharp or heavy.

My attention drew away with a ring of bells rushing from the hut. I turned to where Toni had broken in, the policeman's movement following mine.

My heart sunk at his slow walk towards the door still open wide.

There was no sign of Toni.

I had to do something. I had to warn her at least.

I jumped between the seats, my head spinning as it hit hard against the roof.

Gripping the upholstery hard, I steadied myself, wasting a precious moment for my view to settle. With the spin almost gone, I searched in the back, grabbing a tripod, but it was too heavy to wield. I had no choice and let it drop to the floor, leaping to the side at the last moment so it wouldn't hit my feet.

For a moment my hand hovered on the handle of the rear door, then I jumped back in the front seat.

In the time I'd wasted in the back, the policeman had made up the distance and was a few steps away from the source of the penetrating alarm.

Jabbing my foot on the accelerator, I pushed down the clutch, selecting first gear, forcing the van to lurch forward and hit the fluorescent jacket, sending it disappearing to crunch under the wheel. The tyre slipped and I winced at the sound, trying not to think on what the scene under the van would look like when eventually I rocked to a stop.

With my arms locked out straight to stop me hitting against the steering wheel, the passenger door slammed closed with the force.

Toni, her hands weighed down with carrier bags, appeared at the garage door and looked down at the front corner of the van and to the ground below, raising her eyebrows before looking around.

Movement caught my eye. Staring out, I saw a second policeman coming around the corner. He was missing his fluorescent coat and the left sleeve of his white shirt ran with dark scarlet, leaving a syrupy flow in its wake with his eyes fixed in Toni's direction.

I let the horn sing, drawing the creature's attention.

Toni took one look before running to the van and pulling the door wide to jump in.

"Go," she shouted, slamming the metal closed as she placed the huddle of shopping bags in the footwell.

"Go," she repeated, just as a high voice electrified the air.

Together we turned to see a young woman standing in a thick winter coat, her gloved hand at her face, having come around the opposite corner of the building. She stared at the mess on the ground with her mouth wide as her gaze caught the horror of the policeman who'd turned to check out the piercing noise.

"Leave her," Toni shouted with a force and anger that tugged a memory.

I heard the echo of Toni's screamed accusations as I shrunk back. I listened to my voice through the tears I'd shed and winced at the words I'd sprayed back, remembering the silence as I stormed to my car, barely able to see the road through my anger, my sorrow for another terrible ending; not able to look her in the face as she pleaded through the window for me to come inside so she could make up.

That was the last time I'd seen her. The one-sided conversation I'd calmly spoken down the phone was the last time I'd given her my energy.

I caught the muscles in Toni's face relax just before I turned away with my foot burying the accelerator deep, but saw her hands hurrying on her seatbelt whilst she watched wide-eyed as I turned the wheel not towards the free space and the exit, but to the infected creature whose aim centred solely on the woman standing out in the cold.

"What...?" Toni snapped, her words cutting off at the impact sending her chest into the belt tight across her front and pushing the policeman's hijacked body out of our view.

I ignored her curses, instead turning the wheel, twisting to move the van so my door was alongside the woman who stared with her mouth hanging open and the blood draining from her face.

"Get in," I said, nodding to the back, but she gawked on like I'd just killed someone.

Shouldering the van door open, ignoring Toni's protests, I jumped to the tarmac and held my hands out as the woman stepped back.

"He's not human," I said. "We have to get out of here."

"Are you fucking crazy?" Toni shouted from the passenger seat as she leant forward, her face going beetroot red as I slammed the door shut to deaden her sound.

I stepped forward, stooping to catch the stranger's eye as she stood frozen on the spot.

"Do you recognise me?" I said. Watching, I saw her flinch from the ground to look me in the eye. She drew back and I took a step away. Her eyebrows raised and a slow nod rocked her head.

"Then come with us. We need to get away."

She didn't reply, but let me lead her to the back door. Let me help her up the back step to sit on the chair in the rear.

"What are you doing?" Toni snapped as I jumped back in the front, already manoeuvring the wheels to get us back on the narrow road. "You're letting her out just up ahead," she said when I didn't reply other than to shake my head.

"Jessica," she snapped. "Stop the van."

"Where do you get off ordering me around?" I said, my voice surging out from my throat unbidden.

Silence filled the air. I felt sick, my heart pounding at the realisation of what I'd just said, my grip around the wheel tensing, foot hovering with indecision over the brake in anticipation of what Toni would do next. When she didn't reply, stunned to silence perhaps, I spoke again in a voice I tried to keep calm.

"I'm not going to have sex with her, but if I wanted to then it has nothing to do with you."

There. I'd said it, but I didn't feel better. I'd said the words I'd wanted to all along, to a fashion. Still the nausea rose, threatening to overflow in the silence as I tried to push away the fears roving around in my head.

Toni was driven. Passionate for life. For her field. For science. For me.

She was empathic to a fault. She knew what was going on inside my head, unless the green mist descended. She was caring, brave, honest, but jealous. Toni wanted me all for herself and I was ready to give her what she craved, but only if she could shake off her cross.

It took me a long time to understand that she couldn't or wouldn't change.

Only on her own could she get past the mistrust. I'd never given her any reason to think I wasn't hers. I'd never cheated. Never looked elsewhere while we were together, not that we'd ever been an item for very long. Despite my protests, a phone call, a text message, a look across the room from someone else would be enough for her to think I'd been with everyone else in the world when I wasn't laying in her bed.

I'd leave and we wouldn't speak, until the memories wore thin enough for one of us, usually me, to pick up the phone. We'd talk for hours, slow at first, building it all back from scratch without ever mentioning why I'd run from her bed.

Despite our time apart, she was always there, in the back of my head, in my thoughts every hour that passed. Over the years the arguments came after a shorter time of being in each other's company and I was getting used to having to defend myself with shouted words. I knew I had to stay away from her, have a long break before one of us took it to the next stage.

Toni's barely heard voice cut through my thoughts.

"You were always so weak."

I shivered at the words and knew again in that moment that the decision I'd made months ago had been the right one.

A scream from the back of the van snapped me from my thoughts and we flinched around to see the woman in the back, her mouth wide in terror as she shook. In her hands gripped the empty pistol she must have found on the side, her aim alternating between our faces.

I turned around as I felt the uneven road, twisting the steering wheel to pull us from the grass verge. Looking up I saw the flash of blue lights ahead coming over a hill in the distance.

"Toni," I shouted over the piercing noise.

"Shut up," she called out to the sight of olive drab lorries as they followed the car high over the brow that stole my breath, knowing we had no chance if they chose to stop and check who we were.

36

Pulling over to the verge and with Toni climbing from her seat to the back, I watched the oncoming white of the police car loom into view. It headed a convoy for which I couldn't make out the tail, with more vehicles rising over the crest as the long line continued towards us.

I didn't flinch at the click from the empty gun. Instead, putting my hand to my ear, I moved my mouth as if I was on the phone, taking the time to let a smile out to the flowing traffic as the scream cut short with an abrupt thud against the floor of the van.

The police car didn't stop, didn't pause after the driver glanced in my direction. My gaze turned to the truck at its back and the next as it passed, glimpsing soldiers in full kit in the wing mirror, their faces fixed and serious.

The next truck blocked my view and I looked back through the windscreen, my fear turning to a warm sensation as I counted the trucks full of soldiers who would save the day, who would stop this nightmare. Even though they were too late for me.

Truck after truck kept coming, soon followed by Land Rovers and other army vehicles in their wake. I could feel the smile stretching out my face until the last heavy vehicle passed by with another police car following behind. It slowed as the driver caught my eye.

I twitched the most pleasant smile I could raise in the circumstances, letting my empty hand drop to my side as I told Toni all that happened. Only silence replied from the back.

With the car slowing, I rolled down the window to let the cold in.

"You got here fast," the policeman said as he pulled from the car he'd left in the middle of the road. He was older than me. Late twenties, his face full of a black beard, the top of his head, too. He wore thick, dark-rimmed glasses, the kind kids would have bullied you for at my school. "You know there's a D-Notice in force? You can't use anything you've got."

I let my on-camera smile through, twitching up the side of my lips.

"We haven't got anything," I said. "I'm supposed to be standing by for when you boys want to announce to the world," I replied, bunching up my cheeks. "But I don't much mind for the cold. Do you know any good hotels close?" I added, running my fingers through my hair.

He shook his head, speaking quicker than I expected.

"Don't stay close," he said, his smile faltering.

I pulled a sharp deep breath before reminding myself to keep it subtle.

"What do you mean? Are you saying the chemical spill is affecting people this far out?" I said, letting my voice rise in pitch whilst my eyebrows climbed.

The officer looked to his car and the butch female colleague I hadn't noticed until now in the passenger seat.

"What's your name, officer?"

He returned his look back in my direction, stepping closer to the window.

"Mike," he replied. The name caught in my head and I paused for a little longer than I should.

"Nice to meet you, Mike," I said, pushing my hand out through the window. "So where should I stay?" I heard a noise from the back, the sound of a voice quickly muffled. He gave a nervous smile, raising his eyebrows.

"All I'm saying is there's plenty of nice hotels Exeter-way," he said, leaning in, trying to peer past me and into the back of the van. "Where's your man?"

"Excuse me?" I replied, the indignation in my voice not put on.

"Sorry, your camera man. I mean your camera operator," he said, and I watched as he forced a smile to his face, his cheeks reddening.

I flinched to the police car as the passenger door opened and his female colleague stepped out, her chest barrel-like, not helped by the body armour.

I heard what sounded like something heavy dropping to the floor. The van rocked with the noise and footsteps walked from behind.

A deeper version of Toni's voice came from over my shoulder.

"Camera-woman," she said, and I turned to see her stroking a grey furry windshield from a stick microphone.

The policeman gave a wry smile, his eyes narrow.

Mine, too. She looked like a feral child and as she turned, we saw a line of blood dripping from the corner of her eye.

37

"Oh dear," Mike said at the sight of the blood down her face.

I would have mirrored his words if I'd had any breath.

Toni's gaze flicked between us, surprise not hidden in her brow.

"Are you okay?" the policeman said through an imagined strict frown, but my eyes were too busy pleading with Toni for some well-placed words.

I turned back to the man at the window, watched as he backed away with hushed conversation to his colleague coming around the car. His hand reached down, instinct touching on the top of his baton.

I thought about revving the engine. I could speed off down the track, but realised before my feet could react I'd switched off the ignition.

I turned to Toni's high grin, her hand dabbing at her face before looking down at the sticky red on her finger.

"A box fell from a shelf," she said. "Lady here wanted to drive. It's always a bad idea," she added with a shake of her head and a smirk down in my direction.

I lowered my eyebrows to the officer, his face rising with a knowing grin at my apologetic shrug as his hand fell away from the baton.

"Looks nasty. Someone should have a look at that," came the voice of the policewoman as she came into view.

"It's fine," Toni replied, smiling back.

The woman squinted at the blood, her fingers hooked under the arm holes of her stab vest. After a pause, she turned to her colleague.

"We should go if you've had enough of a look?" she said, raising her brow.

"Nice to meet you," Mike said with a new distance in his voice and turned away. "Get that looked at," he said, twisting round to Toni as he slid into the driver's seat of the police car. His colleague joined him, the engine jumping to life shortly after.

A sudden bang on the back door snapped our gaze around and between the seats to the stranger on her knees, her hand slapping on the thin metal in Toni's shadow.

I twisted around, my face full of alarm, first looking to Toni, but she was already between the seats with great strides to the stranger, whose head had turned around in alarm.

Spinning back, I watched for the police car to make sure they'd gone. Instead I saw their car rock to a halt, Officer Mike's face set stern as he stared towards the back of the van.

I turned the key in the ignition, waved to the officers and pulled away from the lay-by. I wouldn't wait for their next reaction.

Watching in the mirror, I expected blue lights to flash, expected the car to turn and begin the chase.

Instead I saw the driver's door open whilst the car started a slow forward roll. My foot lifted from the accelerator with my gaze fixed in the mirror, watching as the police car jabbed to a stop for a second time.

I stopped the spin of our wheels, barely listening to the scuffle of activity in the back or the muted argument with no voices. My concentration hung on the policeman's walk.

Switching my view to the left-side mirror, I jabbed my foot back on the accelerator when I saw the bush move into the road. I realised it wasn't the foliage advancing with bared teeth towards the poor man who didn't understand what approached him.

Pinned in my seat, something heavy fell in the back and rolled, thudding against the metal panels with each snap left and right of the wheel.

I forced the accelerator hard as I wound around the country road, taking every bend, every junction to put as much distance between us and the terror.

When Toni didn't re-join me as the adrenaline faded, my need to know what was happening in the back grew.

Only when we entered a sleepy village did I feel my right foot lighten and the van slow, coasting to a stop as the road widened.

For a moment I let my breath settle, finding no danger as I scoured through the windows and soon I discovered we'd stopped outside a church with a steeple rising high in to the blue winter sky.

Movement caught my eyes and I sat up straight, ready to push the accelerator again.

I studied the figure's walk, concentrating on the man in a long black coat and a black shirt with a white collar that reminded me of my childhood. It took several seconds with my gaze on the priest before I could let my heartbeat slow; before I could be confident as he drifted between the headstones he wasn't someone who should be buried deep.

I stood, climbing out of the seat and turned to see Toni on the floor with her back resting against the doors. I couldn't quite make out her expression, my body casting a long shadow.

Reaching high to the ceiling, I flicked on the light and gasped for air as I saw the stranger's face held to Toni's chest. A look of terror stared back from Toni. The stranger didn't move, didn't struggle as I watched with my mouth agape.

38

"She was going to scream again. She was going to give us away. They would take you back."

Toni hadn't moved her hand from behind the stranger's head as I stared on.

"What have you done?" I said, my voice high as I kept my feet planted firm. "What have you done?"

"She wouldn't be quiet. I was just holding her down, but she stopped moving. She stopped struggling. I wasn't holding her that hard."

"Maybe she's okay," I said, my legs stiff as I moved between the seats. "Let her go," I said, leaning down.

Toni kept her hand to the back of the stranger's head as she stared back.

Her eyes were wide, brow heavy and lips pursed.

"Let go," I said, raising my voice. "What's wrong with you?" I pushed out my hand to touch Toni's, but before I could she pulled away, leaving the woman to slide down her body.

Turning as her limp form fell, the woman's eyes were open and didn't flinch when the back of her head bounced hard against the floor.

I stared at her bloodshot whites fixed back at me as if asking why I hadn't done something sooner.

"What have you done?" I said, snatching a look at Toni. With her gaze fixed on me, she hadn't looked down at the body. "She's dead," I said, glancing down. "She's dead," I said again, with a rise in volume when Toni didn't seem to have heard.

"Look at her," I said, peering down once more, but still her gaze didn't follow. "Look at her," I repeated, my voice high, almost shouting.

Flinching back, her mouth hanging wide, Toni took a tentative look down, but twisted away and scrabbled to her feet as she spoke in a hurried voice.

"She almost gave us away. I didn't mean to," she said, rushing along the van and between the seats.

I watched as she pulled open the passenger door and jumped to the tarmac. Picking myself up, I followed, slamming the door at my back, my gaze moving across to the vicar paying us no attention as he continued to ramble around the graveyard.

Toni hurried in the direction we'd just raced from, her head shaking and mumbling to herself.

Taking after her, trying my best to match her pace, I called out whilst flinching another look to the graveyard.

I pushed on a fixed smile as the vicar looked up with concern in my direction.

"Toni," I said a little quieter, but still she rushed on, almost running down the narrow road. "Toni," I said as I caught up.

She didn't slow and made no move to acknowledge she'd heard my words. It was only as my hand went to her shoulder she flinched at my touch and let herself slow.

I took her by the upper arms, turning her towards me. Her eyes were vacant as she stared right through me. A mumble of words came from her pale lips.

"Toni," I said, gently shaking her shoulder and she saw me as if for the first time. "Where are you going? We can't go this way, it's not safe," I said, pleading wide-eyed.

She blinked, twisted her head the way she'd been heading and turned back, her face so pale.

"I know you didn't mean it. It was an accident."

She nodded and I tried to convince myself my words were true.

"She would get us caught, then we couldn't break the story and keep everyone safe."

She nodded harder at my words.

"And now we've just got to deal with it."

My words caught up in my head. What was I saying? Toni had just murdered someone and now I was telling her how we would cover it up. Didn't that make me as bad as her?

Bloodied faces burst into my vision. Teeth snapped at me as I remembered how the world had changed. The world I lived in would never be the same, for me at least. I'd spent the day killing already, although they were dead before I did anything.

Toni had taken a life. Why didn't I feel worse? I was going to help cover it up and I hated myself for the thought.

The roar of an engine caught my ear and I turned away from Toni, her head following. A Land Rover flashed into view, speeding around the corner, the side panels scraping the foliage lining the lane.

Great stone sections of wall scraped down the side, sparks flying as the driver struggled to keep control, the windscreen marbled with a hole in the centre. The Land Rover's direction corrected, swerving into the middle of the road, but too quickly. The wheels slid left, then right and for a moment I saw daylight underneath.

Taking a step back, I tried to look at the driver's face. I took another step, my hands clamped to Toni's t-shirt and I saw the red, blinking eyes of a soldier in the driver's seat. He stared back, face white like snow, breath panting. In his terror he hadn't seen us, or didn't care.

With the road not much wider than the vehicle, I lunged at Toni, pushing as hard as I could towards the bush, but I knew there wasn't enough time to save us both.

39

The roar of the engine thundered high as Toni dropped into the bush. About to launch after her, I watched with an ache as she stopped short of safety, her shoulder pushing aside the thick green cover to clash hard with a rigid stone wall hidden under.

With no time for a plan b, no time to change my mind, all I could do was brace myself for the impact and hold back any thought of the crushing weight heading my way.

I'd waited with my eyes squeezed closed for longer than the split second I'd expected for it to all be over.

I turned without thought, instinct taking control. My hands reached up to my face as the Land Rover collided with the wall, sending shrapnel bursting out from its front.

The fearful gaze of the driver stared back and I twisted, without conscious thought, letting myself drop with my arms wide, falling over Toni like a blanket.

Debris peppered my back as Toni writhed beneath my cover.

A few moments passed and I stood with the last of the shrapnel showering to the ground. I twisted and turned, easing out every new ache while I watched steam hiss from the crumpled front of the Land Rover.

With the ring in my ears only just settling, I helped Toni up and she lunged, folding her arms around me and squeezing tight, gripping so hard I felt like I'd been hit.

After longer than I should have waited, I peeled her off and turned back, remembering the poor driver who must have seen me, twisting the wheel at the last moment.

The front half of the vehicle had crumpled like a concertina, the front tyre flat. The rim of the wheel rested in a great wedge; it had been driven into the blacktop. Steam continued to rise, black smoke intertwining and no matter how hard I looked, the driver was nowhere.

I didn't wait for Toni's response before I leapt forward, gripping the door handle tight, my gaze flitting around the inside. There were no loose white air bags that should have saved his life. He'd vanished without a trace.

A groan pulled my attention to the field the other side of the wall. I stepped back, shifting to the front of the crumpled bonnet, wafting away the blackening smoke mixing with the white of the steam.

Turning back to Toni wide-eyed, both of us twisted to the sound of movement and listened to the rustle of leaves and the scratch of vegetation on the other side of the wall.

As I turned, I caught a glimpse of the shattered sheet of glass resting flat on the bonnet.

About to turn back to take a closer look, I heard stones grind and rub together, jumping back just in time to watch as the wall collapsed into the field, stones falling either side.

Toni caught my arm as I was about to step through the settling dust and over the debris, about to race into the field to help the man who'd put himself into the wall to save our lives. I watched as she raised her nose to the air.

I took a tentative breath, coughing at the bitter smoke itching the back of my throat. Despite the caustic scratch, I could smell the rot hanging at the edges.

My mouth dropped and breath stopped as I turned towards the Land Rover and the crackle of flames rising from the edges of the bonnet to dance with the blackening smoke.

"Jess," Toni called.

I turned without hiding my alarm and nodded whilst battling to keep my voice mute, not wanting to attract the attention of what could be the other side of the wall.

Watching the moment she caught up, her hand slammed to her mouth to cut a second call in half. Her head shook and lips bunched tight.

I turned back with a flinch as her hand gripped my shoulder. Stepping from the wall, I pulled at the Land Rover's warming door handle, coughing as my grip got tighter. With the door holding firm, I jabbed at the passenger window, pointing to the rifle laid in the footwell.

Still she shook her head, pulling hard against my arm.

I relented, stumbling back, but as I steadied myself the body of the soldier lunged from the field, his face curtained with blood washing down from a slit in the centre of his forehead.

The solider fell towards me, his bloodied hand still warm as it latched on to my hand and he fell face first across the stones, dragging me down.

40

My gaze fell on the jagged patch of skin missing from the back of his hand as I lurched forward. I watched in slow motion as blood seeped from the wound each time his tendons flexed.

I glared on as exposed bones slid with its grip tightening around mine.

I didn't panic. For some reason unknown I didn't want to scream out. It felt like I was watching a documentary on the Discovery Channel.

My concentration drifted to the pistol holstered at his side as I saw the rocks rising to meet my falling body. My left hand swept from my side, but dragged back by a snatch of Toni's clenched grip.

In amongst the struggle I caught the race of engines echoing down the lane, their volume growing each short moment between the pounding of blood in my ears.

I took no active part in the tug of war. I pulled neither hand either side until my attention snapped to the pain in my right.

Roused from the chaos, awed by the pain, my muscles tightened and almost effortlessly I pulled free of its grip, leaving its face to slap down to the remains of the stone wall.

Stumbling back, Toni caught my fall. Her arms were under mine until I leapt forward, righting myself, not waiting to steady.

Instead I leant forward, bending to heave a great rock from the pile and pull it high above my head before letting it crash down. Flinching away, the legs shot up, then went limp as blood slapped across my bare shins.

Only taking vague notice of the great clots rolling down my skin, I tried to forget the squelch, the liquid slap as the stone hit.

With no time to pause, the sound of engines growing so near, I leapt to the rocks, pulling my glance away from the misshaped head. Seeking the soldier's holster, I pulled the gun into my grip and was through the gap in the wall, turning back only to make sure Toni had followed.

We ran along the hedge inside the wall and despite my steady jog, I knew whoever was following, whatever was chasing after their colleague, they couldn't take their vehicles any further than the Land Rover blocking the road.

Just as the thoughts were helping to slow the adrenaline coursing around my veins, I heard the aggravated bark of hungry dogs in the distance.

When down into a shallow valley we took our first opportunity to peer back and make sure nothing had followed, thankful we couldn't see the scene we'd left behind and they couldn't see us in return.

The pause didn't last long; the breathy barks of the dogs in the distance helped us to swerve across the field, running until our breath couldn't pull any harder.

Coming to rest well away from the hedge, together we leant behind a tall, wide tree, its branches gnarled and bare.

Taking solace in the silence and peering around the tree, my breath rattled my body as I tried to regain control whilst watching the vertical line of black smoke in the distance whiten and soon disappearing altogether. Listening for the snarl of chasing dogs, all I could hear was Toni's deep breaths.

My view turned down to my feet and my ankles caked in mud, peppered with scarlet flecks of clotted blood dried hard, clinging despite my kicks as I tried to hold back the gag.

I turned away, looking around for something to help, something to wipe the mess away. Instead my gaze settled on Toni as she watched, squinting to where we'd come. Her breath had slowed and the darkness in her eyes seemed to have passed.

She turned, her face solemn, a grin rising in the corner of her mouth as she looked me up and down. I did the same, taking in her dishevelled hair, her face lined with darkening blood smudged together with a sheen of perspiration. My gaze fell to her chest and the rip in her t-shirt at the arm. The white of her left cup showed through.

The corner of my mouth wanted to rise, but I forced it down.

I watched as she grinned my way, the way my Toni had done in the good times. The way that used to wind back the clock. I watched as her smile grew and she shook her head until her gaze fell on the pistol I'd forgotten I gripped in my hand. The grin lessened as she pushed out her hand, her eyelids narrowing with the crumple of her face as she reached for the gun.

Despite all that had happened, I felt no hesitation but I understood why my arm was so reluctant to offer the weapon.

Her head turned sideways, her eyes now a pinch as she stepped forward. Her smile was back, but the glow had vanished.

I wanted to pull the gun away. I wanted to release the clip and empty the chamber to the ground, running away so I could keep the promise I'd made to myself before coming to her rescue.

Taking another step closer, her unforgettable scent pulled hard on a chaos of snatched memories. I closed my eyes as her fingers ran light down my arm. My tight tendons relaxed as she gripped the barrel of the pistol and my hand emptied.

Opening my eyes, my gaze fell on the red bloodless teeth marks embedded in the knuckle of my index finger.

She hadn't stepped far and looked sideways to the sky. For a moment she turned her head until she found the low sun halfway around its journey.

I knew the words before they came out.

"We have to get back to the van," she whispered.

I nodded.

"The cameras," I said, whilst still tilting my head, but she raised her eyebrows, turned to the side, righting after a moment.

"Your medicine," she said, her voice lowering. "We need to get it before night fall."

She smiled, bunching her cheeks in my direction. I felt the need to be close to her. A need to feel her warmth, whilst hating myself for how easily she'd undone a year of repair within less than a day.

I stepped closer as she peered in the direction we'd been running before snapping her gaze back my way as I touched her forearm. She flinched away before I could explore her warmth. Her eyes flared wide and brow shot low, curling her features up in disgust as she moved backwards with a jolt.

Unsure at why she'd reacted so strongly, I watched with intent as her features quickly settled as if remembering how she was meant to act. She still couldn't hide the shadow looming behind her eyes and I let the question that had been playing on my mind slip before I had a chance to call it back.

"Why did you call me?" I said with my stomach churning.

Before our last time together, before the time I drew a line, I had always been the one to reconcile. I had always been the one to bring us back together, but a year had passed since that day. It had been a year of self-control and of understanding that we couldn't be together, knowing how it would turn out if I didn't stay away.

Why after so long was I the one she picked the phone up to in her hour of need? Surely she must have understood we just weren't right for each other, no matter how much it hurt?

Toni turned her head to the side, staring back as if she didn't understand the question.

"Why did you call me? Why now?" I said, the strain pulling at my voice.

She shook her head and took a step back, alarm rising on her face.

"I wanted to be with you forever," she said with a sadness in her eyes.

For a moment I stared on, numb, shaking my head, waiting breathless for her to say more and open up. Only when she looked back towards the field did I hear the panting snarl of the dogs again, pushing the rest of the questions to the side.

Together we turned as I backed away and stood transfixed to the Alsatian running across the field. Puffs of vapour poured from its mouth like a steam engine. Its eyes were wide, jaw hanging open. Its tooth-laden mouth gritted and fixed in our direction.

41

"We can't outrun it," Toni said, her voice calm as she stepped back from the tree. With her stare fixed forward, only glancing behind for a moment, her gaze never caught mine.

I watched the dog as its legs pumped hard, its shape getting bigger as each moment passed.

"Run," she said, her voice raising with the weight of the gun towards the field, edging back to get the tree from her field of vision. "If we get split up, meet at the van," she said, her voice sounding only half committed to the words.

I glanced away, looking out to the horizon filled with fields sprawling until they vanished. The countryside rolled up and down as I tried to fix my view, tried to imagine where I'd parked the van. We'd run further than I'd first thought and with only one crumbling building high on the horizon to fix on, I made my first slow steps in its direction.

"I'm not leaving you," I shouted, stopping as her earlier words sunk in.

"Don't be a fucking child," she called over her shoulder. "I'm the one with the gun. You need to run."

"What about you?" I said, exasperated.

"They're trained to go after the hosts. I mean, the subjects. They're part of the plan if it gets out of control."

A numbness came over me as I realised the implications of her words. The dog had been trained to go after people like me. A host. Was I even a person anymore?

With the sound of the dog's heaving breath, my teeth gritted tight and I planted my feet firm.

After a few moments of deep breath, I looked over my shoulder and saw Toni's back. Turning, I watched her arms raise and stretch out. Her head twitched as she checked the view and repeated.

I took one final glance before the hedge lining the long field obscured the dog's race towards us. At least I couldn't see anything following behind the creature.

Only the rise in its pounding breath forewarned its sharp-toothed chase. I wanted to take control. I wanted so much to run, to outrun, leaving the creature alone; dragging Toni with me and overpowering her protests.

All I could manage was a slow pace backwards whilst shaking my head. I was a passenger.

Toni took small steps towards me, her stare facing forward, never leaving the direction of her outstretched arms.

Putting my hands to my face, the dog appeared, taking the corner wide with a speed much greater than I could have imagined. Toni let off a shot without delay.

The explosion shook through me. As did the next when it was clear the first had missed. The second, too.

The dog took a course neither of us had predicted as it continued to ignore Toni and the gunshots altogether, instead making a wide arc around her, its legs pumping, pushing hard in my direction. Its heavy pant turned to a snarl, glaring its long teeth as it sped unrelenting to fill the space between Toni and I.

The third shot exploded with the gun pointed in my direction. The dog's teeth barrelled into me, pushing me to the ground and sending my head spinning as the world turned over, Toni's scream the only sound.

42

I felt the pressure of the explosion through my body as the ground rose to smash against my shoulder. The shock wave forced the pain from elsewhere, but only for a moment.

I tensed, made for the fight and I was ready as I ever would be to take the pain. To kick and scream until it gave up. Or *I* had to.

As the echo of her voice died away in my numb ears, I forced my eyes wide with the pain subsiding.

Toni's hand filled my view. Air sucked through my lips as it felt like blades sliced down my shoulder with her pull from the ground.

The dog lay lifeless, its long teeth hidden over hanging lips. A spray of red cursed the grass. On my legs were long scratches falling down to my ankles and new elongated splashes of blood criss-crossed my skin.

Turning my gaze away when I saw the wound to its head, I looked to the ground with a heaviness in my chest. A sore shoulder was a small price to pay, but the dog didn't ask to join the military or the police, or whoever sent it chasing after us. This was something else Toni's mother would have on her conscience. I would make sure it sat heavy.

I looked up to see Toni already making her way across the field, the barrel of the gun tucked into her waistband. I stood waiting for her to twist around and check I was okay. To make sure I had followed.

Sucking up the pain, I twisted back the way we'd come, slowing my breath as I listened, my gaze hanging on the horizon, not able to stop wondering what played out beyond the view.

Would life ever be normal again?

To the sound of distant gunfire I could only just hear, I turned and followed in Toni's path. She continued to trudge ahead as if she had no doubt I would be there in her wake.

With her pace slow and easy to catch, I hung a few steps behind and she knew, her legs speeding as I joined.

Nothing followed. Nothing tracked behind, despite the noise we'd made in our defence. Still, we didn't rest and had soon climbed up to the building, a ramshackle shed whose roof had caved many years before.

Looking through where a fourth wall had once been, inside lay a long-dead animal. A sheep perhaps. Its bleached white skeleton the only remains.

The building marked the edge of the village which started over the crest, twenty or so houses arranged around a tee junction. The road headed across our view. The point of the tee ran almost to the shed, but finished with tarmac only halfway, the rest running to gravel.

Crowded around the junction, a post office bunched up tight to a local shop with bright orange signage. The shop sat alongside a public house. A lion roared out from the red board hanging on the side. My gaze fixed on the tall steeple just slightly removed from the rest of the village to the side.

Toni gave a sharp look in reply as I pointed out our destination. My growing anger at her scowl dissipated at the sound of a pack of ferocious barking dogs. We both took a step closer to each other, sharing the concern on our features. Toni's hand reached around for the pistol, but before she took hold, the fearful sounds lost their strength, echoing into the distance.

With my heart calming and about to set foot to make our way, a scream cut through the air and the unmistakable boom of a gunshot followed.

The calls became a chorus with a second soon joining. We tried to find the source, tried to peer around the building. Only as two women rounded the corner of the T-junction in the distance, coming from the right and running down in our direction, did we know where it came from.

But it wasn't just these women making the terrible noise.

The women were joggers, if their tight shorts and figure-hugging bright tops were anything to go by, and sprinting as if their life depended on their hobby. Their view twisted backwards, issuing screams to echo out each time they saw what we still couldn't make out.

Doors of a few of the houses opened as the background of screams grew more feral, not abating.

We looked to each other, knowing opening their doors was the worst thing they could do; knowing some wouldn't live long enough to regret their actions.

The cause of the terror could only be one thing. We stood in silence, watching on with a fascination we had no time to take, but neither of us could pull away from the view.

Something must have nagged unconsciously, as we started a slow walk down the side of the hill, sidestepping the crunch of the gravel and walking toward the danger the two joggers were about to know all too well.

Watching, we stopped again. By now half of the houses had their doors open. People stood on their doorsteps looking around, glancing to each other and at the two women. None could figure out why they were making such a din.

It wasn't long before they got their first sign of what should have told them to get behind their doors and hide away. None of them reacted to prevent their deaths. All continued watching on with hands at their faces, wide-eyed at the ear-piercing shriek that told us we couldn't outrun what chased. We knew our only chance was to find sanctuary, but that meant racing toward the noise.

We ran, gazes fixed on the first house. A middle-aged man stood at the door with a woman of a similar age at his back. Both wore dark Christmas jumpers with festive patterns inappropriate for the peril.

As we ran, they saw us, but took little notice, looking back towards the jogger's screams which were now so high, looking to each other, neither sure what to make of the situation.

Their glances hung as the feral shriek lit the air again. Their faces turned wide. Mouths hung open, fixed as we ran, not waiting to see, but already knowing one jogger would be flat on her face with something resembling a human dog tucking into her flesh.

Neither of us were wrong as we caught a glance just before we pushed past the couple and ran into their house.

43

"Close the door," I heard Toni's sharp command and watched the guy's eyes follow as she led the charge with his face indignant to the invasion.

"Mary, ring the police," came the man's voice, his gaze snapping to mine as I followed behind.

"Shut the door," I said through heavy breath, trying my best to keep my voice level. "Is your phone working?" I quickly added.

"Close the door," the woman begged as I passed, her hands grabbing the man's upper arm as she sunk at the knees.

A chorus of screams lit the air outside and I ran past Toni as she stopped in the hallway, peering back and letting her breath settle. I stopped only when I came to the kitchen and ran out of space.

"Close the door," Toni repeated, her voice even sharper than before.

The screams dulled as the door slammed shut and the locks clicked into place. I turned to the back door and the empty mortice lock, noise flashing high as I pulled it open, slamming out the blast of cold air blowing off the rolling fields beyond the garden fence.

"Where's the key?" I shouted, my voice racing away.

Toni arrived first, joining my search of the room before heading back through to the hallway.

"Toni," I snapped, and she turned, looking to my hands gesturing to her waistband at her back. She untucked her t-shirt to cover the gun.

I continued to search the kitchen, pulling open drawers, rooting around for the key while listening to the man's bluster in the hallway.

"It's not working," I heard him say.

"Mobile?" came Toni's reply.

"Not out here," he said, his voice growing in volume.

The woman, Mary, marched from the hallway, projecting her hand out whilst the other clamped firm to the side of her pale, white face.

I took the key and turned it in the lock, testing the handle twice before I moved away.

"What was that?" she said with a tremble in her voice as I drew at her side. Her eyes held wide, dropping while her head twisted and eyebrows fell. "Are you from the telly?" she said, taking a step back.

I gave a shallow nod, no time for the usual smile everyone expected to be in my company.

"What is that thing?" she said, her voice trembling.

Toni arrived at her back just in time. The man followed. Both the couples' pale white expressions were ridiculous in their Christmas finery.

I didn't reply; instead looked to Toni for answers.

The man asked the same unanswered question, but before he finished, Toni walked back into the hall. I followed her into the living room.

A great tree blocked the view through the front window, the light on to compensate. I caught sight of the TV news. My colleague of two years addressed the camera, dressed casual and wrapped in a warm woollen coat with his back to frost-covered parked cars. The millennium wheel loomed in the background as he presented the annual stock piece, giving out advice for the night's celebrations. Not once in those few moments did a body cross the screen with his hands raised and a fractured jaw hanging wide.

The picture soon swapped to a roadblock across the entry ramp to a motorway. A double line of cones and red signs blocked the path as a pair of stern-looking police officers surveyed the view from behind the line, looking everywhere but at the camera.

My heart raced even further as I blotted out the hurried voice of the man at my side, the conversation he was having with Toni or his wife. I peered forward, concentrating on the words of the reporter I couldn't recognise from the voice, or their business-like face as the camera panned to take in their view. He talked about the worst outbreak of foot and mouth disease. He talked about the strictest prohibitions enforced in decades.

The story was still mine. For now. A double-edged sword. For the one who broke the news, their career would go into orbit, but any more delay and it could be too late to save anyone.

Toni shot past me as I watched. The husband made noises of complaint and followed her up the stairs, his tone changing halfway as he stopped.

"What's that?" he said, the words tailing off. "Mary, no don't," he said to stop her following. "Lock yourself in the downstairs toilet."

"What?" was her only reply.

Both moved swiftly out of my way as I bounded up the stairs to catch up with Toni in what appeared to be the master bedroom. My gaze soon turned away from the chintz velvet wallpaper, dark gaudy flowers on a light background, then from the black silk sheets, my corner-mouth smile dropping as I stared into the distance and the dish on top of the van right where I'd left it.

Toni swept the net curtains aside as I joined her, leaving the window open to let the wind rush over us, ignoring the sharp cold air, our focus fixed on the scene before us.

The fallen runner lay motionless on the ground, her bright orange top split in half with a great round wound to her back, welts of skin ripped off. The white of her spine and ribs exposed. Great chunks of flesh were no longer where they had grown.

I followed the dark marks to the road, the red and white of skin left lying on the hard ground surrounded in oily puddles; what looked like pink kidneys discarded on the creature's journey to the house only a few doors down and the only house where the door remained open.

"Now," Toni said with a sharp twist in my direction.

I replied wide-eyed.

"The van," she said. "We can make it."

My heart raced even harder, lungs pulling shallow breaths.

"We're saved," said the man as he joined us at the window.

We'd turned away, but twisted back at his words. Mary pushed past me to get a look. I followed their overjoyed faces along the road to the scatter of soldiers, the vicar in the lead as they headed down from the church.

My heart sank and I gave a heavy breath when I saw their slow, slack-jawed movement. My stare caught as doors along the street opened and people ran from their houses, arms open in the soldier's direction.

44

One after the other, people streamed from their houses, doors opening across the view. Whole families ran breathless, racing from safety, not caring for the bloody trail and the obvious danger still hidden beyond the door that had never closed.

The husband stepped away from the window with Mary following as he jogged to the hallway.

Both Toni and I grabbed a shoulder each and she stopped, eyes wide with fear as she looked back.

"They're not what you think," I said as I snatched a look at Toni. She stayed quiet as if unsure of the words to use. "Look," I said, pulling the woman around as lightly as I could whilst pointing to the slow advance from the church.

As she turned, her eyes squinted out to the crowd of soldiers. Her gaze lingered for a moment before twisting to check on her husband.

As she returned to the view, I leant out of the window.

With Toni watching on and shaking her head I shouted, "No."

An echo called back.

"Get inside, it's not safe," I said, stopping only when Toni gently pulled me inside.

No one had responded. No one gave any sign they'd heard my words.

With the wind gone from my face, I followed Toni's outstretched finger to a woman about our age.

She dragged a boy of maybe seven or eight behind her whilst she ran towards what she thought were her saviours. I urged Mary to look on, adding my pointed finger at the soldiers. I begged her to watch their walk. To see their hands empty and any weapons in sight hanging useless around their backs, despite the danger.

I urged her to look at their injuries, the blood crowding each face. I pleaded with her to take in the same pale, lifeless expression they all wore.

"Ray," Mary screamed in the heartbeat when it all came together, and disappeared from the room to find him.

She came back with her husband behind her just in time to see the thirty or more soldiers heading towards the woman who'd only just slowed, her attention on the child kicking and screaming behind.

After a few paces she turned and saw the obvious. She slowed and let go of the boy's hand. He'd known long before and took the chance to run, the desperation clear in his pace. He tripped over his feet, falling forwards and I wanted to race down the stairs to sweep him up.

I knew Toni would grab at my arm. Maybe there were enough people down there already to help. One of the ten or more of their neighbours who'd realise soon enough. They would soon understand there wasn't a fairy-tale ending to this bulletin.

The first scream shattered the new calm moments later. The mother had held her ground, had stared on, still trying to get her mind to fix on what she saw.

Hands reached from the crowd of soldiers and fingers scraped out at her throat. A second and a third grabbed around her neck and she disappeared, overcome by the surrounding dead bodies stood on two feet.

Her pained screams cut through the forest of camouflage to remind us she wasn't out of her misery yet.

I felt Toni's fingers wrap around my wrist. She held firm, but not gripping tight. It was like she could read my mind. Like she knew I could run at any moment and leap from the window to my death. She knew I would hope to survive for long enough to do the right thing. To pick up the boy; scoop him into my arms, not turning like the others running for their lives.

A heavy thud shook the floor and broke my concentration. I could barely bring myself to look back and see the man lying on the carpet. No one else had turned, their eyes fixed forward on the boy and the encircling masses.

"Run," I screamed out of the window as he vanished from our view. I pulled against Toni's grip to get a better look whilst holding my breath. I saw his face between the forest of legs, his hands swiping as the creatures bent and stumbled over themselves to get at the child.

Toni pulled me back as he scrambled out. He was on his feet and running, his eyes darting around for the safety.

A moan called out from the floor at our backs, but still no one turned, each of us too busy urging the boy on as he tripped over his legs, sending his knees scuffing to the hard ground. The procession of ex-soldiers were not far behind.

A second moan called to my ears with a reminiscence; a sound I'd heard so much in such a short space of time.

Toni twisted her view and I watched at my side as her hand reached, pulling the gun free and pointing to the floor.

Our breath relaxed as we saw the husband's wide-eyed stare. His mouth had turned to an oh as he recovered from his feint and looked up at the gun pointed in his direction.

Sharing a look of relief, Toni and I turned back, but my body tensed as we fixed on the snarling creature at the open door across the road.

Its leathered face dripped red from its forehead, blood falling from its chin.

I followed its gaze as it tracked across the road, its head moving in time with the fastest moving object in view.

I closed my eyes and took a deep breath. I didn't need to look to know it was about to pounce toward its target.

The running child.

45

Toni's hand shot out of the window, the gun climbing high as she pulled the trigger, the sound like it would shatter the glass.

No one saw where the bullet landed. All eyes, including those bloodshot and bounded by heavy hanging lids, fixed upwards for enough of a moment. At least I hoped.

I couldn't see the child.

I couldn't take my gaze from the snarling creature whose legs were bent, primed and ready for the chase as he blinked, staring in our direction.

I couldn't stop staring down its throat as it let out a scream, sending a shiver along my spine.

Only as it leapt into the air, covering half the ground between us in one great bound could I avert my gaze from the doorway, thankful we were the new target.

Mary didn't see it that way.

With no time for her to let out a scream, she collapsed at our feet. If I had a spare second, I would have let out a great sigh. I would have mumbled under my breath, applauding her for playing up to the bloody stereotype.

Instead I had my energy fixed on grabbing for the handle dangling at the window and dragging it closed. Toni moved out the way as I slammed the double glazing hard into the frame.

I felt the wave of pressure as the glass flexed inward, the room dark for a moment as the creature's bulk loomed across the pane. Blood sprayed either side with a slap against the window as its face hit hard on its second bound.

Its expression didn't change as it hit, the hunger I recognised all too obvious in its curled features. With its will clear as it slid down the glass, blood smearing until its clawed fingers hooked to the sill.

I glanced to Toni and she looked back with a question on her lowered brow. We had it point blank with a chance that didn't come often. We just had to sacrifice the safety of the house.

"We're leaving anyway," I said in answer to her look and she raised the gun before my last word. We turned, cringing back, ready for the sear of pain to our ears.

Instead she paused as we stared at the smear of its victim's blood. The sounds of footsteps heavy on the roof coming a moment later told me why she hadn't fired.

Our look headed out across the sea of soldiers heading in our direction, until our attention drew downward by a light but frantic call of a hand against wood.

We moved in unison, looking over the sill and saw the back of a little figure, hearing his sobs rising. His hand slapped in time with the noise coming from the front door.

I ran, not waiting for permission I wouldn't get.

I ran, not being careful with my feet, ignoring the complaints of the husband only just rousing from the floor.

I ran, hearing Toni's calls through the window. She was calling out the beast, distracting for a second time.

Leaping halfway down the stairs, I saw the boy's tiny shape through the misted glass. With hands on the banister propelling me toward the ground floor in two great leaps, I caught the black shape fall from above to cast a dark shadow through the glass at the short figure's back.

A great explosion filled the air, heard from outside and above at the same time. The shapes were too indistinct behind the misted glass to see anything other than their collective flinch. I didn't know what I'd see as I pulled the door wide. Still, I raked open the wood without a pause.

The kid had turned his back to the door. I lunged my arm around his chest, drawing him over the threshold and into the warmth; into our safety and away from the creature who seemed fixed in an upward look.

As I scrabbled backward, my hand reaching for the door, its face turned down in what seemed like slow motion as its mass fell forward, pushing the door back open before it could slam.

I saw the bullet hole through its forehead. A smile appeared on my face as I stepped out of the arc of its death.

"Great shot," I said under my breath to Toni, who must have shot from above, forgetting the kid folded in my arm.

At the same time, I caught a gust of foul wind and heard Toni's shout from above, calling with urgency for me to close the door.

I hadn't noticed the crowd edging ever forward. Their stumbling pace had brought them up to the garden path. I turned and ushered the kid up the stairs. I had to call for Toni to help him up as I turned to push the door closed, only to find the creature's lifeless lump of a body had fallen across the threshold.

No matter how hard I pushed and shoved the warm flesh it wouldn't move. No matter how hard I heaved at the door, shouting the air blue as I prayed to a God I hadn't believed in since I was six, I just knew I didn't have enough time to heave it out of the way before the crowd would be on me.

46

Sweat poured down my face as I pushed and pulled at the cooling flesh. Where had my newfound strength gone? The dead weight wasn't moving quick enough.

As I looked up with each touch a new wave of its stench raked at my nostrils. I tried to listen to Toni's calls, but they barely broke through the low moans vibrating through my chest.

I struggled on. What else could I do?

With one last shove against the limp shoulders, it gave but not enough. I looked up as light blocked from the doorway to see the first dead soldier trip over the step and fall across the threshold.

With defeat resting heavy, I turned and ran. Climbing the stairs two at a time. I chanced a glance over my shoulder just as I turned back to the bedroom. More of the horde had already fallen, tripping over the body I couldn't move.

Another crossed behind, stamping along its former colleague's spine, with its milky white eyes fixed in my direction.

Slamming the bedroom door at my back, Toni looked on, her eyes almost as wide as the kid's tear-streamed face, her arms wrapped across his chest.

Shaking my head, I swiped my brow with the back of my hand and dabbed my eyes along my sleeve.

"I couldn't move him, couldn't shut them out," I said, trying to hold back the exhaustion.

Mary was first to react, lifting from the silk sheets next to her husband, swapping dazed looks between each of us.

"Andy," she said with surprise. "What are you doing here?" she added, lowering her brow.

The boy looked at me and then up to Toni.

"Come here."

I saw the recognition as he pulled away from Toni's grasp and he ran into Mary's wide arms, while I leant my back heavy against the door and fixed my hand to keep the handle upright.

"What are we going to do?" I said, looking only at Toni.

She shook her head, turning to the window.

"We need to get out. We've got to get back before nightfall," she said, turning back with her concern obvious.

I avoided her stare, looking over her shoulder at the sun hovering over the horizon.

"We might need to think again," I said, raising my eyebrows. "In a minute those things," I said, exaggerating the last word, "will be here and this door won't hold for long." With my eyebrows raised, I wasn't able to stop myself glancing to the child still buried in Mary's arms.

Before Toni could speak, I lifted my hand, raising my index finger to my mouth as I turned my ear to the door.

"The window?"

Toni turned as I finished, peering over the sill and shaking her head.

"There must be over a hundred out there. Even if we survived the fall, there's no way we could win a fight."

"Toni," I said, my voice sharp.

She turned, watching with a lowered brow as I gestured to the kid. She dismissed my concern with a shake of her head, pulling the clip from the gun.

I glanced to the couple's wide eyes, staring on as Toni turned the clip lengthwise and counted the bullets.

"Fifteen rounds. It's not enough," she said, shaking her head.

She still had a lot to learn about being around others.

I looked towards the ground, straining my ears to noises somewhere beyond the door, when the squeak of the little boy's voice cut through the air as he shuffled out of Mary's embrace.

"Can they climb stairs?" he said, and we both turned in his direction, the couple looking on with bemused expressions.

I swapped glances with Toni, but I was the first to speak. "What do you know about these," I said, slowing to a pause, "things?" I added, not able to find a better word.

"Zombies, right?" he said, without a change in expression.

I looked at Toni, holding her gaze for a long moment before shrugging and turning back to the boy, nodding.

"I've read a lot of comics. My dad has one of those survival guides and he lets me read it."

I couldn't help but look back at Toni for a second time, watching as she took a pace towards me. She pulled up the gun and aimed towards the door as I rested my fingers on the handle.

Air gurgled through my stomach, the sound radiating out into the room. Toni's expression hardened as she turned away from my belly, fixing back to the door before giving a shallow nod.

She watched as I pushed down the handle.

47

I let the handle drop. Slow at first. Bracing for the heave of wood, I counted down the seconds in my head.

After more than I dared to wait, the force I'd expected hadn't come. Hadn't pushed back.

I gripped the handle tight, holding the metal down until it went no further.

Toni hurried me with her frown and I relaxed my hand, realising I still held the door firm with my back. The wood didn't push against me, didn't smash outward. Hadn't forced me to the floor.

I took a breath, letting the ache in my hand dissipate.

Nodding towards Toni, she nodded back with her face full of impatience.

I pulled the door open, holding it firm and I backed into the shadow. Shame rolled over me as I hid behind the wooden barrier to expose the room to the horrors of the hallway.

With guilt crowding my thoughts, emotion battling in my head, I realised Toni hadn't fired. She hadn't launched an assault on whatever came towards us from the other side.

I stepped slowly around the door as she stood with her face fixed with anger and the gun aimed into the void.

Their signature scent carried through the corridor, a low murmur vibrating along flaccid throats.

The stench of blocked toilets billowed out through the open door, but in the dim light their lifeless forms were nowhere as I peered into the darkness.

Glancing behind me, I saw the sun already hiding behind the houses opposite. Toni twisted, following my gaze, returning with a concern common these last few days.

I turned away, taking my first steps over the threshold.

She arrived at my side as I made out the scene, the writhing dark mass leading halfway up the staircase only just becoming clear. Hands clawed in the air. Jaws snapped open and shut, speeding as they caught my sight.

Although their bodies hid in the dark, the soldier's fatigues doing their job, I could still see pale fingers scraping at the stairs carpet, clawing for traction.

Toni and I swapped a glance, but we both turned back to their slow advance; as if in competition, they rose towards us. Their progress unnerving.

Splitting, we ran to different rooms. I took the back bedroom, Toni the bathroom, but soon she arrived at my side, joining my lingering stare out of the window as I peered down the tiles of the extension roof.

Toni dragged the chest of drawers under the window, pushing me out of the way before I had taken my gaze off the tiled slope below. By the time the plan formed, she had already dragged a chair across the carpet to use as a step up and was urging me to climb with the point of the gun.

If it was a threat, I couldn't tell. Had she left the gun in her hand in her urgency to get me to safety?

My breath stopped as anger balled in my stomach. I let my foot rest on the chair before stepping down, not listening to her call my name as I ran from the room.

Whilst I gripped the front bedroom frame, I shouted at the three to come, spit flying from my mouth as I screamed to urge them on, saying the words I didn't want the kid to hear only when they wouldn't budge.

"Run, or you'll die."

The kid was the first, pulling from Mary's arms and followed my pointed finger in Toni's direction as I stooped, smiling encouragement as he ran past.

"Your choice," I shouted, stepping back.

Peering to the stairs, I saw they'd risen three quarters of the distance. I tried to hold back my shock at their quickened pace.

Giving one last look back into the bedroom and raising my eyes, without voice I pleaded for the couple to wake from their trance.

Neither did, their staring expressions fixed toward the ground. I ran the few paces back to the bedroom and found Toni helping the kid onto the chair. She held his hand as he eagerly climbed to the chest of drawers.

"Wait," I said, and grabbed the kid under the arms, glaring at Toni, but not saying the words I was desperate to voice. Flinching around, my heart rate spiked, dropping only when I found Mary rushing through the doorway.

"You first," I said to her, ignoring Toni's protests as I held the kid back. "And we'll lower Andy down the roof to you."

Toni quietened.

Mary was easy to get on to the roof and made no complaints as we helped her up. She gave no protest as we lowered Andy down once she stopped slipping along the tiles.

"You now," Toni said, her head twisting back and forth to the entrance. She disappeared one last time to the corridor as I waited standing on the chair. She came back a little out of breath, slamming the door of the bedroom and leaning against it with her back. "They're almost at the top. Hurry."

I paused, hovering my foot over the chest of drawers.

"What about the husband?" I said, but Toni could only shrug. "What's he doing?"

She urged me on, gesturing the gun out of the window.

I stepped down to the carpet, lowering myself to the floor and watched as she slid her back across the door to block my path.

"We've got to get him," I said, stepping to her side. She slid to follow my course and block the handle as she mirrored my sideways move. "He's in shock. He doesn't understand what's going on. We've got to give him one last try," I said again, with wide eyes and stepping closer.

Toni took a step forward and put her face right up to mine, her sweet breath washing over me.

"He doesn't want to come. He's given up," she said with a shallow shrug. "He'll get us all killed."

I could hear the moans and irregular footsteps growing louder in the hallway.

"You don't know," I said, my senses overwhelmed at our closeness. I could feel energy sparking across my nerves, blood jetting through my veins.

Toni flinched with a gurgle vibrating outward from my stomach as she pulled in a sharp breath.

"It's too late now," she said, shaking her head towards the window. "Too late. Go, please."

I could hear a mix of anger and desperation rising in her voice. I drew a deep breath and, about to turn, I flinched as something heavy smacked against the door.

Deflated, I turned away, raising my foot, leaving Toni to lean against the door with white knuckles around the handle as she fought against its movement.

I stopped my climb when his strained call came from the other side.

"Help me. Please, help me. Open the door."

48

My features dropped as I heard the words, as did the strength from my legs as I tried to raise up to the chest of drawers. Turning towards Toni, I knew she'd be shaking her head, but didn't expect to see the gun pointing square in my direction.

Energised with the surprise, I spoke, the words weak, barely heard over the elongated sound of his voice begging from the other side of the door.

"Why would you?" I said, my eyes squinting, watching a single tear run down each of her cheeks.

"I have to keep you safe," she said, repointing her aim at my chest. Her look followed as I climbed down. My legs shook as the gun traced.

"You won't do it," I said. "We have to save him for goodness' sake." I turned, following the slope of the roof, watching Mary looking up expectant at the window with Andy smiling wide in her arms. "His wife is just there," I said, taking a step towards the door. "We have to try."

I raised my hand toward the gun, but before I could reach, she turned, huffing out a great breath. Taking large steps, she pulled the door open, ignoring the relief of the husband, his eyes wide as he saw us.

Without looking back to the hands scraping on the top step, I watched the elation in his smile vanish as his eyes caught on the gun raised at his head. He'd shown the most emotion I'd seen since we'd met. I ushered him in with a frantic wave of my hand.

The bang came after the bullet exploded out of the back of his skull.

My ears numbed and I fell to my knees, the world enveloped in cotton wool. My senses dulled.

Toni's words, her shouted commands, her tug at my shoulders only half felt as she said she'd seen a bite mark on his arm.

My senses snapped into focus with a sudden slap of pain at my face and saw her open palm complete the arc.

She'd done it. I'd been right all along. I knew a year ago this is how it would turn out if I didn't break the cycle.

I stood, shaking off her grip and climbed the chair up to the top of the chest of drawers. Dropping myself down to my butt, I pushed myself through the window to slide down the roof, past Mary and Andy waiting on the edge.

Falling to the grass, I bent my knees, but cared little for what would happen if I crumpled to a heap.

Slowly rising to my feet, I scarcely noticed as I helped Andy, holding him for a moment before letting him down to Mary as she stood. I followed her gaze as she looked up, trying to see past Toni emerging through the window.

I didn't wait. Didn't linger; just called out to Mary to find somewhere safe to hold up. In the fading light all I wanted to do was get the van and drive away as fast as I could.

Still barefoot, I walked along the grass to the end of the garden, climbing the fence at the back, all the while trying to let the low hum of moans, the sting of the stench and the occasional scream dissipate into the distance.

A new sound cut through the air after a few minutes of trudging through the field. It came from the village.

I didn't look up to see the helicopter for fear of finding Toni following. I hoped she'd taken another path. At the same time some part of me hoped she chased.

The noise of the rotors grew too strong and I glanced to my right, watching as the green helicopter hovered over the centre of the village. A figure in a flight suit leant out of the open side door; even though they were quite some way off, I thought I could see, or sense, the horror in their expression.

The helicopter flew away after a moment, moving high along the road with caution and the figure still at the door.

I couldn't imagine the crazed conversation as they tried to explain over the radio what they were seeing. Still, I walked on at a pace, covering a quarter of the distance to encircle the village. When I came to the road bisecting the settlement, I stood at the roadside, leaning against the brick of the last house.

Pausing, I couldn't help turning back the way I'd travelled and with surprise I saw Toni hadn't been following. She hadn't appeared as I lingered on, and staring out as far as I could to where I had come, I swallowed down a rising guilt that I hadn't pulled Mary and the child along with me.

Still she didn't appear as I waited; as I tried to reconcile why she'd pulled the trigger. The husband had made his mind up. He'd chosen life. He'd chosen to join us in our escape.

Despite her actions, when she hadn't appeared I felt so exposed.

Taking a deep breath, I told myself nothing had changed. I told myself I needed to get to the van. Toni would be there waiting impatiently for me with a scalding look, drawing the anger from where I kept it hidden. When we met again I would find out her reason. I would get the missing information only she knew; the real reason she killed that man.

I'd seen no bite mark.

Peering around the wall, I saw the thinning crowd of dead soldiers, each still turning right into the cul-de-sac, following their dead colleagues to torment any residents still alive.

There were only a few by the time I walked toward the white of the van. I could just about make it out around the twist of the road on the other side of the village by the church. Toni was probably already there, ready to grab me when I arrived and tear off a strip for going it alone, or shower me with an apology.

She wouldn't be the only one raising her voice. I would make it clear things had gone too far.

I meandered, hugging the buildings to avoid putting my bare feet on the gravelled edges of the road. Using the line of detached houses for cover, I stopped each moment at the sight or fear of a soldier's glance with the lolling roll of their heads. I ducked into doorways. After checking the coast was clear, I stepped back into the road.

Passing in front of a dark house, I didn't see the door hanging open before it was too late; before a pale hand shot from the darkness, yanking my arm to drag me, my feet smacking against the concrete step to envelope me in the shadows.

49

He was alive, his hands warm to touch. I tried to let my breath catch, tried to push away the musty tang of dust in the air. I tried to let my chest relax as I sat on the floor, staying where I'd landed on the carpet in the stranger's hallway.

"I saved you," the man's voice said in a thick, west country accent, his body just a wide shadow at the door.

"Thank you," I said, my breath yet to slow. "I'm okay, but thank you."

"There's too many of them," he said, still staring through the open door, his head darting left and right. Abruptly he turned, stepping back into the hallway.

The room was too dark to see very much, the carpet a shade of grey. Dark, damp stains clung to the walls. The thick air only helped my conclusion. To my left stood an open door, another to the right at the base of the rising stairs.

"Thank you again," I said. "But I've got to go. I have a friend out there. She'll want to make sure I'm okay."

He paused and I watched his head twist, but the light was too dim to catch more than a pudgy outline of features as they lingered in my direction. He turned around in the doorway, took another look left and right, pausing in each direction before he let the door close at his back. The silhouette of his hands turned and pulled the key from the lock.

"I've really got to go," I said, my heart rate still not falling. My heels stung as I pulled myself up.

"Wait for help here," he said in a breathy, asthmatic voice, offering out a hand while he pushed the key into his pocket with the other.

"I insist, but thank you," I said, already at my feet without his help whilst trying my best to keep my voice even.

A shadow passed on the other side of the front door's three thin windows, and then another. I thought about screaming, but I could have read this all wrong. My first fears could just be a hang up.

I felt annoyance creeping in.

"Look, I'm thankful for your help, but I have to insist you open the door so I can re-join my friend."

"Insist all you want, you're not going anywhere."

Bile rose in my stomach, but I held back from my gut reaction to scream and call for someone to come to my rescue. This guy just needed to be told to stop being such a prick. What could he do anyway, the size of him? He looked like if I said boo he'd have a heart attack and fall to the floor clutching his chest.

"I'm going. Now get out of my fucking way, you big fat creep," I said, taking a step forward. "I will scream this place down and you'll be surrounded by those things."

Despite the darkness, with my first foot forward I saw the concern on his features and the bunching in his cheeks as his hand pulled something from behind him before pushing it out towards me.

He mumbled under his breath with all but an aura of light around his wide frame blocking the doorway. His face lit from below. His chins hung heavy from his shadowed features as the crackling blue light of electricity arced between the two prongs of the Taser in his hand.

I turned and ran to the back of the house. Racing through the hallway, I knocked a thin, tall telephone stand to the floor, the bells pinging as the Bakelite hit the carpet.

In the kitchen I had my hand on the back door and pushed down the handle whilst pulling as hard as I could.

It was locked. Of course it was.

I picked up a bowl filled with rotting fruit from the kitchen counter, raised it above my head with both hands, but felt his grip against my wrists and his pull backward as my legs buckled from under me.

Screaming, the air went from my lungs before I could get any volume, each of my muscles contracting and relaxing at the same time as the electricity took over my body. All I could do was listen to the concern in his voice.

"It's for your own good."

50

My vision blurred. Sounds rolled into one. His stench felt thick in my face, his breath heaving as he carried me over his shoulder in slow, painful steps, each one higher than the last.

I kept silent, not able to talk, not able to think what would come when we reached the top. Tears boiled over as he laid me down in a dark room. The musk of months-old bed clothes surrounded me.

I tried to fight as he grabbed at my hands, but when his face lit up with an arc of electricity, I let him take them and seal the Velcro around my wrists, clipping the cuffs to straps either side. My instinct told me to kick out, but the memory of the spasm won and I let myself go.

I shuffled up the bed, resting my head on a pillow to get a better look. I tried to bring my hands together, but when I could almost touch my fingers, the straps stopped my progress. A lamp clicked on to my side, its long arm tilting with a hand wrapped around its shaft. The light fell to my body, turning me away from the brightness and he disappeared into the dark.

I heard his weight rest in an armchair, the leather creaking under his mass. A huff of air came from his chest as it pushed out the effort, leaving just the rattle of his lungs with each laboured breath.

I looked to the window to see the daylight had almost gone, what remained of the light doing nothing to help me see the room.

"Just wait it out here," he said.

"I'm sorry but you've got the wrong idea."

"What wrong idea?" The words came out questioning and breathless.

"I just need to go. I need to meet up with my friend."

"You're safe here. I'm sorry I had to use the stinger. It's for your own good. You don't know what they are."

"I do. I do. I really do. Please just let me out," I said, my voice rising as I pleaded.

"Please keep quiet or I'm going to have to cover your mouth."

I held back the words and slowed my breath as he spoke again.

"You don't want to attract those things. Trust me on that."

I waited with nothing else I could do, the grate of his breath somehow reassuring me that he was still sat there and not coming closer. He wasn't the worst thing I'd had to deal with this day and I knew with certainty I would deal with worse before all this was over. I told myself again and again this was just another story to tell. The underbelly of rural England. Of humanity.

With a great bubbling surge of noise from my belly, his breath paused, the silence disconcerting, leaving me with a rising pain.

I thought of Toni out in the darkness alone. She was safe. She had the gun, but her worry would be uncontrollable. By now she'd be at the van for sure. She'd be searching and I listened out for the distant call of my name.

The void had grown in my stomach, a cloud descending into my head. I remembered the first time I'd had this feeling; the first time I'd experienced the alien depth of want in my belly.

Anger surged as I pulled at the bounds around my wrists.

"Is this the only way you can get girls?" I blurted out, regretting the words as I heard a deep breath and the complaint from the chair, air hoofing from his lungs, the floorboards creaking with each movement.

I looked into the darkness, following as the noise travelled around the room, but the bedside light was too bright to make out any shapes in the shadows.

"You've got the wrong idea," he said, and I flinched at the words coming somewhere to my right, the view masked by the bright light.

I screamed with all the effort I could muster, but all I got was his breath running harder as the noise tailed off.

"Please don't," he pleaded as the floorboards creaked to the sound of a tape being ripped from the roll.

I kept still, knowing I would need my energy soon to stop myself destroying this man and diving too deep into what I could feel coming.

With surprise, his hands didn't appear in the light, but as I heard the floorboards creak again I couldn't hold back my voice.

"No," I said. "Please, no. Untie me. Let me go," I added as I tried to listen for a reaction, whilst knowing he was staring back at me from the other side of the light. All I could hear was the slow breath.

His wheeze had gone, his breath so shallow.

His odour was changing and with every breath I could taste the richness of his sweetening meats.

A sheen of sweat glistened on my body, despite the cold, each of his breaths sending a fresh wave of sensation through me and it felt as if saliva poured into my mouth.

His podgy face peered in from behind the light with wide eyes and confusion staring back.

"Are you feeling all right?" he said, but before I could snap my teeth forward he stepped back without a pause, withdrawing from the light and leaving me with just an empty pit in my stomach.

I could hear his movement, swifter than I could have imagined and he was around the other side of the bed, swiping the lamp off, plunging the room in complete darkness.

This was it. This was the time. The event to change the way I saw the world was about to happen, one way or another.

Instead of him coming near I listened as he ran from the room. He must have heard something before me, some pre-warning I hadn't caught.

Only now could I hear the glass shattering to the floor somewhere downstairs.

51

Toni. It had to be her.

She was here to save the day, to take care of me.

The freak couldn't hide his motion down the stairs. She would hear him coming long before she would see the massive target lumbering forward with the Taser. She would shoot him down before he had any chance to react.

I screamed, louder and longer than I thought I could. The gunshot came sooner than I could have hoped, the second soon after, quickly followed by the third, leaving only silence after the echo died.

I listened hard. I listened long and let myself relax, taking deep breaths though my nose. The last of his fresh scent had gone, leaving only the odour I tried to ignore.

Was there another mixed in with the musk?

Could I smell Toni?

The memory of how she would taste sat in the forefront of my mind. The scent to which all others fall short.

No, I couldn't make her out. I couldn't find her, my palette blank.

Then it came. Not the smell, but the noise. I heard the hum, the motion of the masses beyond the walls. They'd followed the sound and sought the cause of the loud noise, but they would stay to get at what created the glorious smell. I heard movement in the house too, controlled, not frantic; the scrape of heavy furniture.

At first I pictured Toni hauling heavy cabinets across the room, moving solid wood to block the door she'd just smashed open. But why wasn't she racing to find me? Why couldn't I taste her on my lips?

The hunger was great enough, the chasm in my belly bottomless, my need singing out for her. Maybe it wasn't Toni after all and the nightmare was about to start over, but this time worse when they saw me bound and helpless on the bed.

With a smirk, I pitied whoever else would come into the room, picturing me tearing their face off as they came near.

I tested the bounds at my arms, pulling hard against the strain. I tried to judge if I let go, if I let the beast inside grow at its will, could I pull free? Would I be submitting myself to the creature I wouldn't be able to turn off when I needed?

No, I told myself. I must fight on and concentrated back on the noise. I could hear definite footsteps coming from the hallway. The steps were so light compared to what had come before.

So calm.

I caught the first scent, the glorious smell so intoxicating. It was Toni standing there in the doorway; hers was the slender figure I could just make out in the last ebbs of the light through the windows. But why was she at the end of the bed not saying a word?

"Toni," I said without question, but she didn't respond. "Toni. Let me out please."

The figure moved with a grace only confirming what I knew, but with an unhurried pace I couldn't understand. Why wasn't she rushing to free me?

Instead, as she grew near, I felt her fingers on my ankle, tracing with a light touch against my skin, the electricity stronger than the Taser's punch. My nerves were on fire as her taste sparked the inside of my nose, energy coursing between my legs.

I raised my hips up and down as she travelled with her fingers as a guide, getting closer to where I was desperate for her touch.

She raised her hand as she was about to arrive, my body aching, hips bucking to find her touch again, but she'd gone and I couldn't make out her form; only knowing she was there in the shadow, her smell almost solid in my mouth.

The light burst on and I squeezed my eyes closed. The lamp moved toward the ceiling and I opened my eyes to see Toni looking me up and down, a playful grin on her face.

"Let me out," I said with a stranger's low tone.

She shook her head, the smile gone in an instant.

"I think you better stay there for a while longer," she said, but when she didn't raise her eyebrows, didn't give a childish giggle, my face screwed up and I shook my head.

I didn't want her to take away my senses on fire, to take what I had. What I could feel.

I bucked and I pleaded as her fist came down to my thigh, the syringe of the red liquid curled in her fingers as I snapped my teeth towards her hand.

52

Surrounded by a sea of creatures of the night, the starless dark sky all around me, I stood on a stone column rising high above, in a white shimmering lace nightgown, watching as they clawed at the air. With their disfigured, rotten faces melting to the floor, I had no emotion, didn't fear, didn't want for anything; the hunger in my belly satisfied.

As I watched, my head turned down without my will and I saw my once-pristine white gown dripped with blood, congealing as it rolled down my front. My fingers came away from my face wet and sticky. The pads of each were red as I looked, the scarlet darkening, cracking as it dried before my eyes.

My focus fell to the floor far below. The creatures had parted, were spreading wide, each running away from the naked body lain at the base of the pillar. My vision zoomed and as it did, I saw the creatures had changed, screams raising from their voices. They were human now. Real. Alive, and running for fear of the body surrounded in a spot of light. I couldn't look up to see its source.

Dumbfounded and unable to find breath, I could only stare down. I couldn't look away as I saw a woman on her back, naked, her white pale skin perfect in every way; her mound of hair trimmed to a line, her breasts the perfect size. Not too big or too small. Her arms spread, hands upturned at her side.

I knew it was Toni, despite not being able to see her face; the skin missing, leaving just the sculpt of her bones and a ragged mass of flesh.

It was Toni, her scent undeniable. Thick, strong, shivers ran down my spine as I stood there on the pillar, now less than a foot high, the darkness empty of all but her slain body.

I wanted to stare on. I wanted to take her in, but something drove me forward, my hands stuck behind my back and I felt as if pushed from the plinth. I screamed with anger, with pain, tears rolling from my eyes as I opened my mouth. With no breath, I panted for words as I lunged, my face forced to her fleshy stomach as she called out my name.

"Jess," she said, and I opened my eyes to the darkness.

I lay on my side with my hands bound around my back.

"Jess," she repeated.

I blinked to take in more light.

My legs were free, my feet bare, but I was still on the bed as the shadowy shape of the room came into focus.

"Jess," she said one more time.

I nodded, afraid I would have no voice.

"They're here," she said.

"Where?" I replied, surprised at my voice. "Who?" I added as I processed. "My hands?"

"How you feeling?"

I sat up, my abs aching as I pulled up to sit. I remembered laying on the bed. Remembered my wrists bound.

"Hungry," I said, realising they were the wrong words as the shadow I could only just make out stepped back and pushed out something square in her hands.

"Eggs, bacon, that kind of thing," I said, not knowing how else to express myself.

I watched as she relaxed and drew in close. Her scent had gone, the powerful elixir only a dreamlike memory.

"Good," she replied. "It only took half the time." I could hear the warmth in her voice. "That's good. It means it's having an effect."

"What time is it?"

"One," she replied.

"Can we have more light?"

"Power's out."

"My hands," I said, shaking my wrists to make sure it hadn't been part of the dream.

"Soon," Toni replied. "I had to be sure."

I nodded in the darkness.

"Who's here?" I said, remembering her words. For the first time I could sense someone else close.

"I am," came a woman's voice, pulling at a memory, sending the blood from my face as I twisted around to the doorway.

"Toni," I replied. "What's your mother doing here?"

A rumble of laughter came from the woman's throat and I struggled to turn my legs, shuffling to the side of the bed.

Bright torch lights beamed at me from the doorway as my feet found the floor after too long. The lights were moving and figures were around me.

A hand gave a firm grip around the cuffs, pushing my arms up my back, forcing me forward as I stood. Pushing me towards the door.

"Toni?" I said, pleading.

"Come quietly." Toni's voice breathed low from somewhere in the room. "I told you we had to find her."

"And here I am," said the woman, her smile obvious.

53

"Not like this," I said, the chasm in my stomach growing.

"It's okay," Toni replied to the background of low laughter coming from beside the doorway. "You're not helping," she said, but in a different direction.

The laughter slowed.

"Not like this," I repeated with my voice low. "Why didn't you tell me?" I replied, twisting my body and testing the grip on the cuffs.

"You were dead to the world," Toni replied. "I got a call."

"You didn't have a phone," I said, failing to keep the emotion from my voice. I waited for the reply, but it didn't come. "You could have waited, discussed it. Like adults do."

There was no reply other than a snort from the doorway.

"Please," Toni pleaded.

"Why am I so shocked you've let me down again?" I said out loud, shaking my hands, but the bounds held firm.

"Jess, don't do this."

"No. You don't do this, Toni," I said, letting my anger build. "You told me they'd pull me apart. They'd want to find out why your medicine was working when the others hadn't."

"I promise you'll be okay. We'll look after you. I'll make sure you'll be fine."

"They win again. You chose them over me."

"Jess, please."

"But it's what you do, right? It's what you have to do. You always fuck us up."

A huff of air came from the doorway.

"Please, ladies, stop with this sickly crap. We need to hustle. We've got the fate of humanity in our hands and I haven't got time to listen to this disgusting, deviant talk. I've told you she's just a phase, Antonia. You'll get over it. We'll find you a nice man and you'll never look back. Trust me."

"Are you going to let her talk to us like this?" I snapped, trying my best to shake my hands from the hold.

"Stay out of it, Mother. It's not a phase," Toni shouted, her words caustic, but then I heard her voice turn in my direction. "Jess and I are meant for each other."

The words sounded more like an accusation than a declaration.

"My hands, Toni? We've obviously got lots to discuss," I said, trying to let the whine out from my words as I looked in the general direction of where her voice had come from. The lights still dazzled bright in my eyes.

"We'll have plenty of time to talk," she said, but before I could question her meaning there was a gruff call from below; a man's urgent shout for everyone to get moving. Something was coming and it didn't take much to know what.

The lights from the doorway disappeared down the stairs and I pushed back against my braced arms, wincing as my wrists pushed upwards and forced my shoulders down.

"Really," I said through the pain.

Toni's voice came more distant this time.

"I said not to hurt her," she said, her voice more than a little childlike.

I couldn't tell, but the mother must have given a wave or some other signal to let the pressure on my arms relax enough for me to stand up tall. I tried to twist, but the hand on the cuffs and my shoulder held me firm.

"So you don't need me to film this shit now?" I shouted as I fought against the hold. "No more bargaining required, or have you already struck a deal? What have you sold to the Devil, Toni?"

A low rumble of laughter came from close by. Her mother had neared.

"What are you doing, Toni?" I said as my voice settled back. "How can you trust this woman after what she did to you?"

Toni's voice came back weak, but her mother's voice cut over it before I could hear.

"What I did?" the mother said. "Get her to the truck. Stop pussyfooting around. We need to find out what happens if she survives. We need to see if what you're saying is right."

It felt like my insides had drained out. I could hear Toni protesting as she moved around the room; each time I thought I heard her speak, her mother cut in.

"It was your idea," the mother said.

The words cut through me and I felt as if I was about to pass out. My brain numbed; the only hope left was that I was still in a drug-addled dream.

"What?" I said. I wanted to say more, but I had no energy.

"It's okay. It's not like it sounds," Toni said, finally given a chance to speak. "We'll get through this and we can be together again. We'll have the rest of our lives, don't worry."

The questions came thick and fast in my head.

What had she done? How involved was she? Had she set this all up? Was she the reason they had infected me? Was this all just to get me close, to be together, or was it some kind of revenge for leaving her?

Another shout came from downstairs, but with more urgency this time. The figure at my back tried to push me along.

Another call came. We'd missed the opportunity. The air thickened with curses rising from the stairwell.

Whoever held my arms pulled me back into the room as I watched shadows from the beams of light downstairs scattering, hurrying as they danced on the walls before disappearing. I heard the front door slam and a call went up from outside.

I didn't flinch at the gunfire. Instead, I turned around to the window and saw two figures standing either side, their silhouettes hardly visible until the guy at my back glanced their way, his head torch following.

Toni was to the right; that woman, her mother, to the left. Both had the side of the curtain lifted, their faces hidden as they peered out. The guy flinched away when he realised what he'd done and the light was back on me, but it was too late.

Energy flooded back through my veins. I don't know if it was a side effect of the drug, but I could feel an animalistic anger raging inside me. And now I'd seen it was just the four of us in the room.

To the orchestra of gunfire raining lead outside, I dropped to the floor and, rather than being dragged down, he let me fall. Before his breath had huffed out in annoyance and he'd completed his bend to pull me back, I'd twisted around and had my knee in his face.

With our short scuffle blocked from the ear by the explosions lighting up the night outside, I felt bone crack. My knee jolted forward as his cartilage displaced and the nose gave way.

He gave no replay. He was out cold, slumped to the floor.

I paused, watching the line of light from his head torch along the stained carpet.

I saw my chance, my first instinct to run abandoned. Instead, I twisted, squatting backward to the carpet. The pistol came out of the holster much easier than I'd expected.

Ignoring the pain in my wrists as they scraped against the cuffs, I pulled the slide back and hoped it was a Glock. I had no chance to feel for a safety.

Standing tall, I angled my body sideways, my shoulders aching as I twisted my arms behind my back to get the gun pointed toward the window and I swapped between the pair's shadowy positions.

I kicked the head lamp, glancing the guy's head. He didn't complain as the torch spun for a moment. It came to rest facing me, obscuring the tiny amount of light coming from the window.

It was then they first noticed. A shadow turned; Toni first, but the other followed her sharp breath. Despite the chorus of the fight outside, I could tell they were looking my way.

Toni had moved in the last few moments, her voice coming different to how I expected, their shadows now one. I retrained the gun away from her voice.

"What are you going to do with that?" Toni said, her voice calm, somehow heard over the slowing rate of fire from outside.

I looked down past the light. The guy who'd held me had woken and was crawling away towards the window.

"I thought I could trust you. I thought I needed you," I said, pulling in a deep breath, not thinking before I spoke.

"You do need me and I need you. This is for your own good," she replied, her voice moving closer. Her mother gave a push of air from her lungs in disgust, tutting between the slowing shots from outside. I was sure her sound came from the left.

"Did you do this to me?" I said. All I could hear was Toni's feet stepping toward me and the mother's garbled voice in the background. "Did you bring me here for this?"

When she gave no reply other than the movement forward, I closed my eyes and let the gun drift to the left, centring the sight on her mother's shadow, in my mind's eye at least, and pulled the trigger three times.

54

Running down the stairs with tears streaming down my face, my shoulder slid across the wallpaper to keep me steady as I raced to the ground floor. Not able to slow without toppling, no arms to balance, all my hands could do was grip the gun. My upper arm took the force as I slammed hard into the thin toilet door, the hardboard cracking down the middle as it stopped my fall.

With an ache in my hand, I let my grip relax. Head darting left and right, I sought out shadows, but the only disturbances in the light were thin flashes through the remains of the front door's glass to my side.

Twisting my wrists still held tight by the cuffs, I turned towards the back door and my bare feet found the pricking remains of the missing glass panel. Sucking up the pain I stepped with a light touch whilst trying to ignore the tacky suction of the floor.

Passing the sideboard whilst squinting under the stairs, looking for the trainers I'd been wearing or anything I could use to protect myself.

Seeing a rabble of disorganised shoes, I stopped and pushed my feet into a pair of white trainers which were way too big and slid on with no need for my hands.

Urgent but muffled calls came from upstairs and I looked to the back door, hesitating as I ran towards it searching its surface for some lock or a mechanism I could use to slow their return. I found nothing I could operate without my hands. I would have to hope the slowing gunfire had been enough to hide the call.

Contorting my hands around the side, I ignored the tension at my wrists as I tried the handle. I couldn't stop the gun slapping and scratching against the metal.

It was locked. Still locked, I thought, as I remembered the last time I'd tried. The last time I was desperate to escape.

With my night vision improving, I looked to the wide windows at its side, shuffling along the dining table to follow. Not able to raise my hands high, I angled the handle of the old-fashioned window with my nose. It moved just enough for me to push it wide with my forehead, feeling the chill air wash over me. I used my foot to hook a chair from under the dining table. Its metal legs scraped across the tile floor, the loudest sound in the moment. My actions were no longer drowned by gunfire, my noise only competing with the footsteps above.

Teetering for balance on the frame, I toppled headfirst. My hands let go of the grip, the gun landing before my shoulder.

Thankful for grass under the window, I shook off the ache, pausing for the pain to dissipate. Taking a deep breath, I tried not to think what would have happened if it had been concrete under the window.

After the darkness inside, the outdoors glowed bright with moonlight.

Standing, the gun caught my eye. I dropped back to my knees and fumbled it from the ground, adrenaline racing as I heard shouts inside the house, but still no one came racing down the stairs.

Not able to stop myself as I stood, I looked back inside through the window. Ignoring the hurried sounds, I froze on the fat guy's body; his face a bloodied mess, his mouth hanging open, jaw at a contorted angle as he lay on the floor. I knew who had caused the wounds. I knew who had gone to town on his face. I knew she wouldn't have been able to control herself when she saw what it looked like he was so close to doing.

It was his blood sticking to my feet and I didn't know how it made me feel. There was no space in my head for any more right now.

I ran, could do nothing else, but instead of trying to figure how I could climb the tall fence growing in my vision, my mind played over the three frames of light as the bedroom brightened in each of the bullet's flashes.

The frames hung for a second at a time and I fixed on Toni's evolving expression with each pull of the trigger; her body forced back, unable to absorb the momentum while she watched as I desperately tried to correct my aim to my intended target.

55

The smash of glass brought me back to the present. Still running and with no time to turn and check the source of the noise, I was upon the fence, blinking away the tears.

With my face set with no expression, I felt numb to emotion as I looked left, not slowing until my shoulder hit hard against the wood. Pain forced through the ache I already felt as the wood stayed firm, not creaking as I slammed hard against it. My wrists screamed against the cuffs.

Running to the left and the neighbour's boundary, there was still enough light to see the fence was only half the size and made from wire mesh.

I was over without slowing.

I'd expected the fall. Expected the agony, but did my best to roll as I landed.

Shocked at my grace, I was up again in one swift move and amazed the trainers had remained on my feet, the momentum still with me as I headed towards the next line, a bushy barrier I wasn't prepared to find out what lay beneath.

The garden's rear fence was just as tall as the last, but my excitement grew as I spotted a wooden structure only half as high in the corner; the type used to store bikes or other garden clutter.

At the base, a haphazard collection of pots stood with wooden boxes I hoped would make the perfect set of steps.

As I ran, I tried to think the motion through. There wasn't enough time to do anything but give myself a yes or no.

I committed, buoying myself up, taking comfort in the graceful forward roll I'd just accomplished only seconds before.

Plotting the line, my right foot aiming for the larger box, I would push up as hard as I could, expecting to land my left on top of the roof, leaving myself to hope I hadn't lost my athletic, school-aged skill. In my head I'd Fosbury Flop over the next fence, but didn't care to think about the landing.

With the time to plan over too soon, I committed and any more thought would just add corrosive doubt. I had it all planned out in less than a second.

I took a great breath of air, filling my lungs in more than just a symbolic act. I adjusted my stride so my next footfall would be on the wooden box whilst trying not to envisage its collapse under my mass.

It took the weight of my body and right foot. It didn't collapse as I pushed off, but my left foot went only as high as the lace caught under my right would stretch. My leg stopped before the top of the box and my shin smacked against the roof of the container. The momentum carried my knee down the sandpaper-like roof before my right foot raised.

Skin scraped away as I came to a halt, but my concentration was elsewhere as I tried to stop my nose cracking to the wooden roof, with my torso falling forward and hands not able to break the fall.

I paused, took a breath of thanks I'd turned away and let my right shoulder bear the brunt.

Holding there for a moment, I relaxed the grip around the gun, surprised I'd kept hold.

The sound of a pack of dogs barking pulled me out of the pause, the noise getting greater, the chaos racing ever closer.

With air sucking through my teeth, I stood and took a single glance back, watching torch beams scour the garden I'd left. I let myself flop over the tall fence, bracing for whatever came next.

Thorns. A blackberry bush, or something else with spines. My shoulders were thankful for the jabbing; much better than being crushed hard under my weight for the second time in a row.

I rolled off the thorns, landing on my knees with my breath still intact, the gun still tight in my hand.

I ran as hard as I could along the fence in the darkness, lunging forward every other step to keep my balance on the uneven ground. When I caught the first hint of the stench, I veered off into the field.

The only feature on the horizon, apart from the dark rolling hills was the silhouette of a tree and that's where I headed. I didn't look back. Nothing had changed. I had to run. There was no other choice.

The tree was a great wide species that had been there for years. Like me, it was alone in the wild, its branches bare and gnarled and sloped heavy to one side.

Fighting against my breath, I let the solid trunk take my weight. Leaning with its girth between me and whatever chased, I gripped the gun and peered around the bark.

I saw nothing but the building darkness, heard the dog's calls getting louder, remembering their training.

The thought passed with Toni clear in my thoughts; her eyes wide in the flash from the muzzle, reflecting my alarm as I tried to move the gun whilst my finger pulled at the trigger with a mind of its own.

I'd yet to prove what she'd done, the bullets not intended for her. Her mother's part already clear. Now I wouldn't be able to question Toni; couldn't give her a chance to tell me I'd got it all wrong.

I wouldn't be able to fix us.

Was I as bad as her?

The urgent call of dogs gripped my insides with fear as Toni's vision fell from view.

I ran with the new rumble of engines and looked to the sky, looked for blinking lights on the horizon. The hard, cold ground became tarmac as I stumbled and a joy filled my chest as I scoured the road.

The engine noise grew, as did the cacophony of barks with smaller, whining notes.

I imagined motorbikes chasing after the hunter dogs they'd let loose and turned again to see two headlights bright and coming towards me.

Standing in the middle of a road, my feet fixed to the spot, I couldn't move.

The lights were so close I could see the young driver, his face pale and white. His gaze disbelieving as he raced towards me, eyes locked with mine.

56

My lungs emptied as I hit the bonnet.

Instinct bent me at the waist to slow the impact as the bumper hit. It worked and worked well; so well it took a few seconds of resting on the warm bonnet to realise the car had slowed before it hit.

My feet were still under me. The borrowed shoes scraped along the floor. I felt no pain as I pushed up from metal and stumbled back into the blinding headlights.

I listened to the click of the driver's door as I struggled to walk sideways out of the dazzle. The man climbed out of the car, but he'd turned away. Instead, his gaze snapped toward the way he'd come, looking long into the distance with his neck extended, his head pushed out like a meerkat.

The rev of motorbike engines grew stronger and he turned away as if he hadn't noticed me, his brow low, forehead pale and bunched in the near darkness.

About to jump back in the car, he hesitated before looking again in my direction where surprise lit his face.

"Get in," he said, his voice higher than I'd expected and full of confusion. "Quick," he added, when I hadn't moved.

He didn't wait and was back in the car, leaning over the seat to push open the passenger door. I lingered, my ears ringing with the sound of the small, high-pitched engines.

I stared past the car, searching out what he'd been looking for. The car rolled forward and he nodded with impatience to the open passenger door.

Motorbike engines continued to ring through the night. Dots of light bounced over the countryside, not so far in the distance. I swear I could hear the heavy breath of the four-legged beasts racing in our direction.

I had no choice.

My butt scarcely touched the fabric before being forced back in the seat, my hands crushed together against the gun as the car sped. Lunging forward, metal clattered in the footwell as he dabbed the brakes and the door slammed at my side. With no seat belt to hold me back, I caught the mirror image of ambling legs in the red light's glow before being enveloped again by the darkness.

"Where are we going?" I said, my voice unsure as I stared out of the side window to search the dark horizon. I caught the tang of alcohol in the air. My gaze roved along the line of the land in the distance, lingering on every imperfection as I squinted. The car moved too quickly to make out all but the direction we were heading.

When he hadn't replied for what seemed like a long time, I turned to watch his profile. I stared at his concentration, trying to get a measure. I studied his clean-shaven face, his smooth skin as he leant forward with his muscular chest pushed up towards the steering wheel, peering out wide into the distance.

The beat in my chest refused to settle, doubt filling my mind as I looked at his face, only just more than a silhouette.

Had I left the hornet's nest only to jump straight into the web of a poisonous spider?

From what I'd already seen, he was young, a similar age to myself. In the darkness he looked like he'd not seen the sun in years. He was tall, but not lanky and wore a black t-shirt under a dark shirt half tucked into his jeans. His short back and sides hair matched the black of his clothes. If first impressions were anything to go by, he didn't look like he scared easily.

I'd seen many men like him before; had felt sorry for their choices in my early days as a court reporter.

"Where are we going?" I said again.

This time he replied, his voice calmer than his focused expression portrayed.

"Anywhere," he said, coughing away the tremble in his voice as it wavered. "You saw those things? Right?" he said, as he gripped his hand back tight to the steering wheel.

He turned to catch my reply and I nodded. "What are they?" he added, his eyes wide on me for the first time.

I shook my head and he turned back to the road, leaving behind a feeling of unease I just couldn't shake. With the moon high in the sky, my night vision had improved. His must have too and he turned back, for the first time seeming to take note in the dark, looking back with what could have been concern at how I sat uncomfortable with my hands at my back.

The car slowed as we took a corner, both of us pulled up in our seats as we couldn't help see the floodlights lighting up the road ahead, the dark trucks parked across its width. Dots of figures moved around in the light. A roadblock.

His hand jumped at the switch for the headlights and he slowed the car to a stop. Twisting around, his brow furrowed in my direction.

"What's wrong with your hands?"

I took a deep breath, my options racing through my head. I could jump from the car and run in to the darkness. The dogs would have lost the scent by now. We'd travelled far enough to get from what had frightened him, but would he risk following me? It all depended on his intentions.

I shouldn't take a chance. I should run, my gut told me over and again. If only I could get the door open.

I twisted in my seat, showing my cuffed hands, leaving the gun still resting in the small of my back. I waited for his reaction, trying to suppress my urge to scream as I questioned why I was giving myself up to him.

"You weren't running from those…" He paused with the same hesitation I'd seen before; the same stall in the brain people have as their minds try to come to terms with a new reality. "Those things?"

I shook my head whilst trying to keep calm, opening my eyes wide and holding my breath.

"What were you running from? Did you escape from the police?"

I gave a shallow shake of my head.

"A man," I said, letting my voice catch. "He tried to...," I said. "He... He..." I stuttered.

"It's okay, you don't need to say," he said, pushing out his hand in my direction.

I backed away, pushing myself to the door, conscious of the pistol pinching in my back as he snapped his hand away.

"But, he, he's a soldier. I can't," I said, looking up to the roadblock. "I can't let them find me," I said, peering straight into his eyes. He stared back, then looked down to my hands still twisted down on show at my side.

He turned to the lights ahead, twisting back to me with a nod. He grabbed the wheel, pinning me in my seat as he sped up and swung the car out to the side, bumping us off the road.

The car jumped up and down, metal clattered in the footwell, the underside of the car scraping against what sounded like giant boulders.

We kept going. Kept bouncing along the rocks. The ground undulated beneath us until the impacts stopped. With a great thud against the tyres I felt the smooth road and our world calmed.

As we drove through the darkness, I felt an overwhelming urge to stop, to get the cuffs from my hands. I had no idea what this guy's intentions were.

"Can you let me out?" I said, as buildings grew on the side of the road.

"Do you know where are we?" he said, still facing forward.

"No," I replied with the truth.

"So you plan on just knocking on doors and hoping they won't turn you in?"

"I think they have more on their plate than me."

He kept quiet for a moment.

"I guess, but do you want to take that chance?" he said after a letting the silence hang.

My turn to pause. I didn't want him to change my mind. I didn't want him to think I was even considering his words.

"I should be able to get those off. The locks are straight forward. If not, I've got a hacksaw at my house," he said, making eye contact.

"How far are we?" I replied, keeping my scowl fixed. I didn't want him to think I took any pleasure from the suggestion, despite my obvious eagerness to rub my wrists free of the ache.

"Five minutes," he replied, turning the headlights back on at the sight of another pair of lights on the horizon.

Flashing a look inside the car as it passed, I could see it was full of teenagers. The back windows were steamed, the driver's face fixed forward. He looked half asleep.

"What day is it?" I said.

He turned in my direction and stared, raising, then lowering his brow. "New Year's Day. Weren't you at a party when all that happened?" he said, looking back down to my wrists hidden behind my back.

I shook my head and turned away to look through my window.

We passed a building on my side, but it had gone out of view before I could take a proper look. Another building shot by and I realised we must be in a village, but the lights were off here too. Even this late, shouldn't there be someone awake on New Year's Day? I caught the guy's concentration just before he spoke.

"Power's out here as well," he said. "I'm just up there."

"Wait," I said, as he slowed the car, pulling up to a house whose front door was level with the thin pavement.

The car stopped with a lurch and he turned in my direction. Twisting in his seat, I took in the view, moving my head slower than I would have liked. But any quicker, I could feel my vision blur.

"It looks clear," I said.

His gaze shot across the view, his face full of panic as if I'd reminded him of where he'd run from.

"It's clear," I said in a softer tone.

He nodded and jumped from the car, still checking the horizon as he jogged around the bonnet.

Taking a deep breath, I stopped halfway through the pull, my bound hands searching the seat, touching at the small of my back as I wriggled to cover every part. My fingers wouldn't connect with the gun.

His hand was at the door. I snatched a look down the right side between the centre console, peered left between the door and seat. As it opened, I looked up at his hand reaching out to help me up. I'd expected the light to come on above our heads so I could get a better look, but it stayed off.

Something made me turn away, a noise in the distance perhaps, but I never noticed the source because as I turned, my foot touched against one of the hard objects out of place.

My gaze followed down to the dark pistol on the floor. Next to it was a long claw hammer and a crowbar and the guy's hand reaching toward my feet.

57

There was nothing I could do.

His body blocked the door.

His arm extended, hand reaching deep into the footwell.

I paused; thoughts of kicking out flashed through my head. Thoughts of propelling myself forward, smashing my head against his. None of the glimpsed ideas ended well; only in more pain with the cuffs still tight around my wrists.

"Mine," I said as he pulled the pistol up, turning it in his hands as he swapped his view between me and the black handgun.

He mouthed a word I didn't quite catch. His face stretched with surprise, eyebrows high on his face.

He stepped back. Turned away, but something made him stop and stare along the road. My heart sank as I thought of the creatures coming our way, the thought of having to run again. This time without the gun.

"Help me out," I said as I struggled in the seat, twisting to get my feet to the road with the memories of my previous plans to escape coming back to ridicule me.

He turned and seemed to remember. He came back to a long-forgotten part of the night and snapped around in a hurry. He bounded over in two long steps, pushing the muzzle of the gun into the waistband of his jeans before taking both my shoulders and hoisting me up.

Out into the night, I twitched my gaze to the flashing blue lights at the far end of the village.

After slamming the car door shut, he hurried me along its length. I let him escort me, the skin of his hands rough on my wrists as he ushered me to a door. His grip didn't release as he pushed in the key and guided me over the step. Only when inside did he let go.

I turned to see the door close, his back leaning against the wood.

We waited. Our breath slowing. The flash of blue growing through the gap under the door.

Together we watched it grow so intense I could see my legs in the eerie blue while listening to the growl of the engine before it died back.

He turned his back and I listened again as he pushed his key, twisting the bolt into place.

Oh shit, I thought.

"They've gone," he said, his voice still quiet. I felt his hands reach out and with a firm touch they were at my forearms, guiding me to turn and urging my back to the wall as he slid past. "Wait here."

I heard his footsteps place with care on the carpet, stopping in a room nearby where I listened to him rifle through the contents of a drawer. I urged my night-vision to improve, but the concentration did nothing for my pounding headache centred on what felt like a melon-sized bruise reaching out from my forehead.

I heard friction from a match striking out of sight and watched the doorway off the hall build with an eerie light. The glow brightened to the sound of footsteps. He was at the doorway with a burning candle resting in a glass tumbler in one hand, a bunch of unlit candles in the other.

The orange of the light made him look so different; his skin fresh and unblemished, making me question if I'd misjudged his age. With the pistol still tucked into his jeans and his mouth in a wide smile, he looked very pleased for himself.

"Follow me," he said, and he stepped into the hall, holding the candle out in front. It felt like I was about to follow a priest to my execution, but what choice did I have?

I took one slow step and then another, keeping my eyes forward, not noticing my foot snag until it was too late. I fell forward, stumbling over whatever was in my path; the object skittering across the carpet until I stepped on it a second time, taking my feet from the floor.

The fall felt like it took an age. The carpet lit as the guy turned, the flickering light revealing the stacks of metal boxes with multicoloured wires coming out of the back. The home electronics with their black cords wrapped around their middles, the stack I'd knocked still collapsing.

As my shoulder hit the carpet, I watched DVD players, Sky boxes, video cameras and games consoles cascade around me to thoughts of the hand tools littering the footwell of his car. His fear of the roadblock. Of the blue flashing lights.

With my wrists scraping hard against the cuffs, I caught his wide-eyed look as his gaze followed me down. With his features shadowing in the candlelight, I felt his hand push against my arm, turning my view down to the carpet.

I'd been right all along.

I'd stepped out of the frying pan and jumped, hands bound, into the witch's oven.

58

"No," I said with the last of my breath, the muscles in my neck spasming as I fought to keep my face from the carpet. My hands darted left and right from the warmth of his fingers trying to get a grip.

"No," I repeated with little success, my fingers going limp as he took a firm grip and pushed my wrists into the small of my back. I tried to scream despite knowing I had no breath.

"Hold still," he said in the struggle, but his words made me wriggle harder against his weight until I felt his pressure release, like I'd won the battle.

It felt like my wrists were coming away from each other. My hand was free. I tried pulling my arm up to my side, ready for the disappointment but my hand came away. I couldn't believe it, despite the ache in my shoulder as I moved.

As the reality settled, I pushed my hand to the floor and rolled, searching in the darkness. There he was, looking down with a heavy brow, his face illuminated by the candle flickering on the floor. His hand offered out.

"Alex," he said, pushing his open hand towards me.

I lay on my back, swapping my view between my wrists, the cuffs still hanging on the right.

I didn't know what to say, didn't know what to do. I'd been so wrong about this guy, about Alex.

My hand touched his and he gripped as I pulled, taking my other hand with his left until I was on my feet. He kept hold of my right before pushing a small key into the cuff's lock.

"You have a handcuff key?" I said, rubbing each wrist as the metal released and working my shoulders around in circles. The relief flowed over my head like cooling water after being in the sun for too long.

"Five pound ninety nine on eBay," he said, pocketing the key.

"Why would you need that?" I said and paused, the question overwhelming my aching senses and my head too busy to think about his words for long. "Jess," I said, when he replied with a flash of his eyebrows as I pushed my hand out again.

We shook, his grip more gentle and more considered than I'd expected.

"Sorry about the..." he said, nodding to the littered floor. "Are you okay?"

I thought for a moment. I felt fine; my head ached a little, the fall not helping. It surprised me enough to keep other thoughts I didn't want to dwell on pushed to the corners of my mind.

Raising my hand to my forehead, I touched at the tender bulge and with relief I realised it wouldn't stop me fitting through doorways.

"I'm fine, thank you," I said as he bent down, piling the household electronics back into neat stacks against the walls. "Can I use your phone?"

He nodded.

"Shall we?" he said as he finished stacking, offering a hand towards the end of the corridor and picking up the lit candle before lighting another and handing it over.

I took the candle and followed him into a living room dominated by a wide TV hanging on the wall. Even in the low light I saw there were no decorations of the season; just a single Christmas card on the mantlepiece reminded me we were supposed to be jolly.

Apart from the TV, a man of Alex's age didn't look like he belonged to the decor, to the chintzy decoration.

He pointed to the rectangular phone on a side table.

"Take a seat," he said as he took my candle, fixing it with dripping wax into a mug resting on the nest of tables at the side.

I did as he asked, choosing the single overstuffed armchair in the corner next to the phone. He went to sit on the three-seater couch, but first had to pull the pistol from his trousers before resting on the edge and laying it to the side.

"My gun," I said, tipping my head towards the pistol.

He looked down at the weapon as if he'd already forgotten.

"You going to shoot me?" he said, raising his eyebrows.

I paused for longer than I should, but instead of speaking I let a smile bloom on my lips as I ran my hands over my hot wrists, head shaking.

He watched my reply before picking up the gun by the barrel and leaning over. The warm grip felt solid and reliable in my hands, its power buoying my insides. Letting my thoughts gather, my options flashed before my eyes. I was back in control.

For a moment I thought about standing. Thought about aiming the pistol in his direction.

I'd been wrong about this guy and looked up to see him watching my every move, his expression intense and not hiding the uncertainty. He'd done nothing to me. Despite my fear. Despite his opportunity.

I lay the pistol on my lap, smoothing down the wrinkles in the skirt either side and smiled back.

Remembering the phone, I turned and picked up the handset, but no tone replied.

"Line's dead. Do you have a mobile phone?"

His only reply was to lean back and pull a thin, black mobile from his pocket. Tapping at the screen, he turned it around to show the *No Service* message staring back.

"Something to do with the power being out I guess," he said.

Noticing my feet, I tied the trainer's laces. I had to prepare for whatever came next; a habit I knew I should get into.

"So you're a burglar?" I said, in a matter-of-fact fashion that took him by surprise.

He stuttered the first words of his reply so much I could only guess their meaning as his gaze flashed to the gun. When I didn't reach for the pistol and take aim, he shook his head.

"No. Why would you think that?" His face screwed up with confusion and his reaction seemed real enough. Judging people's responses was part of my job.

"You don't seem to like authority?" I said, turning my head to the side.

"That was for you," he said.

Not convinced, I nodded.

"Why do you keep the electronics scattered around the house? The house breaking tools in the footwell of your car?"

I watched his smile bloom, then fall again as he peered to the corridor and the stacks of black boxes piled against each wall.

"They were my dad's," he said, his voice lowering. "He'd buy broken electronics from the internet, fix them and sell them on."

I nodded, but couldn't have hid my uncertainty well as he leant over to the mantlepiece and pulled a stack of business cards, blowing a sheen of dust as he brought them close.

He handed over two cards. Angling the top one to catch the light from the candle, I read Bob's Electronics in black letters on the white card.

"He wasn't imaginative with the name," he said, his voice high at first but falling as if some realisation came.

"Where is he?" I said, but soon realised it would be a tough question to ask anyone in the coming days.

"He died last month. Bowel cancer."

"I'm sorry," I replied and pushed my hand out with the cards.

"I used to help him after work. It was the only thing we'd do together. I haven't been able to bring myself to clear his things out."

I nodded as he took the top card, leaving me with the one I hadn't yet read. The word Locksmith stared back at me in bold black letters. I looked up and he turned away as I did, trying to hide a new vulnerability I hadn't seen until now. How wrong I'd been.

I stared back, wondering how after all that had happened I had the capacity to feel such a deep sorrow for what this guy had gone through and still he showed me, a stranger, so much compassion.

"Can I trust you?" I said.

He stared back, raising a single eyebrow.

"I'm not the one running around in the dark in hand cuffs and carrying a gun," he blurted out.

"Touché. Forget that," I said. He'd given me every reason to trust him already, whereas I hadn't. "I need your services," I said, standing. "And bring the handcuffs. They'll come in useful."

59

"Wait, what?" Alex said, standing, his hand reaching out.

I stood, backing away from his reach. My eyes fixed on his scarred knuckles and I looked up only as he withdrew, his intent on the gun limp in my hand.

"You…" he said, but stopped as the churn of my stomach radiated across the room. Raising his eyebrows, a smile widened across his mouth. "Do you want something to eat?" he said, his perfect white teeth gleaming in the candlelight.

My defences fell again, leaving my insides knotted with pain. The feeling wasn't new, but the cramps hadn't been my key concern. Until now my concentration had focused on impending death or incarceration and flashing back to shots I fired in the darkness of that bedroom. A compliment to Alex, I guessed.

Mind and body relaxing, I drew in a deep breath. A few minutes of delay wouldn't hurt, a few hours perhaps. Daylight would be our friend and would maybe give time for the area around the van to clear. He could get me inside, on the assumption they'd locked it.

I nodded and his smile grew wider.

"Sit down. I'll go see what I can rustle up."

I didn't like being in the room on my own. Hated the flicker of the candle and the shadows it cast. The hypnotic movement sent me within myself. The chaotic dance resembled the flashes of light I kept seeing in my head.

In the strobe I saw Toni, her wide-eyed expression, a bloodied wound growing before my eyes, despite knowing my head filled in the blanks. I didn't want to think about this right now. I never wanted to think about it again. I'd spent this last year getting over her, filling the empty void with self-respect and now I'd done something so much worse than she had. Albeit without intention.

Standing, I lifted the candle before the anger or the sorrow grew too loud and, watching my feet, I headed towards the kitchen.

"Gas still works?" I said, as I found Alex stirring a pan in the blue flame's glow, the grill bright below.

"It's pressurised," he said, turning towards me. "Doesn't need electricity," he added, returning to the pan. "You don't have to carry that around, you know."

I looked down at the gun. He was right; at least, I hoped.

"I took the cuffs off," he said, still looking at the stove.

I had my chance and didn't take it. I heard the words only in my head.

"I know, and I'm sorry I didn't say thank you," I said and turned away. "Thank you."

I wasn't ready to give up the gun just yet.

"It's okay. Take a seat," he said, turning, nodding towards a small table on the opposite wall of the small kitchen where he'd laid out a single place with a lit candle in the centre. Behind the table were stacks of pizza boxes piled high like a memorial to a single man's life.

I pulled out the wooden chair and sat, resting the gun on the table close to my hand and watched as he placed a steaming plate of beans piled high on two slices of toast.

"Are you eating?" I said, grabbing the knife and fork, not waiting for his answer before I dove in.

He sat opposite and watched as I ate, but I enjoyed the food too much to hear his reply. Looking up with my mouth too full to add any more, I saw him watching me with a question still hanging on his lips.

"I said when did you last eat?"

I thought back to the taste of food I could remember. The fresh, gamey meats I could smell in my head. The char-grilled BBQ overpowering the tomato sauce and I almost choked as I forced myself to stop those thoughts, remembering the last meal of a cheese sandwich; Toni's smile as she offered out the plate. For a fleeting moment I saw the look on her face she would pull if she could see me now. If I hadn't just killed her.

"Yesterday morning," I said, holding back the cough. I ate the rest of the meal in silence, too distracted to care about my audience and gulping down the water Alex offered.

"So are you going to tell me what's going on?" he said as the last of the water disappeared.

I sat back in the chair, basking in my full belly; enjoying the stretch of my stomach whilst trying to ignore the lack of satisfaction. Trying to forget I may never feel it again unless I gave in to my new urges.

"People have different names for it," I said, and watched him stare as if hanging on each word. "Are you a religious man, Alex?"

He smiled and on the edge of laughter he shook his head, a confusion on his brow just holding back the odd reaction.

"Good, nor me, but don't tell my parents," I said anyway.

His smile grew and I enjoyed his white teeth again.

"It'll make this easier."

His brow grew heavier.

"They are what they seem," I said, raising my eyebrows. "A virus, a plague has taken over the land," I added as I tried to think of how I would say this on camera. "Reports of a deadly virus are coming out of a secret government research facility in Devon."

His thin brow furrowed even further.

"Sources say the plague has infected hundreds of people, but our experience shows it could be in the thousands," I said, the words slow as I chose. "Causing symptoms including reanimation from death." I watched as his mouth dropped wide and he stood, scraping back his chair.

"Oh my god," he said, pushing his hand to his mouth. I could see the colour draining from his face and I made a mental note to tone down the words. "Oh my god," he repeated and peered closer. "Oh my god," he said again, his eyes getting wider, not able to turn away from me.

I stood, scraping back the chair as he drew in close. My hand moved to my face, afraid I was changing, afraid hairs were sprouting out of my chin or my teeth were ripping through my lips.

My hand headed to the gun.

60

"You're from the TV. You're Jessica Carmichael," he said, lifting the candle from the table and holding it towards my face. "Off the news, right?" he said with a new, high-pitched eagerness in his voice. His face contorted as he leant further and further over the table to get a better look.

Sinking back into the chair, I let my hands fall as the air sighed from my chest.

"Oh, my god. I've never met anyone famous before and you're in my house."

I shook my head.

"You are, you are. I watch the news every day. I see you around the world giving all those important people a hard time."

Another sigh escaped.

"Yes, I'm Jess Carmichael," I said, not hiding resignation from my voice as I shook my head.

Blind to my response, he rested the candle back on the table and pushed his hand out with a great smile on his right side as he waited. When it seemed he would stand there forever, I shook his hand with a weak grip.

"We've done this already. You're Alex, I'm Jess."

"Jessica Carmichael. Yes," he said, gripping my hand with a great enthusiasm. "I can so see it now."

He sat back in the seat, hovering on the edge and leaning forward as he swept his arm further across the table. "So all this," he said, his eyebrows raising and lowering. "It's a TV show, right?"

He looked around the room as if searching for hidden cameras or waiting for a TV crew to burst through the doorway.

"No wonder you look so glamorous for this time of night."

I peered down to the dirt and the creases covering my jacket. I looked back up with a raised eyebrow. Maybe this guy wasn't the full biscuit.

"Those things," he continued. "I should have known. How did you do it?" he said, standing and not waiting for a reply. "Oh my goodness, you got me good."

Walking past me, he reached up to a cupboard just at my back. "You like whiskey?" he said, but before I could say anything he spoke again. "Oh shit, can you drink on the job?" he said, his face widening as if I'd taken offence.

"I'm not on the job," I replied, and must have seen the curl of my lip as he reached for another bottle.

"Of course you can, you're not a copper. Vodka?" he nodded, his smile wide again as I replied with a reluctant nod.

"If only," I said, but he ignored my words, pouring a slug of the clear spirit into my empty glass.

"I mean," he said, before having to catch his breath while he poured a good few fingers into another glass grabbed from the drainer, "the make-up is amazing and the smell, oh my god, how did they get it so realistic? Made my stomach turn."

"It's real," I said, letting the glass down, but he carried on talking like I hadn't spoken.

"And you picked me," he said. His smile beamed wider than ever.

I sighed again, turning down to the table as I shook my head.

"It's real," I said, letting the words build in volume. I looked up to see he'd stopped talking, his gaze on me as my head rose, but he burst into laughter as our eyes met.

"You're good. You're so good," he said, taking another look around the room. "So when do they burst in to spring the surprise? Are there cameras hidden all around my house? I hope I haven't ruined this for anyone?"

"Listen," I said, and he was about to speak again, but I stood up from my seat and slapped my hand down on the table, sending the glasses jumping into the air. As the glasses landed without spilling, he paused, the colour draining from his face as the candles flickered.

"It's real. It's fucking real," I shouted, watching his smile fall.

"I'm sorry," he said. His smile crept back, but not building to its full strength.

Anger boiled in my chest. I grabbed the glass and downed the liquid, revelling in the sting as I wiped the back of my hand before letting out a great relief of air.

He looked on, his uncertainty growing as the smile sank. He looked around the room, searching again. I'd had all I could take and hit the table, sending both glasses toppling as they landed.

"On Christmas Day I had a call," I said, my voice quiet, but forceful. "My ex called me. She was in trouble." I did my best to ignore the twitch of his eyebrows. "I raced here to find they had imprisoned her in the middle of a quarantine zone. They held me, too, the government. They conducted tests on me and on my camera team who are both now dead. I barely survived to escape with Toni. There were so many people infected, dying and coming back to life. They attacked us from all sides. We nearly died so many times. This thing is real and if you still don't get it, step outside and it won't be long before you're surrounded. Let one, let all of them bite into your flesh, then you'll know how fucking real this is."

I drew a deep breath and held my lungs full, congratulating myself for holding it together.

He didn't speak, just stared on and I let him. I gave his mind time to get to grips with what I'd just said. It was the first time I'd told anyone. The first time I'd opened up. The first time I'd told anyone so much about me.

I watched the excitement slowly grow on his lips. My chest rising into my mouth, breath constricting with each moment.

"You deserve a fucking Oscar. Where's Toni now?" he said.

I hated the way he exaggerated her name like she wasn't real, like she was part of a lie. I moved around the table, careful to place my feet where I could see. I leant toward him.

"I shot her," I said, letting the alcohol breath pour out before I stepped back.

His smile fell, but not completely as his eyebrows twitched.

"We had to run. We had to run for our lives, but still those things found us. They're everywhere. We got split up and some fat fuck tied me to a bed in a screwed-up attempt to keep me safe..." I stopped as the words caught in my throat. I could no longer see the detail in Alex's face, the rage pumping blood so fast in my head.

I took another step back. "Toni rescued me, but then turned me over to that bitch. I killed her trying to escape. It was an accident, but it was my finger pulling the trigger," I said, raising my palms out towards him. "Does that deserve a fucking Oscar?"

Part of me wanted him to smile. Part of me wanted him to give me a way out, to give a release to my rage.

His smile came and he shook his head as he saw the gun in my hand as it raised. He saw it the same time I did. He saw it as I realised I'd picked its weight from the table when I'd passed to step forward. The smile fell with each angle of the gun rising in his direction.

"If this is a performance, if this is a show, if this is entertainment, this bullet won't kill you."

I raised my eyebrows, his smile no longer there, but still he couldn't help flinching a look around the room as with disbelief I pulled the trigger.

61

The candles stopped flickering. The room fell silent. Dust and smoke rained between us.

Past the barrel I watched Alex standing straight like a statue. His face fixed. Eyes staring. Open-mouthed.

Shaking, I let the gun drop and he bent his neck towards his chest. Trying to someway rationalise what I'd just done, I watched candlelight dance across his shirt, his hand shadowing the light as he scoured for a break in the cloth.

Pulling his shirt high, I saw the pale of his flat and well-defined stomach and flash of a black bra as he swept his hands across his chest, looking for holes that weren't there.

Alex was a woman. How could I have been so blind?

She looked up and my brain caught up from the distraction. Alex watched as I flicked my eyes over her shoulder, trying to regain the anger that had caused me to take the shot.

She twisted as her shirt dropped back down, following my gaze to the wall behind.

Before I could finish questioning how I could have been so blind, how I could have missed the pitch of her voice, or the lack of an Adam's apple, air pulled deep in a gasp and she stared into the cracked plaster as high as her head, her view fixing down the round hole in the centre.

It wouldn't have surprised me if she'd have fallen to her knees. I was ready to catch her head as she turned, but instead she twisted, standing like a statue with her mouth held wide.

"Still think it's a fucking joke?" I said, my eyebrows raised as I fidgeted the gun in my grip. The words had less behind them than I'd expected.

Alex shook her head, eyes flicking to my hand.

"You almost killed me," she said, all the colour gone from her voice as she raised her head.

"I never almost do anything," I replied, but as I made a show of placing the gun on the tabletop, I tried to push away the horror of what I'd done.

I let the air hang with silence, watching the sharp contours of her face in the flickering orange light, looking at her as if the first time. Her soft skin unblemished with stubble. The purse of her lips. Despite the short hair and her clothes, it was so obvious now.

She took at least a minute to move; any longer and I was ready to walk out of the door, the anger returning as the shock of my actions subsided. If she came with me, she'd see so much worse by the end of the day.

Moving to the sink, Alex leant against the metal basin, letting water from the tap dribble into the bowl before pushing another glass from the draining board and holding it until it overflowed.

Leaving her in peace, I waited for the glass to finish; waited for her turn before I spoke.

"I'm sorry but you need to know this is real. The dead walk the streets, infecting more each minute. Tomorrow it will be so much worse, people will wake to the horror and it will overcome them."

She turned back, following my gaze. She'd seen something out there, I'd seen it too. Fear forced her back from the window.

"There are people out there trying to help. The military. The police, but others will use this as an excuse."

White as a sheet, she turned back towards me, but flinched to the window at the sound of a glass bottle rolling along the road.

"And that's not the worst," I said, raising my eyebrows. I didn't finish my words and she didn't ask what I'd meant.

Taking a deep breath and swallowing hard, she was about to speak, but stopped herself as she turned, pushing the glass under the tap until water rolled over her fingers.

"What are you trying to do?" she said once she'd gulped the water down.

I let a smile rise in the corner of my mouth.

"I'm trying to let everyone know. It's the biggest story in history, but unless they see it coming down the road, they'll have no chance. They won't be prepared."

She stared on, her gaze turning down to the gun.

"So why do you need that?" Alex said, her voice soft and slow.

"I need to survive," I replied, my gaze following hers. "I won't give a shit when I'm dead and not in control."

"And why do you need me?"

"I need someone to help me get my cameras back." She raised her eyebrows before letting them fall. "I had to leave them behind."

"Why me?"

"I thought you had big balls," I said, but immediately realised my mistake and she turned her head to the side, squinting. "I thought you would be able to handle it. You have skills I need," I said, shrugging my shoulders. "And I can help you."

She looked down to the gun again before meeting my eyes and I spoke again.

"I'm surviving. I know how to survive. I can help you stay alive."

Her brow furrowed and a question formed on her lips. She didn't give it voice, instead turning to the blue lights building in the darkness outside.

Alex stayed quiet as a strobe of light raced past the window. I knew she would turn as the lights faded, but they didn't disappear. Instead, a great screech came from outside, from beyond the angle of the window no matter how far she craned around.

She twisted back, looked at me as if she wanted to know what we should do, but turned to the window again when I gave no response.

I stood by her side, eyebrows raised. An orange glow mixed with the flash of blue, searing through our night vision with every pulse.

I shook my head and spoke. "I might have been wrong about you. In more than one way."

She twisted back and forth to the window, each time looking at me with her brows low.

"We can't help them," I said, looking to the window, but before the words settled in the air, a shock wave from outside shattered the glass, pushing Alex toward me.

The pressure hit before I could move. Before I could steady myself, a bright light surged through the room.

It took a moment for my senses to recover. It was darker than before, my body covered with a great weight.

I hit out at what lay over me, but it wouldn't move. It lay lifeless across me as my ears rang, the room getting brighter with dust and smoke catching in my throat.

62

"Fire." The word came slow from my dry throat. "Fire," I repeated, heaving against the force on my chest.

Alarms rose and fell in the street.

Car horns bellowed for attention.

Bright lights flashed in and out like a white disco, singing to the music of embers crackling and the burn of plastic. Searing hot smoke thickened and collected in my lungs.

With a great heave I rolled the weight to the floor, glass scratching under my trainers as I pulled myself up against the table. Snatching the gun, I leant heaving for breath while squinting around the room. The pizza boxes were just embers glowing orange, flames licking along the adjacent unit to the microwave, which was already melting, its plastic dripping down the counter to drop liquid fire to the floor.

I turned to the doorway, glass strewn between me and escape. Checking my feet, I found the oversized shoes still there.

My gaze fell on Alex. She had been the dead weight.

I pushed my hand into the crook of my elbow, nudging her hard with my foot. When she didn't respond I admonished myself for a thought even though it had no time to form.

Turning to the doorway, I pushed the Glock into the band of my skirt and gripped her under the shoulders. Nails pulled hard with each tug. Her body moved with each pull, sweeping glass along the floor. Soot smudged in her path, but we were soon through the doorway with only a short distance left to escape.

I fished the key from Alex's pocket and praised my fortune when it turned, smoke billowing from behind me as the first chill of fresh night air sucked deep into my lungs. We were over the step before her body complained, our lungs heaving, coughing as the icy air hit our faces. A cacophony assaulted our ears.

With heat pouring from the house at my back, I stared at the scene of destruction while I dragged Alex a few more steps away from the house. I pulled her backward into the road, the pathway blocked by parked cars pushed over, including hers, which I found resting on its door. The tang of petrol hung heavy in the air.

What I could only guess was once the police car sat in the road just a short step away. Black smoke poured from the multicoloured flames dancing inside its glowing red cage, with no sign of what caused the crash.

Along the street, half the houses, ten or more, whose owners were yet to update to double glazing, had no glass remaining, except for the odd finger dangling down, ready to fall at an inopportune moment.

We were the first out, but not the only house on fire. Two others, both opposite the centre of the blast were alight. Only now people burst into the street, followed by smoke, trailing tears and pained, longing looks for their worldly possessions.

Fingers jabbed at the screens of mobile phones, but I could see even from the other side of the street they weren't able to make the call. Maybe no one would come. Maybe no one *could* come.

Alarms of all tones continued to ring, boxes on the side of houses strobed. The headlights of parked cars flashed. Heat-cracked wood split the air.

As I looked down, I watched Alex sit up. I let my lungs clear with each cold breath, the sting of petrol vapour in each intake. I grabbed at Alex's shirt. She looked up as I shouted and tried scrabbling to her feet, eventually able to get up with my hand as a guide.

"Petrol," I shouted out into the street, pointing back as I squinted to the orange light.

No one took note. My cotton-wool-filled head shook as we got to what I thought would be a safe distance.

"Petrol, get back." I shouted this time, my voice hoarse and with little power.

Alex joined me to make a chorus, but her voice gave little help against the chiming of the bells and the two-tone alarms. I looked around and saw the street filling, everyone at home for the season.

Families stood in their pyjamas, some covered with dressing gowns. People cried, children screamed, others held torches.

Along the road a crowd built. Figures walked towards us, ambling in a daze. The noise had woken the street, had woken the village and the army base by the look of those coming down towards us.

I pushed my fingers in my ears, the chaos enough to wake the dead.

I tried to concentrate. Tried to fix on the crowd, watching their movements with intrigue.

My eyes went wide as the realisation came. I'd seen this before, but from a different vantage.

My hands raised up as the first of the crowd passed into the group of houses. As the crowd spread, turning this way and that, they moved to those standing by the side of the road. Those watching on weren't scared, weren't worried until it was too late. Their screams added to the background.

Only I saw those weren't people. Only I saw those weren't rescuers. Only I saw those were the infected.

I grabbed for the Glock, but it wasn't at my waistband. I scoured the ground, turning to stare across my path, running back towards the house, knowing I must have dropped it inside. I jogged, but fell to my knees, my arms covering my face as the cars on the side of the road exploded one after the other.

63

The heat beat me back. I stood, unsure on my feet with screams and pain radiating, echoing between the houses. I heard the moment the realisation came from the crowd. Panic sparked to life, screams echoing out.

People ran into the dead. When confronted with jaws locking to their fleshy parts some ran to the fires, adding to the orchestra of screams while others ran back to their houses and shut out those who tried to follow, even though hearts still beat in their chests. Some jumped over fences and out of sight. Others stayed put, their feet fixed to the ground in disbelief.

I couldn't watch. I had to turn away.

Taking a step forward to Alex's house, the fire beat me back again.

My thoughts flashed to Alex. I twisted around, searching, but she'd gone. I tried again to get through the heat but still the searing temperature forced me away and I bounded back a few steps until I could just bear the energy pouring out.

I heard a familiar call, an angry shout and turned to see someone in the shadows tussling with one of the creatures.

I watched the pair fighting until with a flash of light from a nearby fire I saw the dark shirt. I saw the long fencepost wielded in the defender's hands, the club swinging left and right. She'd taken down the first and then figure after figure fell, each knocked to the ground.

With pride rising in my chest I saw Alex beating back the onslaught of the dead.

I twisted as many hands gripped at the fence. The fire at my back had died down enough for me to run past the flames, cursing the heat as I scooped up the gun in the hallway and turned back, racing towards the battle.

She'd disappeared again, leaving just a crowd surging forward where she'd been, hands grabbing at those whose brains were miswired, gripped to the spot with fear.

I ran.

A gust of wind almost pushed me over with the stench of the sewers. I looked beyond the front line of the group, high on my toes, but she was nowhere to be seen.

They'd overcome her and I felt disbelief at another life lost before I'd got to know them.

"Jess," a call came to my left.

"Jess," it came again as I searched. Only on the second call did I see Alex beckoning me between two houses as she stood beside a stream of people waving them past her. I took one quick glance toward the crowd and watched, wide-eyed, at a middle-aged man, his face grey, hand clutching his chest. He disappeared, overcome by the crowd of hungry faces bearing down as he collapsed to the ground.

I ran.

Alex followed behind me, the last of those who could still walk. By now the screams had died and the lights had gone dim. Torch beams flickered around the night, dispersing across our view. Sirens and car horns still blared away, calling more of the dead ever closer. We had to get away.

We'd made the right choice to run, not to lock ourselves away hoping the cavalry would come around the corner and save the day.

These are the people that had to be told. It was my job to tell those people who could still hear me to prepare for the worst or die. I had to break the news and save as many lives as I could.

Once between the alley, we filtered through the garden of the house on the right and followed the thin crowd down along the grass and over the tall wooden fence laying on the floor. We were out into the fields. Back where we'd started.

Stumbling in the dark, I felt Alex's strong grip in my hand. She caught my fall as I listened to the sounds diminish behind us with each pace and the smoke thin in the air.

Moonlit figures dotted around the field. Most had stopped and turned back to their village, shining torches across the horizon with sharp pulls of breath following each moment someone caught a fright or saw movement from an unseen part of the field.

Alex stayed at my side, scouring like the others as we slowed. Words in the scattered group built to a hurried conversation and people drew together. Tears fell and rose and fell again as they sought and received comfort, their mouths full of questions.

"What now?" a deep voice said, the loudest of many.

A reply came from somewhere unseen. "Wait for the police," a woman said, her voice on the edge of tears.

I looked to Alex and could just make out her face in the dull glow until a torch shined right on her. She pushed her hand out to block the beam as she turned away, shaking her head. The beam swapped to another face.

"We get away," I said, and the beam was on me, but, used to the brightness, I didn't shy away. "We walk, find somewhere safe. Stay in the fields until it gets light, till we can see where we're going."

A murmur ran around the thin crowd. Tears dried and breath slowed.

"We should get back to our houses," a man's voice shouted towards the back of the group.

"You need to keep your voice low," I said, hushing mine. The crowd seemed to murmur in agreement and took a collective step closer to where I stood.

"What are they?" a woman's voice said close by. Hers the clearest of the many questions pouring in my direction. I paused, not wanting my words to raise their blood.

"I don't know," I replied. "I know what they look like."

Noises of agreement ran around us.

"All I know is you need to stay away. You need to keep quiet. You need to find somewhere safe, somewhere with food until you're rescued."

Voices of encouragement greeted my sentiment. Names of places came from the crowd. The words were loud at first, then repeated quieter until the crowd broadly agreed on a supermarket a few kilometres away.

"Great," I said and stopped. "Which way is that?" I added, watching in the moonlight as many hands pointed to our left. "Okay."

As the crowd moved, following the way pointed, Alex stepped to follow until I put my hand on her forearm and held her back, my finger to my lips as she turned in my direction.

64

In silence she walked in my wake with my hand around her wrist.

I felt her tension, the questions on the tip of her tongue as we headed parallel to the growing amber glow and the cacophony still roaring at our side. With the fade of each short-lived scream, I imagined more people forced out into the open as the fires caught neighbour after neighbour. Under my breath I thanked them for their help drawing away the infected and keeping us safe.

With the amber glow at our backs, Alex twisted from my loosening grip. Before she spoke, I lingered on the halo above the village and the growing plume of dark smoke rising to blot out the stars. To its side I saw distant torchlight flashes, watched beams scanning the horizon and I couldn't help fear the lights were seeking me out.

"Why didn't we go with them?" Alex said in a quiet voice.

I turned, meandering away while my eyes adjusted from the lights.

"I told you, I have something to do. I have to get my cameras. I have to tell the world what's happening here."

"Shouldn't we have brought them with us?"

"It's too dangerous. They're better off doing what I said."

"Isn't it too dangerous for us too?"

"I don't have a choice."

I let my pace quicken.

"And I don't either?" she said, her mouth sounding contorted.

"You can catch up with them if that's what you want."

She didn't reply for a while, her voice quiet again when she spoke.

"You need my help?"

"It's your choice," I said in a flat tone.

"You want me along though?"

I paused.

"I doubted myself back there. It's a lot to come to terms with, but when I saw you with the fence post, I knew."

"Knew what?" she said, her pace quickening to catch up.

"I knew you'd be okay. Knew you've got what it takes."

"Takes for what?"

"To stay alive. To survive."

She didn't reply.

We walked in silence for what must have been ten minutes with still no sign of light on the horizon.

"What's the plan?" she said, catching up after falling behind.

I paused and thought about the question. "Get the camera van," I said. "Do you think you can operate a camera?"

"I guess," she said. "How different can it be to a camcorder these days? What are we going to film?"

I paused again, hoping she was right, hoping that with her electronics skills she might be able to decipher the instructions.

My thoughts turned to all that had happened so far. I thought of all the missed opportunities; each time I should have captured the images. Each time I could have sent them back to London and the rest of the world would have known, would have come to the rescue. I thought of all the lives I'd seen lost. Thought of all the needless death and tried not to imagine the scale, fearing I'd only seen a fraction.

"We film what we see. We won't need to be picky."

She paused again.

"Where's the van?"

I stopped and looked around the horizon, trying to get my bearings.

"The next village over?" I said, the words uncommitted.

She stepped ahead, repeating my turn around the view and pointed to our left, almost in a right-angle direction and started walked.

She spoke as I caught up. "Why the van? Why can't we just Facebook live film it and then it's out there for the masses? I bet you've got a few hundred thousand followers?"

"Two point three million last time I looked," I said, not taking any enjoyment from the words. "But I saw how you reacted and you're here. You've seen it for yourself. You thought it was a prank. How would that appear on the internet?" I let the words hang for a moment. "No. This needs to go through my editor. It needs sending out on the main channels. It needs to be on every screen. Then they'll have to believe. To do that I have to transmit the pictures from the equipment in the van. It has its own satellite transmitter. It has to come from me or it will get intercepted by the firewalls or who knows, maybe the government will get it first."

Alex didn't reply straight away, other than to nod, but she spoke when it seemed as if a thought occurred to her from nowhere.

"Why's this down to you?"

"It's what I do," I replied, the words a reflex.

"What I mean is, if this is so bad, why aren't the special forces down here kicking their asses?"

I thought for a moment and peered up to the sky. I thought of the Home Secretary's expression as I mentioned the headline before I'd started this journey. I focused on the pinprick stars I often stared at to make sure I remembered how minuscule my part in the universe is.

"My thoughts exactly," I said. "And that's what else we'll do."

"Huh?"

"We'll find out why the rest of the country is letting this happen."

"How?"

"I'm not sure yet," I replied, my words slow. "But I've got a feeling if I stick a gun in my mother-in-law's face, we'll know a lot more."

65

"Mother-in-law?"

"I don't know why I said that. I didn't mean mother-in-law. I meant something else. She's the mother of my…" I stopped, the words confused in my head.

Toni hadn't been my girlfriend for longer than two weeks at a time and only way back when we didn't know what happened when we spent long periods together. Long before we ruined the dream.

A fear flashed that I'd already begun to romanticise what we had. Had I already forgotten she'd handed me over to the woman who'd plunged a needle in me, then infected me with a bite? Handed me over to the woman who'd locked me in a cage to see what happened.

I remembered the woman's words. *It was your idea.*

I had to find out what she'd meant. I had to find out what it *all* meant. I had to find out if it was Toni who'd orchestrated what had happened. I had to know; if she had this all planned then why was her face so beaten and bruised? Why was she locked up in that place?

So much didn't make sense.

Breath caught in my mouth as I rambled inside my head. Images of Toni's body stumbling back flashed through my mind. Her hand at her stomach so clear in my head. Maybe now I would never know her side of the story. Never know if she was the one who pulled me to her so I could be part of their experiment.

"Are you okay?" Alex said, one hand reaching for my arm, the other in the small of my back as I bent. With her touch I pulled upright, shaking off her grip.

"I tripped, calm down," I snapped and she pulled away.

She didn't speak and I was glad for the quiet. I needed space to concentrate on pushing away the thoughts as we walked.

As time went on, my mind went over the same questions and I needed her to talk now. What had Toni's first look meant when I caught her gaze as she sat in the orange jump-suit? Why did the sniper help us? What was this all about?

I needed Alex's voice to fill the void left by my feelings pushed down inside. I needed her words as a weight to keep them from rising.

"It's getting light," I said, my voice low, not turning to see if she'd been watching the first glow of orange on the horizon.

"Yes."

"Sorry I was short," I said. "I've got a lot to deal with, you know. It's no excuse, but…"

She quickened her pace to catch up.

"It's fine. As long as you don't try to shoot me again," she said.

Dread washed over me at the thought of what I'd done, but with surprise I heard the smile in her voice and saw the curl of her lips as I turned. Still too dark to make out the detail, I could see no blame in her features. She didn't look like she'd retaliate with a verbal attack at any moment.

I looked ahead, revelling in the relief, but could see nothing on the horizon as we climbed. The rising light highlighted the clean line of the hilltop. There was still a long way to go.

"So you want to talk now?" she said; her words seemed genuine enough. I couldn't sense any accusation.

I nodded.

"Do you feel better now you know I'm not a man?" said with a smile in her voice.

I couldn't look at her, the embarrassment forcing my mouth closed.

"It's okay. I get it a lot. I don't exactly help myself."

I turned towards her to see her grin and I got the feeling she loved wrong-footing everyone when they first met.

"My parents were set on bringing me up gender neutral. I had transformers and dolls. Now I just can't bring myself to wear a dress."

"I'm sorry I just assumed. You don't have to explain," I said turning to her as I walked.

She nodded and gave a shallow raise of her eyebrows.

"But *you* do," she added, jogging past me and turning to me as she walked backwards. "What's all this about? What do you know?"

Of course she wanted to talk about the one thing I'd had enough of.

"What do you mean?"

"You said something about what's going on, the dead reanimating. I've seen for myself, but I need to know more. And from the beginning."

I got it. I would be the same. I was the same.

"It's patchy, but I'll do my best," I said and turned to see her nodding out of the corner of my eye. "From what I can gather, it started in a laboratory near to the village we're headed to. The scientists were doing work on a virus, trying to find a cure." I heard Toni's voice correcting the words in my head. "An antidote or a vaccine. Maybe both."

She nodded, only moving her eyes from me to check her footfalls as the ground undulated.

"It got out of control. They argued about how to deal with it. The scientists squabbled about the best approach. I got a call, my girl…" I paused on the word. "Toni, was in trouble and I rushed here to see if I could help."

"Your girlfriend, right?"

I closed my eyes and drew a deep breath.

"It's complicated," I said, shaking my head and opening my eyes as the sole of my trainer kicked against a stone. "What they were doing in there…" The words felt heavy in my throat. "They were testing on people. Live people." I stopped walking and she stayed at my side, her gaze fixed in my direction.

"Their tests created something. Some things," I said, correcting myself. "These things are like a hybrid, a mutation and they're so much more powerful than when the disease, the virus, takes over a dead body. They overran the facility. Not even the Army could deal with it."

"And that's when you escaped?"

I nodded and walked on.

"Why you?" she said as she followed.

I shrugged my shoulders. "Wrong place, wrong time."

"Where did it come from? The virus, I mean," Alex said.

I paused. Had Toni said something about the Amazon? It was one of many questions I would ask when the gun was in the doctor's face. I shook my head.

"I don't know," I replied. "All I know is you have to damage the brain to kill them."

"Like in the movies?"

"Like in the movies, yes."

"So..." she said, stalling for a moment. "They're zombies, right?"

I didn't reply, but my shoulders gave an involuntary shrug. The name had been on the tip of my tongue since I'd first seen them, but to use the word to describe the creatures seemed both perfect but too cartoonish; too trivial at the same time.

"They're the dead come back to life?" Alex said, with an eyebrow raised.

"Apart from those who escaped the facility, yes."

"They've got an insatiable thirst for flesh?" she said.

I chewed my bottom lip and gave the slightest tip of my head.

"What happens if you get bitten?"

"Okay," I said. "I get it." The world obsessed with zombie culture on the TV, in books and in film. Now they'd need to obsess in real life, too. "Call them Zombies if it makes you happy," I replied.

The silence hung for a few hundred metres.

"Is this legit?"

"In what way? Do you mean am I telling the truth? Let's not start that again."

"No, no, no. I've seen it with my own eyes. I've smelt it. I've felt their cold skin. I get it," she said, holding up her palms. "I mean the work they were doing, was it legit? Is it the government doing this to us, or is it some rogue outfit?"

I thought about her words. Another sensible question.

"Like a super villain?"

She laughed. I wasn't smiling.

"I guess, but less like a comic. If they sanctioned this work, then surely they would be better prepared. They'd have protocols for protecting against a release. A back-up plan. Enough protection, enough troops to contain any situation."

"You don't know the government like I do," I said. "But still you could be on to something."

I looked up, realising the light was rising quickly and we were heading downhill, the sun blueing the sky enough for us to see the buildings looming large. My gaze drew to the dark smoke-columns rising on the horizon.

With each step I could make out more detail. Houses. A tall metal fence wrapping around the village, only breaking where the original wooden fences took up.

It hadn't been there when I'd escaped, nor had the olive drab trucks I could only see the tops of over the other side.

I saw the wooden fence over which I'd jumped and where I'd run along. The house I'd run from.

Its sight sent a shiver down my spine.

I slowed, gripping the gun tight. Alex kept at my side, staring at the tops of the heads just visible over the fence as they moved in the streets, our brains trying to find any other explanation; looking for any other reason than a sea of zombies looking nothing like they did in the cartoons.

66

"What now?" Alex said, but I hardly heard the words, my concentration fixed on scouring everywhere but the house where I'd been held. The house where I'd shot the gun. The house where I'd done what I couldn't bring myself to think about.

Glad of her interruption, she spoke again.

"I have a cousin in the next village over. We could hold out with him?"

I sped my pace, twisting back to see her face in the burgeoning light and her soft complexion for the first time without the shadows. Still I had to remind myself Alex wasn't a man without facial hair and a protruding Adam's apple.

For a moment my mind drifted, mood lightening as I stared, until something reminded me of Toni. Reminded me of the look she would shoot in my direction if she could see me holding my gaze on someone other than her.

"Nothing's changed," I said.

"You're looking at the same place?"

I nodded and she stared back.

"They're packed in like kippers."

"Sardines," I corrected.

"Yeah, whatever. Fish in a tin. They've shut them in there for a reason," she said, looking to the sky which had more than a hint of blue.

"I get it," I said, and sped my descent towards the village.

"And you're still going in?" she said, hurrying at my side.

"I have no choice."

"We can get another camera," Alex said, but by now I was jogging. The distance between us grew as I closed in on the village.

"I need the van. I have to send it via the equipment in the van," I said, shaking my head.

With each breath of wind I caught the concentrated foul odour and I could hear the low grumbling moan. The ground itself seemed to rumble as if to complain at the weight of the creatures.

As I drew closer, I could see the metal fence panels swaying in and out, the creak of the metal clamps scratching to keep hold.

Through the gaps between the metal sheets clamped together to the vertical poles, constant movement passed back and forth.

Somehow I knew Alex was about to talk and I turned to see daylight full on her face. Her mouth stood wide, words ready to spring out, but she paid attention to my request; to my index finger held to my lips.

I pointed to the slow sway of the fence and she changed course as I did, heading to the right and the tall wooden panels marking the start of the village's gardens.

Not slowing from the jog, I followed its path. I still couldn't see over, but I could feel the house. Cold sweat ran down my spine and I picked up the pace, slowing only when the fence turned a corner. Around the turn, the fences were lower and made from chain-link. The house's deserted gardens were easy to see the other side.

I kept my gaze flitting to the windows, watching for movement and any signs of life.

There'd been many people. Tens of villagers caught up in the fright the last time I'd been here. Was it only a few hours ago?

I wanted to see movement at the windows. Wanted to see hands waving, people trying to get our attention. I didn't want to see open-mouthed stares of the people I'd helped survive their fate once already. I needed to see reason for the Army not to forsake this place, to lock it up, light the blue touch paper and stand well back.

If we found people still inside, they'd evacuate first, right? Then again, if that woman was in charge, maybe my hopes would be unfounded.

We ran on with neither of us speaking, not even when I saw the familiar row of houses. The row Toni and I had first come across. Where we'd stood and seen the two runners chased and dropped to the floor. Where we'd watched at least one of their lives end. My thoughts turned to hope for the woman who remained.

I saw the back of the house where we'd escaped over the roof. I saw movement, the memories of that time clear. The house a bust. We'd run because I'd let them in to save the boy.

For a moment I wondered if he was safe and if the woman was alive. Guilt welled when I couldn't remember her name.

"Jess."

Alex's sharp but quiet call pulled me back from my memories. About to admonish her for breaking the silence, I saw her reason. My gaze ran along her outstretched arm to her finger, pointed at another metal fence cutting across the gravel road where we'd first walked into the village.

A woman stood with her back to us. I could see her spine pronounced through the thin bright running top. Two great rends of flesh ran across her back to expose skin and what it was meant to protect underneath. The second jogger.

I let my eyes close, but just for a second and took a deep breath. I had time, I told myself. She hadn't seen us.

I imagined her turning. I imagined her drawn features, her mouth hanging slack as her attention focused on the metal fence which hadn't been there last night.

She was different to the others we'd seen. She wasn't trying to escape. Instead, trying to get in.

I stopped. Alex halted. I pulled myself away from the danger, turning to watch Alex's wide eyes lurching across the view and searching out the overgrown grass for anything she could use as a weapon.

I pulled the gun from my waistband, but knew I couldn't fire. Knew it was a last resort. We had to get inside without making a sound or risk calling the dead towards us like a dinner bell.

I took a step and the snap of a twig rang out from under my foot. I stopped, cursing myself for not taking more care.

Holding my breath, I flashed a look to Alex.

Twisting back, the dead woman still hadn't turned. Movement pulled my gaze to where the fence disappeared around a corner and I saw another creature staring in our direction as she walked towards us.

Her hands rose in the air as my gun fell from my grip. My stomach stabbed as if hit with a bolt of lightning.

Her face was red with blood, shredded with deep scratches. Patches of hair were missing. Great welts of her scalp were gone and I could see the white of her skull on show. Her stomach an open cavity, her intestines uncoiled like a rope dragging behind.

Still I knew it was Toni.

67

"No," I shouted, as Alex reached for the gun on the ground.

With no pause in her reaction, her hand froze, hovering just above the black of the pistol. Our gazes caught, breaking off as the sound of movement came from in front. The sound too loud, too busy for what we'd seen.

Alarm lit our faces at the crowd of bodies ambling around the corner in her wake, none of which had been there only a moment before. With my breath already caught, it felt as if a vacuum pulled my lungs from my chest as I saw Toni again, this time following behind the first woman, her chest rendered wide, ribs pulled clean of flesh with a blanket of thick, clotted blood covering her face.

I looked to the first Toni, pulling her intestines behind her; snatched a look straight back to her double with the white of her ribs bared.

I knew only one could be Toni, despite what my eyes were screaming at me. I knew even when I saw her for the third time, her clothes a perfect match. At least what remained. At least what I thought the colours would be underneath the blood and dirt.

I saw her head on every other body. Saw her smile on mouths hanging slack.

Looking between each, I stared at the face of a soldier. The face of a man dressed in military fatigues, a rifle hanging loose around his front. He wasn't her.

I would have calmed. Should have calmed. Should have taken a deep breath and centred myself, but Alex had taken my pause to reach for the gun and she'd raised up and pointed it out to the crowd.

Blinking, her motion slow, all I could do was observe. All I could do was seek her line of sight and follow where she pointed.

With alarm, I saw she pointed her aim straight at Toni.

"No," I screamed, regretting the volume as the world came back in focus. I grabbed both hands around her upper arm and yanked. The gun went off and I screamed again. "No."

I moved but didn't grab the gun. With a twitch to the crowd I saw the shot must have missed. Each of the creatures still moved forward as I pulled Alex's arm hard. Letting go with one hand fixed tight, Alex followed as I dragged her along.

A few paces from the low fence I took faith that she'd follow and let go, jumping as high as I could and pulling my legs around the side, barely stumbling as I landed. I kept running, racing through the garden, chasing down the house; eyes fixed on the bright green back door, only looking back as I pushed the handle down and it held under my weight.

Alex had followed. Relief raised the corners of my mouth until my focus fell at her back to the creature stumbling forwards over the short fence.

The resemblance still held as they floundered to their feet the other side, our side, already making their slow but dogged journey in our direction.

Alex's hand grabbed at mine, pushing the gun into my grip, her other at my back, drawing me away from their route, pushing me in front and down the side of the house and the second short fence.

Numb to the climb, numb to the cautious raise of my leg, I stepped over the chain-link while Alex held it low.

I didn't look on to where I'd landed. Didn't pay attention to the other side while Alex climbed. My gaze fixed on my thigh, exposed by the long rip up the side of my skirt, rising to the waistband. I tried to think back to when it happened, knowing Toni would be cross. If she had lived long enough.

"Jess," Alex said, grabbing me by the shoulders, shaking.

I looked up and saw her concern. She shook my shoulder for a second time. I watched her face, but didn't realise I'd been anything but wide awake.

I turned, grabbing her wrist despite her running parallel to my side and not needing my encouragement. My gaze ran across the view, jumping every few steps to launch over the bloodied mess of bodies littering the once sleepy village street.

I'd seen the tee junction. I'd seen the steeple of the church, but couldn't quite see the white of the van. I'd seen the street thick with the creatures, but hadn't connected that they'd give us no safe route.

The pull of Alex's wrist guided me away from the junction as I stared out to the road littered with the smoking remains of Land Rovers and trucks and black sticky piles of charred remains with steam rising.

She'd turned us around. She'd had no choice, could find no alternative. All but one house on each side of the once quiet street had their doors open and I could see movement inside. We had nowhere to go but back the way we'd come.

We ran, repeating the journey in reverse. We slowed when we saw the creatures which had followed from outside of the village climbing up from the grass as they pulled from their fall on our side of the second, short chain-link fence.

I looked to the sky for a miracle. I looked down to the blood-soaked ground at my feet as we slowed to a stop. I looked to Alex and her eyes twitching to every point in view, then peered to the gun.

I didn't know how many bullets remained. I hoped we had enough to make sure we could choose our own ending.

68

I'd let go of Alex's wrist but still felt her body twisting as she searched for a way out. While I tried to slow my breath, I felt her warm grip tight in my hand. My hand followed her pull, my body too and feet soon after, if only to stop me falling face first to the tarmac.

She'd taken control. She had me completely. I gave no resistance as she dragged me toward the row of houses. My feet barely kept up as we headed to the opposite side of the street to where we'd arrived, heading to the false hope of the closed doors, behind which we didn't know what survived.

To our right, the metal fence rang with the scratch of fingers, hands slapping, shoulders barging as teeth snapped open and closed. Metal pulled its grip against the wooden posts, sending them rocking, swaying with each wave of effort.

Arriving at another house, Alex's hand released and I slowed. A weight pulled at my chest as if I'd lost my gravity. She didn't slow and continued to race past the garden gate, shoulder first, not stopping to test the front door handle.

I could hardly believe it when the door gave with a dull thud. As her shoulder connected, the wood sprung wide, the frame splitting at her side as she took the barrage in her stride. Not stumbling. Not faltering. Her only pause was to make sure I'd followed.

Alex ignored me as I stepped over the threshold while she pushed what remained of someone else's front door back into its hole, then rushing back past me to the living room to grab at the straight-back chair and heft it in front of the door. She barely took note as I climbed the stairs.

With sweat beading at my forehead, I toured each of the rooms, making sure they were clear, the view from the front bedroom doing nothing to calm the heat building as I slowly recovered my breath.

Pulling off my jacket, I turned away from the view to let the cooling relief take effect.

Alex joined me after a moment to the sound of the furniture she'd pushed at the front door slowly scraping along the wooden floor. In her hand she held a packet of digestive biscuits.

"I found these," she said, but the rest of the words didn't come. "Your arm," she added, and I tensed at the sound of concern in her voice, following her gaze down to my right arm and the pink new skin of the bite mark. "When were you bitten?"

"I'm not going to die," I said, after waiting for a moment to let my adrenaline relax after hearing her voice, then watched as her brow furrowed and her head moved to the side.

Now was not a time to be coy. She deserved to know the truth for staying at my side; still, panic flushed through my chest, spiking my heart rate and sending the hairs on my body to stand tall as I thought of the words I would use.

"The tests?" she finally said as her hand went out to touch the pink scar from the wound that started this all off.

I nodded, raising my eyebrows.

"What did they do to you?"

I paused, speaking to stop the words rolling around in my head.

"They gave me medicine."

Her eyes went wide.

"So it works?" Her voice came out high, words coming quick; her face alive, animated and lit bright, but shrank away at my reluctance to reply with anything but a shake of my head.

"No. It's a vaccine," I said, looking away despite the stiffness in my neck. I didn't want to see the thoughts running through her brain, the twitch of her brow as she tried to figure out my words.

"You were bitten after they gave you the medicine?"

I turned back to see her eyes widening and I nodded.

"They were testing the vaccine," I said.

"That's horrible, but," she said, pausing, "good at the same time, right?"

"It wasn't ready."

She shook her head, her features bunching.

"We need to move," I said on hearing the furniture scrape again.

"It'll hold for a little while longer," she replied.

We both paused our words and listened to the thud of bodies slapping against the front door.

"Eat," she said, holding out the open packet in her hand.

"No," I said. "We need to get to the van. I need the cameras."

"Don't be in such a hurry," she said, taking bites from a digestive.

"I'm on a course of treatment. The last dose is in the van too. I need it before nightfall."

She didn't speak at first. Instead she watched as I relented and ate, head shaking from side to side.

"And if you don't get it? Sorry, stupid question."

I knew what I should say. I knew what I wanted to say would be too much. The words should be too much for anyone to take and so I watched as she raised her eyebrows in our silence.

Still her expression told me she expected an answer. She deserved an answer.

"Do you turn into a werewolf?" she said. I could tell she'd forced the laughter that came after.

Part of me was glad when I heard the front door collapse under the continued assault, but I soon changed my mind when she dropped the packet to the floor, taking my hand and pulling me out of the room, giving me no time to protest.

Her pace hurried as the scrape and moan rose from the stairwell. We were soon out the other side and in another light room. The windows were wide open and after handing her the gun I balanced on the window ledge, daylight bright in my face. Cold air stole what remained in my lungs as I stared out at the view of the drop that swam beneath me to my left and right.

"Give me your hands," she said.

I turned, looking down to the flat roof.

"Give me your hands," she repeated.

I could do nothing else but what she told. With a firm grip, she lowered me down, relief coming as my feet touched the cushion of the roof and her hands released.

Wobbling to the bitumen roof, I leant against the brick to slow the vertigo. The flat roof felt as if it gave way for a moment as Alex let it catch her weight. Relief let me breathe when it held.

With my head settling as I pulled at the fresher air, I took in the view and the sight of the van glistening in the bright morning light.

It was in one piece, but may as well have been on another continent. Several gardens stood in our way, each teeming with a writhing mass of dead bodies whose stench filled my nostrils anew. Even if we could get through their masses, we'd have to scale the hastily-erected metal fence hemming in the densest collection of the creatures I'd ever seen.

The van rocked side to side as repeatedly the walking dead crashed and bounced off its paintwork.

69

Stepping back from the edge of the roof, I looked away from the impossible sight, Alex's hand stopping me from falling over the edge as my shaking legs struggled to hold my weight.

The stench built to a thick soup as it rose from the bodies crowding between the houses. My gaze sunk to the bloodied hands pointed straight in the air, the fingers clawing, scratching at the brick as they clambered for traction to get at our flesh.

I knew any moment I could see her face in the crowd.

Waves of the dead rippled forward in every space, every patch of ground covered with the creatures eager to get to where we stood. I turned back to the van, frantic to seek a possible path through the seething collection. My mind raced to find how I could get to the goal I had no choice but to reach.

In front of us were six houses between us and the van; their back gardens at least. Each had a single storey extension, more or less as deep as the one we stood on, projecting out from each original house. All but one had a flat roof, but it didn't matter; the gulf between each structure much larger than we could dream of ever reaching without help.

I turned to Alex and our eyes locked.

"What now?" I said and turned away, frustration racing my heart each time I stared out, not able to find a path free of the swarm. Our only choice would be a deadly dash through the scratching, grabbing hands, biting teeth surging for us even now, despite being out of reach.

I looked around the garden to my right, but only with half a heart. It didn't matter if an aluminium bridge lay on the grass; the teeming crowd of scraping clawed hands and snapping mouths would get us the moment we dropped to the ground to retrieve it.

Despite that, I didn't find what I needed, only piles of old paint pots along the fence line.

I turned at a strange high sound ripping over the low, background moan. With surprise, I found Alex not standing at my side and panic sprinted up my insides until I saw her kneeling by the edge of the roof as if she were about to climb down to her certain death.

"What the hell? You won't stand a chance," I said, rushing towards her. With each step I felt the roof compress under my feet.

About to grab her arm, she lifted and as she did, pulled up a sliver of bitumen felt.

I stood back, regarding her curious smile, letting myself calm as I fixed on trying to figure out why she was pulling the roof apart with us on it.

"What are you doing?"

As I spoke, I moved beside her to get a better view.

She didn't speak at first, her breath lost in the effort as she stood, the muscles in her arms tightening against her shirt as she heaved, stuttering the felt up and sending nails popping as they gave out their grip.

"We need to get something to bridge the gap. I think there might be tools or a ladder in this house," she said, flicking a look over her shoulder. "Can't think of anything else. You?"

I ignored the question and she didn't linger for my reply, instead she discarded great rips of dark tar-backed felt before leaning over the result of her destruction.

I peered in to look for myself.

Beneath the felt were chipboard panels, their surface swollen with water and peppered with stubborn nails still surrounded by skirts of felt.

"What now?" I said stepping back.

Alex didn't answer, but the wood beneath her feet did. As did the dust spraying out of the gaping hole she disappeared through.

70

Jumping back to the wall of the main house, I stood wide-eyed with my hands flat against the cold brick. Breath fixed in my throat as I willed for the dust and chaos to settle whilst listening, keen for Alex's call, letting me know she was still okay.

The dust stopped falling, but the commotion had whipped the surrounding crowd to a frenzy. Still, I hadn't heard her voice.

Taking a tentative step forward, I didn't want to join Alex's side and land on the floor next to her body I imagined spread out ready for the chalk outline.

Sinking to my knees, I crawled, spreading the weight across my limbs in hope, in desperation, to get close.

The surface gave just a little with each of my movements, feeling as if with just a little more pressure I would be by her side.

Creeping slowly forward whilst pausing every other moment, I could hear the racket of creatures crowding, their ragged low moans not falling back.

I shot a glance backward, peering up to the window of the main house, cursing my caution when I saw no shadows behind the glass and sped up my movement toward the edge of the gaping hole.

Split, dark sodden wooden sheets lay under the great hole, each folded, bent or buckled, broken apart and sprinkled with the white dust of plaster. Loose remains fell from the ceiling as I edged closer.

Squinting at the neat lines of thick wooden beams on the roof below me, I followed each line covered with a dark frosting of mould where the chipboard had gone from between.

Laying my front flat to the wood, I edged further forward, urging the pile on the ground to move.

Paintbrushes, rollers and tools lined the walls hanging on metal hooks. A wooden bench ran along the closest wall, its surface notched and paint flecked from years of hard labour. I could think of so many ways we could use the sharp tools.

Shaking my head, I tried to clear the thoughts when I saw the metal step ladder sat in the corner at an angle, its length too great to fit flat to the wall. It would be perfect to bridge the gap. Perfect for Alex to climb out. All she had to do was rise from the pile as long as her heart still beat in her chest.

I saw movement in the room at the bottom of my vision, not in the centre as I expected. A boot rose and fell as it tried to mount the pile, but somehow it couldn't get high enough, couldn't coordinate its movements.

Why was Alex standing at the edge of the room? Were those the boots she'd been wearing when she fell?

I crept further, despite knowing I was already overhanging the beam and gambling how far the rot had affected the structure.

With the improved vantage, I regretted my movement, regretted the blood-soaked trousers connected to the boots. I regretted the second pair of legs joining at their side and the realisation surged through my chest.

It wasn't Alex but a creature from upstairs, or fresh through the front door. Now the pile below me rose. Another groan added to the low moans already filling the air.

Alex's short hair came through the rubble dusted with white as she sat up, her face covered in plaster, giving her an even more pale complexion, her features much like the creatures at her front. The only colour came from a line of bright red dripping from a wound to her forehead. If she hadn't died from the fall and turned, she would soon fulfil the fate unless I did something.

Scrambling to my feet, I took little care with their placement. Clenching my teeth, I wrapped my hands tight around my chest and jumped.

71

I'd like to say I fell with grace, keeping an elegant line while the chipboard crumpled, not waving my arms wild at my sides as I abandoned the previous second of planning.

I'd like to say I didn't scream, not turning the air blue as I cursed in a shrill call.

I'd like to say I watched the fall. Stared with my expression fixed. A picture of composure as the floor raced towards me, watching as I knocked the ghouls off their feet instead of arriving to curse the slap of the ground to my knees; broken bones only prevented by the crack of plasterboard catching my fall.

Alex stood as I raced to my feet, knowing either side the creatures would climb to their own; their slow, toddler awkwardness my only advantage.

Fists balled, I stepped forward, my glare fixed on her dazed expression, seeking hope, recognition. Searching for any sign of humanity.

She blinked.

I racked my brain for meaning. Was this only a human action? Had I seen the creatures blink? The dead ones at least?

"Speak," I shouted, knocking her sideways as I jumped over the mound, my hands landing either side of the cold metal ladder.

Still, she hadn't uttered a word as I swung the awkward load whilst separating out each half and thrusting it to the floor. My feet were already to the second rung as it landed, swaying to the side with each rubber shoe resting on the uneven ground.

Back on the roof, I crawled to my front, twisting and turning, scraping my chest across the sodden board as I landed. I peered below, anxious with my hands to the top rung and ready to hoist it high if Alex didn't have the will to follow.

She stared up, mouth wide and coughed.

The dead didn't cough.

"Alex," I shouted, her stare snapping to her side.

The creatures were on their feet, teetering for traction on the edge of the rubble.

Alex blinked. I saw recognition, her upturned expression as she looked at me.

"Alex," I shouted again, ignoring the harmonising calls.

She turned, twisted sideways, face alarming as she caught the sight.

Grabbing the rungs, she sprung alive with action, her feet kicking as pallid hands reached out to her dust-ridden clothes. Slapping away hands before they could get a grip, dust rained down as she climbed to the edge to follow my lead. Spreading herself thin, she scrambled to the roof.

I turned away as soon as I knew she was out of their reach. Pulling at the aluminium, yanking hard from their grip.

Hands reached high and I pulled. Alex's plaster-coated hands joining mine and together we swatted clawed fingers before the ladder clattered to the roof as we let go.

Our breath took time to settle and we lay with our backs to the felt, staring skyward, cursing each deep pull that drew in the foul smell.

Alex rose first and pulled up the ladder from the roof.

"I'm sorry. I should have told you what I was doing. It was stupid," she said as I got to my feet, careful to rest each where I knew the beams ran beneath.

I shrugged and spoke with my voice low.

"Let's work as a team. But it wasn't that stupid. At least we got the ladder."

Nodding for a moment, her movement stopped as her glance fixed down the hole. I followed her look, my gaze ignoring the bloodied creatures still clawing towards the opening, instead fixing on the shape of the gun frosted in a white dusting.

I let out a deep breath before I spoke.

"We need to be careful."

"I'm sorry," she said and I turned away.

Alex joined me and together we held a side of the ladder each, carefully lowering across the gap to the next flat roof. Our grips held until the angle grew too great, its length too far for us to do anything but hold back the fall and guide the drop with a hope it would reach the other side.

It did, but only just, the width of the top rung barely at the edge.

Hands clawed to the air. Bloody fingertips scraped and tapped at the metal. We had to race. We had to get across before something tall, something with long arms came along and grabbed a leg or tipped our bridge as we clambered over.

"I'll go first," I said, looking to Alex.

I slipped on the first touch. Falling forward, I watched the river of upturned foul faces, their outstretched clawed fingers racing toward me as I descended.

72

Despite her efforts, she couldn't catch me. Couldn't stop my fall as I raced down face first to the rungs.

I collapsed to the metal, my hands grabbing a hold either side, gripping hard. The sting of the skin on my arm tightening as I took the weight.

The two halves of the ladder clattered against each other, the metal jumping before snapping back.

I held firm, waiting for the ladder to turn and twist and fall into the crowd who would frenzy over my body, pulling flesh from my bones.

The ladder stayed put, despite the claw of nails down my face as it felt as if hundreds of fingers willed me to the ground.

"Go," came Alex's voice from my back.

I shot a look behind to see her kneeling, her weight on the edge of the ladder, holding it firm.

I pushed up with my arms outstretched, the tips of my feet on top of the rungs and surged forward, giving full respect to the ladder as it stayed in place. With my feet slipping against the metal, I recovered over and again until I found the rough purchase of the solid roof the other side.

Turning before I calmed, fear rained down as I worried for the strength of the wood underneath my feet. It hadn't collapsed yet and held my ground, watching as Alex followed on her hands and knees to scamper to where I stood.

As the ladder slipped with her last step, falling until I bounded over, forgetting my fears, I skidded to my knees and felt the sting of skin coming loose, but I had the cold metal in my hand and stopped the fall.

Alex helped me to pull it free from the tangle of hands and arms and heads slapping it side to side.

She helped me to my feet. She helped lift the ladder, settling it down to the roof. Together we peered back to the wreck of the roof we'd left behind, the felt ripped away with two great holes where there hadn't been before.

I pushed away the guilt at what we'd done to someone's house, knowing we had to save our lives and turned my back to survey the next challenge.

The pitch wasn't too steep. If we could get onto the roof, it was shallow enough for us to climb with probable ease and little fear of slipping down, but for the life of me I couldn't figure out how the hell we could rest the ladder on the angle.

At least we had time. At least we were safe for now. I turned on the spot, Alex mirroring my search for inspiration. With a shake of her head, I knew she'd come up as empty of suggestions as I had.

I looked to the windows just above our heads and saw the single panes of glass in the main house of the extension roof we stood on. I looked to Alex, annoying myself for seeking confirmation as I quickly turned away, but not soon enough to see her raised eyebrow.

Nodding, she came around me, opening the stepladder and setting it underneath the nearest window. I rose, squinting to the darkness inside.

A double bed sat in the centre with the quilt ruffled, the sheet cast half off. I could see a mattress. I could see a dark, abstract pattern on the white. I saw the near-naked man sitting cross-legged on the bed, his gaze fixed at me through the window.

I stumbled down a rung of the ladder, breath rasping and body shaking but already disbelieving what I'd seen; questioning if the man who'd rested on the bed really had blood trailing from his mouth to matt down his front. Already asking myself if those two shapes beside him, covered in a dark blanket, were just folds on the duvet. Wondering if my look to the carpet as I'd instinctively dropped had actually seen the great inkblot, or the bleached white bones piled in its centre.

As if from a remote location, Alex asked what I saw to make me draw back. She asked if I was okay when I didn't reply.

Instead, I looked up as a bloodied face appeared at the window, its forehead surging toward the thin layer of glass and our only protection.

73

The scream came next, sending daggers across our senses. A shrill call in tune with the outward spray of glass.

I stumbled back, pulling the ladder with me as I lunged for safety. Still, I fell.

Alex caught my weight and together we collapsed to the roof, the cold metal following.

With no chance to recover from the shock or to be thankful the roof held in place, I peered up through the rungs while I pushed the ladder from my chest. Willing my ears to close off from the pain of the shrill call, I fixed on the window as the creature burst out in a blur, sending the remaining shards in its wake.

My legs wheeled in circles as I struggled to my feet, Alex's arms in the same frenzy, her words shouting disbelief.

Scrabbling to her feet with her hand on my arm, at my side I saw her twitch her view between me and any sight of the creature who'd jumped right over us but was now out of view.

Gaping to each other, then to the window empty of glass, we turned to the back garden. My feet weren't willing to take the steps needed to peer over the edge.

With my brain frozen, locked up, I had no idea what would come next, my head still reeling from the sight which disappeared as quick as it arrived.

The shrill call had relented, but how long ago wasn't clear. The echo continuing to ring true in my ears. Alex's head seemed in the same state, her feet unmoving at my side.

After what seemed like an age, but was more than likely just a fleeting second, I found clarity and fumbled at my feet for the ladder. Alex grabbed the other side when she saw me moving, but just as she took a firm grip a shadow cast on the brickwork and the flat roof bounced under the extra weight.

We turned, swapping the ladder between our hands and saw the creature standing before us, its bloodshot eyes wide and chest heaving for air. This was a living creature, despite the outward appearance.

With a smooth scalp and the remains of a once white shirt around his shoulders, a dark soaked tie loose around its neck, he looked as if he'd just stepped away from a grotesque table after digging into a banquet with his bare hands.

Behind the bloody covering across his face, some of which still oozed from the lesions in his cheeks, I watched veins pulsing just under the skin as he glared and bared his teeth.

At first I couldn't believe the pause. Could this be because I had been infected by the virus and it couldn't quite decide if I would make a decent meal?

Looking to Alex I remembered when I saw her ashen face that this was her first view of *these* creatures.

I'd seen many already. Enough for a lifetime. I'd shot one over and again and watched it stay upright, charging onward with a fury that would be at home in a horror film. Now this stood before me, its blood-drenched belly sagging heavy out in front. With each of its shallow breaths, long streams of vapour plumed into the cold air; for the first time I came to understand what I would become if Toni's vaccine wasn't up to the challenge.

Competing against the realisation, I still had the wherewithal to marvel at its pause. Watching its slowness to react as if tired and lethargic from a full stomach.

Instinct came back and I didn't wait more than another a blink of its eye before surging forward. With Alex still holding the other end of the ladder, gripping tight, she took no time in reacting to my plan.

The creature could have jumped. It could have charged forward, but instead just watched and issued a dulled call. The weak scream cost it more time and precious breath.

Unable to hold us back, its feet fell from the edge of the roof and it dropped to the ground.

We didn't look over. Instincts told us it shouldn't be this easy; instead, our insides screamed for us to run and act, knowing we'd soon be dead if we didn't take full advantage of the gift.

Alex let go of the ladder so I could take hold and I hopped with wide steps across the roof, planting the feet of the ladder as I pulled apart each half. Running, I clambered up the rungs, jumping in through the window as I reached the final step, somehow missing the glass still left around the framed edge.

As I landed, I didn't look down. I already knew the reason the floor was sticky and wet; instead, I fixed my concentration on the door I needed to put between us and the creature when it followed.

Through the open door my gaze flitted back to the bedroom and latched on to the two bodies side by side laying on the bed, their faces thick with a mask of blood.

Alex's landing to the floor pulled my stare from their death and to her curled lip and wrinkled nose as she crouched in the mess, trying to wipe the sticky blood from her hands.

"Come on," I said, trying to keep my voice low. I knew I should just go. I should run. I knew it was her choice to hesitate. She wasn't my responsibility. Mine was the bigger mission. Mine the higher cause.

Still, I waited, willing her on and shouting for her to stand.

Eventually she jumped up as if she'd only just heard my voice, her feet slipping as she struggled for traction in the slick.

Bursting through the doorway, she pulled the door closed before settling back against it to join with my pressure.

With our lungs pumping the surrounding air, I was desperate to slow the pull and the whistle of wind. I knew full well the creature would follow and we wouldn't get another chance like this again.

But we weren't followed, the house silent. The building empty, if we believed our ears.

The low rumble of breath over dormant vocal cords had become the norm. With its absence it felt like something was missing. Something wasn't right. At least when you could hear their low hum you knew where they were and could prepare.

In the silence I felt blind. My mind questioned if they were around but just being quiet. I'd grown to prefer open spaces.

A drip of sweat drifted down my forehead as I looked along the hallway, trying to will my vision to peer down the stairs, the top of which was at the end of the passage.

I looked through the window at the opposite end. I watched the village; the roofs of the houses at least.

Staring out across the view, I knew it would have been the same days ago when all people had to worry about were trivial things.

With an already clammy hand, I swatted the droplet away as I shook my head with breath still refusing to slow. I pulled at Alex's arm, pointing to the stairs.

She looked, her head darting in the direction, but she didn't move from the door and turned back as my breath continued to race.

The room spun and I could feel my hold at the door lessening each time I failed to fill my lungs.

Raising my hand to my face, I saw Alex's raised brow as she grabbed my wrist and pulled my hand away.

I lifted my left to take its place and she grabbed that too. For a moment my breath held back from clawing at the air. My lungs stopped altogether as I reacted to my wrists being gripped against my will, again.

I should have been angry. I should have felt the need to lash out and I felt bile rising as I headed that way.

Somehow the warmth of her hold had the opposite effect, my breath back; even and controlled.

She released. The sense of loss took me by surprise until a thump landed heavy on the other side of the door, sending a solid vibration through my back to evaporate my thoughts.

74

As the vibration dissipated to fear, adrenaline exploded upward to send a surge of energy, clearing the vision I hadn't realised had blurred.

Alex released my wrist as she snatched a look to the door and by the time she turned back, I'd leapt away in a desperate search for our escape.

Ignoring the pound of my feet on the floor, I raced into the next room at our right.

Thump came a heavy weight at the door I'd just left. Energy surged as the vibrations rattled the house.

Shaking my head, I looked around the bedroom I found, but I couldn't see anything to wedge at the door where Alex stood. I couldn't find a way to bind it closed.

Thump came the same call again and I shouted for Alex, no longer with any use for being quiet.

She followed, eager to slam the bedroom door closed and add her weight to push the chest of drawers across the opening.

Thump came the call for the fourth time and I thought I could see our door bow inwards, even though it still hadn't breached the first.

With the chest of drawers barring the way, I took in the room and the window with the single pane looking out over the extension roof from where we'd come, looking out on to the roof next door where we wanted to be and down at the sea of dead which hadn't thinned since we'd been inside.

Thump. The sound seemed to change. I had to hope it wasn't the door already weakening.

I pulled out the drawers of the chest we'd shoved across the door, raking out clothes despite not knowing what I looked for.

Moving my attention to the wardrobe and pushing aside its hanging contents, I jabbed at the buttons on the small electronic safe without thought to what help it would bear, all to the vibration of the continued assault.

When it didn't open with a random series of numbers poked at in desperation, I looked up and with a flash of clarity, my smile gleamed at the sight of a long leather gun case and a baseball bat resting on the top of the metal in the corner of the dark wardrobe.

With both in hand, I passed the case to Alex. She soon had it unzipped with her head twisting to the door each time the thud came.

When her expression didn't light with glee, I snapped a question.

"What?"

"It's an air rifle," she said, shaking her head.

Fighting back the disappointment, I drew a deep breath.

"Better than nothing. Any bullets?"

"Pellets," she said, as upending the case over the bed I watched a bag of tiny metal balls fall to the covers.

Running to the window with a plan quickly forming, I cursed the poor view through the glass showing only gardens edged on the vast space of the moor. The not-so-distant thump against the wood rattled the glass and I ran to the chest of drawers.

Without dropping the bat, I struggled to pull the drawers from across the door. Alex's help came a moment later and we stood, wide-eyed, staring at each other when the wood out in the hallway gave an ear-splitting crack.

"No," Alex said as my hand went for the handle. She didn't hold me back and the handle twisted. I wasted no time pulling the door wide, leaving Alex fumbling with the plastic bag.

Stepping into the corridor I saw the great crack running through the wooden door we'd first come through and I ran to the right when with the next thump I saw the shadow of movement in the widening gap that I knew couldn't hold it back for much longer.

With the bat leading the way high over my head, I stormed into the third and last room on this floor. Finding the front bedroom and after a quick scan left and right, I raked the curtains to the side and saw the road teeming with dead soldiers and residents, some of which I recognised from our last visit.

I didn't linger on their faces for fear of what my mind would project. Instead, I fixed on the cars parked outside each house, most of them only a few years old; most of them perfect for my plan.

I turned to Alex when I heard the door slam into place.

"You any good?" I said, nodding to the rifle gripped hard in her hand.

She looked down at the gun as if she'd forgotten she held it, shrugging her shoulders as if it was a stupid question.

"I can give it a go," she said, flinching back, her head still concentrating on the battering at the door across the hall. Still concentrating on the sound which seemed less bass with each successive hit, with each the wood opening wider in the countdown for it to give.

I turned away, quickly scanning the view again. Soon I pointed the bat's length to the furthest away car; a Freelander in a dark red, but the details didn't matter.

She didn't ask questions. She didn't look confused, but I had to make sure she understood.

"The windows, right?"

I saw the realisation ping on her features and she nodded quickly, the silence from the hallway speeding her hurry to the window.

Covering our faces as best we could with our arms, I jabbed the baseball bat at the glass. It gave so much easier than I thought it would and I soon had the edge cleared of shards as I circled the wood around the metal frame.

As the musical shower stopped on the pavement below, the corridor came alive with another heavy thud, followed by what could only be the door slapping to the carpet as it finally gave way.

"Do it," I shouted, holding back the full force of my voice.

I turned around the room, cursing for not blocking the doorway before and searched, frantically trying to find the large piece of furniture I needed to block the door.

There was nothing, the room just filled with a lightweight divan bed. A cheap wooden frame surrounded in thick cardboard.

"Do it," I said as I turned my back to Alex and raised the bat high over my head, ready if the creature finally realised all it had to do was turn the handle.

I heard the puff of air from the rifle and waited, forcing myself to take a breath whilst urging the car's alarm to scream.

75

The wail of the alarm didn't come. Only silence screamed from the gaping window, its lull peppered with the slow fall of feet and what I hoped wasn't the enquiring intake of breath, searching out what I knew first-hand would be our provocative scent.

"Again," I shouted, regretting the volume. I couldn't take my gaze from the door to check Alex was doing as I urged.

I heard the rustle of the plastic bag, the patter of metal pellets forming a pile, but still I couldn't look away; I could only listen to the silence as the feet stopped moving the other side of the door.

Air rushed from the barrel a second time.

Nothing other than Alex's curse replied.

I shot her a look, eager to take her place whilst listening for any sign of movement.

Alex twisted, resetting her aim to a different target. An easier option, I hoped. As she snapped the air rifle in two, pushed the pellet in and cracked it closed, I held my breath and turned back to the door.

"I can't become them," I said under my breath, regretting the words as the shot didn't come.

About to turn to question the pause, I watched the bar of the door handle move. Stepping closer, I leant out my trainer to push against the base of the door whilst trying to keep the bat high over my head.

Air rushed from the barrel as the handle twisted and a scream replied, a shout of fury from behind the door whilst Alex congratulated herself.

It was when the scream faded, the piercing volume receding, I heard the call of the alarm outside.

She'd done it.

"Another," I shouted. There was no need to hide now. I heard foot falls heavy on the other side of the door;

then glass shattering somewhere in the house turned my expression wide.

"Another," I said as she looked toward me with a question set on her features.

"Another," I repeated, until she backed away from the window, snapping the rifle in two to push another pellet home.

The second call of an alarm added to the chorus and her smile. She didn't need to be told again and reloaded.

Three alarms sang out into the street, echoing off the buildings, the cycling klaxons pulling at my senses.

Grabbing the door handle, I let my toes relax from the door and waited to feel a response from the other side. When none came, I took a step back, letting my grip loosen but ready with the bat over my head should I have been wrong to think the creature had left the building.

When the door didn't burst wide, I turned towards the window and Alex, my view flinching back to the door then out to see the lumbering crowd of creatures drawn like steel to the magnet of screaming cars.

I'd been right and let a smile pull at my mouth as I lightly tapped Alex on her upper arm. She'd done it, but breath paused and the corners of my mouth dropped as I saw the beast, his engorged, blood-soaked belly swinging side to side as he climbed to the roof of the closest car with his head raised to the air, sniffing in search of the source of the electronic call.

Creature after creature kept up their slow pace. I watched Alex set her aim again.

"Don't bother," I said, placing my hand on the warmth of her upper arm. "Even if it works, there's a hundred to take its place."

She took a moment to lower the gun, watching as I collected up the pile of pellets from the bed and followed, wordless, as I dragged the door wide and peered through the gap with the bat raised.

The coast was clear, the floor not. Red patches in the beige carpet recorded each of our journeys from the first doorway to this opening and the lone pair carrying on to the window which once kept out the cold at the end of the hallway.

I placed my trainers around the marks and moved toward the second room at the back. I turned away before I crossed in, bile rising in my stomach at the thought of the mess ready to greet us. We had little choice but to climb out the ladder we'd left behind.

The mess was no greater, no worse. The picked-clean bones no brighter, no duller. The red of the carpet no more vibrant. The metallic cloud no thicker, no thinner.

With a glance to my left I saw the two bodies and an unformed question pulled me from my course to the window. Finding myself standing at the foot of the bed I looked at the couple whose ages were obscured by the thin mask of red. More questions raised themselves and pulled me around to the side of the bed, closer to where they lay as I tried to answer why they'd been killed but not eaten.

The answers didn't come. Only more questions and Alex's voice calling me in the background, but I couldn't turn away to check her words. I couldn't take my eyes from their chests when I saw movement. Only when their crystal-clear eyes opened together, pulling apart from the clasp of the dried blood and rearing towards me did I realise they weren't dead, but weren't human anymore either.

Instinct took control and brought the bat down heavy on their skulls, sending dried blood cracking into the air. Two solid thumps each and they were out of their misery.

The questions fighting for attention kept me removed from the deed, the loudest of which was why the creature who'd sat on the bed and attacked us, hadn't ripped these two apart? Had I witnessed something Toni had said was impossible? Had I witnessed one of her creations making more of itself? Had I just witnessed a double birth of these terrible creatures?

76

The car alarms screaming in the background reminded me I couldn't linger on the horror. Using the tips of my toes I trod as lightly as I could through the great scarlet patch to lean out of the missing glass with my hair billowing behind me in the draft.

The last of the creatures were leaving the garden. The last of the creatures were rushing, just a little faster than their previous shambling pace, clattering and bumping to find the source of the noise.

I accepted the mini victory of the step ladder still being in place and I was on the flat roof without Alex's offered helping hand. I took the air rifle as she climbed down and gave it back as I lifted the ladder, whilst checking all around before I placed it to the foot-flattened grass at the back. Climbing down, I peered around the corner and watched the backs of the last creatures moving toward the chorus of alarms.

Up the ladder and jumping down the other side of the fence, I watched Alex repeat the climb and balance on the wood with the thin slats bowing in and out as she took the ladder up before setting it on the other side. I flinched each time the metal gave the slightest clatter, hoping the alarms would be more than enough to mask it.

When both of us landed on the grass the other side with the ladder in hand, I couldn't help think it was going too well. We were three houses down out of six, with three more to go and with the ladder handed into the fourth garden it wouldn't be long before I could get what I needed; the camera equipment and hopefully the last vial of medicine.

My thoughts turned to my happy place, my posture straight as I imagined looking down the camera and telling the masses about the breaking story that would change their world forever.

As the thoughts whirled in my head in a noxious mix of emotions, the chorus of alarms turned to a pair and after a pause to check, became a single voice as I stepped off the ladder and jumped to the paving slabs the other side.

With another step, the last masking call dissipated and the world seemed to stand still.

I didn't panic. My pulse didn't inflate by a wide margin until Alex sat on the top of the fence; until it collapsed as she swayed with the ladder in her hand. The metal slapped down to the flagstones. The cacophony echoed like a dinner bell when Alex landed on top to send a second chorus ringing out.

I listened to the lull as the echo died, fixing my glare on Alex's wide-eyed fright.

We were both afraid to do anything. Both afraid to rattle the aluminium call in our attempt to move. A rising fear told me we'd already done the damage and the creatures, fast and slow, would chase around the corner at any moment.

We couldn't wait to find out. Holding my hand out for Alex, she clambered to her feet, pulling the ladder as she rose. The gentle rattle of the aluminium sounded less than I imagined but still seemed to echo in the quiet air.

We ran.

As I arrived at the next fence, I glanced along the side of the house where grotesque faces met my view as they headed our way and responded with a steady increase in their clamber to get to their meal.

With the ladder planted at the base, I climbed, but my feet slipped as they hit the first step. Swearing under my breath, I raised again, attempting more care to plant my feet with Alex's hands fixing the metal's shake.

Balancing on the top step, I ignored the fence, only peering with a glance over the wood before checking back along the side of the next house where the creatures were already getting within a couple of car lengths from us.

Dropping the baseball bat to the other side, I jumped and a sharp pain rose along my shin as I landed, but I would not die for the sake of a sprain. The faces of the undead spurred me on.

Running, I felt relief as I heard Alex land with a huff of air and the slap of her feet. As I turned, she launched the rifle through the air toward me, her attention turning to leaning over the fence before I'd caught the rifle midway with my left.

Indecision took hold of me for a moment as the crowd were about to pass the house and enter the garden, the stench of the sewer amplifying to catch in my lungs.

With a quick glance to Alex, I saw her struggling to pull the ladder from the other garden and over the tall fence. I let the rifle down to the flagstones and gripped the baseball bat with both my hands, raising it high over my head and took two steps forward.

Two creatures led the advance, shoulder to shoulder between the house and the wooden fence. Others stumbled and fell at their back.

I kept my stare on the tall woman to the right. I watched the barrel of fat around her midriff, her belly button on show through a rip in her shirt. My gaze traced the fabric open from her chest bone to her hips, following a scored, jagged line along her pale skin.

One, I said in my head and moved my gaze to avoid her impassive snarl.

Two. I counted in silence, turning my look to the man tall at her side. His arms were outstretched and his milky white eyes fixed on mine until something drew me to his fingers pointed in different, unnatural directions.

"Three", I said, this time letting it go with volume. I raised the bat higher, stretching out the muscles in my arms whilst trying not to think of who these people had been.

On the fourth number counted in my head, I swung down with all my breath. With the bat flying through the air I couldn't stop myself from imagining who they were before their first death.

The middle-aged mother of two, her children were doctors, one with a kid of her own on the way, fell to the floor as the wood bounced from the front of her skull to send a shiver along the ash.

The young bank clerk who'd lived with his wife and two point four kids seemed relieved when the bat returned from its lift to crack his skull open. His eyes fell closed as blood and lumps of flesh sprayed out with a sound like a melon shattering against the ground.

As the mother whose birthday it would have been tomorrow rose to her feet, I issued a second swing and she went the same way as the guy while I tried to scrub their made-up lives from my memory.

Raising the bat with blood dripping in an arc as I pulled up, my gaze fixed on the next two in line, the fairy tale of their lives already forming when the car alarms took up again in near unison.

The front two kept up their advance, but the outnumbered crowd at their backs took a slow turn, their arms pointing back out towards the road.

I twisted, racing to Alex who was at the next fence, holding the ladder ready for me to climb with the rifle shouldered over her back.

We were in the last garden before the alarms silenced and relieved to see the teeming mass of creatures were dispersing in all directions but towards us.

Alex peeled from my side, shoving the rifle from her shoulder as I peered over the last wooden fence, welcoming the thin smell of creosote cutting through the sewerage taste.

There it stood all alone. The van I'd wanted to get back to all this time.

There it was, a little dirty with red smears and new finger-sized holes near the ladder fixed to the back door, which gave me concern for the safety of its contents.

Still, there it was, a short run from the other side of the fence, with only a handful of creatures who hadn't made the journey towards the alarms.

An unfamiliar electronic song rang off from the road and I turned, catching Alex relaxing the rifle down, a wide smile gleaming across her mouth.

Up the ladder before she reached my side, I watched the backs of the last few humanlike creatures receding.

My breath paused and eyelids batted as I saw the carpet of bodies scattered across the tarmac, the shock soon replaced with a guilt-laced struggle to silence my rising joy when I saw the discarded pistols, fingers gripped around the triggers and the rifles. Real rifles loaded with dead killing bullets.

I knew I'd become desensitised to the worst. I knew my training, my prior experience of what I had called horror, took me further from the person I wanted to be.

Alex took hold of the ladder and pulled me back into the moment. I landed on bent knees in a spot I'd hastily picked out between two bodies I was desperate to consider someone's people.

Shaking away the battle in my head and the pain in my ankle, I focused on the goal. There would be time to work out how I felt. To work out if I was a bad person or if my experiences had killed my humanity, but only if I took action now for those I could still warn and save.

Arriving at the passenger door, I stretched out my fingers and pulled the cold handle. I knew already the locked door would hold firm.

I closed my eyes and my head filled with Toni in the flash of gunfire. She held out the keys in her hand as a patch of red grew around her chest, a smile widening on her face.

77

"Step aside," came Alex's breathy whisper at my back.

"No," I said, regretting the volume as I turned and found the rifle butt filling my view. I quickly stepped between the passenger window and Alex. The air rifle looked so slender compared to its big brothers scattered across the blood-soaked tarmac.

"No," I repeated in a stage whisper. "You're a locksmith and that's your plan?" I said, looking her up and down in a vain search for the tools of her trade, or at least a bulge in her trouser pocket to show she'd brought something useful with her.

"I didn't get time before the place burned," she said, struggling to keep her volume from rising through gritted teeth.

"No," I replied as she again raised the butt high. I turned along the road to check I hadn't disturbed the withdrawing masses.

The creatures still crowded, scratching at the Freelander, its hazard lights blinking and electronic beat pulsing out. Each blink drawing the creature's gnarled hands open, clicking their teeth together as they groped at the metal.

The sound soon dulled, in my head at least, as if heard through cotton wool ears. My gaze fixed on the clustered olive drab vehicles and the hint of the house where I'd been taken. Where I'd been held. Where I'd been betrayed.

"No," I said again, snapping back to see her withdraw the butt, confusion thickening on her brow as it lowered. "It's alarmed. You're just going to bring them this way and I need the van, the satellite equipment." I slowed my exaggerated nod up to the roof as her confusion melted, eyebrows raising as she processed the information.

"So where are the keys?" she said as she scanned our surroundings, shaking her head.

Turning to the side, I peered past her to look beyond the flailing mob and stare at the house where I'd last seen Toni.

To the house where she'd died.

To the house she taunted me from.

Her words came back slow and exaggerated.

"No way."

I turned to Alex, eyebrow raised as she spoke again, giving a slow shake of her head.

"You are kidding right?"

I didn't reply. I didn't lower my brow. Instead, through my distraction, I watched as she seemed to contemplate with her eyes unmoving from mine.

"So we'll need another distraction?" she eventually said with her brow furrowed.

I could have hugged her. I could have wrapped my arms around her tight.

I didn't. Instead I left my gratitude to a shallow smile, cheeks bunching as my face relaxed.

I watched her sling the air gun over her shoulder and pick her way around the dead soldiers to pluck a rifle intertwined with its former owner.

"Go around the edge," she said, pointing in the direction a copse of trees the other side of the road beside the church yard. "I'll draw them away," she added, as she raised the long gun and peered through the optical sight.

"No," I replied. "We should stay together."

She didn't listen and was already climbing the ladder bolted to the back of the van, her hands soon on the cold metal rung at the top and pulling herself up by the steel supports of the folded satellite dish.

"No," I repeated. "You should come with me," I said, gripping the wood of the bat as I crept around the back of the van.

She didn't reply, leaving her concentration to lower herself to the roof as she scanned the horizon through the sight.

Pausing for a moment with my eyes closed, I steeled myself as I listened to the background of low-pitch moans and gnashing teeth to take my first steps.

Walking along the temporary fence-line, I stopped only to stare at a soldier's feet as I peeled a pistol from his cold fingers. My first fleeting glance told me his face had gone. I couldn't linger on what was left behind for the sake of my dreams.

I didn't look back toward the van more than once, instead holding my concentration fixed at my feet whilst trying to give as little sight to weave around the bodies.

With my head full of memories I was trying not to make, I hoped Alex had heard my last words as I disappeared into the trees.

Hunger, the type everyone experienced I hoped, left a cavity in my chest and in my stomach as I walked, peering between the thick trunks with the pistol out in front. I fixed my view to the line of houses on my left, trying not to get distracted by the car alarming, its flashing lights barely seen through the crowd five or more deep as they surrounded it.

The alarm halted. I couldn't help taking in the view and notice the lights not stopping their flash. I paused my breath and step, watching as the crowd lost interest without the wail of the alarm and they spread out in what seemed like random directions.

The pain in my chest grew, but I knew it wasn't real. I knew it was just a sensation.

The hunger perhaps?

No.

Anger, maybe, but I didn't have time or the inclination to interrogate the cause.

On my own again and I knew I should have been pleased. Back in charge of my destiny, not reliant on any other. So why did I feel like something was missing?

An alarm took off in the distance and cleared my head as I watched the crowd draw their slow, ragged steps in its direction like fish to food dropped in their tank.

She hadn't needed to stay behind. She hadn't needed to play the hero. She should have been at my side.

I kicked myself as the thoughts returned.

The alarm ceased and my head once again flooded with a dreaded void. The silence broke with each twig snapping, each rustle of the thick undergrowth sounding the dinner bell, but not for me.

I'd known her for less than a day. My ex had been dead for the same time. I couldn't bear to think of her name.

The thoughts vanished again as the house came into view. I leant forward to peer at the dark scorch marks across the front and the shattered clusters of bricks which somehow still kept the building upright.

Moving to stare at each of the trucks, I was desperate not to linger on the smouldering carcasses.

There had been a great battle, the start of which I'd seen. The soldiers hadn't been the victors. With so many lain across the street, so many dead now walking, how could they have been?

I tried to ignore the scene, instead looking beyond the chaos to peer through the wide doorway. My gaze caught on the door which lay fallen against great collections of shattered bricks and splintered wood.

I moved, each step helping to dissipate the caution as I readied to make the run, my body preparing for the long strides I would need to get over the corpses.

My heart rate jumped as a car close by lit with sound, the alarm calling the dead again. About to take this as my starting bell, I heard footsteps behind and I couldn't help turn in hope to fill the gap in my chest.

I turned to see Alex, but she wasn't there. Where she should have stood, another did. Someone else walking towards me with his arms raised out. A soldier with half his face burnt beyond recognition and a bloodied, dark mess dried across his fatigues.

I dropped the bat from my hand and raised the gun. Gripping tight with both hands, I pulled the trigger and ran.

Another sound came from behind, heavy footsteps and I dared not glance back for fear of seeing the soldier gaining, but I couldn't just wait until it caught up. I stopped, twisting as best I could and brought the gun up level, already pulling the trigger nearly all the way before I saw Alex's face set in alarm as I hoped the gun wouldn't go off before my finger released.

78

I stumbled backwards, pulling the gun high just as the shot rang out from the chamber.

"Get up. Run," Alex said as her hands collected me up as I twitched, checking for wounds across her chest, but reassured with her words.

With pressure under my arms, my legs were the first to take up, my lungs pumping hard before I realised I was travelling; before I realised I was being dragged. Held up. Pulled along.

My alarm didn't hold back when I figured we were travelling away from the house. We were travelling in the wrong direction.

"No," I shouted. The words came out dry and raw. We slowed as I tried to pull my arms out from her grip. Juddering to a stop, I leant over and gasped for breath.

Alex ignored my protests as my vision cleared. With her back facing me, her head darted along the treeline.

"Hurry," she said.

I stood and looked up to see her still facing the direction we'd come. Eventually she turned, our eyes catching for only a moment until she twisted back away and pushed the sight of the rifle to her eye as she scanned the direction I needed to head.

Despite the car alarms still strong in the background, I drew a sharp breath at the sight of the crowd in the distance. I had no need for magnification, the crowd easy to see at the edge of the wood; the light it shut out obvious as they ambled in our direction.

Instead of speaking, I held my hand out, my finger shaking as I pointed toward the house we had to get to.

Turning back, Alex shook her head.

"Change of plan," she said, her words hurried as she bounded toward me.

"No," I said, pulling myself upright, but I couldn't fight as she hooked her arm around mine and pulled me deeper into the woods.

"No," I said again as I tried to force my steps into a regular pattern.

Alex's pace built with mine, increasing against my will until we were jogging and jumping over fallen trees. Somehow we found the energy to bound over sticking out roots and swerve left and right to avoid the undergrowth. We stopped only as the ground fell away out of sight.

Alex held me back from the edge. She held me too far away to see what waited in the dark.

I turned back, already knowing what I'd see and my lips curled into a painful smile at the light obscured from the treeline.

"Shoot them," I said as I laughed.

Alex looked back as if I'd lost the plot. Perhaps I had.

We both knew even emptying the magazine with a perfect aim wouldn't reduce their numbers to a survivable level.

Was this how it was going to be forever? Running for your life, never catching your breath? Were we ultimately doomed to fail? Was it really worth the constant battle? Did people really deserve to live?

Alex turned away and I watched as she surveyed around us, peering along the ground, head stuttering as she took in the tall trees. I could guess what was going through her head, but instead of joining her to look for a way out, I took in a deep breath.

My gaze came to rest on the surging crowd which had made so much progress in the last few moments. It felt as if the last of my will left me with a breath.

I glanced across the view with Alex tugging at my shoulder, but I refused to hurry back. I refused to rush to the edge of the ground falling away behind us.

I fixed my entire world on a small girl in a pale-yellow dress as she ambled at the head of the group, my only thought that the pretty dress wasn't suitable for the harsh chill in the air.

My mother's words caught in my head. *She'll catch her death*. But the great wound to her forehead meant she already had.

The virus didn't care who it affected. The illness didn't just strike down those who were ill or infirm. It didn't discriminate. Innocent or guilty, it would take everyone. If only there were hope.

The stench rolled in a great gust to my nostrils and I gagged, retching for clean air.

I had been the hope. I had been the one who'd held the power to stop this. I had been the one to warn everyone before it was too late.

My vision pulled back to take in the wider crowd now only a few steps away and wondered why I was no longer the person who would stand up to be counted. Why was I no longer the person who could change the way this would play out?

I couldn't find the reason and I turned to ask Alex the question, watching as she stared fearful to the crowd.

The words didn't come; instead they replaced with a new will to save her life first. To save those who still could be saved. I had to get to the house and find the keys so I could tell the world before it was too late.

I grabbed the arm of her shirt, dragging her stare away and peeling her from the crowd just out of our reach. Without looking to where she would fall, I pushed her over the dark edge, knowing whatever was at the bottom couldn't be much worse than our fate if we stayed put.

With a scrape of fingers to my back, I sunk to my behind and launched myself to follow down the steep incline.

79

Alex and the surrounding water caught my fall. From the chaos of the chill I rose alongside her, spitting the muddy contents whilst batting my lids to peer up to the shadows falling down the bank.

I struggled to my feet, but I could feel my fight was back. My will had hardened once again and grabbing Alex's wrist I splashed through the knee-deep water to follow the slow current heading parallel to the village.

Soon we escaped the full shadow of the canopy. Shards of light peeked through from above to show us the banks were still too steep to climb. But hope lay ahead. Hope stretched out in front as the banks first narrowed, rising higher still, the water deepening with a rapid decline, but beyond we saw the edge of the copse of trees and the sunbathed fields rolling out to the horizon.

Twisting around toward the darkness, I watched bodies continue to roll down the bank, falling into a great mess of arms and legs. Thin light highlighted gnashing teeth as some of their number rose from the murky water to take up the chase. I saw their dreams of our blood coursing, could feel as if inside their riddled minds. Their instinct desperate to pull our flesh open, but at least the dense undergrowth stopped them from following us along the bank.

We slowed with each step, taking our time as the depth grew, turning each moment to check their progress. Most who'd risen were falling again, tripping over their feet, except for two. A man and woman, both early twenties, their faces running with lines of red liquid as they kept up their chase.

Thankful the stench had calmed as they covered with water, with our feet pumping we watched ahead as over the drop the river bore to the right. We stared onward as it swept away from the village, gaining width.

My look ignored the water running fast only a few paces away and disregarded the surface, white with foam which I should have read as a big NO ENTRY sign.

We watched as the banks in the distance fell either side, levelling with the calm flow and calling us with its placid surface.

The slap of feet and the building rumble of the monotone hum from behind spurred us on, although we had no choice. We could stay and fight the two following close on our heels, but would still have to take on the rest of the building crowd whose mass had already built to dam the flow.

I looked down as the thought came to my head. I peered to the water and watched, now sure the level receded. I turned back to where we'd skidded into the river, looking past the pair whose swipes would soon connect if I didn't stop looking.

The water was receding and not because of our steps.

Alex's pull snapped me back in the direction we were travelling and made my legs rise and fall, the resistance against my feet definitely eased. I ran, knowing the gift they had given us; knowing it wouldn't last forever and when it did, I knew it would take us with it.

With every hurried step the splash of our feet grew less intense. With every step I knew we had to quicken, knowing the dam could burst and send a teeming mass of clawing creatures our way.

As we reached where the water had once been white, where only moments before water had cascaded down with the full force of nature's might, we watched the slow trickle as it wound its way through the shining rocks glistening with moisture. Now would be the worst time for the blockage to give way; the worst time for the creatures to catch up.

Bouncing down the smooth rocks on my butt, I looked up as I reached the bottom and my feet plunged to the remaining water. Alex landed only moments after I cleared.

A short sharp breath made me turn, forcing me to watch as one after the other the two chasing creatures went over the edge, with their arms reaching out for Alex despite their tumble.

Forcing myself on, the pressure against my legs gave me hope that those without dexterity couldn't follow. It left just the rising water level as my only concern. And the dam bursting.

I edged toward the far bank on my left; the packed mud rising higher than I could see over even if I stood out of the water. I felt Alex bump into my side. I felt her motion pause, as did mine.

We both heard the rumble of weight around us.

We both heard the rush of water as it charged toward us, sweeping the blockage aside; bringing with it a tumbling mess of death.

80

I grasped for roots in the bank that weren't there. I grabbed for something to pull against as the rumble of pressure grew with every moment. I found nothing but the sheer walls of dense dirt.

Breath pulled in as water reached my crotch.

I felt a shove at my side, but I didn't complain and stopped clawing the air for traction, running as best as I could; as best as my last stores of adrenalin could push.

My next footfall landed higher than I expected and I tripped forward, then was drawn back by the new current and swept along against my will. With my lungs pulling sharp for air as I sank, the water washed over my shoulders.

A firm grasp grabbed at the scruff of my jacket and I was high in the water again, cold wind washing across my soaked clothes as Alex pulled me to my feet.

We raced on, gripping hands as the banks spread, their depth lowering with every step, the flow calming.

The water receded and I gave thanks the worst hadn't come. We would be okay. I could see the shallow bank only a few steps away.

A noise at our backs made me turn. The thunderous sound distracted me from my goal and I watched the cascade of water reach the fall we'd slid down on our butts. I watched as it seemed to ignore the rules of gravity, its weight punching over the edge, bursting out towards us before crashing down and delivering the teeming mass of its passengers to where I'd tried to rise over the steep edge.

I ran on, pumping my legs through the water, knowing the pressure wave of the liquid and its solid load would roll on and push us to the side or gather us up to force an impossible fight with the scratching, clawing fingers and the gnashing teeth.

With a heave I felt myself fall to the side; a sudden lightness around my waist stopped me from falling to the water and instead launched me on to the bank. I turned, still dazed from the sudden change of position, but I had the composure to reach out and grab Alex's outstretched arm and pull her as the tirade of water caught up.

Water cascaded down our bodies as I panted for air. Our wet clothes clung tight, chilling fast in the frozen wind. In that moment neither of us could do anything but shiver for heat as we watched the great wave wash along its course, lapping up at the banks as it delivered the creatures somewhere downstream; delivered them to somewhere where the people were unprepared. To those who wouldn't understand. They would try to help the fallen and I knew what would come next.

Still catching my breath, I stared at Alex, tracing the curve of her soaked clothes across her chest, the tails of her shirt and t-shirt clinging tight to her hips. Hair flat to her face. Eyelashes dark and pronounced. A red shine to her cheeks; a feminine glow.

I watched her as if seeing for the first time.

"What?" she said, shaking her head as her brow lowered, hand brushing either cheek to clear away what she thought I might be staring at.

Broken from my trance, I turned away from the flow as I rose, unsteady to my feet.

I couldn't help but look back again, watching as the water drained from her hair to run down her face. I watched her nod, giving the smallest of smiles as her breath returned.

I looked to the woods, my body still vibrating as the chill bore further in.

We'd done it. We'd thrown them off the scent, or the water had sent them away to be someone else's problem. The only price to pay was the need to find dry clothes before hypothermia took away our choices.

I was the first to run across the meadow. Alex soon joined me as we peered through the trees, our gaze switching ahead every other moment, both of us waiting for when we'd see the creatures again and the process would repeat. I shook away the thought, unwilling to head down that path again.

It wasn't until we cleared the trees, rounding the wood as we headed to the road that we realised we were on the wrong side of the tall metal fence. Movement was obvious on the other side, as were the roofs of the olive drab vehicles crowded near the house I so much wanted to avoid; the house I had no choice but to enter.

Steeling myself with a deep breath, my teeth chattering so much I thought any moment they would fall out, I jumped high and caught the top of a fence panel, hanging from the edge as it swayed under my weight. I felt Alex's hands, warm and large, gripping around my waist as she lifted me until I could get my arms over the top and twist my left over the other side.

The fence swayed with each precarious movement; the concrete blocks at its feet stopped it from toppling.

Not waiting to find out how long it held, I twisted over the edge and lowered myself as I tried to avoid landing on the discarded bodies.

I should have kept my concentration elsewhere. I should have stopped my knees from banging hard against the metal to send out a deep, bass call as I landed.

I couldn't stay and wait for Alex to climb. I knew the drum would have called them near.

Replacing the pistol lost to the water was easy. Pulling it from the dead body's holster soaked in blood was not. Despite my best will, I couldn't take my eyes from the empty cavity where its owner's organs should have sat.

They kill every time. I said in my head. Why didn't it devour those two earlier?

Picking my way around the truck blocking my view, I ran toward the first house but ignored it. Instead, I fixed my gaze on the wide-open door to its side whilst trying to stop my running breath from pulling in their toilet smell and the decaying flesh everywhere I looked.

Peering through the open door, I saw straight through to the garden and the place where I'd run. In my head I recounted my escape after killing the woman I once thought I loved.

Had loved. Continued to love after I'd called it off, but couldn't bring myself to take another chance on her.

In the background I heard feet landing to the road, but soon a heavy tone in the air took my attention. It was a low hum which could be only one thing, but I took longer than I should have to realise I'd been right as we'd first approached the village; there had been a reason the army penned the creatures in.

The sound grew louder as Alex arrived at my back. She turned to the sky, using her hand to shade from the sun.

The aircraft was there, even though I couldn't see it.

It was there even though it would be too late for us when we could make it out. But we had no choice.

We had nowhere to run and I carried on regardless. Bounding up the stairs I ignored the blood and glass on the floor whilst I couldn't help thinking how Toni would have laughed if the bombs hit as I stood over the place where I'd taken her life.

81

Alex didn't follow. Instead, she dragged furniture in a way so reminiscent, but I couldn't recall from which place or when.

How many times had we repeated this process since the world changed? I didn't know. I couldn't tell. It was all I could do to concentrate on lifting my heavy legs while I thought of anything but what I would find as I entered the bedroom.

I looked to carpeted steps, their pile covered with mud from many boots, but my stare wouldn't stay down, kept creeping to peer to the summit.

Was this the first of the tricks played by my mind? Or was the line of blood widening as it rose real?

I couldn't remember if I'd seen it last time around. Had it been too dark when I was last here?

The question I knew I should ask was different.

Was it Toni's blood? Should I recognise it from the colour? Did it have her delicate scent I was so familiar with?

If I had truly loved her, should I be able to tell?

I couldn't.

Was that my answer?

With another step, I shook my head to clear the questions.

Alex still busied at the foot of the stairs and despite my legs feeling as if gaining weight or my muscles losing strength with each rise, I made it to the top and followed the blood to a pool in the centre of the landing. I had seen this before.

Raising the pistol and pulling back the slide to prime the chamber, I turned left into the bedroom, despite my fear and knowing it was the place I least wanted to go. Knowing it was the most likely location for what I sought; the keys to the van. Or at least I told myself they were what I looked for.

Darkness greeted me, the curtains pulled closed; the air heavy with an atmosphere not entirely projected by myself.

With my feet rooted to the threshold I couldn't see any detail.

Try as I might, I couldn't stop the chatter of my teeth, the constant vibration of my limbs and the wave of the gun as it swayed left and right to counter the buzz of my frozen arms.

Try as I might I couldn't see beyond the bed. I couldn't see past the mattress. My gaze lingered on the space where I'd been held. Where who knows what would have happened if Toni hadn't come.

With one step I drew a shallow breath, my lungs stuttering to take their fill.

With another, I lifted the pistol to point into the vague darkness.

With a third, I let go of the overdue breath, my eyes closing but only for a moment before they shot wide and I surged to her form standing at the window. At least in my head.

My sudden movement stopped the shakes. It calmed my convulsions as I grabbed at the curtains and swept left and right, drawing back as light squeezed my eyes tight.

A single tear rolled down my face, hitting the carpet soaked in blood as my gaze darted between each of the littered bandages and red sodden dressings.

I saw the chaos play out. I watched myself disappear down the stairs. I watched Toni's mother catch her in her arms and lay her to the floor, breathless and silent as she fought to find the wounds.

I watched as more joined the panic. Lights crowding, pouring their beams to the holes in her chest. Her clothes pulled up and discarded.

I opened my eyes and searched the floor, but found nothing but her drying life-force spread across the cream carpet.

Crouching, I drew in air, determined not to let more tears fall as I touched the tip of my index finger to the matted pile. In places the blood still felt sticky.

I watched as the pain drained from Toni's face in the torchlight.

I watched as she replayed my destructive force over and again in her head, her last thoughts before they brought the long black bag; before they zipped her up from heel to head.

The stairs creaked and I looked up, pulled from my moment. They hadn't made a noise as I'd climbed; at least I hadn't noticed.

I looked back down, begging for the pain once more. Begging for the punishment to fill my heart. I couldn't concentrate, the noise on the floor too great.

I stood, whispering her name.

"Alex," I said, in a voice only someone next to me would hear, but the reply was greater than I could have expected.

Alex's voice shouted a hurried command, another's deep panic matching her volume with hurried words.

As I took the first steps with the gun shaking out at my front, an explosion drowned their confrontation and a wave of energy sprayed with razors of glass as it threw me to the mattress.

82

Numb body.

Numb between my ears.

Each part of me felt like I'd lost all feeling.

The smell of burnt flesh, burnt plastic, a cocktail of unpleasantness circled around the room. Swirling, it mingled with the thin smoke clawing at my lungs. A shot of wind blasted against my sodden clothes and woke my senses as the heat turned to a chill coursing along my spine.

Glass fell to the duvet, chattering as I rose from the bed. Every muscle ached as I lifted my head. Arching my back to straighten out the kink, I stopped mid-stretch when I saw the van keys lain on the floor. They were next to the bedside table, half-buried in a pile of glass by the far wall.

A flurry of delight rushed up from my stomach until I realised the van would be useless now. Totalled.

I couldn't help a laugh drip from my mouth, my neck aching as my head shook.

What a fitting ending, an apt punishment for my humanity to end when night fell.

Alex.

Her face flashed into my head and I stood, wanting to stretch out the crick in my neck but instead grasping for the gun just out of reach.

Soon gripping the butt tight I rounded the bed, knowing I needed to save at least one bullet for myself.

With dwindling hope, I scooped up the keys and ran from the room. I didn't look back through the missing window. I didn't glance again to the blood-soaked carpet.

Steadying myself, I bounded over the scarlet puddle in the hallway, searching left and right with the gun following after; the muscles in my neck only just loose enough to comply.

To my right I saw the soles of upturned feet pointed to the ceiling. They were trainers I could guess Alex may have been wearing, the ankles dressed in white socks, disappearing behind a bed.

I took a step, promising to take more notice next time, if life gave me a chance. Glass crushed under my feet, but my gaze drew to the fluttering of the curtain and the plume of smoke passing by the window.

The bomb, the explosive, the missile, whatever, must have targeted the woods, because we weren't dead. I'd seen the result of targeted strikes before. I'd stood dressed in blue press body armour with a bulky helmet. I'd seen the gutted buildings. I'd watched while families picked through the rubble for their missing.

Speeding, I was under no illusion my steps could be the first and last if I heard the roar of jet engines on the wind again, but on my next step a figure dressed in dark clothing emerged from the right of the room, creeping out of a cupboard.

With his hand on his chest, his arm reached down to Alex's gun dropped in the blast. At least I guessed as much as I couldn't see past the bed.

With a blink I pulled the trigger, bypassing conscious thought, the explosive cracking through the air before I realised what happened.

The man slumped to the ground, his opening hand falling as Alex's foot twitched to life.

Bursting forward, I took in the detail for the first time; his black jacket, black trousers, everything dark. Even the paint covering his skin, all but his nose flat to his face, the paint smudged clean off. The wound in his shoulder poured with dark treacle as I grabbed him by the shoulder and rolled him to his back.

It was the soldier I knocked unconscious, his hand holding a scarlet dressing to his stomach. He'd been in the room when I'd killed Toni. It was his nose which popped against my knee. It was his gun I shot her with and now he was here, already bleeding to death.

I slapped him square on his cheek and his eyes flew open. Blood and black paint came away on my skin. For a moment he stared forward, but I caught the point of realisation.

I saw when he remembered, intrigued by what he saw in his head; was it my face as I lay asleep on the bed, bound with my arms spread across the mattress? Or was he the one who disconnected the ropes, only to force my unconscious hands into the cuffs behind my back?

Wherever it was, I only needed him to answer one question.

Balling my fist, I pulled my arm back, but despite all that had gone through my head I couldn't bring myself to let the punch fly.

"Where the fuck has the bitch gone?" I shouted, ignoring Alex's rise and her open-mouthed stare in my peripheral vision.

The guy stuttered, his words caught in his throat as he fought to hold back.

I lingered the gun in his direction. Thoughts of pushing it up to his wound flashed through my mind, but out of the blue my parent's faces peered down from up high, not quite in my vision as they shook their heads.

Breathing a deep breath through my nose, I held my arm steady and spoke again.

"Where the fuck is the bitch?"

He turned his gaze up from the ground and locked to mine; the pain in his expression seemed all but gone.

"Which one?" he said, letting out an exhausted breath.

I switched a look to Alex, who stared back with her mouth hanging open as she climbed to her feet.

"The doctor. The one in charge," I said, turning back from Alex as she edged back and flinched a look out to the window, her eyes shot wide and her finger pointed to the sky.

A wry smile came across the guy's face.

"Hospital, down south. Stage three," he said, reciting words he knew so well.

"Where?" I shouted over Alex's panicked calls to get to the floor.

"St Buryan Hospital. Field trials. The mother, too."

My arm fell under the weight of the gun. The weight of his words.

Had I got this right? Was Toni alive? No, she couldn't be.

The soldier's booming laughter broke my concentration for a moment.

Was she more of a liar than I could have ever known?

I needed to sit.

I needed to think on the words. I had to interrogate further, but first I needed calm.

"Shut up," I said. "Was it you who beat her when she tried to blow the whistle?" The words spat out in his direction.

He continued to laugh; if anything, the pained volume rose.

"No one beat her. No one alive anyway."

I couldn't trust anything this animal said. I needed quiet, a moment to get myself together. But he wouldn't shut up. He wouldn't stop the laughter.

The moment I craved came in slow motion as I sat to the bed. Turning, I watched Alex diving soundless to the floor, despite her agitated breath. I couldn't hear the words her mouth formed, only the shock wave from the explosion ripping the curtains from the window and forcing me sideways into the wall.

83

Still numb, but not from the explosion, I picked myself up. Dust fell to the ground as I stepped over the soldier's motionless body to pull Alex up by the arm as she reached out.

I led the way down the stairs with my ears ringing, my view swimming in and out. I didn't stop to check left and right; I no longer cared if there were dead searching us out. With my view fixed on a patch of white panel and the bold letters down the side I'd clung to for so many years, I trudged on with my hand clasped around hers, pulling, dragging as she stumbled by my side.

In my periphery I saw cars shunted, their windows smashed and heard a cacophony of alarms coming into focus. A great fire consumed the trees and wooden shrapnel littered everywhere I placed my feet.

I saw movement, but didn't watch. I saw the shapes sharpen into the creatures, their bodies covered with red, their skin torn off, stripped bear with the wave of energy.

They saw us and headed our way, stumbling no more, no less than before.

Alex gripped my hand tight by my side as she built her strength. We dragged each other, both knowing our direction as the pace built to a level we could barely manage. Our course steered to avoid the debris, the cars blown in our path. The shards of fist-sized wooden splinters peppering each body panel.

I took no notice as a dead soldier, or at least the half remaining, lunged out to grasp as I stepped over. Alex pulled me to the side just out of its reach. My features didn't react, my mouth didn't turn from its thin line. The only glimpse of feeling I felt was at the sight of the van which had been too far from the blast, its windows still intact.

The keys were in my hand but I had no recollection of reaching inside my jacket. I felt like an observer watching a replay of my actions. Watching as I pushed the thin metal of the key into the lock at the back door.

Twisting and pulling free.

Watching as the handle clicked, my fingers somewhere in the picture. Watching as clawed fingers reached through the gap and a foul odour pushed me back. Waking from the trance a moment later as the door pushed me away and I fell, slamming hard to the metal fence.

I'd forgotten all about her.

The woman we'd picked up. The woman Toni had killed, but I couldn't think her bad for that. I was a killer now, too.

She said it was an accident. I hadn't meant to take Toni's life, either, but now I knew there was more to her. She knew my heart would melt when I saw her wounds. But who caused them? Was it her mother, as she'd said? Or another? No one alive, he'd said. I'd killed him as well.

Still, this moment was not the time to process how I felt. Now was not the time to unpick the story. To replay the soldier's words or to attach any meaning to his incessant laughter just before his death.

Now was the time to stand the hell up. To stop feeling sorry for myself and do something before the woman rising from her feet in front of me launched in my direction and got her revenge.

I stood, still staring on with the last of my days flashing across my view.

Alex charged in from my side, grabbing a pistol from a dead soldier's hand. Without the top half of his head, the soldier had no use for it.

She pushed the woman to the ground and slammed two rounds to shatter her skull.

The explosions woke me to Alex's stare, her furrowed brow asking a question. Was I broken beyond repair?

I answered; I owed this once sweet girl that and much more.

"Thank you," I said. "This is fucked up."

She gave a slow, dazed nod.

"We'd better go," I said, looking to the sky, hoping the new dot on the horizon wasn't another jet.

I looked to the woods, knowing the blackened, smoking creatures walking towards us were what I knew them to be.

She nodded again after following my view, slamming the door behind her as she climbed in alongside me and slid the bolt, following me to the passenger seat.

I would have spoken. Alex would have, too, but neither of us could pull our hands from our noses as we tried to hold back the stench of death left behind.

The engine started and I almost gagged as the breath of relief came, but turned to the window. I knew I couldn't give them even a crack to get their clawed fingers into. I sucked down the bile and heaved the steering wheel to avoid the car pushed up against the bumper.

Swapping glances with Alex, I could see her knuckles white on the armrest and door handle either side.

I closed my eyes as the engine pushed the van backwards and tried not to think of the crushing bones the suspension couldn't mask as it pitched us one way and then the next.

Bumping to the fence, we slammed to a stop, the echo resounding like a bass drum.

Moving forward, I couldn't pretend it was just a bumpy road, despite my attempts. We could see the bodies, those of dead soldiers and residents. Those who had died and stayed dead and those who had not.

The great tyres rolled over in vain of my best efforts to avoid. I guessed there were at least half of the creatures left alive by the blast as they swarmed towards us. I checked I'd locked my door more times than I could have counted while we rolled along, watching the horizon for an opening in the fence whilst keeping an equal look to the skyline, searching for the dot in the centre growing bigger with every moment.

It was then I realised I hadn't thought this through.

Yes, we were safe in the van, despite the surrounding crowd, but we had nowhere to go. We had no chance to get away from the next missile surely on its way.

I stopped with the bonnet of the van almost at the fence, then let it creep forward until nudging contact with the metal.

The metal complained as the bumper touched, but it stayed firm. I thought of the great concrete blocks on the other side. I thought of the huge square containers of water pushing down the uprights.

The dot grew and blackened hands slapped at the windows. Neither of us jumped. Neither of us panicked.

I turned and asked her down-turned face a question. "Is this how it ends?"

84

She didn't reply to my fear-filled question; instead, turning to the hands slapping at the window, fixing for a moment before her head tilted high.

Her move soon stopped with eyes spreading wide.

Mine followed, coming to rest on the growing dot just above the fence line.

"No," she said. The words were much louder than I'd expected. "The gardens."

I twisted in my seat to meet her puzzled gaze.

"Their fences," she added, but still I shook my head.

As her face screwed up, the frustration grew clear, but still I didn't understand what she meant.

She leant towards me. "That's how we get out," she said, the words in a near whisper.

I paused for a moment, her voice catching in my mind as the electrical pulses traced across my synapses, sparking the first trace of understanding. I followed the route appearing in my head, tracking backward through the journey as the crowd scratched at the paintwork.

We turned the corner down the short street, the road turning to gravel and veered right before reaching the metal fence to see the rolling hills over the two sets of short wooden fences.

"Yes," I said, with eyes electrified wide with energy.

The dot had grown even in my moment of pause. It was too slow to be a plane. It wasn't a jet racing towards us to fire another salvo.

I pushed it out of my mind, releasing the accelerator to calm the engine and selected reverse.

Heavy on the accelerator once again, the van moved backwards as I hurried my view to the left mirror, mindful of the cars strewn in our path.

"Holy shit," came Alex's voice. It wasn't the response I'd expected and snapped a look to her. "It's heading towards us."

I looked up to see she was right. The aircraft was larger in the windscreen and pointed in our direction.

Alex's voice hurried. "Can't they see we're moving? Don't they know the dead can't drive?" Her breath ran hard as she spoke.

I turned back to concentrate on our best chance of escape, cataloguing the sight to remember when I spoke to the camera. Or if.

I concentrated on turning the van, on trying to avoid the creatures and the great trunks of trees littering the road whilst maintaining momentum.

With each turn of the wheel, each crunch of the tyres, each time I couldn't avoid a great splinter, a great chunk of concrete, I thought we'd grind to a halt. I knew I had to keep the momentum up. I knew I had to keep our speed as I followed the journey I'd taken in my mind only moments before.

The layout of the road was the same as I'd seen in my head. I don't know why I expected any different. The van was harder to control, the sideways shift of our weight greater as its bulk listed in the turn, the tyres slipping against the litter in the road.

We leant against the list to balance gravity from taking us over. Somehow we made it, the wheels scraping along the kerbstones to aid us upright.

Still, I continued to pile on the speed with my gaze fixed on the last-minute change of direction I'd need. The turn we'd have to make. The second leap of faith we'd need to take us through the fence and into the garden and beyond, through the next and out into the freedom of the grassy hills.

We made it almost intact, just leaving the air from the front left tyre behind with the impact of the last low fence.

The suspension fed us every lump in the grass. Every divot. Every hole bleeding speed with each revolution of the rim, despite my foot being flat to the floor.

I had little control, but somehow kept us facing out to the moor. Kept us heading away from the village and the great gaping hole I'd made in what had kept us safe; in what had kept those around us from the horde.

With no barrier in their way, what remained of the creatures, burnt and skinless, would be free to roam if they survived the explosion, whose shock wave seemed to touch every atom in my body.

Slowly we recovered from the blast and I realised I'd taken my foot from the accelerator and the van had come to a rest. The wheels just slipped as I tested the pedal.

With a quick glance in the mirror at the creatures I could have guessed would make their way along our trail, I leapt out, Alex throwing me the pistol as she followed.

Whilst she dived underneath the van to search for the spare tyre, I took slow paces toward the first creatures making their way and the procession which had already formed a long trail.

Counting thirty in their slow amble, I tried to work out if we had enough time. I tried to work out if I had enough bullets, then hoped in vain I could put three down with each.

85

At my command, or it seemed so at first, an explosion detonated at the far end of the undead procession. Disintegrated flesh flew skyward in a foul spray, slapping down to the ground in a shower I could only use my forearm to protect against.

Ignoring the stench of burnt flesh, I looked up to the drone whose shape was now more than obvious.

I wanted to wave at the pilots. I wanted to see their faces so I could thank them. I wanted to shake their hands and put them on camera to tell the nation not to worry because they were on the case. I wanted to tell the world they had our backs, even though they were in no danger of contracting the terrible virus themselves.

With those thoughts running through my head, I looked back to the trail and counted what remained. A laugh lifted from my chest when I saw I only had to put two down with each of my shots.

Stepping back, I waited, hoping for the next launch to even the odds. I was ready to turn and take cover from the spray of barbecued stink.

The whine of the drone's engine changed as I counted in my head, heart fluttering, optimism draining even before I twisted up to the sky. I saw its grey underbelly as it turned away, its thin wings empty of the long missiles which could cut the odds to something more manageable.

Pulling in a deep breath, I glanced behind, but turned away at Alex's frustration. For the second time the jack ripped from under the van as she released it to stop it from sinking through the grass with each turn of the handle.

I closed my eyes and let my held breath out before drawing another, as slow as I could manage though my nose. I regretted the need to pull air when the foul stench came in the breeze.

Opening my eyes, I bit back the surprise as I saw the blackened pack had been closing the gap for longer than I thought.

The creatures were so much closer. In a moment they'd be in arms reach. I had to give Alex time.

I ran at a right angle, heading deeper to the moor whilst watching their heads for a decision; watching what remained of their minds choose who would be on the buffet.

I forced the decision, firing off a shot which glanced off the lead creature's shoulder, despite knowing each shot which wasn't a direct hit in the head meant increasing the number I would need to kill with each remaining round as its blood sprayed in lumps across its companions.

As the ground became more uneven, I had to slow my backwards walk. The first few stumbles were too much for my heart to take. Declaring myself as the tastier treat, I released off a second shot to reassure the handful whose decisions were waning.

The shot took down the lead twice-baked creature, tripping two who followed close behind which gave me a welcome moment to catch my breath.

With one eye on the rising van, I continued to lead them further away. With each step I felt the water still in my trainers and the damp running through my clothes, the rub of harsh fabric seams on my skin.

What I wouldn't give for a rest, a cat nap then maybe a shower, or a soak in a bath surrounded by scented candles, drying myself with a fluffy warm towel and stepping into dry clothes not covered in decaying human flesh.

I thought of Toni; her smile as she knelt down beside the bath, her fingers dancing on the surface of the water, promising her touch. I stumbled back, twisting to see what had caught my foot with my hands wheeling through the air, the pistol heavy until it fell.

At first I thought it was a judge's wig, then I saw the animal's belly wide open; the great rend surrounded a cavity picked clean of the organs, blood and dark gristle clinging to the woollen edges.

I saw all of this before my ass hit the grass to send a jarring pain shooting up through my spine. I froze with panic as I looked to the cloudless blue sky. The view was all too soon interrupted with a blackened, bald head rearing down, its yellowed teeth poking out from burnt gums, snapping open and closed.

My eyes fixed on the pink of its tonsils as the sky blotted out. My hands were blind as they swept the ground for the gun.

86

The fingers of my right hand jarred against something cold and hard, curling around its irregular edges before I knew what I held; bringing it up before I could move my head. Leaving my coordination alone to draw the rock down on the wide jaw, I sent its blackened head twisting around.

With a second blow, my heels pushed hard to get a grip. The rock smashed against its temple and the thick blood spraying out was the least of my concerns. The charred once-human went down, its body dropping where it stood and its heavy head smacked against my empty belly to send a wave of pain and nausea up through my throat.

Still, I was more concerned not to feel its teeth unpicking my flesh.

When pain didn't sear through my once-white vest I knew it was dead for the final time, or at least unconscious, if that was still a thing.

I had no time to think about whether they had a consciousness to come out of before I saw two charcoaled creatures taking its place in the attack, one either side with their hands out in front, lipless mouths wide as they mashed their teeth.

I threw the rock at the head of the one to the left, which I regretted as soon as my fingers released and long before the rock bounced harmless from the side of its face and landed with a thump to my stomach to force the wind from my chest.

With my hands flailing left and right, I couldn't decide what to do next as the creatures loomed down.

My hand slapped hard against something white flashing by to my right, leaving a trail of fumes in its wake and sending pain radiating up my arm as nerves told me of the bones broken into too many bits from the impact, the stars in my eyes only confirming.

Despite the veil of pain pulling at my thoughts, I saw there was only one row of assailants left. To the right I could see the rolling hills of the moor with the village in the distance.

White flashed again. I heard the roar of the van's engine, but this time to the left as I remembered I still had to defend myself, despite having only one usable hand.

As I looked up to the sudden change of colour, I saw the black of the creatures silhouetted against white, the large letters so well recognised hovering above its head.

With the slam of a door, Alex appeared at my side. She punched the last remaining creature square in the temple, then twice more before it went down.

Alex bent and I was on my feet, shoved in through the open passenger door. All I could feel was the oppressive warmth as we bounced over the ground with my hand throbbing as it nestled limp in my lap.

"Are you okay?" Alex said with hurried breath between glances shot my way, first to my face, then to my hand as I cradled it, wincing with each rise and fall over the uneven grass.

I nodded, gesturing for her to look forward, not wanting her to miss some other trap in the road; something else that would block our path or rip the wheels from the axle to prevent our progress.

With my breath settling, I stared at the strewn, lifeless bodies in the mirror, then watched them again as the van turned. The bodies were still.

I watched as we drove past the abandoned flat tyre, the block of wood Alex must have found in the back to rest the jack on top of to stop it disappearing into the grass.

The sky was clear until I peered over to the village, where the wind blew thick smoke in the opposite direction, turning the bright daylight to night. It seemed as if there wasn't a single part of the horizon which wasn't burning, or smouldering with toxic smoke.

I took hope. The bombing had worked, despite our breach in their containment. There were no undead still walking to greet us. Maybe, just maybe they'd put a stop to this before the end.

The pain had dulled by the time we were back on the smooth tarmac, with my gaze scouring the horizon and the sky for movement; for any sign of the living or the dead.

"Thank you," I said.

"No need," she replied. "You gave me the time I needed. I'm sorry about the hand. How is it?"

I looked down, afraid of what I'd see, but it wasn't deformed or out of shape. The skin was darkening underneath and swelling as I watched.

I tried a tentative movement. I was brave enough to make sure I could see the first signs as I wiggled my fingers.

"I don't think it's broken, but it fucking hurts."

"I'm sorry," she replied.

"Rather pain than death."

"And," Alex said, then stopped.

"I'm fine," I replied, knowing she couldn't bring herself to ask how I felt otherwise. And I was fine. The pain in my hand totally distracted me from any other sensation.

Her only reply was a shallow nod as her head fixed forward. She placed the gun which had been resting on her lap to the seat in between us without moving her view.

"What now?" she said, as she slowed for a T-junction with no signs showing the way.

"St Buryan," I said, pulling out the Sat Nav from the glove compartment and handing it over to Alex after trying to turn it on with my left hand.

She nodded and found the town. Letting the minicomputer choose the route, she took the first left on the deserted road.

As the van rolled forward, I watched the numbers in the corner fall from sixty.

As we drove along, I felt restless in the seat. I couldn't get comfortable, despite my fidgeting. It wasn't the pain in my hand, but something else I couldn't put my finger on that wouldn't let me settle.

"We're stopping for a change of clothes, too," she said after a few moments.

I closed my eyes, the thought of the candlelit bath coming into focus.

"And painkillers and food."

I let a smile bloom as we rolled down the narrow country road which was only just wide enough for the white lines to mark the two lanes. The stretch of my lips fell as Toni's image appeared in my mind; her bruised face and curled lip drew my guilt back from where it had rested.

I heard her voice as she made the call which brought me here. The call that tempted me back to her. I'd fallen all the way down the rabbit hole at her command. She'd called me for help. She said she needed me, but was it the reason I came? Or was it the want of a story or a break from the monotony of my life?

Alex said my name, pulling me from the trance and I turned from the window, opening my eyes even though they hadn't shut.

When she didn't speak again, I drew back to the road and saw the junction leading four ways. I looked to the little screen and saw we needed to head straight over, but the giant concrete cubes blocked the way and even if we could get past, cars were parked the other side with their doors open, boot lids high, glass missing from the windows. Bodies lay across the road, more adding to the total in my head as the van trundled on, slowing with each passing moment.

I saw soldiers, civilians and a tear caught in my eye as I watched a young body in a red top, its colour leeching to the road. My gaze caught on a column of black smoke rising in the distance, then on another.

Five more fires scattered across the view, but it wasn't until I saw a figure walking towards us from between the cars, a line of blue seen through the great hole in their once pristine white coat, that the emptiness returned to my stomach and I closed my eyes.

"Oh my god, Toni. What have you done?"

87

"Get the camera out," I said, turning to Alex.

"What, here?" she said, staring back wide-eyed as the van rocked to a stop.

"We've got to film this," I said, motioning out to the roadblock. "We've got to let people know. This is how we can help. This is how we can make a difference."

Alex stared at me for what felt like a long while, but as we both turned to the figure, I could see she'd only made it a few steps closer to us.

Alex wiped her mouth on the back of her hand as she took a hard swallow.

"This is…," she said, but couldn't finish. "Back there…" she said, trying again. "Wasn't that the end? I thought we'd seen it all. I thought we were heading away from the trouble."

I nodded. I'd thought the same. I'd thought we were in the middle, the epicentre, but here the military had been stopping people getting out of somewhere we wanted to go. They were stopping people going north and it wasn't difficult to guess why they were trying to get away.

"So did I," I said, sliding along the seats. I twisted toward her, sucking back the pain as I placed my left hand on her shoulder. "There's no dressing it up. This couldn't be worse. It could be the end of the country. The end of the world. But imagine if people could know what's coming. Imagine if they had a chance to prepare, or to even just lock their doors because they know what's heading their way. If we," I said, giving as much emphasis on the words as I could spare, "if we could expose what's happening and who's pulling the strings, we might stop it from going any further."

If only I could live through the night without killing you.

For a moment I wasn't sure if I'd voiced the last words.

Alex looked to my good hand as it drifted down her arm and I pulled away, watching her brow lower.

"We need to tell the world," I said. I wasn't ashamed of the pleading in my tone. "We need to find those who did this. We tell everyone what they've done."

Alex turned back to the road without a reply. I watched as her gaze fixed on the child's body which lay alone. I watched as she followed the road before lingering on the creature, stumbling every other moment as it passed between the concrete blocks, its white eyes fixed square on our windscreen.

Alex nodded, but didn't turn in her seat.

"But not here. We need to keep safe," she said, her voice flat and void of emotion. "We need to find somewhere to rest and get out of these wet clothes." She nodded as she spoke. "We need food and to figure out how these cameras of yours work."

I looked out through the windscreen with a slight smile rising on my lips. She was right. If we did this right here, we were likely to mess it up through fatigue.

I didn't complain as the wheels rolled; instead, I forced myself to look at the child and to take in her pale cold face. I forced the memory to form so I could describe her in great detail to the people of the nation.

We varied our journey more times than I could count to avoid roadblocks found at almost every turn, my gaze flitting to the rising and falling number in the corner of the Sat Nav and the sun sinking further with each passing moment.

A feeling nagged just out of reach.

After two hours we'd cleared ten miles, but we should have been in the hospital carpark setting up the camera rather than watching from so far away as the sun touched the horizon.

When we came across a lone cottage on the side of the road, we both agreed without words we should stop and do the things we knew we should.

Alex hadn't slowed the van for long before we saw the long line of blood covering the path which led to the front door.

Darkness fell soon after we moved on, leaving only our headlights, the stars and the moon, half bright in the sky. Alex drove with care, knowing we had no spare tyre, careful to avoid debris between the cars littered to the side, each pushed at rough angles down ditches and into hedges to clear a path.

With little other choice, she pulled the van into the car park of a wide single storey white building. The headlights were bright on its sign across the front, giving more than a flutter of optimism at the words 'Cash and Carry' in yellow on the dark board.

Alex drove around the perimeter in slow motion, turning the wheels for the headlights to scan every surface. The shutters at the front were down, but two wooden rear doors looked like they wouldn't present Alex with much of a challenge. We parked around the rear.

"You got a toolbox?" she said, looking into the back.

I shrugged. "I guess," I said, and watched her disappear between the seats.

The realisation of what had nagged at my thoughts sprang to the front when Alex switched the light on.

I saw the vial, or what remained, the red liquid soaking into the carpet and already drying around the broken glass edges.

My eyes closed and shoulders hunched as I realised this would be my last night on Earth.

88

"We have to do it now," I said, as Alex continued to search through the racks lining the walls. "We have to…" I said, but the lump in my throat held the rest of the words back.

Alex turned, dragging a small box to the floor which she placed next to the red mess on the carpet. She let the handle drop and turned up to see my gaze fixed to my last hope.

"Your medicine?" she said, her words seemed distant.

I gave a shallow nod. She kept quiet, not replying for a long moment.

"How long have you…?"

A shake of my head was the only reply for a long while as I stared.

"No idea," I eventually said, closing my eyes and drawing in a deep, slow breath as I tried to relax; tried to slow the thoughts racing through my head.

How long did I have?

Could I feel it coming already?

The hunger felt obvious, a sensation I'd learnt to dread, but the emptiness in my stomach wasn't alone, accompanied with a deep pain in my chest and a vacant chasm where blood forced out to my body.

"What can I do?" Alex said, her voice solemn as she put out a hand to her side.

I pulled back a step and out of her reach. "I should go," I replied, with no time between the words.

Alex shook her head.

"You don't understand," I replied, but she wouldn't relent.

"It's too dangerous at night. We'll end up in a ditch on the side of the road or in the middle of nowhere with no chance of help. Is that how you want it to end?"

"If you knew the alternative..."

Alex took a step closer, her hands taking mine.

"You never said what happened if you didn't get the medicine," she said, squeezing my hands and drawing me closer.

I stood on the spot, taking in her words. I had to go.

"I think you know already," I said, biting my bottom lip. If Toni really was still alive, I had to be next to her when it was all over, but I couldn't have Alex near me when the end came. The plan formed as the thoughts scattered across my brain.

I would wait for her to leave to pick the lock. When the door opened and she was inside, I'd take the van and hope I could make it as far as the hospital. I knew Toni would welcome me in. I knew she'd be grateful to see me and then I would change. I would let myself go; go all the way without holding myself back.

She'd be the first victim of the monster waiting to burst out, then I'd end it all. She'd be the one and only.

Opening my eyes, I turned to Alex.

"Never mind," I said. "Let's get inside."

I watched as she smiled, picking up the toolbox before opening the van door and peering either side for a moment.

Soon at the building, she concentrated on the door lock as I moved to the driver's seat, whilst watching left and right for visitors as I practiced in my mind what I would do when I saw her disappear through the door.

She had the door opened before I'd thought it through. Now was the time and I went to put my hands on the steering wheel, but had to stifle the scream as the pain in my right hand told me of how stupid my plan had been.

Alex was already back out, her face beaming, eyebrows twitching when she saw the grit of my teeth on opening the driver's door.

"You okay?" she said.

I nodded.

"You'll love this place," she added, forcing herself to keep her voice low.

I drew a deep breath, pushing up my on-camera smile and let her help me down the tall step; let her guide me through the door as she angled a torch from the toolbox out in front.

Alex's torch pointed out the corridor with doors to the left and right.

I saw the radiators clinging to the walls, wondering if the pipes would be strong enough to hold the cuffs when I tried to rip my hands free.

Alex shone the light on the storeroom packed with rows of boxes on shelves.

I saw the door banded with steel, trying to figure out where the owners kept the key and if the windows were strong enough to keep Alex safe.

Alex marvelled at the rows of shelves containing boxes of food, much like a supermarket, racks of clothes on rotary hangers, giant numbers corresponding to multipack boxes at their side.

I saw the lack of bolts holding the steel to the concrete floor, knowing I would pull it free. Knowing I would drag it behind me when I turned.

"It's great, isn't it?" she said, looking back with almost a skip in her step as she pointed to a row of torches hanging on shelves by their fabric cords as she passed.

"Yeah, great," I said, my underwhelming words quiet once she'd gone. "A great place to die," I said, scanning the shelves, not taking any notice of what I'd seen.

I wandered through the aisles, catching sight across the shelves as Alex made trips outside, her gaze finding mine each time she came through the door carrying the plastic equipment boxes from the back of the van.

After locking the door closed, she toured the aisles with her white smile beaming as she bundled blankets, food and water into her arms before heading to the back of the shop.

I slowly toured the aisles, finding scarlet trousers to near enough match the jacket to replace the skirt I wore with the great tear down the side.

After what must have been half an hour, Alex came to find me. She carried two lit torches in her hands and passed one over as she guided me to the rear. I couldn't stop my mouth forming a smile as she shined her torch beam on the nest she'd been building.

Alex had cleared away racks of clothes, pushing them to the side. In the space she'd piled ten or more blankets on the floor to form two rectangular beds, both spaced a good distance apart. Around each bed she'd placed unlit candles, batteries and boxes of food beside bottles of water and a first aid kit resting on the top of the bed to the left.

My eyebrows raised at the jeans and T-shirt spread in the centre.

I twisted toward her. "Risky business."

"Huh?" she replied.

"Choosing a lady's clothes," I said, and couldn't help letting a gentle laugh trickle after.

"We should change," she said, her voice quiet and stilled as she watched my eyebrows raise and my face contort as I winced with the lift of my hand from my chest.

"I can…" she said, then stopped, filling the air with a pause. "I can help, if you don't mind," she said. The words were slow and broken.

Her voice caught me by surprise. Well, not the voice itself, but my body's reaction. In the silence I could hear her breath; hear mine, too, but I hoped she couldn't sense the sudden race of the engine in my chest.

This wasn't a good time for life to get more complicated.

89

My eyes closed despite the darkness when she threw the lit torch to the makeshift bed. Her fingers crept along the hem of my vest. I slowly lifted my arms as her hands climbed, my skin prickling with heat. Goose bumps rushed across my torso and not just because of the cold air licking at my damp skin.

The sensation kept my mind from the pain and I lifted both my hands high before sinking to my knees, the vest rising over my head.

She stood at my back, throwing the top to the pile with the jacket.

I waited, listening to her breath as somehow the calm air brushed across my body to lick away the last of the moisture, my skin alive with sensation; every inch prickling with electricity.

"Your bra?" she said, her words slow and punctuated with a heavy swallow. The deepness of her voice forced a pull of breath.

When I didn't speak, I felt the tension in the wet strap release.

With a rip of plastic, she pulled a t-shirt from its packet and I knelt in front of her, opening my eyes with my breath catching in my throat when I saw her outline. She was looking with her head shaking from side to side, the room brighter than I'd expected. I could see more detail than I thought possible. So could she.

In the soft light from the torch and with my hands still to the air, I looked up as she concentrated, my body tensing as she guided the fabric first over my bad hand.

I stood, letting my hands relax. She took one side of the hem and I took the other. Together we dragged the top down and I tried not to react as the fabric snagged on my nipples.

The rest I could manage and I let the skirt drop, my left hand hovering at the band of my knickers. I don't know why my mouth curled or why I'd bitten down on my bottom lip as Alex stared at my silhouette with my shadow looking back.

Eventually she bent to the side and pulled a pair of fresh underwear from the pile.

"Do you…?" she said.

I held back my reply, instead taking a moment to swallow down my thoughts and confusion at my body's reaction.

"No, thank you. It's fine," I said, and took the cotton from her hand and disappeared behind an aisle of clothes to finish dressing. I waited longer than the time it had taken to dress trying to resolve the feelings in my head.

"Thank you," I said, pretending to myself I felt no disappointment when she'd already changed as I arrived back to see the candles flickering in the clearing.

We ate cold beans from cans without talking. I didn't care, each mouthful soothing my pain as I listened to the air void of sound other than from my companion eating. Tiredness fogged my thoughts. I hadn't slept since I didn't know when and I could feel myself drifting, eyes heavy. My heart rate spiked as I thought of waking and not knowing who I was.

"You need to tie me up."

Alex sat up straight, not giving a reply.

"I need to sleep," I said, but she didn't get my meaning, her brain clearly frozen on the words. "It's not safe to be around me. You need to tie me up in case I can't control myself."

I felt frustration bubbling in my belly; at least I hoped it was the reason for the feeling. I saw the confusion on Alex's face, along with the smile she was trying to force down.

"I won't fuck you," I snapped, the raise of my voice echoing across the room. "You're safe from my advances, but if the medicine I've already had isn't enough, then you won't know what hit you."

Her face fell with my words and the abrupt change in mood. She stood, disappearing out of the light. Her voice carried softly from the darkness.

"It's not like that," she said. "You're safe from me, too. I'm not into…"

The words vanished to nothing as I closed my eyes. Letting go of a deep breath, I used my good hand to rub the water from my eyes.

I heard her before I saw her shape in the shadows. I heard the rattle of the chain before I saw its gleam in the flicker of the candle.

By that time I'd already clipped the cuff around my good wrist with the empty bracelet, ready to clip to the free end once its length had encircled the pipes leading up to the radiator on the far wall.

With the bracelets fixed, she hadn't said a word and I lay down, turning back and forth to find comfort and closed my eyes.

I couldn't think of her feelings in that moment. All I could concentrate on was what it felt like to feel human and hoping I would see the morning with the same perspective.

***

I opened my eyes.

I was alive. I was me. I was the same as when I'd fallen asleep. I felt no need I hadn't felt before this all happened. Toni had lied about so much; maybe she was lying about the dose I needed.

An engine revved too hard close by, but it was moving away.

The room was the same, but different in every way. Daylight poured from the skylights I hadn't noticed last night. I turned for Alex to shout for her to wake, to call out so she would know someone was stealing the van.

Her hand-built bed was empty, the gun missing from where it had rested at her side.

If this wasn't a dream, I'd made it through the night. But if this wasn't just inside my head, I'd not only scared away my camera operator, she'd abandoned me and left me for dead.

90

The pain in my hand told me it wasn't a dream. The dull ache in my swollen fingers was an improvement on the sharp stab with each pump of my heart before I'd slept. The rattle of the chain as I sat up rang high in my ears, confirming it wasn't the result of chemicals forming pictures in my mind; as did the hunger deep in my belly when I surveyed the ruffled blankets where I'd slept to see if she'd at least left me the key.

She hadn't.

I should have known. Why had I trusted someone I'd only just met, despite what we'd already been through together in the short time? Maybe Toni had been right all along. Maybe I couldn't be trusted not to stray given half a chance. Maybe I trusted too easily, despite what I'd seen in my career and the training Toni had inadvertently given me. Why did I throw that experience out of the window any time someone paid me any attention?

I laughed whilst shaking my head. Was it only a day since we'd met? But my thoughts darkened as the sound of the engine faded further into the distance.

Why had she left? I still struggled to think of her as a woman, despite the evidence. Had I damaged her ego when I said those things? The way she reacted to my words. Had I seen things between us, from her, that weren't there? Had I scared her off with thoughts she didn't want to bring to the surface?

Or was it all in my head?

Pressure rose in my chest; the knot in my stomach grew at the thought of her not even unlocking my bounds or leaving me the key. She knew I would be at the mercy of the first person to come through the door, alive or otherwise.

Since I'd been a teen, I'd needed no one. Never a man or a woman before now and I hated Toni even more for putting me in this position. I knew she'd always wanted me in her control. Our fights, the end of our serene weeks together came, at least partly, because I am my own person. Toni could never call me hers. I would never submit myself to another. I would never stop being me until my heart ceased beating in my chest.

At least that phrase still had meaning. Although the dead rose, they weren't the people they were when they'd lived.

Standing, I traced out a semi-circular path the extended chain would allow. I swallowed down the rising bile and tried to reach out for the shelves as the chain links scratched against the pipe jutting to the wall, the metal like an amplifier. Still, I couldn't reach any of the potential tools my imagination hoped could help free my bounds.

My gaze fell on one of the rugged plastic boxes Alex had opened by her bed and the smallest of the cameras set up on a tripod, the lens pointing down the aisle.

I held my gaze, stopping my survey and taking a deep breath when I saw the manual open on Alex's makeshift pillow.

Why had she bothered to try and figure out the camera when she was planning to run in the morning?

The thoughts fell as I heard a gunshot outside. A second came soon after with the crunch of gears in the distance. A third followed, with barely a space as another shook the air, turning me to the windows blocked by the shutters.

I pulled hard on the chain, yanking till the tension was too much for my wrist when it hadn't come loose, hadn't released its grip.

I drew a deep breath and held still to welcome the silence, suddenly aware of my noise inviting unwelcome guests.

I listened for more gunfire, for engine sounds and I tried to keep still while searching around.

My gaze fell on anything heavy. Water bottles. A can of beans still sealed. Anything I could wield one-handed.

I continued to search for what would give me the best defence against whatever made the slow footsteps coming from the corridor.

91

The tin of beans weighed heavy in my hand, adding to the downward pull of the chain clinging at my wrist. With the footsteps getting near, I daren't raise the tin high, too afraid the rattle of the metal links would further advertise my presence.

Breath caught as I heard another sound, the drag of something bulky along the floor behind each echoing step. I tried to ignore the worst pictures forming inside my head with each passing moment.

Searching left and right, I was desperate to find a space to hide; to find somewhere to give cover, somewhere I'd overlooked all this time. No matter how much I checked, my gaze flitting around the clearing, no miraculous safe room appeared.

Movement flashed into view through the doorway and I raised the can, the chains coming alive with song as I propelled the tin as best I could towards the figure until the cuffs snapped back at the full extent of my reach. The can bounced off the torso, splitting against the tiles and sending tomato sauce flooding the floor as it skidded to a stop.

I stood open-mouthed, Alex lifting her head as if struggling to raise it. The first stage of a bruise reddened her cheek.

My gaze followed down her arms, skipping from the gun in her right to the bundle of heavy clothes held in her left. A mop of mousey brown hair fell around her hand as she held the bundle by the scruff of a jacket, a trail of blood left in their wake.

I backed away until the chain would let me go no further. Fear raged through my chest until her gaze found mine across the room. Her eyes wide and seeking my attention.

Alex threw the gun to my bed and bent down, turning the sack over and sweeping the hair to reveal a young woman's dirty face.

Watching on as Alex bent over and slid up the blood-soaked left leg of her own jeans, she looked up as I peered at the black shard of metal stuck in the side of Alex's ankle below the stark black of a tattoo, whose shape I couldn't quite make out.

Alex's hand reached out for the first aid kit beside my bed. I rushed over, the chain rattling in my wake.

She shook her head, the pain obvious as she pushed her hand to her pocket and pulled out the handcuff key to swap it for the open green box.

"What happened?" I said, with the key, sticky with her blood, held in my good hand whilst looking at how I was going to get the lock open with the swollen fingers on my left. "I woke and you'd gone. I thought..."

She didn't reply. Instead, shook her head as she rifled through the contents of the small kit, letting the packages spill to the floor.

As she pulled apart the foil of an antiseptic wipe, she nodded over to the girl who still hadn't moved.

"Is she okay?" I said, peering over.

"Is she okay?" Alex replied, the words darting from her mouth.

I looked back at her leg. "You're fine. Looks like a scratch," I shot back.

She raised her eyebrows and I raised mine back, mimicking her expression until her face melted to a thin smile.

"You were tossing and turning. That bloody chain kept me awake all night. I ended up spending most of it getting the camera to work."

My eyes widened, head rising and she nodded in reply.

"When I finally got to sleep, I woke to the sound of the van's engine. I darted out of bed and there was this little shit driving off in it."

"You ran after her?" I said, a smile rising.

Alex nodded, turning down to the wound, clenching her teeth as she pulled the jagged triangle of metal and dropped it to the tile with a high clatter.

"She couldn't get the gears working. I bet she's never driven before. I caught up with her, yanked the door open."

"You shot her," I said, looking back to the gun as I tried to reach out to check her over, but the chain held me back.

"No," she said, her tone defensive. "She tried to grab the gun and we got into a scuffle. It went off, the bullet bounced off the metal of the van, then this," she said, looking to the wound.

I looked down at the slumped body which still hadn't moved and raised my eyebrows.

"Did you hit her?"

"No," she said, bunching her features in my direction. "As soon as the gun went off, there were creatures coming out of everywhere. We ran and she fell, banged her head. I took two out, but I bet there's more on their way. We should go," she said, hurriedly nodding back towards the door.

"If she can't even drive, then how did she get into the van?"

Alex didn't reply immediately.

"She can't drive, but she can hot wire?" I added.

Alex turned her head down, wrapping the bandage around her leg and drawing in sharp air through her teeth.

"I may have left the keys in the ignition last night," she said, her voice quiet.

I raised my eyebrows, biting my tongue, but my joy at her return held back my outpouring.

"I told you, you'll be fine," I said. "I thought you'd left," I added, regretting as soon as I heard the words.

Alex looked up, her head turning at an angle. I could see her forcing the smile not to grow.

I held back a frown, but couldn't as I twisted to the shutters when they clattered with a heavy bang. We knew what it meant and together turned to the corridor, but stopped as the sack of clothes jumped to the air with the coat unfurling and the long triangle of a kitchen knife glinted in the sun pouring from the skylights.

Her bright-blue eyes fixed wide in my direction, dirt smothered cheeks that went taught as her mouth gaped, staring towards me with her feet frozen to the spot.

The chain rattled as I moved my arm and she turned as if woken from a trance. Features bunching with rage, she twisted to Alex with her shining white teeth bared and knife rising above her head with each bound.

92

"No," I screamed, watching as Alex stood tall with her brow lowered as she tried to tense for the attack. Pain etched across Alex's face as she steadied herself on her injured leg.

I grabbed for a thick candle resting on the floor, the heaviest object in reach, and hurled it in the rising woman's direction as I screamed for her to stop. In that moment I couldn't tell if she was human or something else.

The bulk of the candle thumped against her shoulder. The stranger flashed a glare toward me, her eyes wide and nose screwed up. By the time she'd turned back, Alex had surged forward and slapped the knife from her hand, sending it skittering across the floor and wrapped the stranger in a bear hug, squeezing hard against her convulsions.

Hurrying, I bent at the knees, snatching up the simple key I'd dropped as she'd leapt, swapping it to my ballooned hand, which looked like I wore five pairs of skin-coloured gloves. Clenching my teeth against the pain, I fumbled it into the lock to the sound of angry calls to be freed.

Relief flooded as the lock snapped open and I could let go of the key, freeing the stars from my view as the pain subsided. I drew a deep breath before leaping the few paces to Alex and the woman, still flailing in her arms, screaming vulgarities on the edge of making even me blush.

"It's okay," I said, being careful not to get too close as she kicked out. "It's okay," I said again. "We're not going to hurt you." I tried the softest voice I could manage, but each word seemed to just amplify her distress. The rattle of the shutters and the rise in the ferocity of their beat did nothing to help her calm.

Trying again to normalise my tone, I looked up to Alex to see her face bunched with the effort.

"Did you lock the door?"

"Shit," Alex said from somewhere in the tangle.

"It's okay, we're leaving anyway," I said, then pushed my good hand out to the stranger's shoulder. I drew back as her eyes locked onto my fingers and she surged her head forward, snapping teeth together. "You can come with us," I said, ignoring Alex's shaking head and the noise I guessed was another protest.

"Let her go," I said, looking back to the knife, making sure I knew exactly where it was. "You can't stay like that forever. We've got to go."

Despite Alex's protests, I leant in closer.

"It's okay. I'm from the telly," I said, looking up to Alex with a shrug of my shoulders.

The stranger's eyes opened and she held my gaze, her motions slowing as she let her legs take her weight. I didn't see that moment of recognition as she examined my face, even when I pushed on my full white-tooth TV smile and nodded up to Alex.

Alex spread her arms and jumped to the side, but I could see she was ready to leap between us if the stranger tried anything.

Taking a step forward, I held my hand out to keep Alex back, despite the shake of her head.

"It's okay," I said again as she continued to stare in my direction. "What's your name? When did you last eat?"

There was silence between us, but the clatter of the shutters didn't let up as her glare stayed fixed in my direction. Eventually I moved away; we didn't have time for this.

"We're going," I said. "Grab food and go on your way, but you're much safer with us than you are alone out there."

The rattle of the shutters stopped and I scooped up the knife, wrapping it in my red jacket still damp at the edges. Out of the corner of my eye I watched Alex move away from the girl, the woman. I couldn't quite decide her age as she stood, her head bent low as she peered around the room through a tangled mop of brown hair.

"You thought I'd left you?" Alex said as she picked up one of the cases in one hand and lifting the camera still connected to the tripod in the other.

I looked sideways at her, but didn't answer.

"I would have left you the key," she said, flinching her survey back to the stranger.

Guilt at my thoughts when I'd woken with her missing kept my words from coming. All I could manage was a grateful smile in her direction.

"Just friends," she said, shooting me a grin, the smile falling as she turned back to the stranger.

I followed her look as she stood with the hair brushed from her face, her gaze roving over the rows of shelves, but flinching to me every other moment.

"Take what you need," I said. "It's yours."

The stranger didn't reply, instead turning on the spot with her hair trailing behind as she twisted to face the corridor, wide-eyed.

We knew what she saw and swapping the bundle of clothes to rest on my other arm, I walked beside the young stranger and pulled the knife from between my clothes to offer the handle out with Alex shouting at my back.

"No."

93

The young woman's eyes were wider than I imagined Alex's were at my back. The stranger's surprise greater than Alex's when I returned the long knife. Although the pause between us felt like an age, the creatures moving through the doorway had barely taken a step before she'd made her decision.

Surging toward the opening, the stranger blocked my view with her wide coat. Her arms dove up and down, the movement silent except for the slash of the knife as it connected to bone and the heavy fall of the bodies as they went down in quick succession.

Alex stood at my side and we shared the view. She'd had no time to put the equipment down. No time to grab the gun from the bed before it was over and watched with me as the stranger stood, beckoning us through the corridor as thick blood dripped from the knife.

This wasn't the first time she'd had to defend herself from those things.

With the gun in my hand, I followed with Alex laden behind. We found the stranger outside, scouring the side of the building for threats. She nodded towards the van and my gaze fell on the dark blood dripping down the side by the driver's door and the wide hole in the metal.

I climbed in the back, Alex insisting I go first as she took the driver's seat. She didn't start the engine, instead looking to me for the answer as we watched the stranger, the girl who we still didn't know, slip back in through the open door of the building.

"Wait," I said, when I saw Alex go to turn the key.

In silence, my gaze drifted to the skyline. Columns of smoke lined the horizon.

As my heart slowed, I could taste the thickness in the air while watching the rainbow of depressing colour flowing from black to white across the spectrum. The green fields were void of life as they rolled out to disappear where they met the dirty, cloudless sky. The road seemed to sleep, empty of traffic as it travelled relentless left and right.

The image had a certain perfection and I looked towards Alex, about to prompt her to set up the camera, but the girl, the woman, rushed from the building, her arms laden with bags bulging at the edges. She stopped as she spotted us in the van, surprise turning her head to the side, her smile dropping from the corners of her mouth.

She'd thought we would have left her and with the raise of her eyebrows, I was sure I could see her eyes glinting with hope as she stared in our direction. The sight broke my heart. Had it only taken a few days, a week at the most, to strip this girl, this woman, of her faith in humanity?

Her features hardened and she let her hair drop back to cover her face while she moved past the van, striding away. I ran through the back, regretting my enthusiasm as I jumped out of the doors, jarring my hand, but sucked down the pain as I called after her, not holding back my voice.

"Come with us."

She turned with her lips curled down. What I could see of her face had twisted feral, but she didn't linger on mine for long, snapping her head around the view.

I shouted again and watched the anger rise in her stride. I forced down a smile as I saw movement from around the front of the building, but instead of focusing on the chef whose uniform no one could call whites, I shouted again and jumped back in the van, not lingering on the crowd gathering at the chef's back.

"Start the engine," I said, and Alex did as I asked, the grumble of the mechanics coming to life only spurred on the middle-aged man with a rend in his great belly and his followers not wanting to be late to the feast.

The girl, the woman, scowled at me through the glass, but she ran to the back and slammed the doors closed after she jumped in, her reluctance obvious in her scowl.

Alex pulled us in a wide arc away from the chef.

"You're safer with us," I said, joining her as she stood in the back. "We're safer with you," I added, pushing my hand out with a wide smile on my lips.

She stood in the corner, clutching the bags to her stomach as her gaze flitted around the shelves and the stains on the floor

"Sit. Eat. We can talk when you're ready."

We drove for five minutes before she let the bags drop, before she sat on the floor and pulled out a can of corned beef, turning the key to release the meat.

I tried not to watch her. I tried to stop my mouth from wanting the food. Instead, I asked her name again, looking away when she didn't answer and the van slowed.

"What is it?" I called out, and stood when Alex didn't answer.

Arriving between the seats, I felt the blood drain from my face as I stared on at the white coach wedged side on with an olive-drab truck and a thick stone wall either side. Together they blocked the narrow road and despite the dark interior, I fixed on the writhing masses inside.

My heart jumped as a delicate voice spoke from behind, almost fainting as I processed the words.

"We're going the wrong way. We're supposed to be getting away from the doctors."

94

"What did you say?" I said, spinning around to find her standing to peer past me to the block in the road, the knife scraping around inside the tin.

"You need to go the other way," she said, dropping the can to the thin table mounted to the side of the van, her voice high and adolescent, like you would expect narrating a Christmas tale.

"No," I said, stepping forward. "What did you say about the doctors? Who are you talking about?"

She raised her left eyebrow, her gaze meeting mine for the first time as she licked the meat from the tip of the knife, letting her right-hand drop and with it the knife as her left swept hair from her face one side, then the next. Tilting her head, she looked past me to the windscreen and, nodding forward, she spoke.

"You know who I mean. They know you," she said, with both her brows raised. "That's where they were going," she said. "That's where I don't want to be."

"Who?"

She narrowed her brow as I spoke.

"The doctors," she replied with a force behind her words.

I took a step toward her, a beat pulsing in my ears. "What do you know about the doctors?" I said, raising my voice.

She lifted her brow, pulling herself up to full height, which was only just a little shorter than my five foot ten.

"Speak, for goodness' sake," I shouted when she didn't reply.

Her chest thrust forward as she filled her lungs, her hand tensed around the knife as she studied my features.

"I'm sorry," I added, pushing out my palms despite the pain. "They did things to me, the doctors," I said, softening my tone as I watched her slowly nod. "I need to find them. Make them pay." Her brow fell; the nodding stopped. "Did they do things to you?"

She squinted and her forehead creased as her fingers tightened further around the knife handle.

I took another step towards her. "You don't have to say if they did, just tell me what you know. Tell me where they are."

The van rolled, but in the wrong direction. I turned back to see the coach and the truck receding in the view.

"No," I shouted, jumping the few steps back between the seats. "We have to find a way. What if this is our only way of getting through? It could take hours to find another."

The van rocked to a stop with Alex remaining silent, only her frown showing her discontent. When light came from behind and the lock clicked, I span around.

Racing through the open doors and jumping to the tarmac, breath pulled as I tried to follow the woman running down the road. She'd dropped one bag already and soon dropped the last as I called after her.

I stopped giving chase. "Please, I need to know."

I watched as she slowed, her head turning over her shoulder. Her gaze fell from me to the bag and its contents spilt on the floor at my feet.

She kept walking.

Drawing a deep breath to hold back frustrated tears, I turned back to make sure Alex had done nothing stupid, like getting out of the van and following.

Picking up the bag, my eyelids batted together whilst a single tear fell to the tarmac as I lifted the tins of food and pushed them back into the bag.

As two dirty trainers arrived at the top of my vision, I stood up straight, wincing with the pain, but offered out the full bag as I drew a breath.

She stood at my front with a crisp white handkerchief offered in her hand. I set the bag down between us and I took the folded square from her dirt-clogged hand, dabbing at the moisture on my cheek.

"Thank you," I replied, her gaze fixed on me as I wiped my face.

"Why do you want to find them?" she said, her soft voice lost in the wide-open space. "They're terrible people. The worst."

"I should know."

"You don't know the half of it."

"Tell me then. I'm a reporter."

"I know."

"They did bad things to me," I said.

She nodded and spoke.

"They did bad things to many people."

"They did this," I said, sweeping my hands across the view, taking in the columns of smoke.

"I know," she replied. "But what are you trying to achieve?"

"I want the world to know what they did. I want the world to know what they're doing so we can stop them and people can prepare. I want to destroy them and make them pay."

She nodded, but kept quiet.

"Tell me," I said, knowing the answer before I asked the question. "How do you know all this?"

"I've seen your picture in her office. I've seen the grand plan spread across her wall."

"How?" I replied.

She took a deep breath and swallowed down hard. "I used to be one of them, before the place was lost," she said, cutting herself off to draw the knife up high, but my head was too fogged to give any reply.

Eventually I spoke. "Come with us. You can help. We'll keep you safe."

The woman burst out laughing. "You don't know anything," she said, stepping back as she bit her lip. "Who's going to keep me safe from you?"

"Me?" I replied. "I won't hurt you."

Then the realisation hit. She knew. She knew what I was; what I'd become. What they'd done to me.

"Please, you have to tell me everything you know." I saw her chest filling out; fear stopped her words from flowing.

Anger grew inside me. "Tell me," I shouted.

She didn't reply; instead took a step back, shaking her head.

"Stay away from me." Her voice was high.

"What is she doing at the hospital?" I said, ignoring the glint of the knife raised above her head, with her whole body shaking as she moved backwards.

I scooped up the bag at my feet and took a step towards her.

"You shouldn't have come," she said, the words muffled.

"I had to. Toni needed me."

I watched as a smile bloomed on the stranger's face.

"She did, but not how you thought."

"What are they doing at the hospital?" I repeated, but then a thought flashed into my head. "She was imprisoned in that place. I helped her escape."

The stranger smiled again and shook her head.

"She wanted you out of here. She wanted you willing. She knew she wouldn't get to see if it worked if they kept you locked up."

I thought on her words but they didn't make sense. I stopped moving. Instead, my gaze fixed to the ground, looking at Toni's eyes staring back.

"She engineered the escape of the creatures?"

"No," the stranger said. "That was an accident. Not part of the plan, I'm guessing. But when they knew the place was lost, was it easy to get out?"

"No. No way. You're wrong. We almost died so many times. If it hadn't been for the sniper who took out those…" My words stopped as breath left my lungs.

The sniper, the soldiers. They'd been protecting us. The soldier had saved us.

I tried to speak but I couldn't think of the words to come back with, the words that would prove the stranger was wrong.

Instead, I watched as with a satisfied smile she scooped up the bag at my feet and took slow steps back. I watched as my chance to get the answers walked out of reach.

"What are they doing at the hospital?" I blurted out.

"Collecting samples," she replied, still taking steps.

"Samples of what?" I said, the words barely voiced.

"Children who've been exposed to the organism," she said, the bag raising through my vision.

That word. The one Toni had used.

"Why children?" I asked, even though I didn't want to know the answer.

She didn't reply; instead, took a step back.

"Why children?" I repeated, looking up and raising my voice.

"Because they're the future. Right? And they make the best ho…" The stranger's words were blocked out by sound of a vehicle horn at our backs and Alex's shout.

"Get down."

I turned to my right as movement triggered in my peripheral vision and I saw a ragged figure heading towards us, a sharp breeze sending its stench our way for the first time.

Without thought I leapt forward to shove the stranger to the road just as the air lit with a gunshot at our backs.

95

She stepped to the side and I stumbled to my knees, her eyes lit with a fire, pivoting between the decaying body settling at our side and me on the ground.

"Don't go to her," she said. "It's what she's wanted all along." She turned and ran, her feet padding to the ground as I climbed to my feet but not chasing after.

I watched, pushing down the questions in my head; I knew where I had to get answers from now.

As I watched her race away down the road, I knew I'd done my job, fulfilled my role. I'd explored my passion to expose wrong and those in authority abusing their positions, but it hurt no less to know such a big part of my life had been false. To know what I'd given, tried to give, had been thrown away.

I questioned if there had been signs of Toni's disfunction. We'd both come close to crossing the line and after that I'd put a stop to it, but before then had my blind feelings put her behaviour down to quirks of personality? I wondered if Hitler's companions had done the same?

I tried to stop my breath flinching at the comparison.

I turned and my gaze fell on Alex at the sound of her trainers on the rungs of the ladder. A smile lifted my lips as I saw her stood on top of the van with her hand shielding her eyes from the bright morning as she peered along the blocked road.

"Can we make it?" I said, calling toward the roof as I walked back, knowing one way or another I was getting through the mess.

She didn't reply and I imagined the thoughts spread across her features. I imagined her scratching her head as I walked along the side of the van, my gaze elsewhere other than the movement in the coach frenzying as I drew nearer.

"Jess," I heard Alex call as I approached the coach, only giving the rattle of the door the barest notice and ignoring the slight parting of the clear plastic as the short bodies clambered to be the first to break through; the first to pierce my flesh. The first to fill themselves with me.

I paid more attention to the paint scraped down its side, the buckled panels and black scuffs running the white length until blocked by the back of the truck. I listened, tried to sense beyond the canvas and figure out what lay behind the musty green cover. What made the truck rock with a gentle movement, but didn't cause the canvas to bulge with hands reaching out?

I heard Alex's steps down the ladder, her feet landing to the road. I lifted my hand behind me, palm out to stop her from getting any closer. When I could no longer hear her steps along the road, I unpicked the string ties with my good fingers, not stopping to take a deep breath as I lifted the musty material.

It was dark inside, but nothing came from where I couldn't see. No fingers jumped out, clawing for the softness of my eyes.

To Alex's soft calls for me to stop, I undid enough ties so I could fit through and I climbed with the awkwardness of using only one hand, but I'd made it into the back still alive. Unbitten.

Welcoming the musty air, I blinked, testing my vision with each opening. Four rows of seats lined the sides and centre, growing clearer in my vision with each flutter of my lids. They were empty, but the space between was not. Instead, boxes stacked high lined the gaps between where soldiers should have sat.

I climbed to the nearest long rectangular box; plastic perhaps, but I couldn't be sure with my thoughts elsewhere and beads of sweat rolling down my forehead as the morning sun trapped under the canvas.

I headed forward, sliding on my knees with my gaze fixed on the edge of light toward the front.

Air pulled sharp between my teeth, forcing myself steady with both hands as my knee found the space between the next row. I wouldn't let it slow me as I bridged the gap and my hand soon grabbed the flap of canvas I hoped covered the window to the cab.

Reaching out with my good hand, I told myself I'd seen the worst. I tried to prepare for the horror I guessed moved beyond the thin fabric, beyond the glass the other side. I told myself the worst I could see was traffic lined up, blocking the road, ending our path and sending us for hours around another way. Blood and guts were nothing new. No injury could top what had already burnt into my dreams.

I took a deep breath before lifting the fabric, but when a pale pink light flashed my eyes shut, I'd seen enough to regret not bringing the gun.

96

Flinching away, I lost my footing, but it wasn't the desperate sight through the glass that sent me back, but the clawed hand shooting out to block my view, the hand appearing from somewhere in the cab.

Instinct forced my eyes wide, sending both hands to grasp for something to steady myself on. Stars shot across my view as pain leapt up my right arm when my puffed grip took hold of a cold metal upright.

I couldn't concentrate on the pain; instead, I watched the clawed hand circle as it felt for flesh, but only wafted the stench of death.

Blinking, I tried to clear the spots of light from my swimming view whilst attempting to steady myself, despite having already fallen to the floor between two plastic crates.

With my back crunching into the cubes of glass and despite my vision still stained with the horror I'd seen through the blood-smeared windscreen, I scrabbled to turn and raised myself up high, leaning back to avoid the arm which was still the only part of the creature that had come through.

I backed up, turned, forcing my trainers to kick out at the stiff canvas, breath ran away, darkness descending as a creature fell through the canvas partition.

I screamed. I couldn't see its advance, but the sound of its crawl was as clear as if I could, as were the scratching fingers as it scrabbled over the canvas seat and the trickle of the glass to the floor as it followed my journey.

Lashing out at the canvas I screamed again, desperate to find where I'd entered and could get back to safety, but everywhere I hit stayed stiff against my effort. The creature was getting so close, the stench of death I would never get used to filling my lungs, bile rising as I coughed between gasps of air.

Amid my panic I saw the faces of my parents. I saw colleagues in their buildings around the world; the buildings they thought would keep them safe with the twenty-four-hour security guards and thick concrete walls.

How wrong they were.

The army couldn't protect us from these creatures. Most of them were the enlisted.

I'd yet to see a battle where we had won. Where the mental jar of the creature's appearance didn't cause us to pause. Didn't stop us from striking out. Didn't prevent wasting those first precious moments.

They were easy to defend against. If only you knew you had to protect yourself. If only you didn't stand there transfixed, eyes wide, trying to figure out if the creature from so many horror movies was real and how it could exist.

Their main advantage was forcing us to kill our friends and family if we wanted to survive. If only people knew they were already long dead.

Choking down a deep breath, I balled my fist, knowing it would be of little use, but at least I would go down trying.

Light came from the front of the truck. A second creature falling through and lifting the flap, but I barely took notice as I saw the first soldier with half his face covered in blood nearly on me.

Throwing myself back against the canvas in a vain hope it would give way, to my surprise it did and I could feel myself tumbling out in the cold air as I hit the road, my left foot taking the brunt of the force.

Alex was by my side, helping me up sooner than I'd expected, sitting me with my back to the hard metal of the truck.

"Can you stand?" she said, the concern in her voice secondary only to her urgency.

I nodded, letting her help me up as I tested pressure on my left foot. I could walk, but only at a slow pace. I followed Alex's gaze to the coach and the heads butting against the glass as we passed, their touch leaving bloody shadows.

So many times I flinched against the pressure, expecting the glass to spray out, forcing us to run for our lives again. Instead, the creatures moved along the inside of the bus not fighting each other, but bumped together like they took no notice of their surroundings other than the feast outside.

Arriving at the coach's flimsy doors, Alex tightened her grip as she hurried me past. What was she afraid I would do?

"Can we get through?" she said, jumping into the driver's seat of the van after letting me down softly on the other.

I stared on through the windscreen. For a few moments I'd forgotten what I'd seen as I peered through the truck's blood-dripping glass. The vision came back in that instant as clear as if still in the moment.

"Yes. We just need to push it out of the way," I said nodding, my absent gaze fixed somewhere unimportant, but snapped back into focus when the doors of the coach cracked apart.

The plastic pushed out under the pressure and the creatures who'd lived such short lives fell to the floor, faces hitting the road, but not flinching, their stares never leaving us.

One by one they struggled to rise back to their feet, despite their similar-aged companions falling to their backs as they stepped off the coach to tenderise the flesh of the new step.

After Alex checked she'd locked the doors and the windows were closed, the engine roared to life and we rolled forward. I watched her expression harden, her lids tightened together and mouth bunching as each of the black-veined faces disappeared below the view, one by one, until our bumper nudged against the back of the truck.

She looked at me and I turned her way, trying to ignore the faces past her which were barely tall enough to reach the window, their hands leaving bloody marks down the glass.

I nodded, as she revved the engine hard before slowly letting out the clutch.

We didn't move despite the smoke soon billowing from the engine, the smell of burning plastic clawing inside our noses.

I coughed, Alex copying my action despite her best effort, but we knew to open the windows would have greater consequences.

I could see she was about to let up when we moved forward. Slow at first, but progress had started. We were pushing against the weight of the truck.

I closed my eyes, trying to ignore what would happen the other side as we rolled, not wanting to see its great mass rise and fall as we pushed on, relentless.

Opening my eyes, I saw Alex steering us close to the coach to despatch the creatures following, heads crushing as the pressure grew too much.

I closed my eyes for a second time to the sound of cracking bone, the faces gone from the window, nausea drawing up from my throat.

On hearing Alex's intake of breath, I knew the time had come to open my eyes and see the other side, but even as we edged forward I struggled to bring myself to face the view again, despite knowing from her quickening breath Alex had taken in the full horror.

97

I heard her exclamation as the roar of the engine slowed. I opened my eyes and tried to force myself to continue drawing in air. With the truck still at our bumper we knew the road was somewhere underneath, the black tarmac through both side windows hidden beneath the blanket of bodies, none with a head intact.

Resting my pained hand on top of Alex's, together we pushed the stick back into gear. I held on as she forced the truck clear, watching the line of water down her face glint in the low sun.

Moving my hand to her shoulder, I gripped tight, my gaze fixed on her face while she turned the wheel to steer clear of the truck. I forced my eyes to stay open as we winced with each rise and fall, each spin of the wheels as they lost traction for a moment.

We stopped when the ride smoothed out, lingering for a long while, not saying a word. She knew without asking I wouldn't let us drive away. She knew I wouldn't leave these people alone without making a record, without putting their horrific deaths to some good.

As Alex filmed out of the open back doors, I forced myself to look at every body and stare at their erased identities. I lingered on flesh turned to pulp from the finger-sized bullets, the empty brass casings littering where the van rested.

With the final shot panning along the side of the road, the camera tracing the river of blood long-dried in the sun, we pulled the doors up as the first of the young creatures peered around from where we'd left them. We drove away as they stumbled to get a footing on the carpet of the dead.

Neither of us talked as the van wound its way around the thin country roads. Neither of us spoke as we travelled, barely making a detour in the hour. We skirted around roadblocks, through fields either side. We weren't the first; instead, following paths smashed through stone walls but from the other way. We were the only ones who seemed to want to go in this direction.

The going was slow, but we weren't in a hurry. Staring across the horizon kept the bodies of the dead repeating over, punctuated only by glances to the Sat Nav and the dot on the white road, the number in the corner ever decreasing.

As the number fell below five miles, we saw the metal fence cutting across our view, stretching out across the road to curve inward as far as we could see either side.

For a moment I thought we might have headed in the wrong direction, but could see no other signs that somehow we'd ended back at where we'd started.

"Left or right?" Alex said, her voice devoid of energy.

Somehow I raised a smile. I'd half expected her to turn the van around.

"You choose. It won't be long now."

With barely a pause, she manhandled the wheel to climb up the shallow grass bank to the left.

"What happens when you've got what you need?" she said, her eyes fixed forward like mine to follow the sweeping metal, tracing the deep ruts compressing the stony mud.

I didn't hold back my reply for any reason other than I didn't know. I hadn't considered a next step. I still didn't want to think of what would happen next.

I hadn't thought I would survive last night without another dose of Toni's medicine. I didn't know if I would survive the next. Now wasn't the time to think any deeper.

I'd spotted the end of the fence, a panel leaning against the side of an olive drab flat-bed truck.

I nodded towards the army vehicle and twisted in my seat to face Alex. She stared forward.

I expected the body to rise from its lean against the fence.

Alex didn't slow. She'd expected it too, but neither of us expected the call from the soldier's mouth, the hasty reach for the rifle. Neither of us expected another to appear around the side, fingers pulling up his trousers' fly in a hurry as he searched for a weapon and found it close at hand.

Alex slowed only at the soldier's demand, her breath remaining calm as I raised my hands to the air.

Alex did the same, but neither of us expected the shot which rocked the van, slamming hard, sending shattered dark plastic shards high in to the air as it hit the engine's grill.

98

They were on us before we had time to flinch. The doors pulled wide and they dragged us to the ground to the shouts I could barely make out for their volume. The soldiers seemed to call for an answer, expecting us to say something.

I couldn't understand the question, their energy masking the words. I kept quiet whilst trying to protect my hand.

The soldier on me pushed me to the side, rolling me around so I could see the barrel of the rifle in my face. His voice blared, spit raining down as he shouted with his view fixed to my left eye then my right.

"Clear," came a strong call from the other side of the van, but I could hear the question in his tone.

"Clear," the guy said, still leaning over me, but the furrowed forehead told me he wasn't sure. His heavy brows covered most of his bright blue eyes.

Then I got it. Although we'd been in the van and we'd slowed when asked, they couldn't be sure we were still human.

Had they yet to experience the life-changing encounter and was it disappointment I read in his face?

"I'm okay," I said with a timid voice, trembling as I guarded my hand.

His brow evened out, his expression falling as he stood upright to draw the long gun around the horizon.

"Clear," he called again, and I heard Alex's voice, her hand reaching down to help me from the ground.

"I'd keep your voice down," Alex said in a light tone, her brow low as she turned to look me up and down. As she did, her mouth formed silent words.

I nodded, confirming I was fine.

"What do you know?" said the soldier, rounding on us, double taking as Alex moved to block his path, raising her head high like a strutting stag.

I smiled within, holding back a flutter of laughter rising from my chest as she drew herself up to protect me.

"More than you, it would seem. They can't drive," she said, keeping her words slow as she tilted her head.

The soldier narrowed his eyes and leant forward, looking like he'd done this in a hundred bars around the world. When the other man arrived at his side, he pulled him away to a huddle for words we couldn't hear, turning back mid conversation with his face lit when he saw me as if for the first time.

He stepped forward, keeping his eyes on mine, a slight smile on his lips but flinching a look at Alex, who flashed a raise of her brow as the soldier stepped past.

Stopping a pace away, he brushed his hand through his short blond hair and narrowed his eyes as he wiped his hand across his mouth.

"Private Jordain," he said, and held his hand out, then looked to his colleague and nodded. "Sheppard."

I smiled, looked to Alex whose eyebrows were lower than I'd ever seen. I looked down to my right hand, still ballooning, and pushed out my left.

Jordain swapped his hands after sucking through his teeth when he saw my injury and gently shook my hand.

"Has anyone looked at that?"

"Jess," I replied shaking my head. "Alex," I said, nodding in her direction.

"Can I?" he said, and I nodded as my gaze fell on the camouflaged bag strapped to his belt with a dark olive cross in the centre.

I sat back in the passenger seat of the van with my legs dangling out, while Jordain took great care checking out my hand. His fingers traced the bones from my wrist to my finger, lightening the pressure each time I winced. As he examined, I watched out across the horizon and Sheppard scouring down the rifle's sight.

"Have you seen any?" I said.

His hands paused and he looked me in the eye before shaking his head.

"You'll know when do you. There's no mistaking."

He paused for a moment, then nodded.

"I don't think it's broken," he said. "Keep it elevated."

I laughed.

"If you can," he added.

Sheppard called at his back. Alex cursed.

"They're attracted to noise. They'll be here soon. The gunfire," Alex said, catching my eye.

I nodded, jumping down from the seat as we stood in a square, our backs to each other, covering all points of the compass.

"Why weren't you evacuated?" said Jordain.

"We've got a job to do," I replied.

"What job?" said Sheppard, and I turned just as Jordain jabbed him in the back with his elbow, pointing to the three burgundy letters on the side of the van.

"Oh," he replied, turning with his eyebrows raising as if he'd caught my eye for the first time. "Oh," he said again.

"Where are you going?" Jordain said.

"St Buryan Hospital," I said after a pause, holding my breath for their response.

Their reply was instant, but not with words. I heard them turn; Alex and I twisted around and we all faced each other. I could see the tension in Alex's fists, could feel mine in the rising beat in my chest, but their rifles stayed pointed to the ground and their faces open with surprise at my words.

"That's our FOB," Jordain replied, the other nodding.

"FOB?" Alex said.

"Forward Operating Base," I said, the words flowing out to leave the soldiers to nod.

"But there may be a problem," Sheppard said. The pair looked at each other, faces turning stern.

Jordain stepped back, sweeping his eyes across the horizon before returning to the square.

"Our Oppos went back to collect more concrete blocks in the HIAB, but we've lost contact with them and Buryan."

"When was this?" Alex said, stepping closer toward the group.

The two soldiers looked at each other, Jordain pulling up and twisting his wrist to look at a bulky metal watch.

"Three hours ago," he replied, his eyes catching on mine.

"You should come with us," I said, seeing Alex flinch at the words.

The soldiers exchanged glances, turning back when I spoke.

"One question, though?" I said, looking to the unfinished wall. "Were you building it to keep them in or out?"

99

As my words finished, the wind blew across my face. On second thought, I didn't need to know the answer. Instead, I watched the concern on his face as he followed mine, turning with his rifle raising in the direction of the gap in the fence.

I pushed my hand out to rest on his forearm, but still it climbed. Turning toward him, I saw the resolve in his eyes as he caught a first glimpse, his training flooding his body with commands to control his grip and take aim.

This was a man who'd raised his weapon in combat before. The lines across his face set with a glare I'd seen so many times in the battlegrounds of Afghanistan and on other faces in other time zones on both sides of the line. It was the look of someone who knew they would take a life. Knew they were putting themselves forward for the ultimate sacrifice.

But I'd never seen the pause. The raise of the head. His eyes widening as he pulled up from the sight. I watched as his humanity caught up before he pulled the trigger, holding back his recent training which told him to put down the woman with half her clothes missing and a great wound on her shoulder. Which told him to pause was to lose the battle.

"No," I said, keeping my voice calm despite my inner panic.

Jordain turned, his fair eyes squinting back a hard question. Inside his head I knew it would be a thought so obvious to anyone looking on, but we knew better.

"We need to run. You'll only attract more," I said, still struggling to hold the panic back.

I turned around and saw I hadn't needed to say the words, watching as others shambled behind the pace setter and passing between the gap in the fence, past the flatbed truck, with it their foul stench greeting us in the wind.

"We need to go," I said more urgently.

Jordain nodded, turning to his left with his weapon gripped hard, but letting the muzzle down to point to the grass.

"Let's go," he said, following my example with his volume. However, Sheppard didn't seem to have heard or taken note; at Alex's side he held his rifle pointed towards the gap as his head shook from side to side.

Alex backed off as we retreated and joined me in the van as Jordain rushed to his colleague's side.

The round went off before he could reach and we watched the woman's head explode, sending her body to the floor as the contents of her skull covered the creatures behind. Jordain stood fixed to the spot with Sheppard stood upright, the weapon loose at his side as they watched the creatures trample the headless body without a pause.

With a sharp blast of the horn from Alex, Jordain pulled Sheppard to the back of the van.

No one spoke as Alex rolled us over the ground with the van pitching up and down to leave the creatures to follow until they shrank to nothing in the mirror. We encountered no more creatures as we skirted the fence line wrapping around the village and soon arrived at the welcome smooth tarmac.

With the engine left to settle to a low murmur, I was the first to speak as I peered over my shoulder and caught Jordain staring to his colleague sat against the rear doors with his gaze fixed into the distance.

"This takes us in a straight line to the hospital," I said, switching a quick glimpse to the small screen suckered to the window.

Jordain nodded as he pulled his gaze around to the windscreen.

"There are three checkpoints along this route. The first should be over the horizon," he said, leaning forward and raising his rifle to look through the scope. "But take it really easy on the approach. They may have seen a little more action than us."

"You mean don't count on them knowing what they're doing," Alex said, interrupting.

I waited for a reaction, my gaze fixed on Jordain.

"She didn't…" I said, but Jordain shrugged and let a playful smile flash across his face before I could finish.

"Touché," he replied. "It might be better if we walk alongside," he added, flashing a look to the back of the van.

My gaze darted around the view as I twisted in my seat to search out across the flat scrub rolling for miles either side.

Unless the creatures hid in the undulating ground, unless they had ducked down ready to pounce, we weren't in immediate danger.

As the thoughts settled, my mind turned to the other creatures; their obvious intelligence, their clear eyes and need to breathe and blink.

A shiver ran along my back as I thought of the moment I discovered their need to reproduce.

They were still human, despite their demonic actions. Were they what I would turn in to?

I flashed back to where this all began, for me at least. The compound where I'd been taken and everything I'd seen. With Toni by my side I'd taken solace that their days were numbered, but now I knew she'd either not had all the information, or it was another lie. My head was so crammed with questions, each fighting inside my mind to be answered.

Humanity is screwed. These things were multiplying, but I could give everyone some hope. Maybe.

Without Alex slowing the crawl of the wheels, the back doors opened and the two soldiers jumped to the road and slammed the doors.

Jordain peeled to our left, Sheppard walking along our right side whilst Alex kept the pace.

"Let me drive."

She didn't hide her surprise at my suggestion as she looked down to my swollen hand.

"It's getting better. Anyway, we're going so slowly," I said, trying to stop the muscles in my face from reacting to the pain as I raised my right hand and flexed each of the swollen fingers. "He says there's nothing broken." The grit of my teeth told another story.

"He also said you should keep it elevated."

"I need you walking alongside. I need you to film what we're seeing," I said, raising my brow as I widened my eyes and smiled.

Her protest sank as the corners of my mouth raised, just as guilt gathered in my chest. She was walking beside Jordain with the camera on her shoulder within less than a minute.

"What's your first name?" I said, calling out through my window whilst I watched Sheppard's slow strides.

With the rifle clasped in both hands across his front, his gaze fixed along the shallow climb and the endless rise as another brow appeared each time we thought it was the last.

"I'm Jess," I said when he didn't reply.

"From the news," he said, still not answering my first question.

I nodded anyway.

"It's just an exercise," he said, his voice flat. "That's what they told us first. Then it was a chemical release as they issued NBC suits and sent us out on patrols. Before we stepped foot outside the complex, we got the orders to build the fences. We're not engineers mind," he said, shaking his head. "He's signals and I'm a chef."

"Patrols came back with fewer men than set out. Then entire patrols didn't return. That's when they started on about the disease, virus or whatever. It wasn't too long before they told us people were being bitten and the dead were coming back to life. We didn't know what to believe.

"They gave us training," he said and laughed. "They showed a fucking horror film for fuck's sake. We all thought it was a joke and checked our watches for the date to make sure we hadn't skipped to April first. We lost comms with our oppos, with the FOB and it all became real."

I didn't fill the pause. I had no words to help.

"I'm sorry for shooting at you," he added, his words soft but distant.

Shaking my head, I was about to say how I understood. I knew how crazy and fucked up the whole situation was, but something distant on the horizon caught my eye. It was a shape on the left side of the road.

I soon realised the building was a shipping container painted dark green, but by that time my concentration had moved to the writhing bodies engulfing it.

Even after all I'd seen so far in these last short days, the sight on the horizon was enough to pull the breath from my lungs.

The first checkpoint lay ahead, but we could barely see the concrete blocks in the road for the dead ambling around. I watched, squinting at the sight I could just make out as one after the other, heads twisted towards us, but when a gunshot exploded at my side, every creature in view turned in our direction all at once.

My scream only added to the call as I saw Sheppard's body settling to the tarmac, his brains only just slapping to the ground as his fingers uncurled from around the butt of the pistol. His first sighting had been too much. How many people would have done the same if they had the chance to take the easy way out?

100

Pushing the van door open, I fell, scattering to the cold road as a flurry of boot steps raced from the other side. Breathless, I tried calling out.

"Pick it up," I screamed at Alex, as I regained my feet.

She flinched upright with the camera loose in her grip and pointing to the ground.

"Pick it up. The camera," I snapped.

Alex pulled out of her stare at the blood pooling on the cold, hard ground and nodded once before raising the camera on her shoulder as I waited for the red light.

"The microphone," I pleaded, stepping forward with her shrug, breath flinching in my lungs as Jordain stood up from the body, his hands stained red.

Taking the microphone in hand, I stepped away from the life gone from my feet, turning my back to the direction we'd headed whilst not looking to see the distance they'd closed. The words already pouring out were raw and unprofessional, less than a rookie could manage. I tried to slow. I tried to cool my hurry, adding definition to the speech I hadn't needed to prepare.

When the flow stopped, I knew I'd done enough. The crowd teeming towards us seen over my shoulder in the distance would have alone done the job, my emotion a ripe illustration of how worried the viewers should be, hoping they listened to my pleading and prepare. Hoping they would not sit back and think they would be served their life on a silver platter. Hoping I'd made them understand life was no longer a right. Life was now something you had to fight for.

Like a director in my ear, the stench told me my time was up. It was time to get the message to the masses.

After moving the van back to what we hoped was a safe distance, I sat in the rear of the van with the door wide as I held the camera on my lap like a new-born. Fragile. Precious. In need of constant care.

We'd taken up our tasks, each knowing what the other was about with no need to ask.

Alex circled the van with a rifle slung over her shoulder, every other moment sweeping the sight across the view, lingering on where we'd come. She estimated we'd have half an hour if they'd continued to follow, but she wouldn't let her guard down; knew the danger could come from any angle. Even the sky.

Jordain worked at a considered pace, taking care with the body as he lay what remained in the grass at the side of the road, covering him with a sheet of plastic, finding stones, boulders to give Sheppard the privacy he deserved.

I played the controls in the back of the van, ignoring the images uploaded to the suite of screens. There would be no editing; a raw version is what they'd get. The images were ready, the van giving the familiar shudder as the satellite transmitter raised.

Until it stopped half way.

Pushing the button a second time, I heard the groan of mechanisms above my head and the whine of gears locked together, unable to fulfil their task. I pushed the system into reverse and felt the shake as the metal settled home. It lifted one more time and I counted the seconds, stopping as it finished before it should.

With a deep breath I stepped to the road, moving away with heavy steps to get a better view. I didn't need to climb the ladder held to the back doors. I didn't need to get up close to see a great splinter of wood which was no shorter than my forearm and lodged in the twisted mechanism, telling me it would never rise again. Just like I didn't need to hear Alex's words; our time in this place was up.

"They'll have what you need at the hospital," Jordain said, his voice close at my ear and I turned to see him staring up at the roof. "All sorts of comms gear," he said. "I can get us on the network. You can still deliver the message."

I smiled at his unbidden words, the weight lifting, if only a little. I turned and took his hand, squeezing through his glove until he pulled away.

"There's too many. I don't think the van can take it. We'll have to find another way," Alex said, as we each scoured the sea of bobbing heads too close for comfort whilst trying not to linger on the detail; the blood matted hair or great rends of flesh blackened and dry, or their slack but determined expressions.

"No," Jordain said as we filled the three seats in the van's front.

"We're going right through them," I said, nodding whilst bracing my good hand against the dashboard, the engine flaring as Alex's right foot grew heavy.

101

I watched on as our speed built whilst listening to the scratch of Jordain's pencil as he wrote instructions of how to connect to the military network. I took in the view, despite my insides gripped with anticipation, head practicing for how the first impact would feel.

The first clash of flesh and bone sent a shudder of emotion though my body, watching each creature mown down, their heads splitting from their bodies at the neck and rolling up the windscreen. I wished I could unhear the solid thumps against the roof as the sounds travelled, echoing the chaos.

I thought of the debris getting caught in the satellite transmitter. I tried to force my imagination not to picture tufts of hair wedged between the mechanical joints, eyes dangling down by connective tissue from where the metal parts met.

With the windscreen wipers fighting to clear the blood, smearing the sticky mess left and right, I could feel the van slowing. The metal complained as I tried to relax back into the seat, tried to let the pressure of my blood release, only to spike again as each new horror presented.

The children were the worst, my imagination fixing panic on their features; setting their hands grasping for parents, instead of their expressions devoid of any reaction. I knew they didn't take notice even as they hit the metal, even as what life remained expired. If you could call it life.

I took a great gasp, imagining nieces and nephews I'd barely spoken with in the past few years, their perfectly formed features showing no sign of affliction, their veins buried deep and out of sight, not raised to the surface, black and bulging despite what my eyes were telling me.

A hand gripped my left. Alex to my right shot a look as I gasped for air, hoping it was my imagination alone which felt our momentum slowing with each hit.

We were slowing. I looked to Alex, then to Jordain to confirm. Neither of them were able to hide the fact from their features as we each tried to look on and beyond the sea of creatures which seemed unending.

"What's your name?" I shouted out above the din of each impact. The complaint of metal. Of plastic. The fabric of the van seeming so fragile.

I didn't look as he kept quiet, just repeated. "What's your name, your first name? It can't end this way without knowing who you are?"

When he still didn't reply, I twisted for a look to see his expression narrowed, eyebrows heavy as he caught my glance.

"Don't you know your name?" I said, nervous laughter spilling up from my throat.

Alex gave a flurry of air from her lungs and I turned to see her lips set in a smile as she shot me a look. But the smile soon dropped as she stared back through the windscreen.

I turned to see Jordain's eyebrows even further down his face, his weathered skin lined across his forehead.

"Liam," he replied, his white teeth on show as a smile soon parted his lips.

Each of us flinched back to the windscreen, rocking against our seats as a dark shape disappeared at the top of the glass to leave behind a great crack radiating where it had hit.

I renewed my grip on Liam's hand, wishing I could hold Alex's in the other, but the tension alone caused pain to pulse up and along my right arm. With the last hit, the van seemed to have slowed more than ever.

There had been hope before. We'd known the crowd of undead couldn't have gone on long enough for us to slow to a stop, but now with the path unending it felt as if we were only moments away from the worst situation.

Just as my mood sank lower than I thought I could recover from, I saw light, saw spaces between the bodies and their grasping hands. Air pulled into my lungs and I raised myself to squint through the sheen of smeared blood.

I was right; the crowd was thinning. I could see the darkness of the road between and we had more than enough speed to carry us through, to knock the bodies to the side. To roll over those who wouldn't get out of the way.

I gripped Liam's hand tight, pulsing my fingers and nodding towards the windscreen in a hope he'd seen the same and would not take the way out his colleague had. Yet, at least.

I turned to Alex. Her face dropped as I caught her view and flinched back to the screen, but nothing had changed.

Our view was still clearing; we were coming out of the danger.

Then I felt it. Felt the rumble of the engine, the hiccup of our movement despite no impact from outside; despite having cleared the last creature Alex just couldn't avoid.

The engine coughed a second time and I twisted around to Liam, letting go of his grip, hoping someone would say something as the engine stuttered again.

Blood drained from my head as on the fourth pause it didn't recover and we slowed, rolling in the silence.

102

It didn't matter which way she turned the wheel or how many times the key clicked in the ignition, the engine wouldn't pay attention to Alex's command. We soon travelled too slow to outrun anything nimbler than a tortoise who'd just woken from the winter.

Heavy breath filled the cab as those we'd barged our way through gathered back around. Their hands slapped, fingers clawed, scratching against our thin metal skin. A rising pressure gripped my empty stomach and a dread expanded deep down inside as the windscreen filled with faces, jaws slack, bloodied teeth bared and broken.

For the first time since we'd stopped, I glanced to Alex and her stern expression toward the gathering crowd. I knew she wasn't really looking. I knew she had something else on her mind.

I turned to Jordain and the blood drained from my face as I watched his hands tracing the outline of the pistol he'd placed on his lap.

"No," I said and reached over to push his fingers from the gun, then turned to lean across Alex and peer at the dashboard with the lights of all colours flooding the view.

The fuel gauge hovered high above empty. It could only have been damage to the front, the radiator maybe, which had been too much. Still the question slipped from my mouth.

"What's wrong with it?"

Alex shook her head, looking down to the rainbow of colours staring back, none of which said anything other than we needed to find another ride.

"I won't know anything until I can have a look," she said. I could barely hear her voice over the groans from outside and that perpetual stink.

To my surprise, she stood and headed into the back. I didn't need to follow to know she was checking the rear doors were locked. I looked to Jordain, watching the raise of his brow. My breath eased when I saw the gun no longer on his lap.

When Alex didn't return to her seat, I felt a shot of energy surging from inside, the van rocking as I twisted and stood, but saw her sat on the floor with her back to the white shelves trying to make herself comfortable.

"How long do you think it will take them before they move on?" I said, cringing each time I picked out a scrape of nails, the echo surrounding us. She lifted her head out of her hands, stopping her search when she'd found me on the floor opposite her.

"I don't know," she said, her voice lowering as she spoke. She stared back and held a question she seemed reluctant to ask. Light disappeared in the rear as Jordain stood between the seats in the cab.

"I can't watch those things," he said, nodding as Alex gave a weak reply and I repeated the gesture.

He sat on the floor, leaning back to a camera case at the front of the van and closed his eyes while mine searched, my body rolling with the gentle shake from side to side as the suspension absorbed the slap of hands and bump of the crowd.

Were there more of them than before?

My hand reached for my stomach as a cramp held my insides to ransom. I hadn't eaten since the night before and the morsel hadn't been enough to hold back the pain. I kept telling myself over and over the same would be true if Toni, her name sticking in my thoughts, had done nothing to me. Anyway, I was cured. Right?

Jordain snored, the noise light and barely there, but from his posture and the slow rise and fall of his chest, it was obvious he was already asleep. My previous experience with the military told me this wasn't an unusual talent.

Rest when you can because you don't know when you'll next get the chance.

Was he right to feel safe with me trapped inside?

Soon, like rain battering the canvas of a tent, the scratch and scrape formed a pattern and although my fear didn't subside, my breath slowed as I concentrated on Jordain's rhythmic rise and fall of his chest and the slow, gentle pace of his breath I imagined over the din as my eyelids grew heavy.

***

I woke to silence, fearing the darkness was a sign of the end. But as my eyes adjusted, light seeming to come from nowhere and everywhere at the same time, I saw both where they were when I'd closed my eyes.

Only then did I realise the scratch and scrape no longer surrounded, but I daren't move, instead sat listening for any clue from beyond the metal. All I could hear was the pair's breathing so clear in my ears.

With each passing moment when action didn't appear, no conversation striking through the quiet, the pair still in their peaceful slumber, I felt the walls surround me and air getting thicker. I felt the pressure in my gut tighten, pain radiating outward and knew it was my body's way of telling me it needed sustaining. But did it have to make me hallucinate?

First came the smell.

Steak fresh from the packet. An odour I'd never taken to and always held my nose until it sizzled in the pan, but now I craved to slide back the plastic and take a deep pull.

The thought caught me off guard, but as soon as I backed away from the image I felt a fist gripping tighter to my stomach, twisting. Licking my lips without command, the smell of a freshly slaughtered lamb came to mind and the pain soon relented.

I stood, hoping to ease the discomfort and watched as Alex stirred, her movement like a bass drum breaking the silence. I stopped my footsteps until she settled, then tread light with every new step, swallowing down the clawing saliva.

With my hand at my chest I looked out past the windscreen. In the darkness lit only by the bright moon, I could see the crowd had dispersed, but I didn't care why. I didn't leap with joy and wake the pair. The creatures still ambled with no aim, but their number was so much less and they no longer cared for the van. It would be a hollow victory if anyone made a sound.

I tapped Jordain on the shoulder and a rush of energy rose through my body, the pain pulling my features down. His eyes lit up, blinking fast to clear the sleep and stood, twitching his head as if trying to figure out my position. The pain deep within me relented with his scent.

In a sleep-waking daze he followed the sound of my steps as I trod lightly toward the rear of the van, his steps in time with mine, mouth widening, pace quickening as I reached for the door handle.

He wasn't quick enough to stop me before light and cold air flooded in.

Before I stepped to the tarmac and left the door wide.

103

Cold air nipped at my skin, but I didn't turn my course or flinch as the road sucked away the heat from my feet, despite my trainers still strapped there.

The moonlight stung behind my eyes, but I didn't back up to the darkness of the van. There was only one thing on my mind and nothing would stay my actions.

Moving to the right and out of the view of the doorway, something brushed against my shoulder and I turned, but without alarm, to see a tall man dressed in a suit, half his face hanging below his chin the only sign of what he'd become.

I didn't take a deep breath. I didn't scream and blood continued to pump at the same pace through my veins as he bounced off to his new course without noting what had sent him in that direction. I left him to walk away as Jordain's boot landed to the tarmac.

The turn of my head was much slower than theirs. Much slower than those who'd been ambling along, waiting for the next meal to come. The creatures had no care for me; I was invisible to them, but the same could not be said for Jordain.

I heard my name on the breeze. I smelt the sweet scent unlatching my stomach, but I didn't rush back towards Jordain, who was still only a few paces away at the open doors of the van. I didn't speed to him, despite being shoved to the side by an eager old man with sagging, wrinkled skin who'd found new vigour in the afterlife.

I didn't see the soldier as Jordain, the man with bright and wide blue eyes with heavy lids, despite the hold of his expression to mine as he tried to figure out if he'd woken or if this was all a dream. Soon his concentration pulled elsewhere, with his hands grasping to pull the pistol and his only chance of survival, from the holster.

Stepping forward, I didn't waste the time on an apology. In this moment there was nothing I felt sorry for. My hands were busy pushing the door closed as the first of the mouths took hold of his flesh.

I didn't waste time watching his reaction, watching his hands spasm to give up on the weapon, then balling to fists and striking out at the growing crowd. I no longer thought of him as Jordain as I gave in and let the last of myself be overtaken and took my place, falling to my knees as he did. I crouched to the ground, my face almost touching the tarmac as I filled like a baby sucking on a teat.

Full.

Senses dulled.

His remains on the road could have been anyone and with my last effort I rolled under the van, my stomach griping with pleasure as it gurgled, excited at the contents.

Coming to a rest in the centre I felt the van's warmth all gone, but I had no care for the cold. I could barely sense anything but the fullness of my belly.

Water rolled to my ears as I tried to remember what he'd looked like before.

I wouldn't let myself linger, pulling away repeatedly as the taste filled my senses and energy radiated up from my core as I turned to my side to dream of those women paying the price for what I had now become.

104

I woke feeling as if the frozen ground had drawn every degree of warmth from my body. I woke with a pressure wave of sound radiating through my brain.

Pain traced my eyelids as they opened, just like when I'd cried the entire night after coming home from a week of bliss with the woman I could no longer bear to think of.

I'd woken. I could still process information. But why?

I wasn't cured, my actions last night were proof enough, but I was alive and felt myself again, with no hunger like I'd felt that evening.

I thought of Alex in the van above and a sudden panic rippled through me. What if I couldn't control myself and she was next?

After a moment the panic passed and my breathing eased when I didn't feel the hunger surging; no urgency to race to her so I could feed.

A bright new day had started, the signs obvious in the fresh chilled air. I peered around between the tarmac and the dark underside of the van, twisting my head and body together to get a full view, despite the tyres and a thin spear of something white hanging from the engine. Turning to the back end I saw a collection of bones and ragged fatigues drenched a dark shade.

I hadn't needed the reminder. The moments were still as fresh as if they'd just happened and I turned away, feeling a rising nausea from my stomach.

My right hand went to my mouth but I pulled it away at the sight of the dried blood caked into the lines of my skin.

Feet wandered across the view, taking my attention from my disgust.

Some wore shoes, some with just their dirty brown skin padding on the ground as they scattered across the view and I remembered in the first few moments last night how I'd been ignored. The creatures had passed me by, taking no interest. Was that because I was one of them now? I shuddered at the thought.

A heavy noise still lumbered in the air. The pounding, rapid battery of pressure pulled me away from my thoughts.

"A helicopter," came a voice. After a moment I realised it was mine and gratefully took it as another sign I hadn't turned into one of those deplorable creatures.

A surge of optimism grew despite the view. Maybe I wasn't going to be like them after all. I would be different.

That was it. It must have been what she'd been trying to do all along. It had been Toni's plan all this time.

I was a host. This thing was not meant to overcome me, it was meant to live alongside me. In Toni's plans she couldn't have meant for me to need to eat human flesh. She must have engineered a way that I could live like a human.

The strength, the tuned senses. The hunger and drive.

She'd told me when she'd first explained that she admired the organism. Only now did I realise how much. She knew we had drifted apart and what better way to keep us together? What better way to keep me at her side? Had Toni thought she'd given me a gift that she couldn't tell me about?

Perhaps there was a way to get through this. Perhaps there was a way I could live with this thing inside. Perhaps there was a way I could do this whilst never having to kill again. I was sure Toni would have the answers.

I was sure she would be in that helicopter and this didn't change anything. I still had a job to do. I still had people to tell so they could be saved, but first I had to do something else. I had to see if there truly was any part of me still human.

Guilt welled again at the sight of the pile of bones. Although it had not been my choice, I should have seen this coming. I did see this coming, but they should be the ones to bear the pain. The regret had to be theirs, not mine.

I turned from the partial skeleton with my head flitting to the sound of the helicopter moving across the sky, but instead my gaze fixed on the long, thin shard stuck out from below the engine.

Crawling along the road on my elbows to the rhythm of the battered air, soon my concentration caught the white bone stripped of flesh, only sinew remaining to hang like thick white hair.

I took hold with my right hand, feeling a wave of repulsion as I noticed the dried blood streaked across my fingers and the jagged nails at the end. It was only then I realised I felt no pain in my hand. My finger and hand had returned to its normal definition. I could grip without being contorted with feeling.

With my smile came the pull of skin across my face, but I didn't need a mirror to know what had dried and soaked into my pores.

With the bone rattling to the road as it dropped, I rolled from under the van, brimming with energy as I stood.

I felt no pain, no aches from last night's effort, the cold air so refreshing, so invigorating as I pulled it deep into my lungs.

My gaze caught on the helicopter, now a dot in the distance as it lowered, the sound shrinking as it fell behind the far away buildings. I smiled. Dried flakes fell as blood cracked on my skin. Pleasure rose from my chest as I knew I hadn't lost my cause.

They were still mine for the taking. They still had to pay, Jordain just another victim of the crime I would make them account for.

Pulling my t-shirt over my head, the cold air sent shivers of sensation across my bare chest. I did my best to wipe my face, but I wasn't hopeful, the t-shirt already too far from its original colour.

The dead still paid no attention as I walked to the back of the van and I stared, taking a moment to linger on the bare bones at my feet so I could let the guilt rise and remind me why I was still here.

Retching at the detail, the body stripped clean, fatigues shredded, the laden holster at his side, I dragged the mass away from the door and bent double.

Tears welling in my eyes, I pulled the gun from the holster still in the pile. With the muzzle facing my way, I laid it in my open palm and I pulled up the handle, the ambling creatures only taking notice as I tapped a light request on the metal.

Alex's bleary-eyed reaction paused much less than I'd expected.

"Oh my god, you're alive."

Her look went from my face to my bloodied chest and to beyond my shoulders, then settled back on the gun resting on my palm. Her hand went to her mouth as I spoke.

"Take the gun."

105

"Where's Jordain?" she said, keeping her hand in place, her eyes locked to mine when I didn't reply and held my open palm out with the weight of the pistol.

"Take the gun."

Lowering her brow, she reached out and gripped the pistol with confusion bunching on her face, not able to think of any other words and I reached out, lifting the muzzle of the gun in her hand so it pointed level with my chest. "I'm so sorry."

I didn't feel the hunger and didn't see her as a meal, but I needed to make sure she was safe if that changed in an instant.

Her gaze flicked to behind me and she stumbled back, keeping the gun level where I'd put it. Pushing the door wide, I stepped up and closed the door so whatever she'd seen wouldn't get near.

"He's dead, isn't he?" she said, her voice muffled with her hand.

I nodded.

"Are you going to kill me?" Alex said, and I could see the gun trembling in her right hand as she spoke.

I shook my head.

"I couldn't control it. I'm so sorry for what I did, but I've figured it out," I said, pushing my palms together and bringing them to my mouth. "Toni made it so I can exist with this thing. It all makes sense now. She wanted me by her side and this was the only way. I couldn't control it back then but she must have made it so I don't have to kill."

"How do you know all this? How do I know you're not going to feel like that again?"

"I get it now, but just in case that's why I've given you the gun."

I watched as her hand dropped from her face and the uncertainty in the squint of her eyes. She looked to the door at my back.

I nodded.

"I won't stop you if you want to get the hell out of here," I said, stepping to the side.

Alex lingered on the same spot, her gaze moving between me and the door.

"And you feel okay now?" she said, the gun wavering slowly down then up again in my direction.

"I feel fine. I feel amazing. Look," I said, raising my right hand up in front.

Alex lifted the gun high at my movement, but it dropped again as she stared on at my perfectly proportioned hand.

"I don't won't to die that way," she said.

I nodded again.

"As soon as I feel anything I'll take myself away. I promise, but I still need to get to Toni. She needs to pay and I have to understand how I can do this without having to take…" I paused. "Without having to take any more lives."

Alex lingered on my face for a moment, the gun still low at her side.

"I thought you were dead. I thought I was on my own. I didn't know how I was going to do this by myself. I guess I have to trust what you say."

I let a small smile fill the silence and she placed the gun on the table at her side and forced her own thin smile as her hands reached to the floor to pull up my red jacket.

Alex had turned away while I dressed, grabbing the pants with both my hands and clenching it hard in my right fist. I took joy in the sensation of working my hand, pausing only a moment before pulling down my jeans mottled with darkness. Turning around, my clothes at least prim and proper again, I saw she was looking back at me, leaning to hand me cleaning cloths and a bottle of fluid intended for the cameras.

The scratch and scrape on the thin metal came back.

"The helicopter," I said, my voice croaking, her head spinning to the windscreen as she nodded. "She's getting away."

"The engine?" she said, with her face in a grimace, eyes wide as they locked back to mine.

"Try it now," I said, scraping the wet cloth between my fingers.

In moments the engine came to life, Alex gripping hard on the steering wheel as we slid sideways and back again to avoid the gathering swarm.

We'd been quick enough not to let the crowd build. Quick enough to find the gap in the blockade, the small groups easy to avoid as we swerved in and around the cars abandoned in the road, leaving them instead to follow on mass in our wake.

We didn't stop at the second olive container by the roadside, slowing only to take the slalom of the concrete blocks without scraping the paintwork. The position had long fallen.

As the road rolled under the tyres, the rest of the streets were no surprise. The desolation. Vacancy. Even the lack of dead bodies walking didn't cause me to look twice. Soon we could see every other panel of the hastily-erected fence had fallen. The outer perimeter had been ineffective and we drove right through a gap, slowing only to stop the skid; no point in swerving the bodies when there was no way to avoid.

Alex drove us toward the white building crowned with the swirled blades of the helicopter, turning away only as I put my hand to her shoulder. She hadn't been able to completely mask the flinch.

With the view in the mirror forgotten until now, I watched the crowd, so much thicker than we'd already failed to get through.

But it didn't matter. I'd seen the communications truck Jordain had mentioned and with my heartbeat racing in my chest, I ran into the back whilst the wheels slowed, watching the equipment's lights flashing green as it picked up the surrounding network.

I straightened my pants and jacket as I jumped to the road, staring into the tall wing mirror, but for the first time ever not caring what I saw, my cheeks red and rosy, with a faint darkness dried into the grooves serving well to highlight and contour.

Energy rose deep from within. I took a breath and with my back to the hospital building, the destruction and carnage all around, I stared out with the morning sun in my face and beamed at the red light shining back from the camera.

106

I'd done it. I'd produced a heart-felt prize-winning piece. The figures, the children, running across the roof in the background were the cherry on top.

I hadn't told the world of Toni's betrayal. I hadn't told them what she'd turned me into so I could be hers forever. I hadn't told them she was creating human-zombie hybrids. I hadn't told them the South West of England crawled with her mistakes and they were multiplying.

I'd told them to stay inside. I'd told them to lock their doors. I hoped I'd given people enough information, enough of a chance.

I almost lost it when I caught sight of someone the right size and height, her hair the same colour; the stoop of an injury. I almost stopped mid-recording and looped the video back.

That's why I'm a professional. I put the needs of the viewers ahead of mine. But now I could see even on the little screen it was her. No doubt. She was in the long line guiding the children to the helicopter.

I carried on talking to the camera, despite the stranger's words from the day before. I took her words the wrong way when she'd spoken. They weren't taking specimens from the children. The children were the specimens.

My power was to let everyone know; to use my words to narrate the story. To tell them what they were seeing in the horrific pictures from our journey. Others could zoom and identify the culprits. They could track the helicopter and end this madness.

They had more time left than we did.

As I thought on, I pushed the play button on the playback machine, used the joystick to zoom and I fast-forwarded, watching what I'd already seen out of the corner of my eye play back in quick time.

As the figure I recognised came into view, I slowed the tape down to half speed, leaning in toward the screen.

It was her. I was sure. A face of perfection, slightly alien with the thick make-up to hide the bruises, but most people wouldn't know that.

Alex left the camera rolling as I waited for the upload to finish and I switched the screen, showing the live feed of the destruction, only turning away as the automatic reply flashed to tell me the editing team had received the footage.

Now it was up to them to do what they had to do. I had to rely on Stan to make the choice to send it out to the masses, to push out my warning as far as it would go.

I let Toni's image play on as if letting her go from my mind.

"What now?" Alex said from the open doors of the van, her voice calming my rising beat.

"There's a thousand, maybe more on their way here," I said, sighing through my smile.

"So what do you want to do? You've done it despite everything," she said, her eyes wide, face beaming a mirror image of mine.

"*We* did it. Thank you."

I let my shoulders fall.

"Do you think they'll use it?" she replied, her face set in a scowl as she nodded to the images still playing on the wall of screens.

"We'll never know," I said with a sigh.

"Doesn't that bother you?" she said, raising her eyebrows.

I nodded. "But what can I do?"

"I don't think this story is over yet," she said, raising a smile in the corner of her mouth.

I glanced to the gun still laid on the table at my side.

"I think you're right," I said.

Alex squinted and turned her head.

"Toni's alive. She got into the helicopter." I could feel the tears running down my cheek, but I couldn't acknowledge them by wiping them away. I didn't have to as Alex leant forward and wrapped her arms around me, drawing out the pain.

"We have to find out how to keep you human," she said, whispering to my ear.

I nodded, but after a moment of relief, the pop of a gunshot came through the speakers, pulling me back to reality. Alex pulled away and together we turned to the screen, watching the wide angle as the helicopter lumbered into the air, bringing back the memory of how the wind had picked up when it happened in real time.

I closed my eyes.

"There's two people on the roof," Alex said moments later, turning back toward me from looking out of the back doors. "A dog, too," she said, uncertainty in her voice. "We should go see if they're okay."

I closed my eyes, taking a slow breath.

"I'm not sure that's such a good idea," I said as I held my hand to my stomach.

Epilogue

The first I knew was the interruption to the police car chasing a joyrider ragged across the streets of London, the banner across the screen turning to words, making me sit up from the sofa.

The warning about the sensitive images made me nudge forward and turn the volume even higher.

The beauty in the centre of the screen, the red jacket and trousers seemed to be all she wore; her features radiating out towards me nearly made me fall to the floor.

The background was a blur. The helicopter with its blades rotating and the people running towards it across the roof were the only details not pixilated.

Her words weren't censored, the emotion in her voice raw as she spoke of the children. The scrolling message along the bottom of the screen saved the need to rewind.

It had happened. It wasn't April the first. I checked my watch twice just to be sure.

A virus raising the dead to their feet.

The end of an era, of our civilisation.

I stood, blood draining from my face, but still I punched the air, a wry smile on my lips as I shouted, "Now who's laughing, bitches," just as the image cut off, the colourful test card taking its place and I ran upstairs to grab my Bug Out Bag.

To be continued…

Check out the next in the series!

Having barely survived leading the children to the military doctors and their promise of safety, and with Cassie still alive despite the creature's bite, Logan's thoughts turn to finding their own sanctuary.

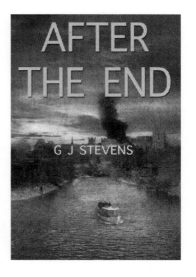

When the hospital soon comes under attack, not only from the demons risen from the dead, but from the bombs raining from above, Logan looks to the reporter in the car park, Jessica, who defied her curse to broadcast the terrible news in hope the public would believe her and protect themselves.

As the world continues to fall apart around them, when it becomes clear Jessica knows more than most, they're forced together despite the questions her actions raise. As Logan discovers the children are not in safe hands and Cassie might be something other than cured, it's a race against time to prevent the children becoming guinea pigs of twisted experiments whilst not only being hunted for their meat, but shadowed by the military. Running for their lives, Jessica can't help but discover more about the monster she has become.

With the odds stacked so high against them, can Jessica control her unnatural hunger long enough to find the secret to living a normal life, and can they rescue the children before it's too late?

Liked what you read?

Please leave a review on the platform you used for the purchase or **Goodreads.com**. Honest reviews are difficult to come by and are so important to indie authors like me.

Visit **gjstevens.com** for news about new releases and sign up to the mailing list to receive a free electronic copy of **SURVIVOR – Your Guide to Surviving the Apocalypse!**

gjstevens.com

Printed in Great Britain
by Amazon

50206010R00246